INTO THE WOODS

INTO THE WOODS

Anomaly Hunters, Book 1

J. S. Volpe

Peridor Press

ISBN: 0615732305
ISBN-13: 978-0615732305

Cover photo: File licensed by
www.depositphotos.com/Cosma Andrei

AH-1

CONTENTS

Part One:
The First Day of the Rest of Their Lives

Part Two:
Winding the Clock

Part Three:
Confrontations

Part Four:
The Other Side of the Door

Epilogue:
Two Endings and Three Beginnings

PART ONE

The First Day of the Rest of Their Lives

Chapter 1

Calvin Beckerman

1

Calvin Beckerman's first hint that his life was about to change forever was the rising wail of sirens as he waited to cross McArthur Road. The sound cut straight through the blare of the song currently playing on his iPod ("Motorway to Roswell" by the Pixies), and with a frown he hit Pause, tore his eyes from the crowd of students filing into May High School across the street, and looked around.

Two police cars were racing toward him down McArthur, their red and blue lights flashing, other cars slowing and pulling aside to let them pass like the Red Sea parting for Moses. In no time the cop cars were blasting past Calvin, the sudden loudening of their sirens making him wince even with the earbuds plugging his ears. The warm, dirty wind of the cars' passage flattened his jeans against his legs and sent whirls of autumn leaves skittering across the pavement.

He watched the police cars recede into the distance. When they were many blocks away, looking no larger now than Hot Wheels cars, they veered off down a side street.

The light changed. Calvin unpaused his iPod and hurried across McArthur, patting road dust from his jeans and his "Cthulhu for President" T-shirt and his close-cropped blond hair. He wondered what was going on. You didn't often see cop cars zooming down the somnolent streets of May, Ohio. Part of him hoped something big and exciting and maybe even catastrophic had happened. A giant sinkhole. A pack of rabid gorillas on the loose. The onset of the zombie apocalypse. Anything to liven up this dull little town. He felt as if he had been waiting all his life for something remarkable to happen, but nothing ever did.

Well, no. That wasn't entirely true. Something pretty remarkable *had* happened recently: Calvin had found the girl of his dreams—his beautiful redheaded fellow senior, Cynthia Crow.

Calvin and Cynthia had spent most of their lives advancing through the May school system together, but they had never really gotten to know each other until this year when they got paired up as lab partners in Chemistry. He was shocked at how well they got along. Both of them were smart and well-read, with creative, probing minds and wry and often irreverent senses of humor. They seemed to be perfectly in tune on some essential psychological level. While they sat there in lab waiting for chemicals to catalyze, they had the most fascinating and wide-ranging conversations Calvin had ever had with anyone. One day after a debate about the existence of ghosts (he pro, she undecided but leaning toward con) he knew that this was The Girl.

For weeks now, he had been trying to screw up the nerve to ask her out. He had never asked a girl out before, never been on a date, never kissed a girl (well, except for that time he kissed Julie Tanner in first grade, but that was just to make her scream and run away). Simply thinking about asking Cynthia out made his heart palpitate and his palms ooze sweat. But he knew he had to try. She was too awesome to let slip away. He lay awake at night agonizing over the best way to do it. He scoured books and websites for tips and methods and reassurances. He tried to embolden himself with positive self-talk. On some level he understood that all of this nervous preparation was a delaying tactic, but he kept doing it anyway.

But then last night, after reading an online sob story about some guy who lost his dream girl because he waited too long to ask her out, Calvin swore to himself he would pop the question at school today. He didn't dare wait any longer. And today was Friday, which was perfect: If she said yes, they could schedule a date for sometime over the weekend. If she said no, he had all weekend to lick his wounds and figure out how to face her on Monday.

So today was the day. No question about it. But when? Chemistry would provide the best opportunity since they had time alone to chat during lab. But they shared Sociology right after that, which meant if she turned him down, they would then have to spend a very awkward fifty minutes sitting two seats away from each other, and he wasn't sure he could deal with that. Maybe it would be best to catch her at the end of school as they were leaving the building…

After stopping at his locker to hang up his backpack and grab the books he needed for his first few classes, Calvin hurried to his homeroom. Cynthia was in the same homeroom, and he was hoping to discuss the latest episode of *MythBusters* with her before the bell rang.

But when Calvin strode into Mr. Quimby's homeroom, he found Cynthia's desk empty. He looked around, thinking she must be talking with someone, but she was nowhere in sight.

Heart sinking, he trudged to his desk, the only other empty desk in the room. The next thirty seconds consisted of him repeatedly swiveling around in his seat to see if she was at her desk yet, seeing that she wasn't, checking the open doorway in hopes that she was even now coming in, seeing that she wasn't, then turning back around to face the front of the room, a little glummer than before. Had he psyched himself up for nothing?

When the bell rang, her seat was still empty. Crap. It wasn't like Cynthia to be late. She must be sick.

He had completely forgotten about the police cars.

2

Calvin was on his way to first-period Trigonometry when a tall, dark figure fell into step beside him. He looked up. It was Brandon Taylor, another fellow senior. Brandon had black-rimmed glasses and a head of thick, dark-brown hair that he had at one time or another gelled into every style imaginable and dyed every color of the rainbow. Like usual, he was dressed all in black, with a black T-shirt, black jeans, black Doc Martens, and a black leather jacket adorned with thin silver chains and a picture of a dancing, top-hatted skeleton on the back. Brandon had painted the skeleton himself. Brandon and Calvin were more than acquaintances, but not quite friends. They hung out together during eighth period study hall and discussed cool bands and horror movies and Brandon's latest offbeat art projects, but they had never met up outside of school.

"Hey, man," Brandon said. "Got a minute?"

"Um, sure," Calvin said. "What's up?"

Brandon leaned in and said in a low, confidential tone, "Well, you know, I was just wondering if you knew anything about what happened?"

Calvin shook his head. "What happened with what?"

Brandon's jaw dropped. "Oh, man. I thought you'd know already, what with you being close buds with Cynthia Crow and everything."

Calvin felt a surge of mixed emotions at this remark. On one level his breast swelled with joy and accomplishment on learning that a third party considered him and Cynthia "close buds." But this feeling was overshadowed by a jolt of alarm at the implication that whatever had happened involved Cynthia.

"What?" Calvin said. "Is she okay?"

"Yeah. Well, no. Well, sort of. It's not her; it's her sister."

Calvin fished around in his memory for the name of Cynthia's ten-year-old sister.

"Emily?"

"Yeah. That's the one." Brandon leaned in farther and lowered his voice even more until it was barely audible in the noisy hallway. "She disappeared. It sounds like she got abducted or something."

"*What?* When?"

"Sometime overnight, I guess. I don't know all the details. I heard about it from Hailie Furness. She was in the office when they got a call about it, right before homeroom. They'll probably make an announcement soon…"

Brandon yammered on, but Calvin wasn't listening. He was remembering his earlier wish that something big and catastrophic would happen. The memory made him squirm with guilt and shame. He hadn't meant something like this. Not something so awful and real. And especially not involving Cynthia.

He hated to imagine what she must be going through. He pictured her huddled on her bed, her willowy body racked with sobs, her green eyes leaking tears. The image filled him with cold, hard determination to do whatever he could to end her pain. Maybe he could even play amateur sleuth and find Emily himself. He envisioned himself striding toward the Crow house with Emily safe and sound in his arms while Cynthia and her family watched in breathless awe from their front porch.

Which he supposed many people would argue was a ridiculously unlikely outcome. But you never knew what was possible till you tried, right?

Calvin vowed to try.

Chapter 2

Cynthia Crow

1

Cynthia Crow sat on the living room couch in the Crow house. Officer Bob Thompson of the May Police sat on the footstool in front of her, frowning slightly as he flipped through a small spiral notebook. Cynthia had given a full statement half an hour earlier, but Officer Thompson said he wanted to confirm something with her. Across the living room her brother Donovan sat in an armchair, looking frazzled and lost and much younger than his fifteen years. Stray wisps of his auburn hair stuck up from his sloppily tied ponytail and glowed hazily against the morning light that brightened the picture window behind him. Outside, a uniformed cop walked slowly along the edge of the woods that encircled the lawn, his head down as he scanned the brush for evidence. In the dining room across the hall Cynthia could hear her father Hannibal's low tones as he spoke to his sister Wendy on the phone. He had called her to make sure she didn't know anything about Emily's disappearance. It wasn't likely; Aunt Wendy lived in Boston. Periodically Cynthia's mom Brenda cut in to tell Hannibal to ask this or that. Her voice was high and urgent.

"Here it is," Officer Thompson said. He set the open notebook on his knee. He was a fortyish guy with a brown mustache and a roll of paunch straining against his blue polyester shirt. Shortly after the cops had arrived, Cynthia's mom had emerged from her state of near-panic long enough to give him a bright, brittle smile and ask him if he had ever stopped eating blue Play-Doh. It turned out that Officer Thompson had been in Brenda's very first batch of students when she started teaching first grade at the May Elementary School thirty years earlier. Thompson had breathed out a small, nervous laugh and said, "Yes, ma'am. I prefer lasagna these days."

That had been the only light moment of the whole morning. And from the look of things probably the whole day. And who knew how long after that.

"I just want to confirm what clothes she's got on before we send out the info," Officer Thompson said. He nodded at the dining room. "Your mom and dad—they're kind of unfocused right now, so I figured I'd better double check the information."

Cynthia raised her eyebrows. "What, you think *I'm* focused?"

He shrugged. "Well, you seem a little cooler-headed."

"If you say so."

"Now, then…" He studied what was on the notepad. "I have her down as wearing a green sweatshirt, blue jeans, white tennis shoes with lightning bolts on the sides, green socks, white underwear, and a lightweight waist-length green nylon jacket. Is that right?"

"Yeah. Well, I think so. I mean, after we discovered she wasn't there this morning, I noticed that her pajamas were folded up next to the bed, so I figured we should check her regular clothes and see if anything was missing. And those are the clothes not accounted for. So I guess if you want to get technical, we can't say for sure she's actually wearing them. They're just not in her room anymore."

"Okay."

There was a thump overhead. Cynthia looked up, stiff, tense. She wondered whether the sound had come from her room or her parents' room. Not that it ultimately mattered; the cops had said they were going to search the whole house, from attic to cellar, even though the family had already searched it before they reported Emily missing. Cynthia listened, head cocked. Another thump sounded. No, it was Mom and Dad's room. Had hers already been searched, then?

Officer Thompson noticed her tension and smiled reassuringly. "Don't worry. They're careful. They won't break anything. They'll put everything back the way they found it."

"Uh-huh." It wasn't the safety of breakables she was concerned about; she was worried that someone would go rooting around on her computer. She hated to be thinking about herself at a time like this, but there was stuff on her computer that would make it clear as day to anyone who looked that she was a lesbian, a fact currently known to no one but herself. If it came down to it, she supposed being forced out of the closet was a small price to pay for finding Emily, but she would really prefer to keep the closet door closed for the moment. She wasn't ready for her friends and family to find out. Especially not her family, and especially not at a time like this. She wasn't sure how to ask if the cops would look on her computer, at least not without making it obvious that there was stuff on it she didn't want anyone to see, which of course would only make the cops want to check it out all the more. "Are they, um, are they looking specifically for Emily, or are they just looking around, or what?"

"They're just looking," Officer Thompson said.

"Sometimes we don't know exactly what we're looking for until we find it."

"I see." Actually she didn't. As answers went, that one was extraordinarily unhelpful.

Thompson began to close his notepad, then saw something written there that made him stop. "Oh, that's right. One other thing. Your mom gave us a photo of Emily. Something we can use to make fliers and send to news outlets. I just want to make sure—I mean, your mom's kind of unfocused, like I said, so I just want to be sure this is a good photo. A good likeness."

He held out a photo. She took it. It was one of the photos Mom had taken during their trip to New England over the summer. It showed Emily in front of the Salem Witch Museum. Her pale face was framed by her long, straight black hair. Her dark-brown eyes were fixed on something slightly above and to the right of the camera. A small smile curved her lips.

"Yeah," Cynthia said softly, staring at Emily. She couldn't help wondering if she would ever see Emily's face again. Her real face, that is. The one that moved and talked and laughed and stuck out her tongue at her brother when he made fun of her inexplicable disdain of fish. Cynthia felt her throat tightening and tears building up behind her eyes, so she thrust the photo back into Officer Thompson's hands before the sight of her sister's face could reduce her to a hysterical mess and thereby destroy her mostly bogus aura of cool-headedness. "That's…yeah, that's a good picture."

As Thompson tucked the photo away, the front door opened. Just like every other time the front door had opened this morning, Cynthia and Donovan shot bolt upright and looked out into the main hall, hoping it would be

Emily.

And just like every other time this morning, it wasn't her. Instead it was Officer Ronald Carter, a young cop with blond hair and glasses. Clutched in his left hand was a large brown paper bag containing something heavy enough to make the bag's bottom sag.

"Where's the Chief?" Officer Carter called out.

"Right here," said May Police Chief Joseph Krezchek as he strode out of the dining room. He was a stocky, avuncular fellow with a head of wavy gray hair and a face that was trying hard to maintain a stern, in-command expression rather than the disorientation he was clearly feeling. The May Police rarely faced crimes more serious than stolen bikes and domestic spats.

Behind Chief Krezchek came Hannibal and Brenda Crow. Cynthia thought they looked even worse than when she last saw them twenty minutes ago. Her dad's eyes were bloodshot and puffy, and his normally neatly combed and parted hair was tousled as if he had just gotten out of bed. Even his mustache looked ruffled. Mom didn't look any better. Her cheeks shone with tear tracks, and there were small coffee stains on the front of her dress. Cynthia wondered if the gray threads in her mom's hair had multiplied or if she was simply noticing them more than usual.

"We, uh, we've got a development," Officer Carter said, glancing around. The hesitancy in his voice and the way his eyes kept flicking toward Hannibal and Brenda, as if he weren't sure he should be talking about this in front of them, made Cynthia shoot to her feet and stride toward the hall. Donovan and Officer Thompson followed. As Cynthia entered the hall, she heard sounds of movement throughout the house—doors opening, floorboards creaking, footsteps thumping. Looking around, she saw cops emerging from doorways and peering over the railing of the balcony that overlooked the hall. Everyone sensed the import surrounding Officer Carter's appearance.

"What is it?" Krezchek asked.

"We, uh, we found something." Officer Carter held up the bag. His nervous eyes swept over the Crows again.

"Where?"

"In some bushes at the edge of that round clearing. You know, the one on Mr. May's property across the river."

"Let's see."

Officer Carter opened the bag. Krezchek peered inside and stiffened.

"Aw, shit," he said.

Brenda and Hannibal craned their heads to look over his shoulder. Hannibal's face went white. Brenda gave a little cry and sagged against her husband.

Cynthia edged around Krezchek and looked into the bag.

At the bottom was a small white tennis shoe with a lightning bolt on the side.

Chapter 3

See Emily Play (I)

1

Brenda Crow couldn't keep standing. The moment she saw the shoe—Emily's shoe, no question about it; Brenda herself had bought those shoes for Emily at the Payless in West River Mall last year—her legs had gone weak and rubbery, and she knew if she didn't get herself into a chair immediately, she'd sink right down onto her bottom on the hardwood floor. So as Officer Carter delineated their other findings in the clearing—a circle of burned grass about two feet wide, some dried blood, torn-up turf indicative of a struggle—and as each of these findings made her legs weaker and weaker, she staggered into the dining room and collapsed into one of the five chairs that surrounded the dinner table.

Five chairs. One at either end, for Hannibal and herself. Two on one side for Donovan and Cynthia. And one on the other side for Emily. Brenda had always thought of the arrangement as a star. Five points, with Emily—special Emily—as the crown.

But if Emily was gone, there was no crown. There was no star. There were four points. A square. A box. A dull, commonplace thing.

She moaned and covered her face with her hands. Her palms quickly overflowed with tears. Horrid rasping sounds were pouring from her throat but she didn't know how to stop them.

Hannibal sat down beside her and murmured vague, meaningless phrases of comfort that he clearly didn't believe himself. Then Donovan and Cynthia appeared, everyone crowding together to comfort her. Or at least everyone from the family: The police had started filing out the front door, speaking in low, inaudible voices. She wanted to follow, to hear what they were saying, but she didn't have the strength to get up.

"We'll find her," Hannibal murmured while his hand robotically stroked her back. "Don't worry. Everything'll be fine."

She nodded. Perhaps he was right. Blood didn't mean she was dead. She might only be injured. Or the blood might not even be hers...

"It might not be hers," Brenda exclaimed, rising from her chair so suddenly that Hannibal drew back, startled. She strode toward the cops. "It might not be hers!"

Chief Krezchek froze midway out the door. "Pardon?"

"The blood. It could be..." She wasn't sure of the right term. "Someone else's. The person responsible's. The perpetrator's. Couldn't it?"

"Mrs. Crow," he said, trying to smile consolingly, "it's far too soon to start hypothesizing about...well, anything. We won't know anything for sure until we do a proper analysis."

"How long will that take?" she cried. She envisioned labs full of white-coated scientists peering stolidly through microscopes and making detailed notes with careful, slow-moving hands while somewhere out in the world Emily was hurt, scared, maybe dying. "We don't have that kind of time!" She realized her voice had risen to a shriek, but she didn't care.

Hannibal's hands closed on her shoulders, and in a gentle voice he said, "Brenda, come on. Let them do their job. If we keep getting in the way, it'll take them that much longer."

She closed her eyes and heaved a sigh. Sometimes she hated his stuffy rationality, but he was right. Not that rightness or truth could do anything to quiet the tempest of emotions buffeting her soul.

He led her back to the table and sat her down while the cops vanished outside to confer and plan. The house suddenly seemed far too quiet.

Hannibal sat beside her again, this time with her right hand in his and his left arm draped over her shoulders. Donovan and Cynthia sat too. Brenda studied the arrangement, frowning. Everyone was in the wrong seat. Hannibal was in Brenda's usual chair. Cynthia was in Hannibal's. Donovan in Cynthia's. And Brenda herself in Donovan's. Musical chairs. Only Emily's chair remained untouched, inviolate. Empty.

Her face crumpled up again. Fresh tears spilled from her eyes. She lowered her head and let the tears drip into her lap while Hannibal caressed her shoulder and squeezed her hand.

A car door slammed outside. An engine rumbled to life. Tires crunched away down the gravel drive. The faint voices of the cops became fainter as they headed off, presumably into the woods to examine this horrible new evidence.

The woods. Of course. It would have to be the woods.

The woods had always made Brenda uneasy. And not just in the typical worried-parent way that foresaw rabid animals and rusty nails and falling branches everywhere.

No, this was a deeper, vaguer, more primal discomfort. There was a sense of alienness about the woods, a sense of things not being quite right. Whenever she had to go into them, she found herself remembering the medieval European beliefs about forests being the home of witches and monsters and child-swiping fairies. Of course, back then people were uneducated dunces and the forests were enormous untraveled things that stretched over most of the continent and were full of genuine threats like wolves and bears and disease. So it was no surprise medieval folks felt as they did. It was ludicrous to feel the same way about less than a square mile of woods in modern-day Ohio. And yet...

Fairies.

2

Emily's obsession with fairies had started when she was five. Brenda had never been able to determine exactly where this interest had come from. She and Hannibal had not yet bought Emily any of the books of fairy tales that now filled two whole shelves in her room. No, the books had followed from the interest, not the other way around. Brenda's best guess was that since Emily had entered nursery school that year, her interest in fairies had been kindled by comments her new schoolmates had made or by stories Miss Rinehart had read to her class.

And yet the first time the subject came up, it had been in connection with the woods.

It had been a sunny Saturday afternoon in September. Brenda was in the kitchen chopping parsnips for that night's dinner when Emily, who had been out in the back yard hosting yet another gathering of her stuffed animals, came bursting through the back door. Emily's eyes were bright with delight, and her big, round, baby-fat cheeks were flushed with excitement.

"Mom!" Emily cried. "I saw fairies!"

"What?" Brenda said. She set down the knife with a baffled frown.

"Fairies! There were, like, a bunch of 'em! They were dancing around some big mushums!"

"Mush*rooms.*"

Emily rolled her eyes. "Mush*rooms.* Sorry."

"And what exactly did these fairies look like?" Brenda expected a description that matched butterflies or fireflies rather than traditional fairies.

Instead Emily said, "They were, like, tiny little people. Little enough to ride a bunny. They had long hair and tiny faces and big colorful wings, and…" She leaned in close and in a gleefully scandalized whisper added, "And they weren't wearing any clothes."

"And where exactly did you see these fairies?" Brenda said.

"In the woods."

"I thought I told you not to go into the woods."

Emily clucked her tongue and let her shoulders sag and her arms flop in a display of unfairly maligned innocence. "I wasn't *in* the woods. I was on the edge. The fairies were right inside."

Brenda stared at her daughter for a moment, then said, "Show me." She figured she had better make sure there weren't any nudist hippies camping out somewhere on the property.

Emily led her across the lawn to the edge of the woods due north of the house, then pointed to a bare circle of dirt amid the greenery a couple of feet inside the tree line. The circle was about a foot in diameter and had a cluster of small white mushrooms in the center.

"They were in that circle there, dancing around the, uh, the mush*rooms.*"

Brenda squatted down to examine the circle more closely. There were no marks in the dirt, no indications that anything (including Emily) had been physically present within the circle.

"Hmm," she said. Her knees cracked as she stood up. "How tall were they exactly?"

"This tall." Emily held her hands about four inches apart.

"I see." The supposed fairies were probably only some kind of insect after all. Or a product of an overactive imagination, something Emily had proven herself to possess in spades time and time again. "Well, if you see them again, just leave them alone. And don't go into the woods."

"I didn't!"

"I'm just reminding you." She looked at the circle again, then added, "And don't eat the mushrooms, either."

Emily looked appalled at the notion. "I would never do that! They're the fairies' mushrooms!"

The incident had an amusing sequel a couple of days later. Brenda had been on her way down to the basement to do some laundry when she glanced out the back door and saw Emily crouched at the edge of the woods. Brenda set down the laundry basket and went outside.

"Emily?" she called as she crossed the lawn.

Emily jerked, startled, then looked around and smiled. "What?"

"What are you doing over there?"

"Nothing."

When Brenda reached the edge of the woods she found that Emily was arranging a pile of Sun-Maid raisins next to the mushrooms around which the supposed fairies had been supposedly dancing. Already a few ants were scuttling forward to investigate.

"What is this?" Brenda asked.

"It's for the fairies. I thought they might like 'em. To eat."

"I see." Brenda figured she had better dissuade Emily from handing out free lunches to bugs. "You know, I don't think fairies eat people food. I think they have a special fairy diet."

Emily's eyes went big with excitement. "Ooh! Like spiderwebs and moonbeams and stuff, right?"

"Um, yeah. Something like that."

"Cool!" She regarded the heap of raisins on the dirt. "Oh, well. I'll just leave those for the ants. They should like 'em."

3

And that had been the start of it. Emily never saw fairies again (or at least if she did, she never mentioned it to Brenda), but her fascination with them continued unabated to the present day. She stubbornly insisted on their reality. And not just fairies, but all kinds of odd things. Things like magic and monsters. Things Brenda wondered if it wasn't peculiar for a ten-year-old (almost eleven) to still believe in in this crass modern world of terrorist bombings and reality TV.

Her thoughts were interrupted by a rising jumble of voices outside. It sounded like Chief Krezchek and his men. Were they back already? Brenda glanced at the clock on the wall and was surprised to see that half an hour had passed since the cops departed for the woods.

The front door opened, and Chief Krezchek came in. His expression was somber and rueful.

"I, uh, I came back to tell you folks that after seeing the evidence in the clearing we're officially labeling this an abduction. We went ahead and notified the FBI field office in Kingwood. They're sending a team over right now."

He said something else but Brenda didn't hear it over the moans that were pouring from her throat.

Chapter 4

Calvin and Cynthia

1

All day at school Calvin followed the developments in the Emily Crow case with keen interest. For a long time there wasn't much in the way of hard facts, but early that afternoon the authorities revealed some significant news: One of Emily's friends claimed that Emily had been planning to meet a man in the woods near her house last night, a man who said he could show her fairies in the woods. Emily had talked to this man sometime yesterday, most likely when she was in Indian Hill Park between four and six p.m.

When school let out, Calvin made it home in record time. He tossed his backpack on his bed, grabbed a quick snack, then set out for Oaks Road, where the Crows lived, where the woods were.

His route took him down Potts Road, which passed through downtown May. A crowd filled the plaza outside the May Civic Administration Building. News vans lined the curb. Here and there news crews filmed live reports. The parking lot of the May National Bank, where Calvin's dad worked as the manager, was crammed with cars, few of which were likely to belong to bank customers. Calvin suspected he knew what his dad would be grousing about during dinner tonight.

Farther down the block Calvin passed Crow Books, the

bookstore owned by Cynthia's dad. Up until a couple of months ago Calvin barely visited the place, preferring to buy his books online where prices were lower. But after his interest in Cynthia had blossomed—and after he learned she sometimes helped out her dad around the store—Calvin found himself visiting the bookstore more often and spending a bigger chunk of his allowance money on books.

Not surprisingly, the store was closed and dark. He wondered how long before it reopened. Hopefully it wouldn't be too long. Hopefully this would all be resolved soon. Maybe Calvin would even have a hand in resolving it.

South of downtown was Indian Hill Park, where Emily was thought to have talked with her abductor yesterday afternoon. The park consisted of a playground, flower beds crisscrossed with walking paths, a gazebo where local bands held concerts in the summer, a baseball diamond, and a few multifunctional fields. The park's southern boundary was the woods where the Crows and old Robert May lived.

Calvin took a quick stroll through the park, but there wasn't much to see. Not even people. At this hour the place was normally packed with romping, screaming children, but parents were keeping their kids at home today and would no doubt do so for many days to come.

No, the real site of interest was the clearing on Mr. May's property. The police said they had found evidence that Emily had been in the clearing last night, but they weren't saying what the evidence consisted of. According to the various stories that had been floating around the high school hallways, the evidence consisted of Emily's clothes, puddles of blood, the remains of a campfire, a bloody knife, a ransom note, and/or evidence of a UFO landing.

Calvin returned to Potts Road and followed it south along the eastern edge of the woods. Soon he came to the Potts Road Bridge, which spanned the Kanseeka River. Calvin paused midway across the bridge and gazed west down the gap in the woods along which the river ran.

The river came into view half a mile away, where, after having flowed generally northward ever since its origin in Blackwater Swamp, it looped east around the base of Indian Hill, a high, steep mound of shale and clay that marked the northwest corner of the Crow property. From there, the Kanseeka flowed east all the way to Kingwood. Calvin wasn't entirely sure where it went after that. Probably Lake Erie.

The bridge shook as a trio of news vans crossed it. No doubt they were on their way to the Crow house. Or at least the street outside it; the house itself was set far back in the woods.

As Calvin resumed his journey south down Potts, he kept his eyes on the vans. Indeed, they turned right onto Oaks Road. So did a lot of the other traffic. It must be a real circus down there.

Calvin's original plan had been to head down Oaks Road to Mr. May's property, then cut north through the woods to the clearing. But now he changed his mind. He didn't want to get accosted by reporters and wind up on the ten o'clock news as a concerned neighbor or something. Plus he didn't want anyone to see him trespassing. He knew he shouldn't trespass at all, of course, but if he was to have any hope of helping Emily (and Cynthia), he needed to get a look at the clearing.

After glancing around to make sure the traffic had thinned out and no one was looking, he ducked into the woods. The sun vanished behind a thick canopy of red and orange leaves. The sound of the traffic dwindled to a murmur. He made his way west toward the river. The murmur faded to nothing. The only sounds were birds singing and trees rustling softly in the wind and twigs cracking underfoot.

Before long the tinkle and gurgle of rushing water grew audible up ahead. The ground began to slope gently downhill. The air became slightly clammy. Then the trees and bushes fell away to reveal the river. At this stage in its course, the Kanseeka was slow and shallow, no more than knee-deep anywhere. The water was green and translucent, and small, water-smoothed stones littered the riverbed.

As planned, Calvin had emerged from the trees near Spirit Cave, a tunnel in the sandstone riverbank due north of the Crow house. The cave ended after twenty feet in a wall of jagged, broken rock. Calvin had heard somewhere that the cave used to lead to a maze of subterranean tunnels but that someone had sealed it up to keep anyone from getting lost in there. Calvin preferred to imagine more colorful scenarios: Perhaps someone had been hiding treasure or bodies, or plugging up the gateway to a blasphemous underworld filled with Lovecraftian slime-monsters. If he had more time, he would have stopped to try to peer through gaps in the rocks at the back of the cave and listen for faint wavering howls and gibbers from deep below. But he had more important things to do today, so instead he made his way southwest along the river to Spirit Falls, a twelve-foot-high waterfall.

There were three ways to cross to the west side of the Kanseeka in this area: the Old Stone Bridge on Oaks Road (the official way); a line of large stepping stones that had been lain across a narrow spot in the river midway between the Crow and May houses; and here at the waterfall, along an alcove in the rock behind the veil of falling water. The alcove extended all the way across the falls. Its floor was uneven and somewhat slippery, but as long as you were careful it was a convenient and picturesque way to cross the river. It was also the wisest way at the moment. The others entailed getting too close to the Crow house, the cops, and the news crews.

Stooping down to clear the overhang, Calvin made his way across the alcove. The alcove was dim and dank and loud with the echoing hiss of the falls. The spray from the falling water left tiny, chilly droplets on his bare arms.

On the other side he headed straight for the clearing. He was on Robert May's land now, and for some reason the woods on this side of the river were denser and darker than on the Crow side. Calvin had no idea if this was a naturally occurring phenomenon—maybe due to environmental differences on either side of the river—or if it meant only that the Crows had felled more trees and cleared more brush over the years. Either way, he preferred the May side. It looked older and creepier and cooler.

As Calvin drew closer to the clearing he began to see traces of human activity. Much of the brush was tramped down and broken, and there were areas where the dirt was churned with footprints. At one point he saw a blue latex glove caught in the branches of a bush.

He spotted a flash of something yellow moving amid the trees up ahead where the clearing was. Not the warm, sunny yellow of the autumn leaves, but a garish, artificial man-made shade of yellow. Were people still here?

He slowed down and advanced more cautiously, craning his head this way and that to see around the brush for a better view. He soon discerned black letters on the yellow and realized it was police tape bobbing in the breeze.

He started to relax, but then caught a glimpse of something else moving. Some*one* else. Amid the foliage he saw what looked like a white T-shirt. Blue jeans. A bit of a bare arm. A skinny arm. A girl.

Then he saw the long, red hair that haunted all his thoughts these days, and his breath caught in his throat. It was Cynthia.

A few more steps forward brought her fully into view. She stood on the edge of the clearing, her back to Calvin, her hands resting lightly on the police tape that was strung at waist level from tree trunk to tree trunk around the clearing's perimeter. There wasn't anyone else in sight.

He had been trying to keep quiet, but now he deliberately scuffed his feet on the ground to alert her to his presence.

Cynthia jumped and spun around, her eyes huge with alarm. Then she recognized him and relaxed.

"Calvin," she said. "What are you doing here?"

"Um…" He wasn't sure what to say. Now that he was faced with the reality of the situation, with the police tape cordoning off the clearing, with the woods around him bearing the traces of dozens of smart and well-trained law enforcement personnel, with Cynthia's haggard yet unyielding countenance, all of his amateur-sleuth/young-hero-to-the-rescue fantasies suddenly seemed silly and juvenile. "I, uh…I heard about what happened. I'm sorry. I just thought maybe I could…I don't know, help somehow or something." He shrugged. "But I guess there probably isn't a whole lot I can do that isn't already being done."

She studied him with a narrow, assessive gaze for a moment, then said, "I'm not so sure about that."

"What do you mean?"

She nodded in the direction of the May house.

"What do you know about Robert May?" she said.

"Robert May? Um…I don't know. I know he's old. He's, what, like, ninety-something? Beyond that, not much. I mean, there're lots of stories about him at school. About him being crazy or a Satanist or…" He stiffened. "Wait, do you think he has something to do with what happened to your sister?"

She opened her mouth to speak, then shut it, then sighed. "I don't know. It's just, I'm not sure how much you've heard, but they found one of Emily's shoes here in the clearing this morning. And some blood, too. They still don't know whose it was. The tests'll take a while. They also found some of Emily's shoe-prints in the mud by the riverbank, down by the stepping stones. And then there's that." She pointed at the center of the clearing, where there was a circle of burned grass two feet wide.

Calvin had been so preoccupied with Cynthia that he hadn't noticed the burn till now. He leaned over the police tape for a better look. The grass was blackened all the way down to the soil. Much of it had already crumbled into powder.

"What happened?" he asked. "How did it get burned like that?"

"Nobody knows. At first everyone thought it was a campfire or something, but the guys from the FBI couldn't find any signs of any combustible materials. No wood, no paper, nothing. They said it looked more like a lightning strike."

"Lightning? Seriously?" He looked at the sky, then at the circle again. "But there hasn't been a storm here for a long time. A few weeks, at least."

"I know! But my real point is, this is all on Robert

May's land." She held up a hand as if to forestall any objections. "Now, I know in and of itself that doesn't mean anything. Just because something happened on his property, that's not proof he had anything to do with it. But there're also all those stories about him. Bodies in the basement. Ritual sacrifices. Generations of inbreeding and insanity."

"Do you think all that stuff's true?"

"Well, I don't know about all of it. But have you heard the stories about mysterious deliveries to his house late at night?"

"Yeah. Like, trucks delivering coffins or iron maidens or whatever. It always sounded like something out of a cheesy horror story to me."

"Well, I can tell you for a fact those stories are based on truth. I mean, I didn't see coffins or anything, but listen: One night about two years ago I was coming back from a get-together at Jess Asher's, right? It was pretty late. Late enough that I wound up getting grounded, actually. It was probably around one a.m. Anyway, I was heading east down Oaks Road, but sticking to the shadows under the eaves of the woods so no one would see me. And as I was nearing Mr. May's driveway, I saw an old flatbed truck turn down it, and chained to the truck's bed was this big metal oil drum."

"An oil drum? What was in it?"

"I have no idea! When I came to the end of his driveway, I paused and looked down it. I couldn't see anything because of the way the driveway winds through the woods, but I could hear faint clanks and bangs as they unloaded the truck. Then everything went silent, so I started walking on. I had just turned down my own driveway when I heard the truck pull back out. It was coming my way, so I stopped and waited, and when it drove by, the bed was empty. There were two guys in the cab. One was a skinny guy with a beard and sunglasses—"

"At one in the morning?"

"I know! And the other one looked almost like a gorilla with a blue cap and overalls on."

"That is really weird."

"Exactly. And let me ask you something else: What the hell does he do? What has he ever done? I mean, I assume he's pretty rich because of the brewery his family and mine used to own, but what does he do with all his time?"

"I don't know."

"*Nobody* knows. I've been living next to him my whole life, and I couldn't tell you the first thing about him. He hardly ever leaves his house. And the few times I've seen him outside it, he's always acting weird."

"Like how?"

"Well, sometimes when I was a little girl, I'd be out playing in the woods, and he'd just sort of pop up out of nowhere and start talking to me. Even back then, he looked ancient, all bent and wrinkled and white-haired. The sight of him always scared me. I'd never seen anyone who looked so old. Anyway, he'd come up to me and ask me all these questions about me and my family."

"Your family? Like what?"

"All kinds of stuff. He'd always start out really innocuous, asking me how I was doing, what school was like, how my parents were. Basic neighbor stuff, right? But then the questions would get more probing and specific. I remember one time he wanted to know about my Aunt Wendy, my dad's sister, up in Boston. He seemed especially interested in her seizures."

"Seizures?"

"Yeah, when she was young—way before my time; this was back when she was growing up here—she used to have these, like, epileptic fits or something. I don't think she's had one in years. But Mr. May wanted to know if she'd had any more, and if anyone had ever told me much about the ones she did have. And then this other time he wanted to know if I knew anything about my grandma's death. My dad's mom, that is. He never seemed interested in my mom's family. But anyway, you see my point? It's like he was collecting information on us, like he has a weird fixation on my family."

"And you think, what, he's taken his fixation to the next level now?"

Cynthia shrugged. "I don't know. I just think there's definitely something not quite kosher going on with that guy, something worth looking into."

"Yeah, I agree he's definitely peculiar," Calvin said. "But like you said yourself, he's also ancient. Admittedly I've only seen him a couple of times, but he looks like he can barely stand up without a cane. Could a little old man like that really snatch up a ten-year-old girl?"

Cynthia rolled her eyes. "That's pretty much what the cops said."

"You told them?"

"Yeah, and they just sort of pooh-poohed the whole thing. They gave me that 'we'll take that under consideration' routine, you know? They did send someone over to interview him, but they did that with all the neighbors." She shook her head. "The thing is, he doesn't have to be super-healthy or anything. It looks like Emily came out here on her own. All Mr. May would have to do is just hit her on the head with a rock and knock her out. That could account for the blood. Then he's too weak to carry her, so he drags her off. In the process her shoe comes off but he doesn't notice."

Calvin nodded. It was a plausible theory. Except…

"What about the burned grass?"

"I don't know," she said. Then a light dawned in her eyes. "Maybe he rigged up some glowing pyrotechnic thingie to look like a fairy light or something. To lure her in."

"That makes sense, I guess. It seems kind of unnecessarily elaborate, but…"

"It's better than magical lightning out of a clear sky."

Calvin nodded. "Very true." He regarded the burned circle for a moment, then stared off in the direction of the May house.

"You believe me?" she asked.

"I don't know. I mean, evidence like this can be interpreted all kinds of ways. It's all too inconclusive. But from what you've said, it really does sound like Mr. May merits further investigation. There's definitely something odd going on over there."

Her left eyebrow rose. "You wanna help me conduct a little unofficial investigation, then?"

He looked at her in surprise, all his amateur sleuth fantasies surging to the fore again. But this was even better than his fantasies. Now, not only would he be investigating a mystery and hopefully helping Emily, but he would be doing it at Cynthia's side.

"Count me in," he said with a firm nod.

Chapter 5

Anna West and John Coyote

1

Eleven-year-old Anna West rang the doorbell of the small brick house on Papesh Road that was home to John Coyote, her friend and classmate and a fellow BFF of Emily's. While Anna waited for an answer, she looked over her shoulder and flashed a reassuring smile at her mom Karen, who sat behind the wheel of the silver minivan idling at the curb. Anna felt kind of babyish to have her mom chauffeuring her on a three-block trip she had walked unsupervised a hundred times before. Then again, Anna understood her mom's—all parents'—concern and sudden overzealous protectiveness in the wake of Emily's disappearance. And while one part of her cringed at the babyishness of it, another part was thankful. With a possible child-nabbing psycho on the loose, it was better to be safe than sorry.

The front door opened and there stood John's aunt Colleen Brandt. She was a short, stout woman who always wore dark frumpy cardigans and fluttery ankle-length skirts and whose brown hair was always drawn back in a bun so tight it could have doubled as a drawer pull. Ms. Brandt gave Anna's mom a smile and a wave. Anna's mom returned the wave, then drove away.

"Come on inside," Ms. Brandt said, holding open the

door. "It's terrible what's happened. How are you holding up?"

"Okay, I guess," Anna said as she stepped into the vestibule.

"Both John and I are worried sick." Ms. Brandt glanced at the open door of the living room from which the zany music and crazy sound effects of a cartoon emanated. Then she bent down toward Anna and whispered, "He's not dealing with this very well, I'm afraid. He woke up feeling poorly, and then…" She sighed. "I just hope they find her soon. But with the FBI on the case now, I'm sure it won't be long.

"Yeah."

"Come on." Ms. Brandt turned and led Anna toward the living room. "Perhaps you'll be able to cheer him up better than a superannuated old biddy like me can."

Despite the grim circumstances, Anna couldn't help smiling a little. Only Ms. Brandt would use a word like "superannuated" in conversation. Though she was a sweet lady, she was kind of a weirdo. She was nearly fifty, had never married, and worked as the head librarian at the May Public Library. According to John, she spent most of her free time working on an enormous epic poem about pirates. Apparently she had been working on it for decades. John said he caught a glimpse of the complete manuscript once and swore it was as tall as he was. Plus it was full of words like "superannuated" (and worse). More shockingly, the manuscript was written entirely in longhand, the ultra-old-fashioned way. Ms. Brandt used computers only at work and only because she had to.

Still, for all her quirks, and despite the fact that she probably hadn't wanted any kids, Ms. Brandt had done a fine job raising John after the death of John's parents. No one had ever told Anna the full story of the tragedy, but she managed to piece most of it together from scraps of overheard conversations. Apparently Martin and Sally Coyote and their only child, John, barely a year old at the time, had been returning home from Christmas shopping one blustery winter evening when the car hit a patch of ice and swerved straight into the path of an oncoming pickup. John's parents and the driver of the pickup died instantly. John came through it miraculously unscathed: When fire-fighters tore open the twisted wreckage they found John still strapped securely to his safety seat with not a mark on him.

At least not on his body. For as long as Anna had known him, John had been subject to bouts of intense moodiness, during which he became withdrawn and sullen and almost hostile. Anna had always assumed these moods were rooted in his parents' untimely death, though she wasn't sure if he actually remembered the accident (she sure hoped not), or if he simply knew what others had told him.

She had figured that Emily's disappearance would plunge him into one of these dark moods, but he was even worse than she expected. Anna almost gasped out loud when she saw him. He sat on the living room couch gazing vacantly at an episode of *Pinky and the Brain*. His face was pale and waxy, and there were dark bags under his eyes. He was bundled tight in one of his aunt's homemade black af-ghans. His right hand stuck out of the afghan's folds and lay atop the TV remote on his thigh. With his distant eyes and his pallid skin and the afghan wrapped around him like a shroud, he looked almost like a corpse.

Anna tried to suppress the awful thought. Dead things were nasty. Over the summer she had caught a few minutes of an episode of *The Walking Dead,* and for the next two weeks she had nightmares about zombies pursuing her across dark, desolate landscapes. Many of the zombies were people she had once loved—her family, her friends, even John, even Emily—all of them now transformed into soulless, shambling, dead-eyed things eager to rip her to shreds and devour her still-warm flesh.

"I'll leave you two alone for now," Ms. Brandt said. "Let me know if you need anything." She bustled off into the kitchen.

"Hey," Anna said, crossing the room to the couch.

"Hey," John said, his voice a whisper.

"You're sick?"

His afghan-draped shoulders rose a fraction.

"I don't know. Something."

"Something?"

He didn't answer. His finger pressed a button on the remote, and *Pinky and the Brain* was replaced by black-and-white cowboys galloping along on horses.

"Hurry!" one of the cowboys hollered to the others. "Before that snakey varmint gets away!"

Anna gestured at an empty spot on the couch next to him.

"Can I sit?"

Another feeble shrug. "Sure."

Anna sat.

John's finger moved again. The cowboys were swapped out for a Volkswagen commercial.

"I was worried about you," Anna said. "Especially with, you know, both of you not in school today. I mean, after I heard about Emily, I thought maybe you were…" She shrugged, embarrassed to remember how hysterical she had gotten during her interview with Officer Ritelli in the elementary school's conference room this morning. When Ritelli revealed the reason for Emily's absence from school, Anna immediately feared that John's absence had the same horrible explanation. Her frantic pleas had put a brief halt to the interview while Ritelli made a few calls to check on John's whereabouts. To Anna's relief, it turned out John's aunt had called him in sick this morning. His and Emily's mutual absence was only a coincidence.

Or was it? Could John have somehow unconsciously known what had happened to Emily and become ill in response? Anna had always felt that John and Emily shared a bond she herself wasn't privy to. When the three of them were together she sometimes felt left out, a third wheel. They were all best friends—a three-person tribe, as Emily liked to call them—but John and Emily's friendship was something rare and special. Unhealthily so, perhaps. John and Emily were *too* alike, really. With their black hair, dark eyes, and light complexions, they looked similar enough to pass for brother and sister. In addition, both of them possessed hyperactive imaginations, a fascination with monsters and fantasy and weird things, and a disdain for the suburban blandness of their hometown. To cap things off, they shared the same birthday. Not just any day, either, but October 31st, Halloween. John and Emily saw great meaning in these coincidences, and this led them to cultivate their similarities and see themselves as a breed apart from the boring normality that surrounded them.

Anna tried to be the moderator of the trio, the voice of common sense, the brake on John and Emily's sometimes runaway crazytrain. Often she failed, but she valued the friendship enough to keep trying. She didn't always understand John and Emily, but she loved them and couldn't imagine a life without them. They kept things interesting.

The commercial ended and a show started. There was a shot of a white-coated scientist peering into a microscope, and a deep-voiced melodramatic narrator said, "Who are we? Where do we come from? What dictates our personality, our development, our choices? These age-old questions have puzzled scientists and philosophers for centuries, but now the answer is finally within our grasp."

The title appeared on the screen: *Cracking the Genetic Code*. Dramatic music swelled.

They cut to a shot of some chromosomes, dark rods on a white background. Anna thought they looked like rabbit poop.

"The final frontier lies not 'out there,'" the narrator said, "but within each and every one of us. Within our cells, our genes, our DNA…"

John turned to her. It was the first time he had looked at her since she came in. His dark eyes looked so distant and dead Anna's first instinct was to shy away from him. But she held her ground.

"I saw a light last night," he said.

"A light?"

"I woke up. I don't know what time it was. Really late, though. I woke up and there was a light floating in the middle of my room. A ball of white light about the size of someone's head. It made the shadows of everything stand out really sharp and black on the walls. The light hung there for a minute, and then it just disappeared like a soap bubble popping, and the room went dark again."

He looked at Anna a moment longer, then turned his gaze back to the TV.

Anna stared at his pale profile, unsure what to think or say. The strangeness of the whole thing scared her.

"Are you…" She cleared her throat. "Are you sure it

wasn't a dream?"

He nodded without taking his eyes from the TV, where a DNA helix was spiraling around and around while the announcer talked about things called adenine, cytosine, guanine, and thymine. "It was real."

"Do you think it was…I dunno, like, a sign or something?"

"I think maybe it was her." His voice was barely audible. "A last goodbye."

Anna gaped at him, appalled and horrified at what he was suggesting. He didn't notice her outrage—he was still staring zombie-like at the TV—so she grabbed his shoulder and twisted him toward her. The vacant look in his eyes vanished, and he blinked at her, startled, lucid. She felt glad and almost triumphant that she had shaken him out of his stupor, even if only temporarily.

"She's not dead, John. Or, well, we don't know. We don't really know anything."

He wrenched his shoulder from her grasp hard enough to make the couch shake. "*I* know. The light—"

"It was just a light. If it was even that. Maybe it was a dream. I've had dreams I thought were real." (The memory of her zombie dream floated to the surface of her mind again. She forced it back down.)

"It was…" John scowled. He was mad at her. That was fine. Even if he hated her now, it was better than him being a dead-eyed zombie. "I saw it!"

"You *thought* you saw it."

John regarded her uncertainly for a moment. Then his eyes narrowed. "What are you doing? Weren't *you* the one who told the cops about some guy saying he was gonna show her fairies in the woods? The TV news people said it was a friend of hers who told them that, and it sure wasn't me."

"I…yeah. She called me last night and told me she was gonna have some really cool news to tell me today. I asked her what she was talking about, but at first she wouldn't tell me anything. I kept pressing her, though, and she finally admitted that earlier in the day she had talked to some guy who said he could show her fairies in the woods around her house. I asked her who, but she wouldn't tell me anything more than that. She was so excited. I told her she shouldn't go anywhere with strangers, but she said he wasn't really a stranger. She said she knew him from somewhere. She didn't say where." She shrugged. "But none of that proves anything. We don't know for sure what happened."

John snorted. "Yeah, right." He shot her a contemptuous look that made her feel both angry and embarrassed.

"Who knows?" Anna insisted. "Maybe it was all true. Maybe she did see fairies. Maybe they took her away. I've heard stories about that: people being taken off to fairy land and coming back years later, the same age as when they left." Anna didn't believe those stories, or that fairies might be responsible for Emily's disappearance, but she hoped John might.

He didn't.

"Don't be stupid," he snapped. His eyes glimmered with unshed tears. "It wasn't fairies. It was just some stupid sex pervert. Just another scumbag, like all the rest of them. Like the whole world. It's all nothing but perverts and car crashes and death. Everything good gets destroyed while evil just goes on and on, and there's nothing anybody can do about it."

In a way this outpouring of pessimism was more alarming than his deadness had been. But the pain and despair that lay behind it were clear as day, and they brought on Anna's own tears. She laid a hand on his shoulder, not grabbing now, not forcing. Only comforting. Connecting.

"I don't believe that," she said in a soft, gentle voice. "I don't believe that at all. But you know what? Even if you're right and I'm wrong, there *is* something we can do. We can not let it make us bad, too. And giving up on people is bad. Maybe you're ready to give up hope. Maybe you're ready to give up on Emily. But I'm not."

By the time she was done speaking, her face was wet with tears. Again. It felt like she had done nothing but cry all day. But that was fine. She had every reason to.

"Hope," he echoed softly. The quivering films that covered his eyes finally broke, and a single tear slipped down each cheek. The tears dripped from his chin to dot the afghan, the spots almost invisible on the black fabric. He looked away at the TV. On the screen Frankenstein's Monster was lurching forward, arms outstretched. The narrator was saying something about Frankenfoods and genetic engineering.

Anna edged in closer and put her arm around his shoulders.

"Everything'll be okay, John," she said. "One way or another."

He didn't say anything, but she thought she saw him give a tiny nod.

Chapter 6
Robert May

1

Calvin had never seen the May house before, and when he peeped out of the foliage on the eastern edge of the clearing in which the house stood, his jaw dropped. He couldn't believe he had grown up only six blocks away from such a cool old place without ever knowing about it.

It was a Second Empire structure built of dark-red bricks, and although Calvin couldn't see the whole thing from where he crouched, it appeared to be shaped like a plus sign, its four wings aligned with the four cardinal points. Each wing ended in a porched entrance surmounted by a second-floor balcony. The high mansard roof was covered with dark-gray fish-scale shingles and crowned with cast-iron cresting shaped like alternating circles and spikes. A gabled dormer jutted from the roof above each entrance, while from the dead center of the house rose a four-sided mansard-roofed tower with the same cast-iron cresting. Spaced like sentries around the tower were four tall brick chimneys. Despite its age, the house seemed to be in excellent condition.

Northeast of the house stood a brick carriage house that had been converted into a two-car garage. A small, decrepit wooden outbuilding, apparently a shed of some kind, sat due north of the house, right on the edge of the woods. The shed was leaning to one side, and all around it were bits of broken shingles that had slid off its sagging roof.

Weeds were growing up through cracks in the concrete driveway, which extended from the closed garage door to disappear amid the trees to the south of the house. There were no vehicles anywhere in sight.

The late-afternoon sun was well below the level of the treetops, and the clearing was filling with shadow. When the wind stirred the trees, a few irregular patches of dim yellow sunlight flashed on the grass and the driveway. But then the wind died down and the shadows returned. Aside from the leaves, nothing moved. Every visible window of the house was curtained tight. Calvin's tension was a knot in his gut.

"So what now?" he asked Cynthia, who was crouched beside him and likewise peering through the foliage at the May house. She was so close to him he could smell the herbal shampoo she used, could see a tiny mole on the edge of her left eyebrow, could hear the faint click and see the slight bulge of her throat when she swallowed. The sleeve of her T-shirt brushed his, and even that indirect touch made his heart leap. For a moment he forgot all about the gravity of the situation and felt only a flutter of delight that he was with her, next to her, sharing this singular moment with her, a thing they alone would share forever. When she turned to him to respond, he had to look down for a moment so he could clear the inappropriately dopey, spacey look from his face. He needed to focus on the task at hand.

"I guess we should try to see inside," she said.

"Does that mean actually breaking in?"

"I don't know." She frowned uncertainly, as if only

now realizing the possible complications and consequences of the path they'd chosen. But then conviction hardened her face, and she nodded. "I guess if we have to, yeah. I mean, I'd rather wind up getting in trouble and—and—I don't know, going to jail or whatever, if it means at least finding out the truth. Even if she's not in there and Mr. May has nothing to do with it, we have to find out." She paused, then shrugged. "Or, well, *I* do anyway."

"No," he said. "I think at this point I do, too."

She gave him a small, grateful smile. He smiled back. Her smile faded and her expression clouded over as if she had thought of something that troubled her. She turned to look out at the May house again.

"We should probably check the garage and that little shed, too," she said. "Rule those out first."

"Yeah. Plus, those'll give us some good cover to approach the house. Everywhere else it's just wide-open space. We'd be spotted in a heartbeat."

They retreated a couple dozen paces into the woods, circled around the clearing until they drew parallel to the shed, then crept forward to the edge of the woods again.

The rear wall of the shed was blank, just dry old boards shedding decades-old white paint, but the east side sported a single bleary window in a rotten frame. Calvin and Cynthia rounded the corner and crept to the window. From here, they were in sight of the May house's eastern porch. No one was on it, but that didn't make them feel any safer. All Mr. May or anyone else inside had to do was step out the door and the jig would be up.

Calvin and Cynthia cupped their hands around their eyes and peered in through the window's dirt-smudged glass. Calvin made out the dim shapes of hoes, shovels, a stack of crates, what looked like an old engine on the floor.

Everything was old and filthy and festooned with webs full of spider eggs that looked like desiccated chickpeas.

"This place hasn't been touched in years," he said.

"Let's check the garage."

That was easier said than done. To get there, they would have to cross forty feet of open grass that would leave them in full view of the rear of the house. Pausing at the southeast corner of the shed, they took one last look at the May house, then one last look at the grounds around them, then one last look at each other. Calvin nodded. Cynthia nodded. They sprinted for the garage.

As Calvin ran he kept glancing at the house, sure a door would fly open and someone would come charging out with a shotgun. But no one appeared and nothing changed, and in surprisingly short order, Calvin and Cynthia were flinging themselves flat against the bricks of the garage's rear wall. They remained there a moment, chests heaving, breath loud and fast, then glanced at each other and nodded again.

There was a door in the back wall of the garage, but it was padlocked shut. Next to it was a window almost as bleary as the one in the shed. Calvin and Cynthia peered through it. The garage's shadowy interior was dominated by a long boxy shape draped with a white sheet. A car. A big one. Maybe a Cadillac or an old Thunderbird. The garage's walls were lined with wooden shelves laden with gas cans, funnels, spray bottles, an oil pan, and similar items.

Calvin grunted. He had been hoping they would find some firm proof of either guilt or innocence without having to get too close to the house.

"So," Cynthia said. She looked as nervous as Calvin felt. "The house, then."

"Yeah."

They slunk to the northwest corner of the garage and peeked around it at the May house. Nothing had changed. Everything was silent and still. The house's curtained windows dimly reflected the sky and the woods.

They withdrew behind the corner again.

"I don't know that we're gonna be able to see in very well," Calvin said. "Not with all the curtains shut like that."

"I know. But that's kind of telling in and of itself, don't you think? It's not like there're lots of passersby who might glance in through the windows. I mean, this place is about as isolated as you can get around here, and yet he still religiously keeps every single curtain shut tight. Why?"

"Some people are just really private."

"True," she conceded. "Either way, we should still try to look in through the windows. The curtains might not be too thick. We might be able to see through them. Or there might be gaps we can look through."

"Yeah." Calvin peeked around the corner again for another look at the house. Each wing sported six tall, narrow windows on the first floor: two on either side, and two more looking out onto the porch. Chest-high bushes ran along the sides of the wings.

He drew back next to Cynthia.

"I'm thinking we should avoid the porches for now and just stick with the side windows," he said. "That way, we can stay behind the bushes, out of sight."

"Good idea."

Both of them took a deep breath, then slipped around the corner and raced across the lawn toward the house. Like before, Calvin eyed the windows and doors as he ran, more certain than ever that someone would catch them, but they made it to the house without a hitch. They ducked behind the bushes that lined the east side of the north wing, then hunkered down in the narrow gap between the bushes and the house's outer wall. The wall's dark bricks ended a foot above the ground. Below that were big gray foundation stones. The ground was littered with crumbly brown leaves from autumns past. Calvin and Cynthia's fast, ragged breaths were loud in the confined space.

After they had caught their breaths, they inched to the nearest window. Unlike the ones in the outbuildings, the windows here were in good shape, with clean glass and sturdy wooden frames free of rot. The frames could have used a new coat of paint, though; the light-green paint that covered them was cracked and flaking in places. Bits of it dotted the ground below.

Calvin and Cynthia looked through the window. The curtain was thin and slightly translucent, but not enough to show more than dark, vague shapes. Fortunately the edge of the curtain fell slightly short of the window frame, leaving a half-inch gap they could peer through.

Inside they saw a swath of a white washing machine, atop the closed lid of which sat an empty brown plastic clothes basket.

"Laundry room," Cynthia muttered.

"Let's try the next one."

They made their way to the second window on this side of the north wing, but this time there was no gap to see through. They moved on, following the wall to the right-angle bend where the north wing met the east wing, then along the north wall of the east wing. The first of the two windows on this side of the east wing likewise had no gaps to see through. But the next one did. In fact there were gaps all the way around the curtain, giving Calvin and Cynthia a decent view of the room inside. The room had speckled gray carpeting, a huge fireplace with a stuffed eagle mounted on the wall above it, a pair of red leather wingback chairs, and an antique-looking dark-wood table bearing a Tiffany lamp with a gold-and-green dragonfly on the shade. Every surface in sight was dull with dust.

"Why is everything so dusty?" Cynthia said.

"Are you sure he's still alive?" Calvin asked. "When was the last time anyone saw him?"

"That's a good question." She thought for a moment. "The last time *I* saw him was…geez, five or six months ago, I guess. Back in the spring. I was coming home from school one day, and I spotted him prowling around in Indian Hill Cemetery, right across Potts Road from my house. God, for all I know, he might've been waiting for me, spying on me. I mean, he must've known what time school lets out."

"Either way, has anyone seen him since?"

"Not that I'm aware of."

"Hm. Well, let's check some more windows. Maybe we'll have better luck closer to the front of the house. I mean, this place is pretty big and it's just one old man. Maybe he just doesn't use most of the rooms."

They rose from their crouch, ready to move around to the front of the house, but froze dead when they saw Robert May standing on the other side of the bushes, watching them with an amused smile.

Mr. May was said to be nearly a hundred years old, and he certainly looked it. He was small and thin and bent, and his face was a network of wrinkles, like a piece of paper that's been crumpled and smoothed out over and over again. His hair was fine and white like eiderdown. A pair of bushy white eyebrows overhung his moist brown eyes. He wore a black suit with a thin black tie, and leaned upon a black, silver-handled cane.

"Let me guess," he said. "You're here to tell me I need new double-hung vinyl replacement windows."

"We—" Cynthia spluttered. "We were—we just—" She scowled at herself, then balled her fists and lifted her chin and said, "Do you know where my sister is?"

Mr. May grunted.

"Why do you think I would know where your sister is?" he asked. Cynthia opened her mouth to respond, but before she could say anything, he held up a finger and said, "Wait, let me see if I can work out your reasoning." He began to pace back and forth as he spoke, his cane moving at his side in short, swift arcs. He looked like a geriatric lawyer delivering a closing argument. "The shoe and the signs of activity in the clearing point to her being on my property last night, yes? And more importantly, I'm weird and old. The strange elderly hermit who never hangs around at the local coffee shop, or wherever folks gather these days. I must be antisocial and thus a horrible person, right? Never mind that I can barely walk."

Cynthia blushed. "It's more than that," she protested. "What about your obsession with my family?"

Mr. May looked baffled. "My what?"

"I remember you always pumping me for information when I was a little girl, asking all kinds of nosey questions about my family and what we were up to."

He stared at her with surprise, mouth wide, eyes blinking. Then he emitted a small, soft laugh and nodded. "I see. Psychological relativity at work."

"What, you're saying you don't have some kind of interest in my family? That I'm only misinterpreting something?"

"No, I do have an interest in the Crow family. But my interest is not quite as sinister as you seem to think." He fixed his gaze on Calvin. "You, however, are not a Crow."

"Um, I'm Calvin. I'm a Beckerman."

Mr. May nodded. "It's nice to, ah, to meet you."

"Likewise."

"Look, do you or don't you know anything about my sister's disappearance?" Cynthia said to Mr. May.

"I might know something, but only in an indirect and thoroughly innocent way. Or rather, I might suspect something." He glanced down at his bent, frail body, then sighed. "If I were younger, I would be out there looking for her myself. I have experience with, ah, investigatory matters. But I find myself rather lacking in mobility these days."

"What, were you some kind of detective or something?" Calvin asked.

Mr. May laughed. "No. Nothing like that." He regarded the duo with narrow, appraisive eyes a moment. Then he stepped back and motioned them forward. "For goodness' sake, step out of those bushes. You'll wind up with bugs in your shoes."

They did so, wriggling out a narrow gap between two bushes, then spent a moment shaking the tiny leaves from their clothes.

Mr. May watched all this with a small smile.

"The intrepid investigators," he said softly.

Calvin glanced up at him sharply, thinking he was making fun of them. But instead Mr. May looked thoughtful, almost wistful. His eyes were distant as if he were remembering something.

"How did you spot us anyway?" Cynthia asked. "I mean, I thought we were being pretty careful."

"Alas, it was merely bad luck on your part. I happened to be out in the woods, taking a look at the Stone Pillar."

"The pillar?" Calvin said. The Stone Pillar was an eight-foot-tall column of limestone that jutted straight up out of the earth in the woods a quarter mile due north of the May house. It was three feet thick at its base but tapered to a mere foot across at the top. Most people believed it was either a marker erected by the Indians to designate an important spot or just geological detritus plopped down in an unusual position by the receding glacier. Calvin preferred to imagine it was the last surviving relic of some ancient, long-forgotten civilization.

"Was something going on there?" Calvin asked.

"I assume you know about the burn in the clearing?" Mr. May said.

"Yeah," said Cynthia. "The police still don't know what caused it."

"I imagine they don't. Anyway, I thought I'd check a few other significant sites around the woods and see if they showed any changes in condition, as well."

"Why do you think other sites would be…changed or whatever?"

Mr. May hesitated, staring at them in silence for a moment as if he were trying to make up his mind about something. Then he turned and waved a hand at the woods.

"This area has a curious history," he said.

"It does?" Calvin said.

Mr. May didn't respond. Instead he fixed his gaze on Cynthia. "Do you know much about your family's history?"

She raised her eyebrows, surprised by the question. "Um…a little. I don't know. About what, exactly?"

"Spirit Cave, for instance?"

"What about it?"

"Do you know why it's called Spirit Cave? Do you know how it got sealed up the way it is now?"

"I remember my dad mentioning something about how a long time ago there were, like, caverns back there or something, and someone dynamited it shut."

Mr. May goggled at her. "That's it?"

"Um…" Cynthia shifted uneasily, looking like a pupil caught unprepared for a sudden pop quiz. She glanced at Calvin, who shrugged. "Yeah?"

Mr. May shook his head. "It was dynamited shut by my great-grandfather, Turner May, and your great-great-great-grandfather, Hamilton Crow, in 1871."

"Oh!"

"And as for why they did it…" He checked his wristwatch. "Well, that's a rather long story. I assume you are investigating Emily's disappearance in a purely unofficial capacity?"

They nodded.

"And now that you have ruled me out as a suspect (I hope), do you intend to continue your investigation?"

Calvin and Cynthia glanced at each other. Calvin saw in her eyes the same conclusions he himself had reached. Though they hadn't ruled out Mr. May in a legal, evidential sense, this brief conversation with him had convinced them he had nothing to do with Emily's disappearance. Instead of the creepy nutjob they had been expecting, they had found a likeable, intelligent man sadly hindered by a failing body. Unfortunately, with Mr. May out of the running, they had no other suspects or ideas about where to look for one.

"We want to continue the investigation," Cynthia said. "Or, well, *I* do—"

"I do too," Calvin interjected.

"But…" Cynthia shrugged.

Mr. May nodded. "You don't know how to proceed

from here, eh? Well, let me tell you, I want to find Emily as much as you do. Obviously I cannot trot about hither and yon as I once did, but you two can. And with a whole lifetime of investigatory experience behind me, I can help guide you."

"But what did you investigate?" Calvin asked.

Cynthia's phone jangled in her pocket.

"Oh, crap," she groaned as she dug it out of her jeans. "I bet I know who that is. They must have finally noticed I wasn't in my room, after all."

"You didn't tell them where you went?" Calvin said.

"They wouldn't have let me go. My mom…" She shook her head, then took a deep breath and answered the phone.

"Hi, I—"

The outraged voice that blasted from the phone was so loud Calvin and Mr. May could hear it a few feet away, though they couldn't quite make out the words. Cynthia winced and moved the phone a few inches from her ear.

"Mom, I just took a walk," Cynthia said the moment there was a lull in the torrent of angry words. "I wanted to—" More angry words. "Yeah, I know, I just—" More angry words. "Mom, I—" More angry words, then sudden total silence. Cynthia put the phone away, then gave Calvin and Mr. May a sheepish look.

"I gotta go," she said. "I don't think I'll be able to get away again today."

"What about tomorrow?" Mr. May said. "Could you come by here tomorrow?"

"Maybe. Probably. I'm sure I can figure something out."

"And you?" Mr. May said, turning to Calvin. "Will you be free tomorrow?"

"Sure," Calvin said. "It's Saturday. I've got all day free."

"Good. Then why don't both of you come by here as early as you can. We'll need lots of time. There's a lot I need to tell you."

"About what?" Cynthia asked.

"About history. About the woods. About your family and mine. About…other things. I can't say for certain that all of it will be relevant to whatever has happened to your sister, but it might be. And then we can figure out how to proceed with the investigation."

Calvin eyed him with wonder. "What is it you investigated anyway?"

Mr. May smiled. "You'll find out all about it tomorrow."

Chapter 7

Donovan Crow
and Violet O'Donohue

1

Donovan Crow sat on the edge of his bed and stared at
Emily's face on the flier that one of the cops had left on
the kitchen table this afternoon. It was the typical missing
child flier, with a photo, the vital stats, the reward being
offered ($10,000 at last report), and the number to call if
you had any info. Donovan had seen thousands of these
things before, on TV and the Internet and the wall at the
post office. The difference was, this one showed someone
he knew and loved. This one showed his sister.

He set the flier aside before it made him start crying
again. He had blubbered more than enough already. The
flier was warped and crinkled from his teardrops.

He took a drag on the Marlboro between his lips, then
gagged at the acrid burnt taste that filled his mouth. His
plucked the cigarette from his mouth and looked at it. It
had burned down to the filter while he had been gazing at
the flier. Shaking his head, he mashed it out in the ashtray
on his bedside table. Then he lit another one.

Normally he was more careful about smoking in his
room. Normally he would have the window open and a
stick of incense burning to mask the smell, but right now

no one cared. No one was going to come up here and check on him. Everyone was lost in their own private hell. At last check, Mom was asleep on the living room couch, having exhausted herself bitching out Cynthia after Cyn had gotten back from wherever the fuck she had gone; Cynthia sat in the armchair nearby watching TV shows she hated, glued there by a sense of guilt and duty; and Dad had retired to his workroom in the basement, ostensibly to do a little therapeutic woodworking, but more likely to get quietly drunk.

And then there was Emily. Wherever she was.

He felt the tears returning. He clenched his teeth and scrunched up his face against them, but this time he couldn't hold them back. They built up in his eyes, ready to spill...

There was a tap-tap-tap at the window.

He looked up, a relieved and grateful smile spreading across his face even though the curtain was drawn and he couldn't see who it was. There was only one person who would be tapping at his window at this hour. Exactly the person he wanted and needed to see.

He set his cigarette in the ashtray, knuckled the dampness from his eyes, then got up and opened the curtain. As expected, it was Violet O'Donohue, his kinda-sorta girlfriend (sometimes she seemed cool with them being a couple; other times she insisted they were nothing more than BFWBs).

Donovan raised the sash, and Violet climbed inside. Without a word, she threw her arms around him and gave him a rib-cracking hug. He clutched her petite figure close, the underside of his chin against the top of her head. There were a few bits of leaves clinging to her long, dark-brown hair, no doubt from the oak tree she had climbed to reach the porch roof and thence his window. He absently picked them off.

"Dude, I am so sorry about everything," she said. Then she drew back and looked him in the face, her green eyes narrowing to slits. "What we gotta do now is get your sis back, then find the motherfucker responsible and beat the shit out of him with pillowcases filled with cans of Coke."

"Yeah," he said with a small smile. It was weird: Violet was the craziest person he knew, but now, amid the sea of bad craziness his life had become, she was his constant, his island of sanity and comforting familiarity.

"Here," she said, digging into the pocket of her jeans. She pulled out a baggie full of pot. "Deb gave me this to give to you. She said you'd probably need it."

"Yeah." He did need it. He had finished off his last batch of weed two days ago. Which turned out to be a good thing. Otherwise the cops would have found it when they were searching the house. "Tell Deb thanks. You know, maybe I should start saving the seeds. We could grow some in the woods somewhere. It's the perfect place." He frowned. "Well, usually." The tears returned. He sat down on the edge of the bed, his head lowered. "Shit."

Violet sat next to him and put an arm around him.

"Why don't you tell me everything that's happened," she said. "All I got at school was a lot of rumors and spin and official bullshit. Besides, talking's supposed to help in situations like this, right? So just, like, start at the beginning."

After heaving a long, shaky sigh, he did.

2

"So, wait," Violet said after Donovan had finished, "you're saying they think she met this guy in the park yesterday afternoon?"

"Well, they don't know for sure," Donovan said. "All Emily told Anna West was that she talked to the guy sometime yesterday. She didn't say where. But, see, the only places she went yesterday were school and the park. She was around other people the whole time she was at school—her friends, her teacher, the other kids—so it's really unlikely she could've talked to some guy without anyone noticing. But at the park..." He shrugged. "I mean, she goes up there and just jumps rope in that corner near the rose bushes. She was there for, like, nearly an hour that day. Anybody could've talked to her."

"Dude, no, the thing is, *I* was in the park yesterday afternoon. Only for, like, fifteen or twenty minutes, but still..."

"You what?"

"Yeah! Remember I was comin' over here? I stopped off at the park on my way over to sort of hang out a little, have a smoke, watch the funny people on display."

"Did you see Emily?"

"Uh-uh. I was right along the edge of the woods about where the walking paths end, so the corner where she was was way out of sight. But I saw other people. I even recognized some of them. One of them might be the person responsible."

"Why the fuck haven't you called the cops about this?"

"Cuz I didn't fucking know they wanted to know about it."

"But it's been all over the news. The cops have been urging anyone in the park yesterday afternoon to come forward ever since late this morning. Didn't they announce it in school?"

"Dude, I skipped school today. And I have better things to do with my free time than sit on my ass watching fucking television or listening to the radio or surfing gay-ass websites like my geektard sister Lauren."

"You have to tell the police about this."

"Oh, come on. Me and cops aren't exactly on speaking terms. You know that."

"Violet." He grabbed her arm, his jaw set, his usual quiet insouciance replaced by a cold, icy firmness that made Violet blink at him in surprise.

"All right, all right," she muttered. "Do the cops have a phone number?"

"Of course they do!"

"Well, how the fuck would I know? I never call 'em."

"There's a tip-line number." He grabbed the flier and showed her the number at the bottom.

Violet sighed. "All right. Fuck. Let's do it. Where's your phone?"

He got out his phone and handed it to her. "What happened to your phone?"

"I kinda lost it."

"Again? Your dad's gonna be pissed."

"Yeah, yeah. When is he ever *not* pissed?"

She dialed the number of the police tip-line. The instant the other end was picked up, she started talking as fast as an auctioneer: "Yeah, hi, look, I was in the park yesterday, when you guys're asking about, and I can tell you some of the people who were there. There were a bunch of kids playing softball down on the baseball diamond. And then there were these two thirty-something chicks chatting with each other by the big rosebushes the city maintenance crews're too fucking lazy to trim. One of the chicks was black and the other was white, and they both had babies in strollers. I think you can rule the babies out as suspects. And maybe the chicks, too, but you never know. Also, there were a couple of people whose names I know. And they were both adult men, which means they are totally the most likely suspects, because we all know the depths of douchiness grown men are capable of. One of them was this dude named Roger Grey, who's got, like, totally nerdy, parted-on-the-side light brown hair and glasses. He looks like the kinda guy who probably hasn't gotten laid in, like, ever. The other one was Theodore Walsh, that fat-ass motherfucker who runs the antique store in the strip mall on Horst Road. That guy is a total fucking wanktard, and you really oughtta look into him first. My guess is, he's the one you want. Did you get all that? Cuz I ain't—" She frowned. "My what? My name? My name is Susan Hubbard. Bye, now." She hung up and handed the phone back to Donovan.

"Thank you," he said.

"You're welcome." She watched him put the phone back in his pocket, then shook her head. "You know, the cops aren't gonna do shit."

"They're doing everything they can—"

"Aha!" She thrust out a finger like a debater about to make a winning point. "The key there is 'everything they can'! They're, like, hampered by too many bullshit rules. I mean, think about it: O.J. walked; Casey fucking Anthony walked; Jack the Ripper never even got caught."

"That was another country and, like, a thousand years ago."

"Cops're the same everywhere. They're either a bunch of power-tripping dickwads, or they're all bound up by shitloads of bureaucratic rules. The sad fact is, most crimes never even get solved. And you know why? Rules! That's why! But me? I don't follow nobody's rules but mine. I think we oughtta investigate this shit ourselves. Cuz, I mean, cops need warrants and crap to look through someone's house. Me? I don't need a fucking warrant. I'll just bust in when no one's home. Boom. Job done."

Donovan shook his head. "Violet, I know you mean well, and I appreciate it. But...well, I never thought I'd ever say this, but I think maybe we should leave this to the cops. They know what they're doing. They have experience in this kind of thing. If we start mucking around, we could, like, fuck up their investigation or something."

She placed her hands on his shoulders and looked him directly in the eye, her expression full of unwonted seriousness.

"Dude, this is your fucking sister," she said. "I understand where you're coming from on this, but the fact is— and I don't mean to be a downer or a complete cunt about this—but the fact is, if she's been abducted by some kinda psycho pervert molester person, her chances of survival get worse and worse by the hour. And while the cops and FBI dudes are noodling around with their fucking paperwork-in-triplicate bullshit and their dainty little regulations, she could be getting killed. Or worse. Now, I know everybody means well, and all those regulations mean well and everything. But meaning well is not gonna find your sister. Me, I'd rather break a few rules and step on some toes in the name of a righteous cause than just sit around with my thumb up my ass and watch a bunch of complete strangers do some frigid little by-the-book investigation and let the moment of action slip away."

"Violet, I don't know…" He shook his head and stared off at the Slipknot *All Hope Is Gone* poster on his wall. Then he looked away with a frown; that wasn't really the most comforting title, given the circumstances.

He sighed with uncertainty. In her usual inimitable way, Violet was right, but she was also wrong. He had heard the same statistics about the swiftly declining chances of survival of abducted children. Not that that was definitely what had happened to Emily, but it was, he had to admit, the most likely scenario. And the thought that he might be letting the moment of action slip away made him feel almost physically sick.

But he also remembered all the cops and FBI agents he had met throughout the day. Behind their by-the-book law-abiding exteriors, Donovan had sensed an urgency to find Emily that nearly matched his own. It was as if Emily were their own kith and kin.

"I dunno, Violet," he said. "I think we oughtta give them more time." Seeing her dubiously raised eyebrow, he quickly added, "I mean, you only just called them with your information. Let's give them some time to act on it. Besides, it's like how you mentioned Casey Anthony and O.J. and all that. Part of the reason they walked in the end is cuz the cops weren't able to make a case against them. If we start mucking around, we might fuck up the case, and whoever's behind this might end up walking because of *us.*"

Violet regarded him in slit-eyed silence for a moment. Then she flung up her hands. "Okay, fine. We'll give them a little more time." She jabbed a finger at him. "But if they haven't found her by tomorrow night, we're gonna start tearin' up this cornhole town lookin' for her ourselves."

Chapter 8

Roger Grey

1

Roger Grey lifted the lid of the large, yellow chest freezer in his basement and looked inside. He had to squint a little against the chilly air that washed over his face.

At the bottom of the freezer lay the body of Emily Crow. She was wrapped in a blue blanket, only her slack, pale face visible amid its folds. A dime-sized spot of blood stained the blanket just above her heart.

The sight made Roger shake his head with anger and disgust. She had been so beautiful, so perfect. Now she was just a lifeless husk. Useless. He had wanted her alive. He had wanted her to scream and wriggle and fight and plead. That had been the whole point. He hadn't wanted to kill her.

At least not so soon...

2

He had desired her from the moment he first saw her six months ago.

It had been a time of change in all kinds of ways. He had just landed a good-paying job at the May National Bank, and to be closer to his new (and hopefully permanent) workplace, he had sold his recently deceased mother's house in Kingwood and bought a cozy one-storey bungalow on Grace Road in eastern May. He enjoyed the thought of assuming a quiet, outwardly normal life among these witless suburbanites. It amused him to no end to exchange smiles and hellos with his neighbors and coworkers while spending his nights fantasizing about the rape and torture of their pretty little prepubescent daughters. He felt like a wolf among sheep.

At times it bothered him that his fantasies were only fantasies, that despite his masturbatory imaginings his life was largely that of the sheep. But he understood that the risks involved in acting on his desires far outweighed the fleeting benefits, and for the most part he had been content to let his dreams remain dreams.

But it had been a time of change in all kinds of ways.

He was thrilled to discover that his new job was across the street from a park frequented by the local children. Rather than take his lunch break at a nearby deli like most of his coworkers, he chose to eat alone in the park. His coworkers probably considered him antisocial, but their opinion of him—of anything—meant less to him than the grass and flowers he tramped as he crossed the park to the gazebo, where he would sit and eat his peanut butter and jelly sandwich and his Lay's potato chips and his Oreos, while he watched the little girls laugh and play.

His third week in May, he was eating his lunch on the gazebo steps when Emily Crow strolled into the park to jump rope.

He couldn't take his eyes off her. She was perfect. He watched, slack-jawed, his sandwich gathering flies in his lap, while she jumped rope, her long dark hair flying, her lithe body working, her flawless skin glistening with sweat.

After that he visited the park with the sole hope of seeing her. When summer ended and school resumed, he hung around the park after work and on weekends, hoping she would visit in her free time. When she did he was elated. When she didn't he was plunged into gloom like a jilted lover. She became the screaming, bawling star of his increasingly violent nightly fantasies. He was smitten.

Via judicious questioning of the locals, he learned who she was and where she lived. A few times he felt bold enough to prowl the woods around her house. He didn't linger long. He felt oddly exposed in the woods. After all, the woods were little more than an assemblage of hiding places. Hundreds of eyes could be watching him from the bushes and shadows. He always wound up cutting these excursions short and hurrying home without a glimpse of Emily.

Despite his reconnaissance, he didn't seriously contemplate making a move on Emily. The vast machinery of law and order arrayed against him was enough to keep him in line, to keep his fantasies only fantasies.

Until two weeks ago.

3

Emily lay on the grass in the clearing, naked and trussed up like a rodeo calf, her sobs and whines barely audible through the gag in her mouth. Roger, too, was naked. They were alone. He could do whatever he wanted with her.

And he did.

The dream had been incredibly long and detailed, more so than any dream he had ever had. He spent what seemed like hours ravishing her delicate little body. He felt every individual blade of grass tickling his bare knees. He traced the path of every tear that spilled from her frightened, pleading eyes. He heard the creak of the ropes that bound her wrists and ankles as she twisted her hands and feet about in search of a release that would never come.

He awoke with a start as he ejaculated—not just in the dream but in reality. For the first time in his life he had been so aroused that he had come without even touching himself.

After that the dream haunted him. The memory of it was always present behind his eyes, no matter what he was doing, a pornographic film loop superimposed upon his every interaction with the world. He would catch himself zoning out in the middle of work as he relived part of the dream, his gaze distant, his mouth agape, his cock an iron rod in his pants He started masturbating three or four times a day. His penis grew red and sore. But even then he didn't stop. He couldn't.

The dream wouldn't leave him alone. Or *he* couldn't leave *it* alone. He saw now that his previous fantasies had been feeble, third-rate inventions with little basis in truth. The dream had given him a taste of the real thing. But a taste wasn't enough. He wanted more. He *needed* more. It was an itch he had to scratch.

He had to act, he realized. He had to make the dream reality. Damn the police. Damn the law. He was smart enough to avoid capture and punishment. He just had to be careful. Meticulous.

He needed a plan. But though he spent many hours crafting scheme after scheme, none of them were good enough. Something was missing.

The something revealed itself a week ago, while he was watching Emily in the park after work one day. She was there with two of her friends—a black-haired boy and a brunette girl, both of them around her own age. The brunette was kind of cute. Not nearly as lovely as Emily, of course, but well worth the occasional supporting role in his fantasies.

The trio of kids had been shit-talking their teacher, an old lady named Miss Dryer. It seemed Miss Dryer had denied the existence of fairies, something Emily vehemently believed it.

"Stupid old bitch," Emily had snapped. "I know fairies are real. I've *seen* them. I saw them when I was a little girl, right in the woods near my house, and—"

"We know," the boy said. "You've told us, like, eight hundred million times before."

Emily stuck out her tongue at him. "Well, I still have to tell you eight hundred million times more, because it's just that important!"

At that point they passed out of earshot. But Roger had heard enough. He already had the beginning of a plan.

4

It took him a few days to work out the plan. To initiate the plan, he needed some time to talk to Emily alone and unobserved in the park. Given the irregularity of Emily's visits and the park's variable attendance, it might take a while before he found the right opportunity. Fortunately, Roger's first two-week vacation at his no-longer-quite-so-new job rolled around, which meant he could spend a lot more time at the park. The timing was perfect, as if it had been meant to be. But since Roger knew there were no gods in the sky and no meaning or purpose inherent in the bland, mechan-

ical world, it was clearly only a coincidence, albeit a delightful one.

Or perhaps not so delightful: The first few days of his
vacation passed without a single glimpse of Emily, and
Roger began to worry that she was sick or busy and that his
vacation would wind up being two weeks of mounting
frustration. But then on Thursday she strolled into the park
around four-thirty and started jumping rope in her usual
shady corner. Roger glanced around. The kids on the baseball diamond were absorbed in their game. The two ladies
who had been taking their babies for a stroll were chattering away, oblivious to everything around them. The fat guy
who ran the antique store and who always spent part of his
afternoon in the park chain smoking and reading Agatha
Christie novels had his bulbous nose buried in *And Then
There Were None.*

Perfect.

Roger pushed himself off the gazebo steps and headed
toward the dim, quiet corner where Emily was. She was
facing the woods, perhaps watching for fairies while she
jumped rope. Roger walked up to the woods about twenty
feet to her right and peered intently into the trees as if
looking for something.

Emily's curiosity was roused, exactly as planned. Out of
the corner of his eye he saw her stop jumping rope to
watch him. Eyes fixed on the woods, he slowly sidled her
way as though seeking out a better view. When he was just
a few feet away from her, he glanced up and jumped a little
as though startled to see someone nearby.

"Oh, sorry," he said with a faint upper-class British accent. His plan required him to adopt the role of the kindly,
introverted scholar, and he figured the accent would help.
"I didn't see you there."

She raised an eyebrow. "How could you *not?*"

He gave a small, embarrassed laugh. "Well, you know, I was a bit, ah, preoccupied. I was rather absorbed in the fairy lights." He gestured at the woods.

"Fairy lights?" She looked into the woods, her eyes huge and excited. "Where?"

"They're gone now. I saw them for only a few seconds. That's typical, though. The moment the fairies realize anyone's watching, they disappear like *that.*" He snapped his fingers for emphasis.

She stared at him with wonder. "You've seen them, too?"

"Yes, of course. Although, uh, I really don't like to talk about it very much. Most people...they just don't understand." He cocked his head. "Am I to understand that you have seen them as well?"

"Yeah! I saw some in the woods when I was little. I've been hoping to see them again, but I never have, even though I live right here."

"Yes," he said with a sad sigh. "Over the last decade or so they've become more reclusive, perhaps because there are more people around than there used to be. Nowadays, you usually see them only late at night when everyone is asleep. Every now and then I come out here around midnight, and I go to one of the spots in the woods where they like to gather. And there I sit and wait and watch, and if I'm lucky I see all the multicolored lights dancing in the air among the trees. It's a beautiful sight."

Hyper with excitement, Emily started babbling away a mile a minute, telling him about the time she saw the fairies. She talked so fast he barely understood her, but he managed to catch the gist of it: naked fairies and mushrooms. He nodded sagely all the while, interjecting comments like, "Ah, yes," and "That's very typical of fairies."

When she was done, he frowned and scratched his chin. "You know," he said. "I'll be coming out here to look for them tonight around midnight. I'd invite you, but it will be quite late, and I'm sure you have school tomorrow."

"No! I can go! I've stayed up that late before. It's not a problem."

"Oh, I don't know…" This was too easy. She had probably been told a million times that she should be wary of strangers, but she had forgotten that, or didn't care, now that she had found an adult who actually believed in fairies. Who believed *her.*

"Pleeeease," she said, giving him a pleading smile. "My birthday's in two weeks."

"Your birthday, eh? I don't know. If your parents were to find out, I'd probably get accused of…of child endangerment or something."

She waved a hand dismissively. "Beh. They won't find out. They'll be asleep. They go to bed really early."

That answered that. "Hm. You say you live nearby?"

"Uh-huh. Right over there." She pointed in the direction of her house.

"Well, that would make it easier, I guess." He frowned down at the ground as though pondering a weighty matter. Finally he sighed and looked at her. "All right. Tell you what: Meet me at the round clearing across the river at midnight. You know where the clearing is?"

"Of course!"

"Okay. Good. If you're not there by five after, I'll go on by myself."

"I'll be there."

"All right, then. Oh, wait. One other thing. I, uh, I'd appreciate it if you didn't tell anyone about what we'll be doing."

"Why not?" For the first time she looked suspicious.

"Well, um…" He grimaced and looked down at his shoes. "The people I work with—my friends—they wouldn't understand. No one else believes, you see. At least not adults. If word got around that I believe in fairies…well, you know how people can be about things like that."

Whatever suspicions she may have harbored were gone now, washed away by a flood of sympathy. "It's okay. I won't tell anyone. Don't worry."

He breathed a sigh of relief. "I wish all people were as understanding as you. Well, then, I'll see you at midnight in the clearing. And please try not to be late."

"I won't."

"Good."

"By the way, what's your name?"

"Huh? Oh, uh, my name's Mark."

"I'm Emily." She held out a hand.

"Nice to meet you, Emily." He shook her hand. It was soft and smooth and warm. There was a sudden swell of pressure in his pants. "And I hope we have good luck tonight."

"Me too!"

They parted with smiles, each of them sure that their fondest dreams would soon be realized.

5

Roger spent the rest of the day preparing for their meeting. He picked out a bunch of old clothes he didn't need anymore and could dispose of afterward. Then he dug out his father's old hunting knife, eight inches of shining, razor-sharp steel that he felt sure would scare Emily into silence and obedience. He hooked the sheathed knife onto the back of his belt, where it would be hidden under his jacket.

Into his jacket pockets went a roll of twine and a few pieces of an old torn-up T-shirt. Into the trunk of the car went an old blue blanket. The plan was to gag her, strip her, and bind her at knife-point, then have his way with her in the clearing. After he had thus made his dream reality, he would wrap her in the blanket—both to obscure her shape should any vehicles pass by while he was carrying her from the woods to his car, and to prevent any hair or skin cells or other forensic evidence from contaminating the trunk, where he planned to put her—then drive her back to his house. There he would keep her locked in the basement, his luscious little sex slave for however long he wanted.

He had been afraid he would be a bundle of nerves once the moment arrived, but as he drove through the dark and silent streets of May toward his midnight rendezvous, he felt calm and powerful, like a shark gliding toward the scent of blood.

There was a grassy verge beneath the eaves of the woods just west of the Old Stone Bridge, and after making sure no one was around, Roger cut the headlights then parked on the grass, his dark gray Ford Focus nearly invisible in the shadows. He looked at his watch. 11:55. Perfect.

He got out of the car and made his way to the clearing. No one was there. The world was silent. Stars glimmered in the circle of sky visible overhead.

Roger positioned himself at the southern edge of the clearing and waited. Time crawled. He kept checking his watch, sure it must be well after midnight by now, but he always found that barely thirty seconds had passed since the last time he checked his watch.

Finally midnight arrived. Then it passed. 12:01 came and went. Then 12:02. 12:03. Where was she? Had she forgotten? Had she changed her mind? Had she fallen asleep?

Then he heard footsteps rustling through the fallen autumn leaves. He peered into the darkness amid the trees, suddenly afraid it was a cop, some mouth-breathing triple-chinned patrolman who had spotted Roger's car parked where it shouldn't be and decided to investigate. But then a small figure materialized out of the darkness. The shoes appeared first, two white ovoid shapes decorated on the sides with bright yellow lightning bolts, then the pale face lit with eager eyes, then the blue jeans and the green jacket, and finally the long hair, which seemed somehow more purely black than the shadows around it. Emily. She had come.

"Here I am!" she said, loud enough to make Roger's heart leap in alarm.

"Not so loud," he hissed. "The fairies might hear and stay away."

"Sorry," she whispered. She looked around. "Where are they?"

He squatted beside her and pointed at the north edge of the clearing. For some reason the faint grapey smell that enveloped her—probably from shampoo or bubble bath—made him dizzy with arousal.

"A few minutes ago I saw some lights in the darkness over there," he said. "I think it was them. If they stay true to form, they'll probably be back any minute now. Just keep watching."

She did. As he had hoped, she took a few quiet, cautious steps forward, allowing him to move behind her and draw the knife from its sheath.

Perhaps he made a sound. Or perhaps she only wanted to ask him a question. Whatever the case, she turned around at the exact moment he pulled the knife out from under his jacket.

She froze, her eyes fixed on the knife. He froze too, startled by this sudden, unexpected exposure. His secret desires were no longer secret. Someone else finally knew. *She* knew. But not in the way he had meant for her to know. He felt small and diminished in some way.

Her eyes shifted from the knife to his face, and what he saw in them was a far cry from anything he had expected. She was regarding him not with fear or anger or confusion or any of the other emotions he had envisioned in his countless mental rehearsals for this moment. Instead she was looking at him with a sort of weary contempt, as though she were disgusted beyond all measure by this crowning betrayal and its obviously sordid motivations.

For a moment Roger felt smaller than ever. He felt an irrational urge to apologize, or justify himself. But then his sense of self-preservation came to his rescue. It was past the point of no return. He had to act now. He thrust his feelings aside and raised the knife.

Her eyes went wide with fear. She took a step backward, and her chest swelled with an indrawn breath, prelude to a scream.

Roger launched himself forward. He slammed into her and crashed to the ground atop her. The indrawn breath whooshed out of her. Before she could draw another one, he clapped his left hand over her face, his fingers veiling her eyes, his palm blocking her mouth.

"Quiet," he snarled. "I'm not going to hurt you. I—"

Her teeth grazed his palm. She was trying to bite him.

He didn't dare move his hand away—the instant he did she would scream—so instead he pressed harder, mashing the back of her head into the ground like a gardener shoving a seed into the dirt with his thumb.

She thrashed violently about. She grabbed his arm and tried to pull his hand off her face. Her legs kicked and scissored.

"Stop it, God damn it," he hissed. "Stop it or I'll—"

One of her sneakered feet slammed into his balls. He yelped in pain and instinctively raised his hand from her face to cradle his crotch.

She lost no time in taking advantage of the opportunity. She turned her head to one side so he couldn't easily clap a hand over her face again, then opened her mouth as wide as she could and drew in another deep breath to unleash a Heaven-shattering scream. Rattled with pain and panic and unable to think of anything else to do, Roger drove the knife as hard as he could into her chest.

She went rigid for an instant, then began to buck like a landed fish. Blood welled up around the hilt of the knife and soaked through her shirt and jacket. Roger let go of the knife and scrambled to his feet. He backed away a few steps and watched with mingled horror and fascination as she flailed about. Her hands clawed up fistfuls of grass. Her heels kicked divots into the dirt. Her blood glistened in the starlight.

Her wild convulsions abruptly ceased. Her body gave a few brief shudders and then stopped moving altogether.

Was she dead? Roger stepped forward again and bent over her for a better look.

No, not dead yet. Not quite. Her eyelids fluttered over her blackly gleaming eyes. Her fingers were twitching like a person tapping out Morse code in their sleep. He could just hear her faint, rasping breath.

Then her eyelids stopped moving. Her fingers went still. She let out one last, barely audible exhalation...

And she died.

There was a bang of imploding air, and a ball of bright white light engulfed her head. At the same time a warm wind blew outward from the center of the clearing, rocking Roger back on his heels and making the grass ripple as if a helicopter were landing. Red and yellow leaves tumbled end over end out of the clearing and disappeared into the woods. The bushes and branches on the edge of the clearing bowed and swayed.

Roger squinted into the light. It shimmered and pulsed like starlight. Except it was far, far brighter than any star except the sun. The shadow of each grass blade stood out long and stark upon the ground.

"What is this?" he said, backing away from the light. He wasn't sure who he was talking to. "What—"

The light exploded outward like a supernova, filling the clearing, engulfing Roger. Everything went white and

6

His next conscious awareness was a burning smell, a sharp ozonic stench that filled his nostrils and dragged him up from the inky depths he was ensconced within.

He opened his eyes and saw the stars in the night sky above the clearing. What had happened?

He sat up with a groan. His head pounded. His mouth was dry. He felt groggy, disoriented.

He looked around. Emily lay where he had left her, the knife hilt jutting from her chest. He got up and took a few shaky steps toward her on weak, rubbery legs.

She was dead. The dark eyes visible through the cracked lids were fixed unseeingly on the stars above. Her mouth was open but no breath passed through it. Her shirt and jacket were wet with blood.

Then Roger noticed the grass. The grass in a circle around her head was scorched black. A few blades still smoldered, their ends glowing like sticks of incense.

"What the fuck?" he muttered.

He didn't understand what had happened (though there was no doubt a perfectly natural explanation; everything had a perfectly natural explanation), but he didn't have time to try to figure it out right now. His only concern was to cover his tracks and get the hell out of here. He staggered back to his car, got the blanket from the trunk, then returned to the clearing. He spread the blanket on the grass and started to roll her body onto it. Then he noticed that one of her shoes was missing.

"Son of a bitch," he hissed, looking around the clearing. There was no sign of the shoe anywhere. It must have flown off while she was thrashing about.

He hunted through the brush on the edge of the clearing for a while, but quit when he checked his watch to see what time it was and found that the watch had stopped, the hands frozen at 12:12 a.m. Shit. He had no idea how long he had been here. He should just go.

He returned to the center of the clearing and rolled up the body in the blanket. Carrying the blanket-wrapped bundle over his shoulder like a mover moving a carpet, he returned to the car and shut the body in the trunk. When he started the car the dashboard clock told him it was 1:14 a.m. Later than he thought. He had been right to quit looking when he did. After all, the longer the car sat here the more likely it would get noticed.

He was so shaky and exhausted that he was half afraid he would wind up smashing the car into a telephone pole, but he made it home safely. He pulled the car into the garage and shut the garage door, then went inside and moved what little there was in the basement chest freezer to the freezer in the kitchen. He had been thinking about selling the chest freezer, one of the many things he had inherited upon his mother's death last year. But now he was relieved he had held onto it. You never knew when you might need something.

He took Emily's body from the trunk and carried it down to the basement. He had to bend her knees a bit to fit her into the freezer. Once she was settled, he parted the blanket so he could see her face.

She was now so pale she looked as if she had been carved from alabaster. Her black hair was tangled and wild. Her eyes were still parted a little, but they no longer gleamed; they were dull and dry. He reached into the cold interior of the freezer and closed her eyelids.

He straightened up and stared at her. His eyes narrowed. His jaw clenched.

"You stupid bitch," he said. "Why did you have to fight?" His anger grew stronger with every word. "Why did you make me do that? You cunt! You stupid fucking cunt!"

Lips twisting in fury, teeth grinding, he kicked the chest freezer hard enough to put a dent in the side. The lid crashed down with a bang that resounded through the workroom like a gunshot.

The sound broke his rage, and he slumped forward with his forehead resting atop his crossed arms on the lid of the freezer.

This wasn't how it was supposed to be. She was supposed to be alive, gagged and scared and bound spread-eagled atop the wooden table by the south wall, her skinny body stretched out like a sacrifice to a cruel and merciless god. The god, of course, being Roger.

But that would never happen now. She was dead. She was ruined. In a weird way, she had had the final victory. Bitch.

He turned out the basement lights and headed upstairs. In the kitchen, he got out a black plastic trash bag, then took off all his clothes, from his jacket to his underwear, and stuffed them into the bag. All of it—not just the clothes, but the body and the blanket and the knife—would be disposed of tomorrow in the deepest reaches of Black-water Swamp.

Though what he really wanted to do was go to bed, he forced himself to take a long, hot shower first to scrub away any traces of the night's misdeeds. Only after he was certain that every last grass stain and smear of blood had vanished down the drain did he towel dry and stagger off to bed.

He was on the brink of sleep when his eyes flew wide.

There's a corpse in the basement, he thought.

His stomach tightened with atavistic dread. His fingers gripped the sheet so hard his knuckles turned white.

A corpse, he thought. *I'm alone in the house with a corpse.*

But barely had that thought sunk in when another one took its place: I *made that corpse.*

A small smile took shape on his lips. His fear ebbed away, replaced by a mad, giddy glee at what he had done. He had committed a godlike act. True, it hadn't been exactly what he had wanted to do, but it was a mighty and irrevocable deed nonetheless. And he had done it. Him. He had altered the course of many people's lives. He had changed the world. Forever.

He fell asleep smiling.

7

That was last night. Today he wasn't smiling at all.

He awoke with the day nearly done. He had forgotten to set his alarm, and he was so exhausted he slept till nearly four p.m. By the time he had washed, dressed, and eaten, the sun was low in the sky, and he decided to wait till tomorrow to make the trip to Blackwater Swamp.

But then he watched the local six o'clock news. As he had expected, the lead story was Emily's disappearance. As he had also expected, the cops had found her shoe and pegged the clearing as the scene of the crime.

What he hadn't expected was that the cops knew that Emily had gone to the clearing to meet a man whom she had met in the park earlier that day and who had promised to show her fairies in the woods.

Shit. That stupid little sow had broken her promise. She had blabbed to someone.

Shit shit shit.

While the newscast moved on to other stories, Roger got up and peeked out the living room window. There were no unfamiliar vehicles parked anywhere on the street, no strangers strolling about. It was the same boring suburban street as always.

But it probably wouldn't remain that way for long. Plenty of people had seen Roger in the park yesterday. And given how disoriented he had been last night, who knew what other evidence he might have left? He had to dispose of the body and the evidence now, today. If he hurried, he might be able to make it to the swamp before it got too dark for him to find his way along its mazy, unmarked dirt roads.

And so here he was, in the basement, staring at her beautiful face one last time and psyching himself up to lift the body from the freezer and drive it away on its final journey.

He sighed and reached into the freezer.

A girlish giggle rang out behind him.

Roger whirled, his heart slamming up into his throat, his eyes as big as moons.

Emily sat cross-legged on the wooden table by the south wall. She was dressed in the same outfit she wore last night—green jacket, blue jeans, tennis shoes with lightning bolts on the sides. But there was no knife stuck in her chest, no blood on her clothes. She was regarding him with a playful, impish smile.

He looked back over his shoulder. At the bottom of the freezer Emily's dead, pale face lay amid the folds of the blue blanket. Roger turned back to the table. The other Emily's smile widened.

"Oh, Roger," she said in a gently mocking tone. "You've gone and done it this time, haven't you?"

PART TWO

Winding the Clock

Chapter 9

Echoes (I)

1

Cynthia rang Mr. May's doorbell, then glanced at Calvin, who stood beside her on the Welcome mat.

"This might take a while," she said.

"Yeah," he said. "He's kind of...slow-moving."

Everybody is today, she thought sourly. She wished they had gotten an earlier start, as they had originally planned. But as so often happened, aligning the lives and schedules of three people took longer than anyone expected. It was already after one p.m. She had been hoping they would have long since heard whatever Mr. May had to tell them and be halfway to finding Emily by now.

"What did you tell your parents?" Calvin asked. "I mean, I assume you told them you were going out this time, right?"

"Yeah. I, um..." She gave a self-conscious shrug. "I hope you don't mind: I used you as my alibi. I told them we were meeting up to go over some schoolwork and then hang out a while."

"Oh, I don't mind," he said. "I don't mind at all." He gave her that goofy, spacey smile he had been giving her every now and then over the last few weeks, a look that he seemed totally unaware of. It was the look of someone who thinks he's found his soul-mate.

She cringed inwardly at the sight. She knew she should tell him the truth: that his having a Y chromosome pretty much nixed any chance of their being soul-mates. It was the right thing to do. But she didn't know how. She couldn't even muster up the nerve to tell her own family she was gay. She kept hoping that maybe if she did nothing and just ignored all of his conscious and unconscious signals of romantic interest, his feelings would dissipate like a fever when it breaks, and they could just be friends like she wanted.

Somehow she didn't think it was going to be that easy, though.

Footsteps became audible on the other side of the door. A moment later a latch clacked, and the door opened, revealing Mr. May, who was as impeccably dressed as yesterday.

"Greetings," he said, stepping back and waving them inside. "Please, come in."

They did, and found themselves in a long corridor that stretched away toward a wrought-iron spiral staircase in the center of the house. Oil paintings lined the hallway, most of them depicting quaint rural landscapes. A few of the paintings, however, bucked the bucolic monotony. One of these showed a pipe-playing satyr gamboling on a rocky riverbank. Another showed a naval battle, the hulking wooden ships reduced to vague and ominous shapes behind the clouds of cannon smoke. Another, which Calvin and Cynthia stopped to look at in more depth, showed a large throne room lined with white marble columns and hung with tapestries. A ribbon of purple carpet extended across the room and up five marble steps to a dais, presumably where the throne sat. But only a sliver of the dais was visible, the rest being beyond the right edge of the painting. Dozens of men and women in medieval finery stood throughout the room, all but one of them reacting with mingled shock and horror to something atop the dais. The one exception was a young woman dressed in a long blue gown and a tall conical hennin. Instead of looking horrified, she was hiding in the shadow of a pillar at the far left edge of the painting and smiling an enigmatic Mona Lisa smile.

Mr. May watched them study the painting with a small smile of his own.

"Do you like it?" he asked Cynthia.

"It's…interesting," she said. "It's very photorealistic. I like that."

"Do you know who painted it?"

"Um…" She peered at the painting, examining the style and dredging up whatever scraps of art history she could recall from various Art classes over the years. She was forced to concede defeat. "No."

"It was painted by your great-great-uncle, Randolph Crow."

"My what?" She looked at Calvin as if she thought he could explain. He just shrugged. She examined the painting again, then looked back at Mr. May. "I've never even heard of him!"

"Well, today you will learn the whole sad story." He beckoned them on. They followed.

Not far beyond the throne-room painting two closed doors faced each other across the corridor. Mr. May led them through the door on the left and into a large parlor with burgundy carpeting and dark wood wainscoting. Most of the furniture looked antique, the only obvious exceptions being a green leather couch situated against the east wall to the right of the door, an entertainment center that took up most of the north wall, and a pair of metal file cabinets that flanked the floor-to-ceiling window in the south wall.

But what caught Cynthia's attention more than anything else was a painting on the wall directly opposite the door. She stepped forward to examine it. Calvin joined her.

The painting showed an old wooden door set into a wall composed of large stone blocks. A door in a castle, perhaps. Or a cellar. The door stood open a crack, and through the crack streamed a line of bright white light that split the shadows of the dark stone room like an axe cleaving wood. The painting was so photorealistic it was like looking through a window into another room.

"Is this another painting by my, um…" Cynthia frowned. "My what was it?"

"Your great-great-uncle," Mr. May said. "And yes. There are two more by him upstairs, actually."

"How come they're over here? How come we don't have any in our house?"

"I couldn't tell you. Maybe after what happened to him, your family saw them as a too-painful reminder of the tragedy and put them in storage or got rid of them."

"What tragedy? What happened to him?"

"We'll get to that. First things first, though." He motioned at the green couch. "Have a seat. Would you like anything to eat or drink? This will take a little while. Or perhaps more than a little."

"No, thank you," said Cynthia as she and Calvin edged around a low, black coffee table to sit down.

"Yeah, I just had lunch, like, half an hour ago," Calvin said. "So I'm good."

Cynthia pretended to have trouble maneuvering around the table and thereby allowed Calvin to sit down first. She was afraid that if she sat down first, he would use the opportunity to sit close to her. Not invasively close, of course; he was a nice guy. But in this case, even a little close was a bad idea.

After he was settled, she sat down an arm's length away. He glanced at her. He looked a little baffled and hurt that she hadn't sat closer. She pretended she didn't notice.

Mr. May carefully lowered himself into a claw-and-ball armchair across the coffee table from the couch. He propped his cane against the side of the chair, then settled back with a small sigh.

"Now, then," he said. "What do you know about this area before the settlers arrived?"

In unison Calvin and Cynthia blurted out "Passenger pigeons!" They looked at each other in surprise, then laughed.

"Why passenger pigeons, of all things?" Mr. May asked.

"Mr. McCready was telling us about them in Biology last week," Cynthia said.

"Yeah," Calvin said. "He said there were flocks of them so big they'd blot out the sky for a couple of days straight."

Mr. May nodded. "I believe I read somewhere that the passenger pigeon population exceeded that of any other animal at the time. There were literally billions of them in North America. There was nothing else like them in the world. So of course our noble forefathers killed them all, mainly for sport. By the time anyone realized what was happening, the birds were nearly extinct and it was too late to change the course of events. The last known specimen died in captivity in the Cincinnati Zoo in 1914."

"Sickening," Cynthia said, shaking her head.

May grunted. "If you want an uplifting subject, avoid

history at all costs. At any rate, it wasn't just pigeons that made their home here in those days. This region was one vast, unbroken forest, teeming with all manner of life. There were elk, cougars, bears, even wolverines. But more importantly, there were the Mima."

"Oh, yeah!" Calvin said. "The Indians. There's a display about them at the library."

"Native Americans," Cynthia corrected him.

He shrugged. "Same thing."

She tutted.

"Technically, neither term is accurate," Mr. May said. "They thought of themselves only as the Mima. They occupied these lands as early as 1200 AD. It is estimated that when the Europeans arrived in North America, the Mima numbered well over a thousand. But the Europeans brought strange new diseases against which the indigenous peoples had no inborn resistance, and plagues spread far in advance of the white man. By the time the first settlers came rattling into the area in their wagons in 1799, barely two hundred Mima remained."

"Yay progress," Cynthia muttered.

"In most respects the Mima were similar to other tribes in this region: They hunted, fished, and farmed, built palisaded villages, had the occasional war with their neighbors, et cetera, et cetera. What is of interest to us are their curious beliefs regarding this area. They considered the land around the bend in the Kanseeka to be sacred, especially Indian Hill. They believed a mighty being called Wakansa dwelt inside the hill or in the tunnels underneath the hill. Wakansa was variously described as a god, a spirit, a great war chief, a giant winged serpent, and the child of a god. He (or it) was said to be sleeping, but would one day awaken during a time of great chaos and lead the remnants of the tribe to a new land of peace and plenty while the rest of the world fell into ruin.

"Spirit Cave was the entrance to Wakansa's lair, but entering it was taboo. And frightening, at least to the superstitious. Back in those days, the cave had an unusual acoustical property. To anyone standing inside it, the hiss of the nearby waterfall was distorted into what sounded like dozens of softly whispering voices. The Mima believed that these voices belonged to the mysterious spirits who attended to Wakansa in his slumber. Hence, the cave of the spirits, or Spirit Cave. The phenomenon was so eerie and convincing that even the supposedly rational white men avoided the cave, and the land around it remained unsettled and undeveloped for decades.

"When the settlers began to arrive in this area, the Mima's chief was a man named Firebird. At first he welcomed the settlers with open arms, but as the trees fell and the animals vanished, he came to recognize that the white men were a threat to the Mima's way of life. Not sure what to do about it, he undertook a vision quest atop Indian Hill, hoping for enlightenment. For several days and nights, he sat alone atop the hill, eating no food and drinking only rainwater when it fell. When he descended, gaunt and half dead, he claimed that he had been granted a great vision, which revealed that the prophesized time of chaos had come and that the tribe must awaken Wakansa so that he could whisk them away to the promised wonder-world of legend. To effect that awakening, a special ceremony had to be held atop Indian Hill, a ceremony unlike anything in Mima tradition. Under Firebird's instructions, the tribe set to work getting it ready. A large bonfire was constructed atop the hill. Special clothes were made. New music, chants, and dances were learned. The ceremony would climax with a special sacrifice to Wakansa, the precise nature of which Firebird refused to divulge in advance."

"Let me guess," Calvin said: "It was one of the settlers, right?"

Mr. May chuckled. "Not quite. The ceremony was held one night in late October, 1804. The settlers knew nothing of it until they were awakened shortly before midnight by manic drumming and chanting. They peeked out of their cabins, saw the bonfire blazing atop the hill and the shadowy figures cavorting in its orange light, then promptly ducked back inside and barred the doors. They lay awake, listening in mounting alarm for over an hour as the music swelled to a wild crescendo and then crashed to an abrupt halt. In the silence that followed, the settlers found it impossible to sleep. The music had been so violent, so frenzied, that they imagined the Indians, stirred to bloodlust, stalking through the woods with knives between their teeth. But the rest of the night passed quietly, and the next day they learned from the confused, saddened Mima what had actually happened.

"The whole tribe had gathered on the hill, and the ceremony was performed according to Firebird's instructions. As the ceremony reached its climax, all eyes turned to Firebird, eager to see what the sacrifice would be. Firebird strode up to the edge of the bonfire and cried out a last plea for Wakansa to arise. Then he drew his knife, drove it into his heart, and plunged dead into the fire. The music stopped. The dancing stopped. Everyone stared in horror as the flames consumed Firebird's corpse."

"Holy crap!" Calvin said.

Cynthia shook her head, frowning. "I don't get it. Why would he do that?"

"He thought he was doing what was best for his people," Mr. May said. "If you believe in magic, the act is not without its logic. Magic is said to work best when it involves the arousal of psychic or emotional energy, and the quickest and easiest way to arouse such energy is via the breaking of a powerful taboo. That's why human sacrifice and various forms of sexual debauchery figure into so many magical rituals. In this case the human sacrifice was the magician himself."

"How do you know so much about this stuff?" Cynthia asked.

"I'm well-rounded."

"Do you actually believe in magic?" Calvin asked.

Mr. May hesitated. "Let's not get sidetracked at the moment. We have a lot of history to cover. Suffice to say, Firebird's particular brand of magic won't be winning any converts. As a glance out the window will show, the ceremony was an abject failure."

"I'll say," Cynthia said.

"The final fate of the Mima isn't really germane to what I have to tell you, but it's briefly stated. After Firebird's death, the Mima fell under the sway of Firebird's eldest son Ten Bears. Ten Bears hated the whites, and on the eve of the War of 1812 he convinced most of the tribe to pack up their belongings and head west to join Tecumseh's Confederacy against the Americans. The Mima made it only halfway through Phoenix Township before they were ambushed by a gang of settlers who had learned of the Mima's plans. Trapped in a clearing with the settlers firing upon them from the surrounding woods, every last Mima was massacred in less time than it takes to tell."

Cynthia's upper lip drew back in disgust. "That's awful."

"In all fairness, it was a time of conflict, and the

Mima's intentions were decidedly hostile."

"You said he convinced 'most of the tribe' to go," Calvin said. "What about the others?"

"The others consisted only of Firebird's younger son Laughing Fox and his family. Unlike his belligerent brother, Laughing Fox was a quiet, thoughtful man who had always gravitated more to the invisible world of the shaman than the blood-and-guts world of the warrior. On the same day Ten Bears led the rest of the Mima on their ill-fated journey, Laughing Fox and his family visited a settler named Klaus Kirchener. Kirchener had always tried to maintain friendly relations with the Indians, and he and Laughing Fox had developed a peaceable, respectful relationship. Laughing Fox told Kirchener that he was taking his family to safer climes and had stopped by merely to thank Kirchener for his kindness over the years and to wish him farewell. Touched, Kirchener gave Laughing Fox and his family some extra provisions to help them on their journey, then bid them adieu and watched them ride away southward.

"And with that the Mima vanish from history."

Chapter 10

Echoes (II)

1

"I'll bet Laughing Fox and his family got massacred, too," Cynthia said with a sigh.

"Perhaps," said Mr. May. "But there's no way to know."

"Or maybe they went underground," Calvin said. "And they've been, like, building up a secret society to overthrow white America and put the Indians back in charge."

Cynthia smiled and shook her head. "You've been reading too many comic books."

"That doesn't mean I'm wrong."

"So what happened next?" Cynthia asked Mr. May.

"What happened was, the township (which was then known as Indian Hill) was overrun with settlers who cut down most of the trees, used the dead trees to build cabins and mills and stores, held elections, worked, drank, bred, and so on and so forth. Our ancestors"—he said this with a nod at Cynthia—"Nathaniel Crow and John May, arrived in 1829. There isn't much to say about them, really. They were old friends and business associates from Maryland who came here because they thought there were heaps of money to be made along what was then the frontier. And there was. For them, anyway. They bought up vast swaths of local real estate, built a hemp mill—"

"Hemp?" Calvin exclaimed with a grin.

Cynthia clucked her tongue. "They didn't *smoke* it. They made, like, clothes out of it. I think." She looked at Mr. May. "Right?"

"They made all kinds of things out of it," Mr. May said. "Clothes, rope, paper. Even early American flags were made from the stuff. It was—and is—a useful substance. Unfortunately, it wasn't useful enough, at least not then and there, for the mill lost money, and John and Nathaniel were forced to close it down after a while.

"Being stolid, unimaginative fellows, John and Nathaniel didn't give any credence to stories about whispering spirits, so they bought up all the land around Spirit Cave and built large houses there. There's an old story handed down in my family that not long after settling here, John tried to tear up the Stone Pillar. He hitched a team of oxen to it but they couldn't budge it. He dug around its base, hoping to unearth it, but it extended down and down into the earth with no end in sight. Finally he gave up and left the pillar where it was. I have no idea if this story is true. I never made any attempt to confirm it, though perhaps I should have. If he wanted it removed, though, one wonders why he didn't simply smash the aboveground portion to bits with a sledgehammer and leave the rest in the ground like an old tree root."

"It would've sucked if he had," Calvin said. "I like the pillar."

"As do I. Which is why I'm reluctant to start digging around it merely to check a probably apocryphal story.

"Anyway, lest this turn into some tedious blow-by-blow of family history, let's fast forward to 1871. By this point Nathaniel and John were dead, and their sons, Hamilton Crow and Turner May, had assumed control of the family fortunes. And under their guidance, the fortunes had grown quite large. In 1853 Turner had had the idea to convert the hemp mill into a brewery, and the May-Crow Brewing Company was born. It proved a resounding success. Booze is always big business. The town and the two families grew fat and rich practically overnight. In an expression of gratitude the town officially changed its name to May in honor of Turner.

"But not everyone was fat and rich, and instead of gratitude some felt only envy and spite. One such man was Luther Jones, a down-on-his-luck drifter who had come to town in search of a job in the summer of 1870. He had, in fact, found many jobs, but hadn't been able to hold any of them longer than a few weeks thanks to his chronic drinking and explosive temper. There are also references to his engaging in long, heartfelt conversations with people no one else could see or hear, which suggests he suffered from some form of mental illness. Jones had most recently been fired from a job as night watchman at the brewery because he spent the whole night drinking the very product he was meant to be guarding. It was Turner May himself who had caught Jones, and as a result Jones came to loathe Turner, not only for catching him but for being everything Jones was not and would never be: rich, powerful, respected.

"Tragedy struck on October 8, 1871. That night, after a dinner at home, Turner May and his oldest son James headed over to the Crow house to discuss business matters with Hamilton Crow. This was around seven-thirty p.m. They remained at the Crow house until nearly eleven, and then the three of them headed to the May house to round out their evening with a sample of an imported brandy Turner had recently bought. They planned to do so quietly, for they expected Turner's wife Abigail and the other three children to be in bed.

"When they entered the clearing in which the May house stood, they spotted Luther Jones darting into the woods on the north side. A moment later they saw firelight flickering in the house's first floor windows. While Hamilton set off in pursuit of Luther Jones, Turner and James raced into the house to rescue their family. They found Abigail's nude corpse laid out on the dining room table, the silver candlestick that had been used to bash in her skull lying on the carpet nearby. They tried searching for the children, but fires blazed everywhere on the first floor, and the stairs to the second floor, where the bedrooms were, were blocked behind a wall of flame. They shouted the children's names, but received no reply before the choking black smoke forced them outside.

"Turner sent James to find help, then continued calling for his other children in hopes they were only asleep and he could awaken them in time. But the second floor was as still as a tomb except for thin wisps of smoke curling out from the bottoms of the windows. He grabbed a ladder from the shed out back, but by the time he had dragged it into position against the side of the house, flames were already licking the insides of the second-storey window-panes. He clambered up the ladder anyway, hoping against hope. As he neared the top, the window above him burst, spraying him with glass and flames and sending him crashing to the ground. Aside from a sprained wrist he was physically unhurt. But psychologically he was devastated, for he knew there was now no hope of saving his children. He sank to his knees, screaming, as his neighbors, roused by James, came rushing into the yard to help. It was, of course, too late for help, and all they could do was comfort Turner while his world turned to ash. As for young James, after hysterically awakening half the town, he was taken to the Crow house, where he remained all night, looked after by Hamilton's wife Deborah."

"Are they sure the other children were in the house?" Calvin asked. "I mean, did they actually find their bodies?"

Mr. May nodded. "The bodies were found in the wreckage later. Given that the house had collapsed by then and the bodies were burnt to cinders, it was impossible to tell whether the children had been alive or dead when the house burned, or even precisely where in the house they had been. The sad and awful truth is, the details of whatever happened in the May house that night—what Jones's purpose was, why Abigail was positioned on the table like that, what if anything Jones had done to the children—all of that will remain forever unknown. Perhaps it's best that way."

"I hope Jones got what was coming to him," Cynthia said.

"Indeed he did, but under quite unusual circumstances. Hamilton Crow's pursuit of Luther Jones ended when Jones, apparently thinking himself unobserved, crossed the river beneath the falls, ducked into Spirit Cave, and slipped through the narrow fissure at the back and into the tunnels beyond. But Hamilton saw him enter and stood sentry at the mouth of the cave to make sure he didn't leave. A crowd of townsmen soon joined him, and they fell to debating the best way to apprehend Jones. Should they go in en masse? Should only a few carefully selected men go in? No one had ventured very far into the tunnels before, so no one knew the exact layout or how deep the tunnels went. And many of the older residents, recalling the Mima's tales of spirits, were afraid to enter the tunnels at all. As they debated these matters, Turner appeared, bearing two lanterns, two rifles, a knife, and a large spool of twine. His eyes blazed with bloodlust as he announced that only he and Hamilton Crow would enter the tunnels in search of Jones. Everyone understood that he meant to kill Jones and perhaps even torture him first, and no one voiced any disapproval. They just watched as Turner and Hamilton took up their rifles and lanterns and entered the cave."

"What was the twine for?" Cynthia asked. "To tie him up or something?"

"No," said Mr. May. "The twine was to find their way back. As they made their way through the tunnels, they sliced off lengths of twine and placed them at strategic points to mark the correct path back to the surface."

"Like the trail of breadcrumbs in the fairy tale. Except no birds ate it, I hope."

"No. No birds. They made it back to the surface safe and sound. Or, well, perhaps 'safe and sound' isn't exactly accurate. When the two men emerged from the tunnels four hours later, they were dazed and weary and covered in grime. 'He's dead,' Turner told the expectant crowd waiting outside the cave. And that was essentially the first and last public word on the subject. Hamilton never spoke about the incident at all as far as I can tell. No one really asked for further details anyway. They simply assumed the two men had found their quarry and given him his just desserts.

"But toward the end of his life, Turner kept a journal, and in it he wrote a strange, rambling account of that night. By then he was in terrible health and half insane. He was wracked with pain and hallucinations, so it's hard to know how literally to take his tale. Still, however delirious he was when he wrote it, there must be a core of truth to the story. I have the journal in the library upstairs, but like I said, it's quite strange and rambling, almost completely incoherent in some places, and rather than read it to you, I will only summarize."

"Aww," Calvin said. "I'm kinda curious to hear what the rambling's like."

"I can remember some of it. For instance, his description of passing through the fissure at the back of the cave reads more or less as follows: 'One by one through the nightslit, the evil eyeslit, lenticular black aperture and we with our firelanterns and fireguns and lights and knife, we entered one by one with eyes watching behind, those pairs of eyes, in a pair we went one by one into and through the hole, the one.'"

"It's like bad poetry," Cynthia said.

"The full account of their journey in the tunnels runs to over a hundred pages in Turner's tiny, crabbed handwriting, all of it written in exactly that style. It's entertaining to read at first, but trust me, it gets quite tiring after a dozen pages or so.

"Anyway, the gist of his story is this: For two hours they made their way through the branching, twisting tunnels in search of Luther Jones, the way sloping steadily downhill all the while. If we are to trust Turner's account, he and Hamilton encountered huge colonies of phosphorescent fungi, caverns crowded with stalactites and stalagmites, and at one point (if I'm interpreting his words correctly) a vast underground river. Over time the composition of the tunnels changed from a mix of shale and sandstone to fine-grained limestone and then, near the end of their descent, to granite, which suggests they had penetrated quite far underground, possibly as far as the original Precambrian bedrock.

"Eventually they caught up with Jones, who Turner says was 'squatting like a frog in the dark, talking and tittering loudly to himself or to unseen no ones.' When Jones saw the men approaching, he sprang up and raced away. They chased him down a long, curving passage that ended in an archway that seemed too smooth and regular to have been formed by natural processes. Beyond the archway was a cavern so large its edges were lost in the shadows beyond the lanterns' light. Jones fled straight across the cavern. In the dimness he collided with a wide, low object and tumbled to the ground, which allowed Hamilton and Turner the moment necessary to get within shooting range. By the time Jones had scrambled to his feet, Turner had raised his rifle and taken aim. He fired. Jones's head snapped back and his brains splattered the cavern floor."

"Good riddance," Calvin said.

"Turner and Hamilton had little time to savor their victory, for no sooner had Jones collapsed to the stone floor than a gigantic dragon-like figure appeared out of nowhere right in front of them. The dragon—or whatever it was—sported scaly, gray-green skin, long leathery wings folded upon its back, and a pair of thick, curved black horns. Its eyes were blood red, the pupils vertical slits. Its huge coffin-shaped head loomed above the two men atop its sinuous neck, its horns nearly scraping the roof of the cavern. After regarding Turner and Hamilton with its red eyes for a long, silent moment, the creature vanished as abruptly as it had appeared."

"Wakansa!" Calvin cried. "It's Wakansa! A giant winged serpent! That's how the Mima described it, isn't it?"

"Oh, my God," Cynthia said. "That's right."

Mr. May nodded. "Yes. Turner made the same connection in his journal. He seemed to be of the opinion, though, that this creature was not actually a god but was some strange life-form that the Mima had seen in the remote past and then woven myths and stories about. In fact, he even went so far as to suggest that this specific creature was the origin of *all* dragon myths the world over."

"That seems a bit…excessive," Cynthia said.

"That was my reaction, as well. In any case, whatever it was Turner and Hamilton saw down there, it wasn't enough to scare them off. After the creature vanished they spent some time examining the cavern, and what they found was in some ways more mystifying that the supposed dragon.

"The object into which Luther Jones had stumbled turned out to be one of a pair of low stone altars about three feet high and eight feet long. A giant skeleton lay on each altar."

"Giants?" Cynthia said.

"Indeed. About seven feet tall and very slender, with unusually long skulls, limbs, and fingers. Perhaps the strangest thing about the skeletons, however, was not their size, or their proportions, but their composition. The substance of which they were made was brown and dense and smooth, something halfway between polished stone and bone. Hamilton was convinced it *was* stone and the figures simply weird carvings. Turner, however, who knew far more of geology than his friend and had never seen a type of stone like that before, was convinced they were genuine skeletons, remnants of some fabulous prehistoric race of beings whose biology was totally unlike our own.

"The two altars were situated about six feet apart in the center of the chamber, and they rose seamlessly from the floor, having been carved from the living stone. What's more, there were eight niches cut into the wall of the chamber at regular intervals. Each of these niches measured roughly eight feet tall, three wide, and three deep, just about the right size for a being of the dimensions of the two skeletons. All but one of the niches were bare. The one that wasn't contained only a heap of ash at the bottom, as if a fire had once burned there."

"What does it all mean?" Calvin asked.

"It's hard to say. I've mulled it over many times, but can reach no definite conclusions. A dragon. Two altars. Two bizarre skeletons or effigies of skeletons. Eight niches. A huge dome-shaped room so far underground it staggers the imagination. But we can discuss these matters later, once I've told you everything I have to tell you and the larger pattern of events has become clearer.

"A few days after the tragedy, Turner and Hamilton returned to the cave and detonated an entire crate of dynamite inside it. Not only did this seal up the entrance to that mysterious underworld, as intended, but it altered the acoustics of the cave, forever silencing the whispers of the 'spirits' who dwelt there.

"For the next year Turner and James May lived with the Crows while a new May house was built. Turner himself designed the house." Mr. May waved his hand in a broad, sweeping arc. "You can see the result. Twenty-eight rooms. Four wings. A porch on every side. A tower at the center. All of it for one man and a teenage boy. I've never been sure whether there was some cryptic meaning to his curious architectural decisions, or whether they simply reflected his growing derangement.

"At around this time he also began to study magic and spiritualism in hopes of finding a way to access other levels of reality and possibly contact his deceased family. He amassed a huge library of occult tomes, most of which are still here in the house. He experimented with many of the rituals found in the books, and as his familiarity with the subject grew, he rewrote many of the rituals and even crafted new ones.'"

"Sort of like Firebird with his all-new ceremony for raising Wakansa," Calvin said.

"In a way, yes. This history is full of odd echoes of that sort, as you shall see.

"Turner's occult studies came to a head one night in the summer of 1872. Somehow he persuaded a very reluctant Hamilton Crow to assist him with a major ritual which he believed would finally provide him with all the answers he sought. Shortly before midnight the two men descended into the Crows' basement, where Turner had been engaging in most of his occult practices."

"Which room in the basement?" Cynthia said. "Do you know?"

"I'm not entirely certain. In any case, I know your house was extensively remodeled in the early 1900s, so the layout may have changed."

"Oh. So what happened with the ritual? Anything? I hope they didn't, like, raise the forces of darkness in my basement."

"Apparently something did indeed happen, but like so much else in this history the precise details remain unknown. Hamilton never spoke about the events of that night, and Turner made only puzzlingly vague comments about it in his journal as if for some reason he was reluctant to say too much. He wrote that a hazy white glow suffused the room as the ritual progressed and that the ritual climaxed with 'a visitation,' though by whom or what he fails to specify, saying only that it constituted 'proof of worlds beyond this one.'"

"Great, it probably *was* the forces of darkness," Cynthia muttered.

"Turner and James moved into the new May house in the fall of 1872, and for the next eight years Turner rarely left it. He alternated between fits of manic energy and immobilizing depression, and he continued studying and practicing magic with unknown results—his journal entries on that subject are few and brief and often incoherent. He completely ignored the brewery and other business matters, forcing young James to handle them in his father's stead. The townspeople were convinced that Turner's losses had completely unhinged his mind, and while they sympathized, they shunned his house. His only regular visitor was Hamilton Crow, who for a while stopped by once a month to check on his old friend. Eventually, however, Turner's deteriorating mental state became more than Hamilton could bear, and his visits grew more and more sporadic and virtually ceased altogether.

"In 1878 Turner's health began to decline rapidly. Though no proper diagnosis was ever made—Turner refused to see a doctor—descriptions of his symptoms strongly suggest intestinal cancer. He lapsed into a coma and died on September 25, 1880. We can only hope he is with his family again."

Chapter 11

Echoes (III)

1

"That's pretty depressing," Cynthia said.

"Alas, there's more of the same to come," Mr. May said.

"Oh, joy."

"Are you sure you don't want to take a break, if only to stretch your legs?"

"No, that's okay. Let's just keep going."

"And you?" Mr. May asked Calvin.

"I'm good," Calvin said.

"Very well. Next we need to backtrack slightly. While Turner lay on his deathbed, the Crow family suffered a loss of its own: Olive Crow, the daughter of Hamilton and Deborah.

"Born in 1859, Olive was a frail, sickly girl who seemed to fall ill every time someone sneezed. Too weak to travel far, she was schooled at home and rarely strayed from the grounds of the Crow estate. She spent most of her time in her room reading. When the weather was good, she would take a book to the riverbank and while away the afternoon there.

"No one could figure out what was wrong with her. Her parents took her to countless doctors, each of whom ascribed her sickly state to a different cause, and each of whom prescribed a different remedy, none of which worked. In the end her poor health was chalked up to 'innate constitutional infirmities,' whatever that means.

"After the May house burned down and Turner and James moved into the Crow house, Olive, then twelve, grew nervous and jumpy and began to suffer from nightmares that vanished from her mind the moment she woke up (or so she claimed). During these nightmares, she sometimes talked—or more accurately raved—in her sleep. Deborah kept a record of these ravings in hopes of making sense of them, but she never did and later destroyed the notes. I wish she hadn't. I'd love to know what Olive said. At any rate, Olive's nightmares and jumpiness vanished shortly after the Mays moved into their new house."

"Maybe it was connected with Turner's magical rituals," Calvin said. "Maybe she was sensitive to the mystical energies or something."

"Actually," Cynthia said, "I was wondering if maybe Turner or his son was, you know, molesting her."

Calvin sat forward excitedly. "Or maybe Turner was using her in the rituals! He could have been, like, drugging her and sneaking her downstairs every night."

"What is this, Gothic melodrama now?"

"All are definite possibilities," Mr. May said, looking amused. "But I think both of you are overlooking the simplest and most obvious explanation: that Olive was an incredibly introverted and reclusive person who felt threatened that virtual strangers were invading her house, her safe haven."

"Yeah, that makes sense," Calvin said. Then he frowned. "But it seems almost too coincidental that she was raving about weird stuff, just like Turner May wound up doing before he died."

Mr. May nodded. "It does. That constitutes yet another of those odd echoes I mentioned earlier. But we can discuss such matters later. For now, let's move on with the history.

"As she got older, Olive grew increasingly remote and disinterested in everyone and everything except her books and her occasional trips to the river. For the most part her family left her to her own devices. Everyone was happiest that way. Hamilton turned all his attention to his son Stephen, whom he was grooming for a career in the family business. As for Stephen himself, he harbored an inherent dislike of his sister and avoided her whenever he could, as if afraid her 'constitutional infirmities' were contagious.

"Deborah, however, refused to give up on her daughter so easily. She believed that Olive should get married and have children, sure that the assumption of these 'womanly duties' would infuse her daughter with purpose and health."

Cynthia rolled her eyes. "Oh, give me a break."

"It was a different era," Mr. May said.

"You can say that again."

"Deborah was especially keen on making a match between Olive and James May. She constantly dropped hints about it to both James and Olive, and even contrived for the two of them to be alone together on numerous occasions. James was not averse to the idea and made several advances over the years, but Olive always rebuffed him with as little emotion as if she were shooing away a fly. Eventually a frustrated Deborah gave up trying to play matchmaker."

"In July, 1880, when she was twenty-one, Olive's health abruptly worsened. She suffered from chills and headaches, she threw up most of her food, and she was so fatigued she could barely sit up in bed. By the end of the month she had a raging fever that left her delirious and unable to recognize those around her. In the depths of her delirium she insisted that she could hear music coming from somewhere in the woods. At times she hummed an unidentifiable tune over and over, presumably the music she claimed to be hearing, and then broke down giggling or weeping. Hamilton and Deborah called doctor after doctor, but none of them could help her. Most of them agreed that Olive was dying, but they couldn't explain why.

"The end came on August 1, 1880. Olive slept almost all day, awakening only once to sip a bowl of broth her mother brought her. That night a violent storm broke. On their way to bed Hamilton and Deborah checked on Olive to make sure the storm wasn't upsetting her as had happened in the past. She was sleeping peacefully. Or at least she seemed to be.

"Sometime around midnight Deborah was awakened by a repetitive banging sound. She went downstairs and found the front door swinging to and fro in the wind. Thinking it simply hadn't been shut properly, she closed and locked it, then mopped up the rainwater in the hall. On her way back to bed, some parental instinct impelled her to look in Olive's room. Olive wasn't there. Fearing the worst, Deborah woke up Hamilton. He went to look for Olive outside and soon spotted the imprints of her bare feet in the mud. In the slashing rain, he followed the prints west to the river. They led straight into the water.

"Hamilton raced along the riverbank, scanning the storm-churned water for any sign of Olive. He found her limp, sodden corpse washed up by the mouth of the cave he had dynamited shut nine years earlier. The coroner's examination of the body the following day confirmed that she had drowned."

"But if she was so weak she could barely sit up in bed, how could she make it all the way to the river?" Calvin asked.

"The coroner's hypothesis—and though it has its flaws, I can see no reason to doubt it—was that the violence of the storm had agitated her enough to provide a brief and final burst of strength that enabled her to stagger away in search of the music she often claimed to hear."

"That's...creepy," said Cynthia.

"Indeed it is," Mr. May said. "Actually, I have to admit, I'm a little surprised you haven't already heard about any of this."

"I don't know, I guess no one in my family is very big on genealogy. I mean, I know we co-owned the brewery and we were kind of hot stuff in the community way back when, but that's really about it. Oh, and we had a mayor. Stephen. Was that the same Stephen who was Olive's brother?"

Mr. May nodded. "Yes. Stephen Crow. He was the mayor of May during most of the first decade of the 20th Century. There isn't much to say about him, to be honest. At least not vis-à-vis our topic of discussion. Nor is there much more to say about his contemporary, James May. It's their children who are of interest to us. Or rather one child of each: Anna May and Randolph Crow."

"Randolph was the painter, right?" Calvin said, nodding at *Door*.

"Correct. And despite what you've seen so far, his favorite subject was not doors or medieval throne rooms. It was his neighbor and peer, Anna May. Which isn't much of a surprise. She was a beautiful girl with long chestnut hair and dark-brown eyes. Like Olive Crow, she often visited the woods, but unlike Olive she was full of life, preferring to climb trees and chase squirrels than sit reading by the river. More than once she was compared to some Greek nature spirit, and such was her beauty and grace that nearly every eligible young man in town took a shot at wooing her, all to no avail. Anna dismissed them all without a second thought. She preferred to spend her time with Randolph Crow.

"Tall and slim, with black hair and dark eyes, Randolph was a brilliant painter whose canvases typically depicted fantastical scenes from mythology and folklore painted in a photorealistic style. Randolph's artistic bent was a source of constant irritation to his more prosaic-minded father, who had hoped his eldest son would follow him into the family business. But even Stephen had to admit that Randolph was a gifted artist.

"When they were children, Randolph and Anna often spent whole days together in the woods, exploring, swimming in the river, and pursuing hapless squirrels. As they got older and hit puberty, their meetings grew less frolicsome and more cerebral. Where once they played, now they just walked and talked for hours on end. Sometimes Randolph would set up his easel in the woods and Anna would pose for him while he painted her as some white-clad woodland spirit. As I mentioned earlier, I have two more of his paintings upstairs. Both of them feature Anna May. Perhaps I can show them to you later, if there's time.

"Randolph and Anna seemed perfectly matched and clearly preferred each other's company to that of anyone else. It seemed all but certain that the couple would take their relationship to the next level, and both sets of parents eagerly awaited an announcement of Randolph and Anna's engagement. But no announcement ever came. And as time wore on, everyone wondered why. Admittedly, Randolph and Anna were free-spirited sorts, not given to conventional mores, but it still seemed odd that such a well-matched pair would keep their relationship purely platonic."

"Maybe it wasn't platonic, but they were keeping it secret for some reason," Calvin said, unable to refrain from glancing at Cynthia.

Cynthia frowned. "Maybe they just weren't interested in—in taking things to the next level. I mean, is everyone sure she was—or him, too—that they were heterosexual? Maybe she liked girls, or he liked guys. Or both. Or maybe they just didn't want to ruin a perfectly good friendship."

"But they wouldn't spend that much time together if there wasn't some kind of, you know, *interest,*" Calvin said.

"What, you think men and women can't be friends?"

"I…" Calvin squirmed. "I don't know. It's just, you have to admit the relationship between the two of them was…unusual."

Cynthia wobbled her head about in a sort of grudging nod. "I guess. But that doesn't make it *wrong.*"

"I didn't say it was wrong. I said it was unusual."

Mr. May, who had been watching all this with interest, now interjected, "Fascinating as this little debate may be, we should move on."

"Sorry," Calvin and Cynthia said in unison.

"So what happened next?" Cynthia asked.

"Next came the influenza pandemic of 1918."

"Uh-oh." She and Calvin glanced at each other. "This isn't gonna be good, is it?"

"Not even slightly. I don't know how much you know about the pandemic, but it was devastating. I believe I read somewhere that it killed around five percent of the entire world population. The United States was hit particularly hard in the fall of 1918. As the plague swept the country, people died faster than they could be buried. For a while it looked as though May would escape the worst of it: There had been only a few cases of the flu, and the town had adopted strict measures to keep it that way—restricting travel, quarantining suspected carriers, even prohibiting people from spitting on the sidewalks. But in late September the town was hit hard. Hundreds died in only a few weeks. Businesses shut down. People locked themselves in their homes.

"At the height of the epidemic in mid-October, Anna May fell ill. The hospitals were full, so she was treated at home by a local doctor. Though she was supposed to be under quarantine, Randolph visited her every day. He fed her, read to her, talked to her, hoping that his love and care would help her. But her condition only worsened, and it soon became clear that she was dying.

"Randolph channeled his anguish and rage into a new painting. When not at Anna's bedside, he locked himself in his workroom in the basement of the Crow house and worked furiously without food or sleep. He wouldn't let anyone see the painting before its completion. He said he was creating it only for Anna and would give it to her before she died. No one thought he would be able to finish it in time, but the manic, obsessive pace at which he worked ensured he did.

"When he presented it to her, hanging it on the wall opposite her bed so she could look at it, members of both families braved the risk of infection to view it."

Mr. May half turned in his seat and pointed at *Door*.

"That's the painting."

"Wow," Calvin said. He and Cynthia stared at it with

114

something approaching awe.

"Randolph told the assembled Mays and Crows that the painting represented a doorway to a better world. Anna smiled weakly and whispered, 'It's perfect.' Those were the last words she ever spoke.

"Less than half an hour later, she slipped into a coma. It was as if she had been waiting to see the painting before allowing her illness to make its final advance. The doctor was called but there was nothing he could do. She died a few hours later without regaining consciousness. When the doctor pronounced her dead, Randolph stared silently at his painting for several minutes, then strode out of the house. Everyone assumed he was heading off to mourn alone, but a few minutes later a gunshot rang out in the woods to the north of the house. After a short, frantic search, they found Randolph slumped against the Stone Pillar. He had shot himself in the head with one of his father's revolvers.

"The May and Crow burial plots in Indian Hill Cemetery adjoined each other, and the families arranged for Randolph and Anna to be buried side by side.

"This particular tragedy marked the beginning of a long, bad period. In the wake of Randolph and Anna's deaths came Prohibition, which forced the brewery to close and threw the two families and the town itself into a steep economic decline. Just when things were starting to pick up again the Stock Market crashed and the Depression hit. The Mays and Crows weren't wiped out, exactly—they were still better off than most of Depression-era America—but their glory days were over. But none of that is relevant to our specific line of inquiry."

"It isn't?" Cynthia said. "I mean, they were still bad events that befell the families, right? Isn't that the common thread of all this?"

"Not exactly," Mr. May said. He looked at Calvin. "Have you discerned the pattern?"

"Um…" Calvin shrugged.

"Well, we'll discuss it later. For now, let me finish up. We're nearly done, actually. There isn't much else to say about my family. Michael May, Anna's brother, lived a long, uneventful life, got married, begat yours truly, and then passed away. And as for me…well, we'll discuss *that* later, too.

"Turning now to the Crows: Randolph's brother Alexander begat Hardesty—"

"That was my grandpa!" Cynthia said. "Finally someone I know."

"And Hardesty begat you father and your aunt Wendy. It's your aunt who is the final focus of this long, strange history. Or rather, her and her husband."

Cynthia goggled at him. "What are you talking about? She's not married!"

"Not anymore. Not after her husband Eugene died."

"Who?"

Mr. May cocked his head. "You don't know any of this?"

"No!" She sank down in her seat, shoulders slumping. "Nobody tells me anything!"

"Well, since Wendy is still alive, it's no doubt a rather sensitive subject. And a mysterious one, to boot. People usually prefer to sweep genuine mysteries under the rug and pretend they never happened. It's safer that way. But you know about her seizures, right?"

"Yeah." She frowned. "Well, just the fact that she has them. Or used to have them. I don't know any actual details."

"Then it's time you learned. Wendy's first seizure struck in 1963, when she was seven years old. She was out playing in the woods late one autumn afternoon, with strict instructions to stay near the house since dinner would soon be ready. But when dinnertime came she was nowhere in sight. After a panicked search, her parents found her on the path that connected the Crow house to Indian Hill. She was writhing and gasping, foam flying from her lips, eyes rolling and white. As Hardesty was about to race back to the house to call for an ambulance, the seizure ended, and Wendy sat up, wondering why her parents were standing over her looking scared out of their wits. She remembered nothing of her seizure.

"From then on she had seizures at seemingly random intervals. Sometimes she would have three in one week, sometimes months would pass without one. The official diagnosis was cryptogenic epilepsy."

"Cryptogenic?" Calvin said.

"It means they don't know exactly what caused it."

"Oh."

"The doctors gave her medications which lessened the severity and duration of the seizures but didn't stop them completely. Her parents home-schooled her until she was fourteen. At that point they learned of a special boarding school that catered to students with medical conditions that prevented them from attending regular school, so they sent her there. She thrived in her new surroundings. She got excellent grades and wound up the class valedictorian. During this time her seizures gradually vanished."

"Wait!" Calvin said. "Did she stay at the boarding school all that time?"

Mr. May nodded, a small smile on his face as if he understood where Calvin was going with this and was pleased. "She spent the school year at the school, from September to June, and spent only summers and holidays at home."

Cynthia saw where Calvin was going with this too. "It's because she wasn't *here* anymore, right? The seizures were, like, environmental. They were caused by something about this area."

"It's certainly the most logical conclusion, though there's no way to be sure. The disappearance of the seizures could also have been due to age and to the various physiological and psychological changes associated with adolescence."

"Did she have the seizures when she came home for the summers and holidays?" Calvin asked.

"No. But if one accepts the environmental hypothesis, the seizures could have occurred only after long-term exposure to the conditions in question, like a sort of toxic buildup. Spending months away might have eliminated the metaphorical buildup, and when she returned home it would have been like starting over with a clean slate. After she started going to the boarding school, she never spent more than three months in this area. That might not have been long enough to restart the seizures." He shrugged. "But like I said, this is all hypothetical.

"Whatever the cause, the seizures were gone by the time she was eighteen, and she enrolled at Ames University, majoring in Graphic Design. Two things of note happened while she was at Ames. First, she began to manifest psychic powers."

"Psychic powers?" Calvin said. He looked at Cynthia. She nodded.

"She exhibited a wide range of psychic talents," Mr. May said. "Precognition. Clairvoyance. Telepathy. But most of it was frustratingly sporadic and uncontrollable. She would foresee the most trivial incidents with incredible clarity but completely fail to foresee major, life-changing ones. It's that way with a lot of psychics, actually. It's often more curse than gift."

"But still," Calvin said. "Wow. That's kinda cool."

"Yeah, kinda," Cynthia said with a shrug. She didn't want to admit that she was glad Aunt Wendy lived far away. Cynthia hated the idea of someone being able to see into her thoughts, however randomly and unintentionally. When the family visited Wendy in Boston during their summer vacation, Cynthia had spent the whole time dreading that Wendy would have one of her "insights" and realize that her oldest niece was gay and unwittingly blurt something out in front of everyone. Cynthia had breathed a huge sigh of relief when she saw Wendy's house shrinking in the rear window of the family minivan. And now the whole damn process was about to repeat itself because...

She shot bolt upright. "I almost forgot!" she said to Mr. May. "You'll probably want to know about this."

"Know what?" Mr. May said.

"My aunt's coming to visit tomorrow. To help out with things and maybe try to, you know, see something that might help find Emily. Psychically, that is."

"How long will she be here?"

"I don't know for sure."

He grunted. "It'll be hard for her, staying here."

"Why?" Calvin said. "I thought the seizures were pretty much gone."

"The problem isn't the seizures. It's because of what happened to her husband."

"Yeah, what happened with that?" Cynthia asked. "I mean, whatever it is, it must've been pretty bad, seeing as how no one in my family has ever mentioned it."

Mr. May nodded. "That was the other notable event that happened while Wendy was at Ames. During her freshman year, she met a fellow student named Eugene Scott, an aspiring pianist. By all accounts it was one of those rare cases of love at first sight, and after only three months the couple got married."

"Three months?" Cynthia said. "That's insane."

"That was pretty much Wendy's parents' reaction, as well. At least at first. When they finally met Eugene, they changed their tune. Eugene was a rare man, always smiling, always friendly to everyone, always choosing to find the best in the worst the world could offer. He was the sort of person only the bitterest misanthrope could dislike. Plus he was an incredibly talented musician whose bright future seemed all but guaranteed."

"But it wasn't, obviously," Cynthia said.

"Sadly not. Tragedy struck while the couple was staying at your house during the summer of 1978, at which point the couple had been married for barely more than a year. The visit had been fine, with no problems or acrimony. Everyone was getting along well. No one seemed unhappy. Eugene had been in fine spirits the whole time.

"But late one night toward the end of the summer, Wendy was wrenched awake when Eugene violently scrambled out of the bed they were sharing in the second-floor guest bedroom. Groggy and confused, she asked him what was wrong. At first he didn't respond. He merely stood there, shaking and covered in sweat. But finally he muttered, 'It was just a dream. That's all.' Then he told her he going to get a bite to eat and slipped out of the room. She was on the brink of sleep again when she heard a crash. She got up to investigate and found Eugene sprawled in a pool of blood in the middle of the first-floor hall, dead. He appeared to have jumped or fallen off the balcony overlooking the hall and smashed his skull. It seemed unlikely that happy, well-adjusted Eugene would have committed suicide, no matter how bad a dream he had had, but given the height of the railing it was virtually impossible for someone to tumble over it by accident."

"Yeah!" Cynthia said. "I was gonna say, that railing is, like, chest-high. There's no way someone could fall off it. Unless you were climbing on it for some reason."

"Indeed. The whole thing was a mystery. It was ultimately ruled an accident, but the truth is, no one knows for sure."

"God, now I understand why Aunt Wendy hardly ever comes out to visit. Between Eugene's death and the seizures..." She shook her head. "And she's coming out here tomorrow. I almost wish she wasn't now."

"Yes, she never really got over losing Eugene. He was the love of her life. After his death, she took to wearing black constantly and swore she would never remarry—a vow she kept. To the best of my knowledge, she never even dated again."

"*That's* why she's always wearing black. I thought it was just a fashion thing."

"No. It's mourning. Perpetual mourning. At any rate, with Wendy we have come to the end of this strange, sad history."

"So what about you?" Calvin said.

"What about me?"

"You said you'd tell us about yourself and what it was you used to investigate."

"Ah." Mr. May grabbed his cane and pushed himself to his feet with a grunt. "It's best if I show you rather than tell you. Come along." He hobbled toward the door.

"Show us what?" Calvin said as he and Cynthia got up off the couch to follow him.

Mr. May glanced back at them with a smile.

"Things you've never even dreamed of."

Chapter 12

Blackwater

1

Roger Grey stood at the top of the basement stairs, his heart pounding as he stared at the poorly lit, concrete-floored corridor stretching away at the bottom of the stair-well. From this angle he could see only the bottoms of the two doors that faced each other halfway down the corridor. The door on the left led to the laundry room. The one on the right led to the workroom where the chest freezer was.

Where Emily was.

The dead one, at least. He wasn't sure about the other one, the one he saw or thought he saw last night. After smiling that devilish smile and telling him he'd gone and done it this time she had vanished right before his eyes, one moment there, the next gone. And the next moment Roger had been gone, too, scrambling out of the basement as if it were on fire. He didn't remember switching off the light on his mad dash out of the room, but apparently he had, for only darkness showed through the gap under the workroom door.

The other Emily hadn't reappeared, but that hadn't made it any easier for Roger to get to sleep. He had lain in bed for nearly an hour before he felt comfortable enough to switch off the bedside lamp. He had always been a ra-tional man who scoffed at the supernatural. Ghosts, magic, astrology—it was the province of witless peasants. But the only conceivable non-supernatural explanation to last night's events was that he had been suffering from bizarre and incredibly realistic hallucinations. He wasn't sure if he liked that explanation any better than a supernatural one.

Despite his anxieties he eventually managed to fall into a deep and dreamless sleep, and when he awoke this morning with golden sunlight filtering in through his blinds, he felt better, refreshed. He snickered and shook his head at his fears. Yes, he had had a few minor hallucinations, no doubt induced by the abnormal amount of stress he had been under. But it was over now. Now he could dump the body as he had been planning to do before his little…episode.

The twelve o'clock news underscored his need to dispose of the evidence posthaste. During an update about the hunt for Emily, a spokesman for the FBI told reporters that the authorities were making excellent progress in tracking down anyone who had been in the park on Thursday afternoon.

"We've gotten some good, specific information from several park-goers," the spokesman said. "We've already managed to identify most of the people who were seen there, and we are in the process of interviewing them."

After hearing this, Roger had wolfed down some lunch, then grabbed the trash bag that contained Thursday night's clothes and slung it into the trunk of his car.

That left the contents of the freezer.

He had made it this far, the top of the basement stairs, and then stopped, his heart suddenly hammering, his legs rooted to the landing, all his gung-ho, can-do determination forgotten.

"God damn it," he muttered through clenched teeth.

He told himself he was being irrational, giving in to childish fears. He was letting a brief mental misfire get the better of him.

His feet refused to budge. His eyes were wide as he stared at the bottom of the workroom door, as if he expected it to swing open and a pair of small feet—one in a white sneaker, one in a green sock—to shuffle out.

"This is fucking ridiculous," he growled to himself.

His anger overrode his fear. His left foot rose from the landing and swung out over the first step.

From somewhere in the basement came a faint high-pitched trill, like the giggle of a little girl. Roger's foot zipped back onto the landing and he stumbled backward until his butt thumped against the wall.

Then he got control of himself and shook his head. No. The sound had been the chest freezer. He had heard it do that before. It was a loose belt or something. He didn't know exactly what. He wasn't a mechanical-minded person. But that was all it had been. Just a bland, quotidian thing. Nothing more. Not a ghost. Not a ghoul. Not even a hallucination.

Nevertheless, he decided to dispose only of the clothes right now and deal with the body tomorrow, or perhaps the next day. Clearly he was still too jumpy. If he tried to transport the body in his current state of mind, he would probably wind up wrapped around a tree. Better wait a little longer, then. Let more time pass. Let the weirdness become a cold and distant memory.

It was the rational thing to do.

2

A twenty-minute drive south on Route 7 brought Roger to Riddle, a tiny town in the most sparsely populated corner of Bard County. He wasn't even sure "town" was the right word. The place consisted of a single intersection surrounded by a cluster of stores and run-down houses, which in turn were surrounded on three sides by weary-looking farms and overgrown wastes. On the fourth side, the south, was Blackwater Swamp.

Riddle was a rustic, reclusive place, untouched by fast food restaurants and strip malls, and it seemed destined to remain that way. Years ago a half-hearted effort had been made to attract tourists with a small museum that displayed Indian artifacts found in the swamp. But few people knew of the museum and fewer visited it. Roger's mother had taken him there once when he was eleven. The museum had been small and dimly lit and definitely not worth the fifty-cent admission fee. Cobwebs and dust had shrouded the display cases, and the artifacts themselves had been broken and dirty, looking as if they had been thrust into the cases mere moments after they had been plucked from the mud. Young Roger had hated the trip. The whole town had felt diseased in some way, as though tainted by the fetor of the neighboring swamp. He had been relieved when they headed home.

The town hadn't changed one bit. Half the stores were vacant and boarded up. Frowning faces watched from grimy windows as his car passed by. A knot of wrinkled bent old men in overalls stood on a warped porch staring at him expressionlessly. He half expected to see a gape-mouthed Mongoloid kid with a banjo in his lap.

In no time the town was behind him, and Route 7 came to an end at an unnamed dirt road. Roger turned down this road and followed it straight into the swamp.

The sun vanished behind a canopy of thick fleshy green leaves. Gnarled, moss-hung trees bent over dark scummy pools. Birds croaked strange songs from the treetops, while down below unseen shapes rustled through brown weeds three feet high. Entering the swamp was like entering another world, a dark sinister place untrodden by man, though the effect was periodically broken by the sudden appearance of a dilapidated shack sinking into the muck or the rusted remains of a car sitting amid the plants like some forgotten jungle idol.

Here and there dirt paths branched off the main road and extended away along elevations in the soupy landscape. Roger turned down one of these paths and maneuvered the car along it until he was deep in the heart of the swamp. He parked beside a large stagnant pool covered with greenish scum and ringed with thick brush. He got out of the car and looked around. He was completely alone. He might as well have been the only person on the face of the Earth. Perfect.

He took the trash bag from the trunk, stuffed a couple of rocks into it to make sure it was heavy enough to sink, triple-knotted it shut, and then tossed it underhand toward the center of the pool. It sailed through the air, black plastic flapping, then splashed into the water and was gone.

Roger watched the spreading ripples for a moment, almost hypnotized by the way they separated the surface of the pool into alternating rings of green scum and dark water. He was half afraid the bag would bob back to the surface, buoyed by trapped air or something. But it didn't, and the water began to return to its previous stillness.

He turned away and circled around the car to the driver's side door. As he grabbed the handle to open the door, he glanced over the roof of the car for one last look at the pond.

Emily stood on the surface of the pond. Her white tennis shoes rested motionlessly on the circle of scum-cleared water at the center of the concentric rings, which were still languidly spreading outward. She was smiling at him.

Roger staggered backward, a scream rising in his throat. The scream was cut short when his right foot met air, and he realized he was about to topple right off the roadway and into another pond. He heaved himself forward just as his left foot started to slide over the edge, sending rills of dirt and pebbles slithering into the filthy water. He thudded to the ground, his face only inches from the front tire of his car, so close he could smell the rubber.

From here, he could see straight under the car to the pond where Emily stood. But Emily wasn't there. The surface of the pond was empty now. The ripples had stopped. The water was still.

He looked all around to make sure she—it—hadn't moved somewhere else, but there was nothing to see. He was alone again.

He shut his eyes and took a long, deep breath. When his heart rate had returned to something resembling normality, he picked himself up and brushed the dirt from his clothes. He took one more look around. Nothing.

Of course. There had probably never been anything there at all. He was just seeing things. It was the stress.

Of course.

In his hurry to get the hell out of there, he nearly fishtailed right into one of the ponds.

3

He was on Route 7, barely five minutes from home, when he heard Emily's voice say, "You'll want to be careful."

He gasped and looked around. Emily sat in the passenger seat, her hands folded in her lap, her smiling face turned upon him. In his startlement the car veered into the next lane. A horn blared behind him. In his rearview mirror he caught a glimpse of a middle finger waving in front of a sneering face.

Roger somehow managed to get the car back under control and in the correct lane. He felt half sure that once he had done so, the apparition or hallucination or whatever it was would be gone, its job of sowing havoc done, but when he glanced at the passenger seat again, she—it—was still there, hands still folded, mouth still smiling, eyes still upon him.

"Leave me alone," Roger spat. "You're not real."

Her smile widened as her black eyebrows rose.

"Then why are you talking to me?" she asked.

He barked out a laugh, then winced at how cracked and mad the laugh sounded.

"You're not going crazy," she told him. "Trust me."

He wanted to believe her. But of course why would he trust the word of the girl he had murdered? And in any case, the fact that she knew what he had been thinking suggested that she herself was a product of his mind.

The car he had cut off sped past him. The driver, a middle-aged woman with witchy brown hair and a thick blotchy nose, snarled something at him in the process. He couldn't hear her through two closed windows and ten feet of highway, but he quite clearly lip-read the word "mother-fucker." Oddly this touch of ugly, banal reality comforted him. It helped balance out the madness that sat smiling at his side.

"I can prove I'm not a figment of your imagination," Emily said.

"Oh, yeah?" Roger said, striving to adopt a breezy tone to prove he wasn't too bothered by any of this. He frowned slightly at the highway in front of him as though he needed to focus on that and thus couldn't spare even a glance at his unwanted traveling companion.

He waited, expecting further comments, expecting the proof. When the silence dragged on, he briefly hoped that she had vanished.

But no: He could still see her out of the corner of his eye. She was waiting for him to ask.

Bitch.

He didn't want to give her the satisfaction, to give her the win. But he had to find out if she was telling the truth. And if she was, then what exactly *was* she? Not the real Emily, that was for sure. She didn't talk like Emily. The words and the tone were too mature. And the look in her eyes was far too canny for a ten-year-old. No, this wasn't Emily Crow. More like Emily *Faux*.

He smiled at the thought. Giving her a snide nickname made him feel a little better, a little more in control.

"So how can you prove it?" he said.

"By telling you something you couldn't possibly know."

"Yeah? What?"

"That they're waiting for you at your house," she said. "The FBI."

"*What?*"

"The FBI. They're waiting for you to come home. They

want to talk to you."

Roger stared out the windshield, his thoughts racing. If she were telling the truth, going home was the last thing he wanted to do. But if he didn't go home, if he drove past his turnoff and spent the day somewhere else, he wouldn't know for sure whether or not she was telling the truth and thus whether or not she was real. Of course, he could always drive past his street and see if there were any unfamiliar cars parked anywhere, or—

"You should go home," Emily Faux said. "You should talk to them."

He snorted. "Yeah, right. And get arrested."

She shook her head. "No. Not if you answer their questions the right way. I will help you with that. I will be there for you."

"Why would you want to help me?"

"I have my reasons. I'll explain later. For now, just go home."

And with that she vanished again. One moment he was looking right at her, the next he was looking at the empty bucket seat.

He gritted his teeth and stared straight ahead at the highway traffic for a moment. Then he flipped on his blinker to move into the right lane for the upcoming turnoff to May.

4

The moment Roger turned onto his street, he saw an unfamiliar black sedan parked at the curb in front of his house. Two men were inside.

He pulled into his driveway. As he got out of the car,

the sedan's doors opened and the men stepped out. Both of them wore black suits and trench coats. One was a lanky guy in his mid-to-late twenties with a crew cut and a ruddy boyish face. The other was older, probably in his forties, with thinning grey-brown hair and a soft, sad face that reminded Roger of a basset hound's. The man's blue eyes, however, were sharp and alert and didn't look like they missed a thing. Roger realized he had seen the older guy on the news yesterday. He was the agent in charge of the investigation. Roger's heart began to pound and his palms to sweat. He tried to hide his dread behind a pleasant smile. He had no idea if he was doing a good job or not; he feared the smile was a forced, crazy-looking thing.

"Roger Grey?" the younger agent said as the duo approached.

"That's me," Roger said, cocking his head in what he hoped was a good imitation of benign puzzlement. "Can I help you?"

"Maybe so." The two men stopped in front of him. The younger one thrust out a hand. Roger took it. "We're with the FBI. I'm Special Agent Schmidt. This is Special Agent Rowan."

Roger was relieved when Agent Rowan made no move to shake but only gave a small nod. Roger reciprocated.

"Do you have a little time to talk?" Agent Schmidt said. "It shouldn't take long. Just a few quick questions."

"Um, yeah, sure."

"Invite them inside," Emily Faux said. He looked over. She stood on the front steps. She nodded at the front door and then vanished. He looked back at the FBI agents, wondering if they had seen and heard her, too. But they were only looking at him expectantly.

"Would you like to come in?" he said.

For some reason he expected them to decline the offer—after all, "a few quick questions" didn't really merit a living room sit-down, did it?—but Agent Rowan spoke up for the first time, saying, "That'd be nice, thanks."

It was only as he unlocked the front door that Roger thought to wonder if he had left any evidence anywhere in sight. He was fairly sure he hadn't. But he couldn't help fearing that there was something he had dumbly overlooked, something he had grown so used to seeing that he no longer even registered its presence.

As he ushered them in, he glanced around but saw nothing. Nevertheless he worried that the FBI agents' training and experience might enable them to spot subtle details no normal person would notice. Maybe they would even realize there was a corpse in the house. Maybe they would smell it or sense it somehow.

But if they noticed anything amiss, they gave no sign of it. They sat down side-by-side on the couch, Agent Schmidt smiling pleasantly, Agent Rowan looking almost bored.

Roger settled into his recliner. When he looked up at the two FBI agents again, he nearly gasped out loud to see that Emily Faux had reappeared. She stood in front of the couch right next to where Agent Rowan was sitting, and she was regarding the two men with a cool, calm expression, her hands clasped behind her back.

Roger looked at the agents to gauge their reactions. Agent Schmidt was glancing around the room, the pleasant smile still fixed on his face. Agent Rowan, however, must have noticed Roger's brief flash of surprise at the sight of Emily because he had turned to look where he thought Roger had been looking—not at Emily, but out the picture window. Agent Rowan couldn't see her. Neither of the FBI agents could. Only Roger could.

Emily looked over at him. Her long black hair shone bluishly in the light from the window, just like real hair, just as if she were actually physically present.

"Ask them what they would like to know," she said.

"So, um, what is it you'd like to know?" Roger asked.

Agent Schmidt leaned forward, his elbows on his knees. "As I'm sure you probably know by now, we're in town to investigate the disappearance of Emily Crow, and we were led to understand that you were in the park on Thursday afternoon."

"Tell the truth," Emily said. She was staring at Agent Rowan again, her head cocked a little as though listening to a faint, distant sound.

"Yeah," Roger said. "That's right."

"What time did you arrive at the park?" Agent Schmidt asked.

"Um…"

"Keep telling the truth," Emily said. She leaned in toward Agent Rowan, her gaze fixed on his left temple. Or on the brain and thoughts behind it. Was she reading his mind the way she had seemed to read Roger's in the car?

"I think it was somewhere around three-thirty," Roger said. "And I was there about an hour, as I recall."

"Did you see Emily Crow?" Agent Schmidt asked.

"Yes," Emily said.

"Yeah," Roger said. "She was jumping rope in the southeast corner of the park, right by the woods. At least I think that was her. It looked like the girl on the news."

"Did you see her talking to anyone?" Agent Schmidt said.

"No," Emily said.

"No," Roger told Agent Schmidt. "She was just jumping rope."

"Did you interact with her yourself in any way?" Agent Schmidt said.

"No," Emily said.

"No," Roger said.

"Do you go to the park often?" Agent Schmidt said.

"The truth," Emily said.

"Yes, I do," Roger said. "I'm there nearly every day. I work at the bank across the street, and when it's nice out I like to eat my lunch in the park."

"But you weren't eating that late on Thursday, were you?" Agent Rowan asked.

"Oh, no. Actually I'm on vacation right now. Two weeks off, thank God. I went to the park that day because it was so nice out. I figured we might not get many more nice days like that this year, so I'd better enjoy it while I could."

"What, no big trip for your two-week vacation?" Agent Schmidt asked.

"On my salary? Please. I'm lucky if I can take a trip to the supermarket."

Everybody laughed. Except Emily, who nodded approvingly and said, "Good." She drew away from Agent Rowan and walked past him to Agent Schmidt. Neither man noticed anything. They kept smiling and looking at Roger. Emily leaned toward Agent Schmidt the way she had with Agent Rowan, her eyes on his forehead, her expression blank and unconcerned.

Roger couldn't help feeling gratified that he had earned her approval and that he seemed to be doing a decent imitation of Joe Citizen, even though he suspected much of the FBI agents' good humor was feigned. Especially Agent Rowan's. Watching them, it was clear that Agent Rowan was the sharper of the two. Schmidt did most of the talking, and thus attracted most of the attention, but that was a feint. While all attention was focused on Schmidt, Rowan was quietly watching the interview unfold, stepping in occasionally to ask a question, usually a very apt one. Rowan was the one to watch out for.

"Do you recall who else was in the park that day?" Agent Schmidt asked.

"Tell them," Emily said without looking away from Schmidt's head.

"Um…" Roger sat back with a frown, thinking hard. "There were two women, as I recall. One was, um, African-American, the other white. Each of them had a baby in a stroller. I think they arrived separately, but they stopped to talk to each other for a while. Frankly, they were kind of loud."

"The babies or the women?"

Roger chuckled. "The women. They were laughing and cooing at each other's baby. You know how women get around babies."

"Yeah."

"And let's see. There were kids playing baseball down on the baseball diamond. Oh, and there was, uh, that fellow who runs that antique store downtown. I'm not sure what his name is. He's in the park a lot, just like me."

Emily Faux turned to him. "Tell them there was a man in his late thirties or early forties in the park when you first got there, but that he left after about ten minutes, or at least you didn't see him anymore."

Roger repeated this to the FBI agents.

"Can you describe this man?" Agent Schmidt asked.

Repeating whatever Emily told him, Roger described a slightly pudgy white man with short receding brown hair, blue eyes, and a light-colored button-front shirt.

"He was just walking around and around on the paths," Roger concluded, per Emily's instructions. "That's why I noticed him. He passed by me, like, three times. I kind of got the impression he was looking for something, or waiting for someone, or something like that."

There was a brief silence. The two FBI agents were staring off at the floor, thinking. Roger hoped they were about to take their leave to discuss this new information. Or rather *dis*information.

Instead Agent Rowan looked up at him and said, "You say you were on the gazebo?"

"Um, yeah," Roger said, rattled by this sudden change in direction.

"The whole time?"

Emily looked sharply at Rowan as if she had sensed a thought she didn't like. She turned to Roger and swiftly said, "Tell them no. Tell them you got up and strolled around a few times."

Roger repeated this. As he did so, Emily watched Rowan closely. The moment Roger finished talking she turned to him again and said, "Tell them you wandered over to watch the kids play ball."

"In fact," Roger said, "I, uh, I strolled over to the baseball diamond to watch the game awhile."

"You were impressed with a home run hit by a red-haired boy," she said.

"It was a good game," Roger said. "This little red-headed kid hit a great home run."

"It went into the woods."

"The ball went right into the woods."

Agent Rowan nodded. His expression didn't change, but Roger sensed him relax a little as if a suspicion he had harbored had been allayed by Roger's answer.

"I think those are all the questions we have for now," Agent Rowan said. He stood up. Agent Schmidt and Roger did likewise. Emily Faux stayed where she was and watched the trio move toward the front door.

"Thanks for your help," Agent Schmidt told Roger. "We may want to come back and ask you a few more questions at some point."

"That's fine," Roger said with a fake earnest nod. "Whatever I can do to help."

5

After seeing them out, Roger returned to the living room with a huge grin plastered on his face. He—they—had successfully fended off the FBI. The stupid bastards had sat there, and he had lied his ass off, and they had swallowed every word, and all the while Emily's body had been almost directly beneath them. Fucking morons.

He wanted to gloat to Emily Faux, and to thank her, and to ask her again why she was helping him (she said she would explain, after all), but when he looked around she was nowhere to be seen.

He waited until he heard the FBI agents' car start up and drive away, then said, "Emily?"

There was no answer. He called her name again, louder. The sound of his voice ringing in the room made him realize how strange and ridiculous the situation had become. Here he was, calling out for the ghostly doppelganger of the girl he had murdered. If she hadn't been right about the FBI waiting for him and if she hadn't helped him answer their questions, he would assume he was going mad.

He searched the whole main floor. She wasn't there. He stood at the top of the basement stairs and looked down at the concrete hallway. He wasn't afraid of going down there anymore. Not now. Not after she had helped him.

He went down and searched the laundry room and the workroom. He didn't find her.

At least not the ghostly one. The real Emily was still in the freezer, looking exactly the same as before.

He reflected that since he had successfully fended off the authorities, now might be the best time to dispose of the body.

But what if Emily Faux's appearances were somehow connected with the presence of the body in his house? What if dumping the body severed whatever link he had with her? Then she wouldn't be able to help him if the FBI came back. And they would almost certainly come back.

He turned in a circle, looking all around the workroom.

"Emily!" he called.

His voice echoed in the silence.

Chapter 13

House of Mystery

1

"I won't give you the grand tour of the house," Mr. May said as he led Calvin and Cynthia out of the parlor and down the painting-lined corridor toward the spiral staircase. "We don't have time for that, and large swaths of the house aren't terribly grand anyway. Old Turner incorporated too many damn rooms into this place, far more than I can possibly use, with the result that many of the rooms currently exist only to provide a landing platform for dust. There's a game room and a smoking room and a study and a host of other completely useless rooms. Perhaps someday you can see them, but not right now. Right now there are only a handful of rooms you need to see."

"*Need* to see?" Calvin said.

Mr. May looked at him over his shoulder. "If you want to understand why I am uniquely qualified to help you investigate Emily's disappearance, then yes."

"Wow, that's a pretty bold statement," Cynthia said.

"You'll see."

The spiral staircase stood in a circular space at the center of the house. From there, they could see down all four corridors to the four porch doors. Calvin expected Mr. May to lead them down one of these corridors, but instead the old man headed straight for the stairs and began to ascend.

The stairs wound downward as well as up, and as he followed Mr. May, Calvin peered down the shaft to the bottom of the stairwell. All he saw was a bare concrete floor. He remembered the rumors he had heard over the years about Mr. May burying bodies in his basement, and he shook his head at how absurd those stories now seemed.

It took a while to reach the second floor. Mr. May moved slowly and with great care, planting both feet on each step before moving on to the next. Calvin couldn't help wincing at the sight. Mr. May probably navigated these stairs on a regular basis; it was only a matter of time before an accident happened. Calvin imagined Mr. May slipping and falling, the old man's old bones snapping like kindling on the metal steps.

"Have you ever thought about putting in an elevator or something?" he said.

"I thought about it," Mr. May said, his voice breathy with exertion. "But I don't want to destroy Turner's design any more than I already have. As it is, I regret putting in the modern bathrooms and making a few other changes."

On the second floor was a circular area identical to the one below, with four corridors stretching away down the house's four wings.

"This place really is symmetrical, isn't it?" Cynthia said.

"For all his seeming madness, Turner loved regularity," Mr. May said. He hobbled off down the east wing. Calvin and Cynthia followed.

Halfway down, a pair of doors faced each other across the hallway. Mr. May stopped before the door on the south side of the corridor and laid his hand on the knob. He looked back at Calvin and Cynthia. His eyes were bright and nervous as if he were about to bare his deepest, darkest secrets. Calvin wondered what the heck Mr. May was about to show them.

"Here we are," Mr. May said. He turned the knob and pushed open the door. "The Collection." The way he said it made it a proper noun.

He led them through the doorway and into a large room whose walls were lined with floor-to-ceiling wooden shelving units. There were also rows of freestanding shelving units running the length of the room, forming aisles like in a library. But the shelves bore few books. Instead they were crowded with a bewildering variety of items. The first shelf Calvin and Cynthia paused to examine held a stuffed and mounted seven-headed rattlesnake, an old dirt-smudged baseball, a sealed glass jar in which a coiled foot-long worm floated in a translucent pink liquid, a six-inch-long humanoid figure made of white wax, and a lidless white cardboard box containing five ceramic tiles, a bunch of red threads in a clear plastic bag, and a small plastic dolphin. The shelf below it held a Polaroid Sun camera, a brass carriage clock that displayed thirteen hours instead of the usual twelve, a frog mask, a coffee can full of pennies from the year 1898, a boomerang, and another white lidless box, this one containing half a dozen audiocassettes, a book of Asian love poems, a fist-sized chunk of granite, and an eight-inch-long segment of a tree root. The rest of the room's hundred-plus shelves held equally weird and diverse items. On the shelf in front of each item or boxed batch of items was a white sticker with a number on it.

Calvin and Cynthia glanced at each other in bewilderment, then at Mr. May. The old man was eyeing them closely, watching their reactions. He looked more nervous than ever. Clearly their response was important to him.

Calvin realized that the Collection—whatever it was—was the real key to understanding Robert May. Everything downstairs—the antiques, the paintings, the old-fashioned atmosphere—all of that was secondary, if not an outright façade. The Collection was the central fact of his life.

Calvin shook his head. "What is this? Some kind of museum or something?"

Mr. May waved his arm at the assembled mass of items. "These are anomalies, mysteries, oddities, or at least artifacts relating thereto. I have spent my life investigating anything the standard view of reality regards as bizarre or impossible. These, in my opinion, are the true wonders of the world. Each item in this room has a unique and remarkable story." He took a large, flat rock from a shelf and held it up so they could see the fossilized fern on its surface. "For instance, this fossil was found in strata over four hundred million years older than when ferns are thought to have first appeared."

Cynthia shrugged. "Well, that's not too amazing, is it? I mean, the fossil record is still kind of spotty, right? So maybe they just don't have all the dating worked out quite right."

"Oh, no one would deny that the fossil record has its gaps and inconsistencies. But still, ferns in the Precambrian? Try arguing that with a geologist. You'll get laughed right out of the room. And that is among the least of the Collection." He picked up an ornate, silver-handled mirror. "What about this? This is a haunted mirror. At certain times, anyone looking into the glass will see the face of the woman who died holding it over one hundred years ago."

"Have you seen the face yourself?" Calvin asked.

"Once. Since then, I haven't been too keen on taking another look."

"Whoa!" Calvin stared at the mirror with his mouth agape, both afraid and hopeful that a rotting zombie face would materialize in the glass.

"And then there's this." Mr. May pulled a vial of thick green goo from a shelf and held it up for them to see. "This was found in the core of a meteorite that fell to earth in Venezuela in 1963. A dozen labs have analyzed it, but none could identify it. They couldn't even conclusively determine whether it was organic or inorganic. It possessed a chemical structure no one had ever seen before."

"Cool!" Calvin exclaimed.

He and Cynthia spent a while exploring the room and examining the items on display: an antique revolver; an earthenware bust of a young woman; formaldehyde-filled jars containing eyeballs, diseased organs, fetuses, fish; an electronic Casio keyboard; a locked, leather-bound diary, its cover crusty with dried blood; a ventriloquist's dummy; a box full of plaster casts of huge bare footprints.

Calvin halted in front of this last item and looked up at Mr. May with big, excited eyes.

"Are these Bigfoot footprints?" he asked.

"Possibly. They were cast from impressions found in a muddy riverbank in northern Minnesota in 1983, not far from a reported sighting of a large hairy humanoid two days earlier. Interestingly there were also strange lights seen in the sky at around the same time."

"Wow. I never would have guessed there was a real-life paranormal investigator living here in May."

Mr. May frowned. "I investigate much more than the so-called paranormal. Many of these items do not contravene any known laws of nature but are simply at variance with currently accepted scientific theories. Anomalousness means far more than groaning spirits and little grey aliens.

The fossil fern, for example. It's not impossible that plant life—and life in general—evolved much earlier than our present data and theories suggest. But at the moment the concept is thoroughly heretical in the halls of science."

Cynthia tapped one of the stickers affixed to the shelves. "So what are these numbers, exactly? Some sort of cataloguing system or something?"

"Precisely," Mr. May said. "The numbers refer you to a file concerning the anomaly in question. I keep the files in another room. Come along. I'll show you."

He led them to the circular area in the center of the house, then down the north wing to a room arranged much like the Collection room, only with file cabinets instead of shelving units. In a corner of the room was a small desk and chair. A closed manila folder sat on the desktop.

"These are all full of files?" Calvin said, looking around.

"Mostly. The file cabinets along the south wall are reserved for magazine and newspaper clippings pertaining to anomalies and mysteries in general. But the rest contain files dealing with all the evidence I have collected. Each file contains a full report on the anomaly, including the date, the location, the circumstances of its discovery or occurrence, and any other pertinent facts. Most files also include photographs. The files are arranged in numerical order, which is also, for the most part, chronological order—number 1 being the first anomaly I investigated, number 3,997 being the most recent."

"There was that much stuff in the other room?" Cynthia said.

Mr. May laughed. "Oh, no. That was only a portion of the Collection. Follow me."

He led them across the hall to another Collection room, which was nearly twice the size of the first one.

While Mr. May watched with a smile, Calvin and Cynthia toured the room, pausing often to inspect some of the more interesting artifacts, among them an unidentifiable animal skull with long, curling horns; a one-foot-square obsidian cube; a Hawaiian shirt; a long thin strip of shiny silvery metal covered with mysterious black symbols; a scrimshaw turtle; a cardboard box full of small, teardrop-shaped stones; and a mummified hand too simian to be human, but too human to be simian.

"How did you get all this stuff?" Calvin asked.

"Perseverance. Luck. Charm. Lots of traveling." Mr. May shrugged. "Having a large inheritance at one's disposal helps, too."

"This is awesome."

"Wait till you see the third floor."

"There's more?" Cynthia said.

"You've seen only about half the total collection. A lot of the really outré items are upstairs."

They returned to the stairs and headed up to a small, square room that had doors in the north, west, and south walls. The east wall was blank.

"How come it's a square?" Calvin asked. "On the first and second floors, the area around the stairs was circular."

"The one in the basement is square, too," Mr. May said. "So there is a weird sort of symmetry: square, circle, circle, square. Then the tower, crowning it all."

"What does it mean, though?" Cynthia said.

He shrugged. "Who knows? No doubt it had some occult meaning to Turner, but I've never been able to determine precisely what."

Mr. May led them through the south door and into a large room that contained the now-familiar wooden shelves as well as many freestanding items too large to fit on the shelves. This room's contents included a full suit of armor; a snow-white animal pelt; an old photograph of a group of men in old western garb standing in front of a dead Pterodactyl that was strung up on the wall of a barn; a jar full of white sand; a harpsichord; a painted plaster statue of a creature that looked like a cross between a reptile and a huge bat; a comic book titled *Spooky Stories;* a silver ring sporting a large, blood-red ruby; and an oil drum on a wooden pallet in a corner of the room.

"Hey, Cyn," Calvin said, pointing at the latter item. "Is that what you saw being delivered that one time?"

She followed his finger, then her eyes lit up.

"It is!" She strode over to the drum to look at it more closely.

"What?" Mr. May said.

"I saw this being delivered here a few years ago."

"Really?" He sighed. "I suppose I've let my caution slip a bit of late." He frowned. "Now that I think about it, I do recall Mike saying something about a teenage girl in the area when he dropped it off. I had no idea it was you."

"Mike?" Cynthia asked. "Was that the guy with the sunglasses?"

"Yes."

"What is he, a fellow anomaly investigator or something?" Calvin asked.

"Not exactly. Just an old friend who sometimes helps me out with procuring and shipping things since I am no longer as mobile as I once was." He shot a smile at Cynthia. "I guess I can see why you were so suspicious of me. I can only imagine what you thought when you saw mysterious metal barrels being delivered to your reclusive old neighbor's house in the dead of night."

"Yeah," she said with a laugh. She ran a hand over the

drum's top. "What's in it anyway?"

"The partly decomposed remains of an unknown life-form that washed ashore on a beach in Brazil. None of the biologists who examined it could figure out what it was, so in a truly astonishing display of scientific laziness they wrote it off as a partially digested jellyfish that had been vomited up by a shark or a whale. I had to pay a pretty penny to get a hold of it, then have it preserved properly and shipped all the way up here. Back in the old days, I would have traveled down there myself and saved half the expenses, but…" A gesture at his cane and a rueful grimace completed the thought for him. He turned toward the door. "Now come. There's more to see."

The next room presented the same eclectic jumble of items, among them an antique telephone; a pair of dusty, sharp-toed cowboy boots with rundown heels; a cylindrical block of marble carved with odd symbols; an assortment of human skulls, bones, and teeth, including one fully articu-lated skeleton sporting bulbous osseous growths; a black leather briefcase on the side of which was a yellow symbol shaped like a Y in a circle; a few mangled pieces of an old silver Porsche Spyder; and a refrigerator.

"Is the refrigerator anomalous, or does it contain stuff?" asked Calvin.

"It contains perishable items," Mr. May said. He opened the refrigerator. It was full of labeled and num-bered metal canisters. The freezer unit contained half a dozen more canisters, plus a large block of ice in the heart of which was a mass of some red gelatinous substance.

"What's that stuff in the ice?" Calvin asked.

"Laboratory tests identified it as raspberry jam."

"What's so weird about raspberry jam?" Cynthia said.

"Nothing, except that the Antarctic ice in which it was

found has been dated as being over forty thousand years old."

"Seriously?"

"Of course. I wouldn't lie about a thing like that."

"But how did raspberry jam get inside forty-thousand-year-old ice?" Calvin said.

"I haven't a clue. Nobody does. That's the point." He headed for the door. "Now come along. We have one last room to see."

The third and final room on the third floor was the biggest Collection room of all. Among the many items on display were a skull carved from a single block of crystal; a typewriter-sized machine bristling with dials, knobs, and wires; a shriveled, green, faintly luminous human hand; a small metallic sphere with three grooves around the middle; a football-sized blue egg with yellow speckles; an ebony box with a stylized gold Z on the lid; a black glass orb the size of a grapefruit; brittle brown fragments of an Ancient Egyptian papyrus preserved in a small glass case; and a black coffin propped up in one corner of the room.

"Um, there's nothing in that, is there?" Cynthia asked, pointing at the coffin.

"Only my pet zombie," Mr. May said.

Cynthia breathed out a small, uncertain laugh. "You're kidding, right?"

"Yes. It's empty. Though it supposedly once housed a vampire, which is why I have it here."

Calvin cocked his head. "You believe in vampires?"

"I neither believe nor disbelieve. I choose to maintain an attitude of utter, unapologetic agnosticism. I have never seen a vampire (as far as I know), but I have seen countless other things that supposedly don't exist or can't happen. The universe is a far, far stranger place than most people suspect. Wonders and mysteries abound for those with eyes to see. Alas, too many people lack those eyes, or lack the courage to use them. They prefer to believe what they're told and not to ask too many questions. Life is safer and easier that way. But there are those of us who aren't content with that, who think their own thoughts and go their own ways and wish to experience the mysteries of the universe in all their mad and fecund variety."

"Yeah!" Calvin said, nodding vigorously, his mouth stretched in a huge grin. He was bursting with excitement. He felt as if the remarkable thing he had been waiting for all his life had finally happened.

Cynthia's response was more restrained. She nodded thoughtfully and said, "This is all really cool and everything, but I'm not entirely clear how all of this connects up with Emily."

Mr. May nodded. "That's what we need to discuss next. The time has come to put the pieces together and develop a plan of action. If, that is, you still wish to proceed. The two of you came here yesterday thinking I was behind Emily's disappearance. Well, now you know (I hope) that I am not the culprit. But you also know that the situation may be far more complex and unusual than you first thought. If you intend to continue investigating—and I hope you do; the two of you have the makings of excellent investigators—then I can help you. I am no longer young and spry and able to gallivant about in search of answers. But you are. And all my knowledge and resources and decades of investigatory experience are at your disposal, if you want them. Bear in mind, though, that the police and FBI won't be terribly happy if they find us sniffing around on our own. Technically that would qualify as interfering with a police investigation, and that's no small crime."

"What about you?" Calvin said. He waved a hand at the Collection around them. "If things go wrong, you've got a lot more to lose than we do."

"I appreciate your concern, but I can take care of myself. Over the years I've faced down much worse foes than the May Police, or even the FBI. But in a way, you do in fact have more to lose than I do: your futures. My life is nearly over, but yours are only just beginning. I want you to be fully aware of the stakes we're playing for and the risks we might face. And not just from the police, either. There are also the unknown forces behind the tragedies that have played out in this area over the last two hundred years. Keeping all this in mind, do you still wish to continue?"

"Of course," Cynthia said. "I'm not backing down now."

"Me either," Calvin said.

Mr. May nodded. "Good. Then follow me, and we'll begin."

Chapter 14

See Emily Play (II)

1

"I quit!" John snapped, flinging away the page of math problems and slumping back against the front of the couch. He and Anna sat on the floor in his living room. The carpet around them was strewn with half a dozen similar pages. "This is stupid. I didn't even get assigned it anyway. I wasn't there. I don't see why I should bother."

"Yeah, but you know Miss Dryer," Anna said. "She's just gonna have you do it when you come back to school."

John rolled his eyes. "Who cares about this stuff anyway? I mean, Emily's…you know, she's out there somewhere. We should all be trying to find her instead of doing stupid math."

"People *are* looking for her. The police and the FBI. We just have to wait and let them do their job. Besides"— she held up the paper he had tossed away—"this'll help take our minds off everything. And it's stuff we should know."

John snorted.

"Look, John, I know how you're feeling. I'm scared for her too. But we can't just sit around and stew. We need to do stuff. We need to keep busy."

John kept his gaze fixed on the carpet, but he could see her staring at him out of the corner of his eye, a small, hopeful smile on her face. It annoyed him how Anna always unquestioningly sided with the schools and the government and society's whole intricate network of silly rules and regulations that forced people to do stupid things they didn't want to do. People who forced other people to do things they didn't want to do were bullies, weren't they? And bullies were bad, weren't they?

For Anna to support this bullyish system was kind of ironic, seeing as how it had been their opposition to a bully that had brought her and John and Emily together in the first place...

2

It happened during recess the third week of second grade. It was a pleasant sunny summer-like day, and John was squatting in a quiet corner of the playground watching little black ants stream in and out of their sandy holes in the dirt. Most of the other students were on the main paved area of the playground some ways off, screaming and yammering and running about and doing all the hectic noisy things they usually did. The only person near John was Emily Crow, who was jumping rope in a grassy area on the other side of some bushes. Every now and then he heard her chanting rhymes as she jumped, most of them idiosyncratic variations of rhymes he had heard other, more normal girls chanting, with absurd, gruesome and/or fantastical words substituted for the more traditional ones.

John knew who Emily was—she was in his class after all—but he had never talked to her and didn't know a lot about her. He knew more about her family than he did about her. This was mainly thanks to Aunt Colleen, who had kind of a bee in her bonnet about local history. One time when Aunt Colleen was picking him up after school, she spotted Emily Crow coming out of the building behind him and then spent the whole drive home prattling on about the Crow family. John had tried to tune most of it out like he usually did when she started going on about stuff like that, but he had caught just enough to learn that the Crows used to be big deals around town because they made beer. "Why, without the brewery," Aunt Colleen had gushed, "May would probably be just a single intersection surrounded by five miles of cornfields." John got the impression that only people who knew much about the past cared about the Crows anymore. And most people didn't care about the past.

John himself didn't care about the beer or the old dead guys who made it or any of that stuff, but he was surprised to find that he was starting to grow interested in Emily Crow. Like him, she was smart and strange, and she often played alone. He felt a weird kind of thrill to find someone else on the sidelines like him, someone he identified with, and he felt an even weirder thrill that this person was a girl. As he listened to her recite her latest goofy rhyme (this one had begun: "Late last night and the night before, twenty-nine hobbits were barfing on my floor..."), he considered going over to talk to her, but he didn't want to bother her, and he wasn't really sure what to say anyway.

A large shadow fell over him. Or rather, one large shadow and three smaller shadows.

John knew without looking up that the large shadow belonged to Buddy Harris. Those rotund curves could belong to no one else in school. Buddy Harris was the class bully, a collection of cruelties and crudities animating a huge blubbery mass that weighed nearly twice that of any other kid in the second grade. His mouth was twisted into a permanent smirk, one that didn't waver even when he was being scolded by the teacher, or when Principal Powell was suspending him, or when someone was slugging him in the face, like Ritchie Givens did last year (Ritchie wound up getting the crap pounded out of him, of course). Above that smirk was a pair of dark, beady eyes that looked horrifyingly blank, like a doll's or a shark's.

Buddy was always accompanied by a trio of smaller, thinner jerks named Scott, Luke, and Nathan. John could never remember which was which. Not that it mattered. They were just interchangeable underlings, like the bad guys' henchmen on the old *Batman* TV show.

John had never run afoul of Buddy, probably because John was quiet and didn't attract much attention. But for some reason John had attracted Buddy's attention today.

"What're you doing?" Buddy said.

"Nothing," John said, standing up. If they discovered he was watching the ants, Buddy would just stomp on them.

"Yeah? Nothing? You're really just sitting over here doing nothing?" Buddy's tone was mocking, snotty.

"Pretty much," John said as calmly and pleasantly as possible. He didn't want to fight. If a fight started he knew he would get his ass kicked by Buddy and his henchmen, none of whom had a problem with unfair fights. John wouldn't have minded a fight—even an ass-kicking—if it had been in pursuit of something worthy. But a fight based on nothing more than the caprice of some surly fatboy was utterly stupid.

It was about five minutes till the end of recess. Under the circumstances, five minutes was a long time, but if John could keep Buddy distracted until then he could avoid this senseless confrontation. After that, Buddy's dull wit and poor memory ensured he would probably forget all about his inexplicable beef against John well before school let out. But what would be a decent distraction?

"Hey, I heard a good joke the other day," John said. "Wanna hear it?"

"No," Buddy said. "I already got a pretty good joke standing right in front of me."

John felt a sinking feeling. Clearly Buddy was determined to start something no matter what.

Still, maybe there was a way out of the situation. Maybe it would be best to be direct about everything. Had anyone ever tried that with Buddy?

"Why do you want to start something?" John said. "What's the point?"

Buddy blinked at him for a moment, apparently taken aback by the question. Then he scowled. "I don't need a point. I just feel like it, that's all." Behind him, one of the henchmen chuckled with approval.

"But why do you feel like it?" John asked.

"Why do you feel like it?" Buddy repeated in a high-pitched mocking voice. Buddy grabbed the front of John's T-shirt in one pudgy fist. "Cuz I do, dickbreath."

"But you must have a reason. You—"

"The reason is, you're ugly and stupid."

Evidently, rational discussion just didn't work with some people. John felt a rush of anger and injustice that he was about to get beaten up over nothing at all.

The hell with it, he decided; he might as well make it over *something*.

"I heard your mom fucked Principal Powell last night."

Buddy gawped at him in surprise. Over his husky shoulders, his henchmen exchanged equally surprised glances.

"What'd you say?" Buddy roared, yanking John toward him.

"Of course, that was after your dad sucked the principal's dick," John went on in a bland, conversational voice. "I guess he wanted to get it nice and wet for when he slipped it to your mom."

One of the henchmen started to laugh, then caught himself just in time to turn the laugh into a gasp of mock outrage. Buddy's dark unibrow descended in a furious glare, while his lips squeezed together into a line as thin and white as a razor scar.

John was trying to decide whether he should now punch Buddy in the face or knee him in the crotch. Whatever he did, he would get the crap beaten out of him—that was pretty much inevitable at this point—but he wanted to inflict enough damage to ensure that Buddy wouldn't want to bother him in the future.

But before he could decide, a girl's voice called out behind him, "I wouldn't do that, Buddy!"

Buddy's gaze flicked over John's shoulder. Then Buddy groaned and rolled his eyes.

"Oh, great," he said. "It's the birdy girl."

John turned his head and saw Emily Crow standing on the edge of the bushes that bordered this side of the playground. Her arms were crossed, and her expression was set and stern. She must have heard what was happening, then circled around and wriggled through the bushes. She was trying to help him. He felt that weird thrill again.

"Get your birdy face outta here!" Buddy snapped at Emily. One of his henchmen added a couple of caws for good measure.

"You shouldn't bother him," Emily said. "He's got

special powers, you know."

Buddy snorted. "What can he do, turn gay?"

All three henchmen found this to be the funniest thing ever and burst into raucous laughter.

"No," Emily said, "but he could probably turn *you* gay. He could probably make your dicks drop off. He comes from a long line of powerful sorcerers."

The laughter stopped. The henchmen glanced uncertainly at each other.

Buddy, however, wasn't swayed.

"That's bullcrap!" he said. He looked John up and down, his smirk more derisive than ever. John just stared back with the same stern, level gaze Emily had adopted, refusing to allow the slightest trace of fear or doubt to show on his face.

"Haven't you heard about the Indian god named Old Man Coyote?" Emily said. "He could do all kinds of powerful magic. He could change his shape and turn invisible and turn people into animals and make people's dicks fall off. Well, that god was John's ancestor. Didn't you ever wonder why John has the last name he does? Old Man Coyote's blood still flows through John's veins."

"What, there was a god named after some mangy dog?" Buddy said. "That's stupid."

"No, it's true, man," one of the henchmen said. "I saw something about it on the Learning Channel."

Buddy sneered at him over his shoulder. "What the hell're you doing watching the Learning Channel for?"

The henchman shifted his weight from one foot to another and mumbled, "I dunno. It was just on."

Buddy grunted, then turned back to John and Emily.

"A dog god, huh? Ooh! I'm scared!"

"You oughtta be scared," Emily said, her eyes dark

slits. "Anyone who messes with him is in for real big trouble."

"What's he gonna do, pee on my leg? And what about you? Are you named after, like, a bird god? Are you gonna poop on my dad's car?"

"Oh, we'll do much worse than that, Buddy. We'll put a curse on you. On all of you. It's the worst curse there is: the curse of ultimate bad luck. It'll ruin your lives forever. The worst part is, you never know exactly what the curse will do. It can cause bad luck in a billion different ways. Maybe it'll give you cancer, or maybe everyone you care about will die and leave you all alone, or maybe you'll just fail at everything you ever try and you'll wind up living in a cardboard box in an alley somewhere. The only thing you can be sure of is it'll always be bad. Real bad. So don't mess with us. Cuz if you do, your world'll go straight to hell and it'll never come back."

John and Emily stood straight and tall and stared down Buddy and his cohorts as if every word she had said were true. And for one incredible moment, John felt convinced that it *was* true, that having this crazy cool girl beside him had made it true, that with Emily on his side *anything* could become true. John thought he felt power coursing through him. Maybe he really did have god blood in him. Maybe Emily did, too.

The henchmen seemed to feel it as well. They were staring at John and Emily with their mouths hanging open. They looked like they wanted to be somewhere else really, really badly.

Buddy, on the other hand, didn't look scared. But he didn't look mocking or angry anymore either. Instead he regarded John and Emily with a closed, distant look. If it had been anyone other than Buddy Harris, John would have said he looked thoughtful.

But then Buddy's lips twisted into a cruel smile.

"Bzzt! Wrong answer!" He yanked John toward him by the front of his shirt and cocked one fist back to punch John in the face.

"Don't!" Emily cried, her stern and baleful aura washed away by alarm.

The henchmen, emboldened by their master's fearlessness, began to circle around Buddy to aid in the impending beatdown.

John tensed up and clenched his fists, ready to blacken as many eyes and bloody as many noses as he could...

And then he didn't need to.

"Stop that!" a voice cried.

Everyone turned. Anna West, another second-grader, was striding toward them. John knew Anna slightly better than he knew Emily. He had at least spoken to Anna a couple of times. Anna made it a point to speak to everyone, even if it was only the occasional "hello" or "how are you?" There was an aura of adulthood about her, of adult concernedness with good manners and fair play. Sometimes she seemed more like one of the teachers than one of the students.

The henchmen swiftly turned away from John and Emily and tried to look like innocent bystanders. Buddy's arm dropped to his side and his fist unclenched as if he were hiding the evidence.

"What do you think you're doing?" Anna said. She stopped in front of them and planted her fists on her hips.

"They—they said they were gonna do bad stuff to us," one of the henchmen said, pointing at John and Emily. John had to give him credit: It was technically true.

Anna raised one eyebrow to show her certainty that

that was far from the whole story. The henchman suddenly found something very interesting to look at on his shoes.

John glanced questioningly at Emily, thinking that maybe Anna was her friend. Emily just shrugged.

"Well, I think you guys had better stop whatever it is you're doing," Anna told Buddy and his henchmen.

"They got this coming," Buddy told her. He clenched his fist again. "They *deserve* this." He raised his fist.

"Is that what your dad says about your mom?" Anna said in a soft, sad tone.

The effect was astonishing. Buddy took a few stumbling steps backward, his flabby belly quivering, his cheeks flushing bright red as if he had been slapped. For the first time John could remember, Buddy looked hurt. An almost haunted look filled the bully's eyes.

For a moment the only sounds were the shouts and shrieks of the other kids playing in the main section of the playground. Then Buddy's face twisted back into its usual smirk.

"Screw this crap," he said. "I got better things to do than waste time with a buncha babies." He turned to his henchmen. "Come on, guys. Let's go see if Cain still has those cards."

They strode away.

"Thanks," Emily told Anna.

Anna just shrugged. "He shouldn't do stuff like that."

"What was that you said about his mom and dad?" John asked. "How did you know about that?"

"Oh, my mom. She works as a police dispatcher. They've gotten a bunch of calls from Buddy's neighbors reporting fights and screams and stuff. 'Domestic disturbances' is what they call it. The cops go and find the place all smashed up, and Buddy's dad drunk, and Buddy's mom with bruises and black eyes and stuff, and Buddy huddled in a corner."

"Why doesn't anybody arrest his dad?" Emily asked.

"Buddy's mom never wants to press charges."

Emily tutted.

They all turned and looked at Buddy as he jabbed a finger at Kevin Cain and said something that made Kevin nod vigorously.

"But if everybody knows what's going on," John said, "why can't someone do something about it."

Anna shrugged. "That's just the way the law is, I guess."

John grunted. "Then the law doesn't work very well."

"It works well enough most of the time."

"Yeah, well, that doesn't really help the people it *doesn't* work for, does it?"

Anna grimaced a little. John couldn't tell if it was because she disapproved of his response or because she shared his feelings.

"Nothing's perfect," she said.

3

John still didn't understand how Anna could support a system that permitted bad people like Buddy and Buddy's dad to get away with their bad behavior and that shrugged off these failures with a lame, lazy "nothing's perfect."

Honestly, Anna wasn't the sort of girl John would have normally chosen to hang out with. The only reason he put up with her was because she and Emily had become best friends. Which in itself was kind of weird; Anna and Emily didn't exactly have a lot in common. But apparently Emily saw some value in Anna.

John frowned. Maybe he was being too hard on Anna and the values she clung to. She *had* driven off Buddy Harris, hadn't she? Permanently, too; neither Emily nor John had ever had a problem with him after that. In fact, Buddy deliberately avoided contact with them.

John looked up at Anna, who was still staring at him with that small, hopeful smile. When she saw him looking, her smile widened.

He sighed.

"All right," he said. "What's the first problem again?"

Chapter 15

Summit

1

Cynthia had expected Mr. May to lead them back downstairs to discuss their next move in the quiet comfort of the parlor. Instead they went up.

"Where are we going?" she asked.

"The tower," Mr. May said. "It has always been my favorite place to sit and think. It offers a beautiful view of the woods. Besides, our progress so far has been ever-upward, from the parlor to the second floor to the third floor. We might as well see our symbolically weighty ascent all the way through to its conclusion."

The staircase ended in a small square room with a window on every side. A telescope on a tripod sat in front of the north window. Between the telescope and the stairwell were a card table and four chairs. Otherwise the room was bare.

Mr. May pulled out one of the chairs and sank into it with a gasp. His breathing was harsh and rapid, and his face was pale and damp with sweat.

"Are you okay?" Cynthia asked.

"Just a little more activity than I'm used to," Mr. May said. "Nothing to worry about." He pulled a handkerchief from the breast pocket of his suit jacket and dabbed at his forehead and cheeks. "I regret not having had the foresight to install the Collection on the first floor. But when you're young you don't think about these things, and by the time I realized the oversight, moving everything would have been a massive undertaking."

"How did you get that oil drum up to the third floor anyway?" Calvin said. "That thing must have weighed a ton."

"Easy. I paid Mike and his friend to lug it up there for me. With enough money at stake, men can accomplish just about anything."

He nodded at the other seats. "Please. I feel awkward being the only one sitting."

Cynthia and Calvin sat down. While they waited for Mr. May to put away his handkerchief and get settled, Cynthia looked around to take in the view. Mr. May had been right about how beautiful it was. Up here they were nearly level with the treetops, and the autumn leaves' reds and oranges and yellows made it look as if they were surrounded by a wall of fire. Cynthia was surprised to see that the sun had already begun to dip behind the trees. It must be at least four p.m. They had been here most of the afternoon. And yet despite all the fascinating things Cynthia had learned and seen today, she wasn't entirely clear how any of it would help find Emily.

"So let me see if I understand this," she said with a frown: "You think whatever happened to Emily is part of some, I don't know, curse or—or some weird ongoing history of misfortune or something?"

Mr. May nodded. "I believe the evidence suggests that, yes."

"But based on what the police have learned so far, it sounds like it's just…" She winced, hating to state the un-varnished truth. "Just some pervert or nutbag who did it.

That's all."

"Yes. And Luther Jones was just an alcoholic drifter. And Randolph Crow was just a foppish, starry-eyed artist. And influenza was just a virus. And the settlers were just honest, hardworking souls trying to get by in the world. And so on. But these seemingly random and inconsequential elements came together in singular ways to form an unmistakable pattern."

"What's the pattern, though? Just, like, weird tragic events in the woods?"

Mr. May shook his head. "You're missing the most important feature."

"What?" She glanced at Calvin. He was frowning to himself, obviously trying to identify the feature in question. She felt relieved she wasn't the only one who wasn't seeing the forest for the trees.

"Visions," Mr. May said. "Hallucinations. Perceptual alterations. First there was Firebird. Whatever he saw during his vision quest compelled him to construct a new and unfamiliar ceremony that culminated in his suicide. Next there was Luther Jones, who in the depths of his drunken deliriums was said to carry on long, involved conversations with people who weren't there. Perhaps it was during one of these conversations that he was inspired to break into the May house and do whatever he did there that night. Whatever it was, the placement of Abigail's corpse suggests odd, ritualistic overtones. Then Turner and Hamilton pursued Jones into Spirit Cave and the tunnels beyond, where they experienced a vision of a giant winged serpent. As a result of these events, Turner began to practice magic in the basement of the Crow house, and one night he and Hamilton had a 'visitation,' which presumably means they saw or heard something. The accumulation of tragedy and strangeness drove Turner mad and he sank into delirium and an early death. At the same time, the inexplicably sickly Olive Crow was likewise often delirious, and her final illness was accompanied by auditory hallucinations of beautiful music that seemed to come from the woods. Perhaps she was heading off in search of this music when she fell into the river and drowned. Then came Randolph and Anna. When she fell ill and sank toward death, he channeled all his rage and grief into a painting—a work of imagination and artistic vision—that he labeled 'a gateway to a better world.' And finally there was Wendy Crow, who first suffered seizures, and then psychic visions, and whose husband died in the Crow house under mysterious circumstances immediately after an intense and disturbing dream."

"I don't know," Cynthia said. "I mean, I'm not saying you're wrong, but some of it just seems a little dubious. A little…thin. Is having an idea for a painting really a vision?"

"It's artistic inspiration. It involves seeing something that is not real or tangibly present. Throughout all of these events we are dealing with manifestations that exist only on a psychic or psychological plane."

"So the vision of the dragon wasn't real?" Calvin said.

"Mental phenomena are real. You just can't touch them."

"Okay," Cynthia said, "so we've got mental or psychic manifestations appearing in and around and under the woods, and most of these manifestations link up with tragic events somehow. Is that the gist of it, then?"

"But it doesn't sound like Luther Jones's conversations with nonexistent people happened in the woods," Calvin said. "And Wendy's visions happened all over the place."

"Well, all the tragic events definitely happened in the

vicinity of the woods, though." Cynthia frowned. "Except the massacre of the Mima." She looked at Mr. May. "But that doesn't quite seem like it's part of the pattern."

"I've never thought so, no," Mr. May said. "It's definitely a repercussion of the events in the woods. But the other tragedies happened in a very small, localized area."

"So did the visions occur to set up the tragedies?" Calvin said.

"No," Cynthia said, shaking her head. "That can't be it. I mean, that makes sense with Firebird and Olive and probably Luther Jones, but it doesn't really work with my aunt's psychic visions, or Randolph Crow and Anna May. Especially Anna May. That was influenza. Randolph Crow had his visionary artistic experience or whatever you want to call it after the tragedy was already underway."

Calvin grunted. "Yeah. I guess the cause-and-effect aspect of the whole thing is kind of sketchy. There're just...connections. Correlations."

"Correlation is not causation," Cynthia muttered, remembering something Mr. Grant, her Sociology teacher, had talked about a couple of weeks ago. "Maybe both the visions and the tragedies are somehow being caused by the same thing."

"Like what?"

"I dunno. Maybe something about this area is making people sick in the head somehow, causing hallucinations. Some kind of, I dunno, emissions from underground or something. Maybe Olive and Anna got sick because of weakened immune systems."

"But why would it be making people sick so selectively? And why would there always be a connection between visions and misfortune? Plus it still doesn't explain the visions that occurred away from the woods."

"What else is there, though? I mean, it seems like the evidence is pointing toward the fact that there's something specific about this area that's behind all this."

"Maybe it's Wakansa."

Cynthia raised her eyebrows. "Are you seriously proposing that a dragon is behind everything?"

"Well, maybe that's only how it chose to appear, but it's really something else. A force of some kind."

"A force? Like what? And besides, this is assuming we even believe Turner's account, which I'm not entirely convinced we should. Considering his mental state, everything in the journal might just be the ravings of a madman."

"Maybe," Calvin mumbled. He looked a little annoyed at the notion that Turner's story might be gibberish. Cynthia could tell that Calvin really, really wanted there to be a dragon and a mysterious underground chamber. "It doesn't have to be a physical force. Maybe it's some kind of energy, or…I don't know. Some kind of psychic presence."

"Psychic? Wait. That gives me an idea. What if, like, my aunt's psychic powers have nothing to do with the woods or any of this stuff? What if they're just a natural talent, and she's inherently sensitive to psychic energy? But maybe it was that sensitivity that gave her seizures when she lived around here. Like, her psychic powers were being overwhelmed by something in the area, and her mind would just sort of periodically spazz out from the overload. In other words, maybe her powers didn't suddenly manifest when she went off to school; maybe that was just the first time they could be seen for what they were, since it was the first time they weren't being distorted by…well, whatever's going on around here."

He nodded. "That makes a lot of sense."

She turned to Mr. May. "What about you? What do you

think? You haven't said anything in a while."

Mr. May smiled. "I haven't needed to. The two of you are doing a fine job without me. You've just covered a series of points and ideas it took me years to think through by myself. I too theorized that Wendy's seizures may have had a psychic origin, but I have found no way to effectively test that hypothesis. I did invite several psychics out here to perform readings. And though some of them reported some unusual feelings, none of them came up with anything terribly specific or dramatic, and none of them had seizures or any other abnormal physical reactions."

"But Wendy's seizures may have been the result of long-term exposure, right?" Calvin said.

"Precisely. Which means that short of having a psychic live here for months or years, there's no way to be sure. Also, at this juncture I should add that several times over the years, I hired people to come out and take various air, soil, plant, and water samples in the woods. They found absolutely nothing worth noting. No toxins, no radon, no carbon monoxide, no radiation, no mind-altering fungi, and no several dozen other things they checked for. On a basic physical level, the woods appear to be completely normal."

"But what about the burned grass in the clearing?" Calvin said. "Doesn't that suggest some kind of physical element?"

"It does. And what creates heat often creates light. I don't suppose either of you are aware of anyone seeing unusual lights in or around the woods on the night in question?"

Calvin and Cynthia shook their heads.

"Mm." Mr. May nodded calmly, though underneath his stoic veneer Cynthia thought she sensed a flash of frustration. "At any rate that brings us to the here-and-now." He reached into his inner jacket pocket and pulled out a pen and a small spiral notebook. "Now we need to focus on the current situation. On Emily." He looked at Cynthia. "If it's not too painful, I would like you to go over everything that has happened, everything you know relating to your sister's disappearance."

Cynthia nodded and took a deep breath. She had figured this was coming but that didn't make replaying the whole horrible scenario any easier.

For the next half hour she walked them through the sequence of events. Some of it they knew from the news. Much of it they didn't. She even told them a few pieces of information the cops had insisted be kept secret.

When the recounting was done, Mr. May settled back in his chair and flipped through the notebook, which was now almost completely filled with his small, spidery handwriting. Seconds ticked past. The only sounds were the rustle of the pages and the occasional creak of a chair.

Cynthia was growing impatient and was about to say something when Mr. May looked up at her.

"Emily believes in fairies, I take it?" he asked.

"Yeah. She's always been kind of obsessed with the subject. Well, lately she hasn't been quite as annoyingly single-minded about it as she used to be, but she still has fairy T-shirts and fairy books and a line of fairy figurines on her dresser. She insists she saw them once in the woods when she was around four or five, and…" Her voice trailed off and her eyes went wide as the full import of what she was saying hit her. "Oh, my God."

Mr. May realized the import, too. He sat forward, his eyes shining with excitement.

"She says she saw fairies in *these* woods?"

"I don't believe it. That's exactly what we've been talking about. A visionary experience. Seeing something not tangibly real."

"Where exactly did this happen? Do you know the details?"

Cynthia told them the story as it had been told to her by Emily: Tiny naked winged humanoids dancing around a ring of mushrooms just within the woods behind the Crow house.

"And no one else saw them?" Mr. May said.

"No. When my mom went to look, there was nothing there. Just the mushrooms."

No one spoke for a moment.

"What does it mean?" Calvin asked.

"It's a vision connected to a tragedy," Cynthia said, putting the pieces together and hating the picture they formed. "Don't you see? It was seeing the fairies that made her believe in them. And it was her belief in them that made it possible for…for whoever it was to lure her into the woods."

"But why? What's the point? And are we saying there's some kind of hidden purpose behind all this, or some intelligence that's directing events?"

"I don't know. And frankly, I'm not sure if that should be our main concern right now. We need to focus primarily on getting Emily back."

"Understood," Mr. May said. "There's the big picture and the smaller picture. The macro-level and the micro-level. For now, our main concern should be finding your sister and the man who abducted her. We need to figure out who he is and where he is and where Emily is. And those are primarily concerns of the micro-level. The whys and wherefores of the situation can be set aside for the moment." He consulted his notes again. "Now, it's possible that the man responsible for Emily's abduction has had his own visionary experiences. Are either of you aware of anyone who has had any such experiences lately? Episodes of seeming mental illness? Delirium? Artistic inspirations? Even drug-induced hallucinations? Anyone who has seen things no one else could see?"

"I can't think of anyone," Cynthia said.

"Me either," Calvin said.

"All right, then," Mr. May said. "I guess we'll need to find a more roundabout means of identifying the man responsible." He looked at Cynthia. "Did Emily frequent the park often?"

"Yeah, when the weather was good."

"Then we need to learn who else frequented the park often. We should also consider checking out businesses near the park."

"Why?" asked Calvin.

"Because the man's interest in Emily was almost certainly something that grew over time. He knew her. He may not have known her personally, but he had seen her before. Most likely in the park. He may have visited the park regularly, or he may have worked nearby. A lot of businesses are across the street from the park. Perhaps he saw her from a window while he worked. Also, bear in mind that he knew the area well enough to know about the clearing, which suggests he most likely lives or works around here."

"Gee," Calvin said with a nervous laugh, "my dad works at the May National Bank. That's practically right across the street from the park. You don't think it might be him, do you?"

Mr. May shook his head. "He's too old. We are most likely looking for a man in his thirties. He's probably introverted, intelligent, very rational, very organized, unmarried, has no kids, and lives alone."

"Wow, you sound like one of those criminal profilers."

He grunted. "In my opinion profiling isn't the rocket science–level ability some people would have you believe. It's really only a matter of basic psychology and some critical thinking skills. At any rate, what about other employees at the bank? Is there anyone there who has been behaving oddly lately? Particularly men who fit that profile?"

"I don't know. I've hardly met any of the people who work there, and my dad doesn't really talk to me about his job."

"See if you can find out."

"All right."

"Why the bank?" Cynthia asked. "I mean, is there some specific reason you think someone at the bank might be involved, or…?"

"We have to start somewhere. We might as well begin on familiar ground. Now, as for you, I want you to see if you can find out who was in the park Thursday afternoon. Check with your parents, or even your brother; the police or FBI might have mentioned something to one of them. We should probably avoid asking the authorities directly if we can help it, since it might rouse their suspicions, and that's something we don't want at this juncture."

"I don't know; the cops haven't been very communicative with us about the details of the investigation."

"Well, try your best. And bear in mind, we're interested mainly in men who fit the profile I outlined."

"Gotcha."

"And then we can meet back here tomorrow afternoon. Hopefully, by then one of us will have uncovered something. In the meantime, if you need anything, please don't hesitate to call me."

"That's all we're gonna do?" Cynthia said, her voice edged with disappointment.

Mr. May gave her a small, sympathetic smile. "I understand your impatience and irritation, but I'm afraid there's only so much we can do at the moment. We need information before we can act. And we need to acquire that information carefully and effectively. If we go blundering about half-cocked, that will only make everything worse."

"Yeah," she said with a heavy, grudging sigh. "I guess you're right. We don't want to be the proverbial fools who rush in, do we?"

Chapter 16

Where Angels Fear to Tread

1

"I'm still not sure about this," Donovan mumbled. He and Violet were crouching behind a bush and looking across a night-darkened backyard at the home of Theodore Walsh, proprietor of May Antiques. Both of them were dressed all in black, with black gloves and ski masks. "If we get caught—"

"We ain't gonna get caught," Violet said. "Trust me. You gotta think positive."

"I still think maybe we should just leave this stuff to the cops…"

Her eyes narrowed in the holes of her ski mask.

"That's just nervousness talking," she told him. "Don't puss out on me. Do you wanna find your sister or don't you?"

"Well, yeah…"

"Then you gotta take the initiative. You can't leave things in the hands of a bunch of tools you don't even know. We gave them their chance. They've had nearly two days to find Emily, and they've accomplished jack shit. We can't keep waiting around. We gotta be proactive. Am I right?"

"I guess…"

"All right, then. Now come on. It looks like the coast is

clear. He doesn't close his store till nine on Saturdays so we've got over an hour to search the place. And remember, there'll probably be, like, hidden rooms and dungeons and crap."

"Really?" Donovan studied the humble one-storey house with a doubtful frown. "You think?"

"Fuck, yeah! These crazy psychos always have shit like that. Now come on."

After one last look around to make sure no one was in sight, she sprang from the bushes and dashed across the back yard. Despite her speed and the poor visibility, she managed to dodge the water sprinkler and bound over a row of potted tomatoes on the edge of the patio with the grace of a gazelle. She hunkered down next to the back door. Donovan joined her a few seconds later. He was grimacing and trying to wipe grass stains off the knees of his black jeans, his journey across the lawn having been considerably less graceful than Violet's due to an unfortunate entanglement with the hose.

"Shit," he muttered. "My mom's gonna wonder what the hell happened."

"You totally need to work on your night vision."

"Yeah, yeah. I'll start eating more fish and carrots as soon as I get home."

They peered through one of the glass panes in the back door. Through the filmy white curtain that hung inside, they discerned the hazy shapes of a kitchen table, a stove, a calendar on the wall.

"So how do we get in?" Donovan asked.

"With this." She pulled up her right pant leg. Taped to her calf was a glass cutter, its blade snugly covered with a blob of putty.

"Where the fuck did you get that?" Donovan asked as

she untaped the glass cutter and plucked the putty off the end, revealing a shiny, brand-new blade.

"Dude, my dad runs a hardware store, remember? He's got, like, a billion tools sitting around the house. And if I can't find it at home, I can just lift it at the store in the course of paying him a sweet, daughterly visit." She raised the cutter next to her face and grinned. "Now watch a master in action."

She pressed the putty onto the pane of glass nearest the doorknob, then carefully cut a circle around it with the cutter. She tugged on the putty, and with a faint scritch the circle of glass popped out, leaving a hole big enough for her to reach through and unlock the door.

"Presto," she said, opening the door.

They stepped inside. The kitchen was dark except for a single light burning in the range hood.

"Flashlights," Violet said.

They pulled small flashlights from their pockets and switched them on, then crept farther into the room. The only sounds were the rustles of their clothes and the faint creaks of the floorboards.

"I don't know..." Donovan said, peering through a doorway into the living room, which was just as dark and quiet as the kitchen. "I don't think anyone's here. This place feels empty, you know?"

"Well, yeah. That's what we want."

"Yeah, but that means Emily's not here either."

Violet stared at him a moment, then frowned and looked around. "Hm. Well, like I said, there might be secret doors or something." An idea struck her and she excitedly shook a finger at him. "Or he might have, like, a cabin in the woods where he's keeping her. Or something like that. I dunno. We just need to look around and see what we turn up."

"If you say so."

They searched the kitchen first. They flung open cupboard doors, yanked out drawers, rooted through cabinets. Donovan checked the refrigerator last. As he opened the door, he leaned away from the refrigerator, his muscles tense, as if he expected to find human body parts on platters inside. Instead there was orange juice, beer, half a lemon meringue pie, a box of Slim Fast, a plate of leftover slices of chicken breast.

"Ooh, chicken!" Violet exclaimed. She reached around Donovan, flipped up one corner of the plastic wrap that covered the chicken, and wiggled out the biggest slice. She whisked off her ski mask and began to wolf down the chicken.

"Violet," Donovan said. "We're not here to eat."

"We gotta keep our strength up. There's lots of protein energy in chicken, you know. You should have some, too."

Donovan just sighed as she crammed the last of the chicken into her mouth. She licked the grease from her fingers, then reopened the refrigerator and grabbed a can of beer.

"You want one?" she asked Donovan.

"Um…" He looked at the beer longingly for a moment, then glanced at the back door and shook his head. "No, that's all right."

She shut the refrigerator, then pulled the tab on her can of beer. There was a crack and a hiss, and tan foam bulged up through the hole in the top of the can.

"Now come on." Sipping at the foam, she strode toward the entrance to the living room. "Let's keep looking."

They spent the next few minutes examining every nook and cranny of the living room. They found nothing of note.

Violet spilled beer on the carpet, the coffee table, and a burgundy easy chair.

Their next stop was the bathroom, which likewise contained nothing of interest except an unusually large and varied assortment of skin-care products. From there they moved on to a rear bedroom which was being used to store antiques. It was packed from wall to wall with chairs, sideboards, boxes full of china, a grandfather clock, a World War I soldier's uniform, and so on.

"Man, this shit's gotta be worth a fortune," Violet said. She picked up a coin with a picture of a chick with long, flowing hair on it. It didn't say what denomination it was, but it had a date of 1794. Violet slid it into her pocket.

Donovan sighed. "This is just stuff. It's not Emily."

"Don't worry. We just gotta keep looking."

The front bedroom was dominated by a king-sized bed with red satin sheets. There was also a dresser, a chest of drawers, and a desk on top of which sat a switched-off computer. One of the desk's drawers was stuffed full of important-looking papers.

"We should go through this stuff," Violet said. "There might be info about his cabin."

"What cabin?"

"The cabin where he keeps his prisoners! I mean, we ain't finding anything here, so he must be keeping her somewhere else."

They spent a while flipping through receipts, bills, auction schedules, correspondence, and similar documents. Eventually Violet got bored and started rummaging through the closet while Donovan continued examining the papers with mounting disheartenment.

His examination ended when Violet exclaimed, "Whoa! Get over here! Check this out!"

He hurried over and found her crouched down in front of a stack of magazines on the closet floor.

"What is it?" he asked.

She handed him a magazine. He took one look at it, then flung it away with a yelp. The magazine was titled *Spank Masters,* and the cover showed a naked middle-aged man kneeling down with his butt in the air, while a leanly muscled young stud in a leather outfit loomed above him, a paddle raised high in one black-gloved hand and a cruel sneer on his face.

"See?" Violet cried. "Didn't I tell you this guy was a creepy perv?" She riffled through the stack of magazines. They were all *Spank Masters* and appeared to constitute a complete run dating back to the late 1990s.

There was a shoebox next to the magazines. Violet flipped up the lid, revealing hundreds of Polaroids of naked men, most of them young and slim and posing in the very room Violet and Donovan were now in.

"Holy fuck!" she cried. "Perv jackpot!"

"Yeah, but he's the wrong kind of perv."

"Huh?"

"I mean, look." Donovan pointed at the photos, refusing to get too close. "He likes guys from the look of it. Guys who, you know, spank. So, I mean, why would he be interested in a little girl?"

"He might swing both ways."

"Violet, I don't think this is the guy. It just…it feels wrong, you know?"

"But I was so sure!" She flapped her arms. "I mean, he's a complete wanktard. You know what he's like. You remember how he acted when he caught me shoplifting. How could it not be him?"

"Well, there's a lot of wanktards out there."

She nodded thoughtfully.

"That is very true. If it's not this one, it'll be the next one." She drove her fist into her palm, producing a loud, sharp smack. Donovan couldn't help reflecting that it was probably a sound heard often in this room. "We'll go through every wanktard in this shithole town till we find the guy!"

Just then the window flooded with light and the sound of an engine grew audible as a car pulled into the driveway.

Violet glanced at the alarm clock on the bedside table. "Fuck, we totally lost track of the time! It's him! We gotta get outta here!"

Leaving the closet open, the shoebox unlidded, the topmost magazine splayed on the carpet, the nearly empty bottle of beer perched atop the dresser, the desk drawer hanging open, and a sheaf of papers arrayed on the bed, Donovan and Violet raced out of the bedroom, through the living room, and across the kitchen to the back door.

The moment Violet flung it open, the front door opened behind them.

"Who—who's there?" a startled male voice cried.

While Donovan bolted out the back door and sprinted away across the backyard, Violet whirled around in the doorway and thrust a finger at Theodore Walsh.

"We are…the Spankmasters!" she intoned melodramatically. Then she spun back around and dashed off into the night.

2

"That was a complete fucking bust," Donovan said as they walked home, their ski masks and gloves safely stashed in their jacket pockets.

"No, it wasn't," Violet said. "We eliminated a suspect. It's one less dude from the park we have to worry out."

Donovan grunted. As usual, Violet had a way of re-framing things that turned even unmitigated disasters into undeniable victories.

"So...what next, then?" he asked.

"Easy. We move on to the next wanktard on our list: Roger Grey."

PART THREE

Confrontations

Chapter 17

The Intrepid Investigators

1

Ever since the meeting in Mr. May's house yesterday Calvin had been wracking his brain for a way to find out from his dad if any bank employees fit Mr. May's perp profile. He couldn't just come right out and ask; his dad would want to know why Calvin was asking, and Calvin knew better than to admit he was helping his secret crush and an elderly local eccentric find Emily Crow. White-bread Mark Beckerman would probably think his son had gone insane. No, Calvin had to gather the info with the finesse of a cat burglar swiping the crown jewels. But finesse, he found, wasn't easy. He had been starting to fear he wouldn't think of anything and would be forced to show up at today's meeting with nothing to offer and thus look like a complete moron in front of Cynthia, but shortly after lunch he hit on the perfect solution.

Calvin headed into the living room. His dad was stretched out in his recliner watching auto racing on TV. Calvin sat down on the couch nearby. His dad shot him a puzzled glance. Calvin normally shunned his dad's Sunday sports-watching sessions.

Calvin and his dad sat in silence while brightly colored cars drove around and around in circles. Finally a commercial came on.

"I want to ask you about something," Calvin said.

"About the race?" Mark Beckerman said with a wry smile. Clearly he knew that whyever his son had come in here, it had nothing to do with auto racing.

"Heh, no. Um, it's just, I was curious about something a kid at school said happened involving someone from the bank."

"The bank?" Mark's curiosity was piqued. "Who?"

"I don't know. That's the point. That's what I wanted to ask you about."

"What was it that happened?"

"Well, this kid said he was sort of accosted by someone he said worked at the bank."

Mark sat forward. The recliner slid into the sitting position with a loud thunk. "Accosted?"

"Yeah. I guess this kid was in Indian Hill Park one day not too long ago, and this guy just starting going off on him. Just, like, yelling at him completely out of the blue. The kid said he was afraid the guy was gonna get violent. He hurried out of there with the guy still yelling at him."

"How does he know that the man works at the bank?"

"He said he'd seen him working there before. He said it was a guy in his thirties?"

Mark shook his head. "That could be a number of people. What exactly did he look like? What color was his hair?"

"He didn't really give a description. But he did say that he was surprised the guy was acting like that since he normally seemed like a very introverted, rational kind of guy."

His dad stared off into space with a frown, his blond eyebrows almost meeting in the middle. On TV, the commercials ended and the race cars started driving in circles again. Mark didn't notice.

"That sounds like Roger Grey," he said. "But I can't picture him doing anything like that. He's very collected, very dependable."

"He hasn't been acting weird or anything lately?"

Mark opened his mouth, then hesitated and shut it.

"Hm. Well, actually, he was acting kind of...spacey the week before last. But I figured that was just because he had a vacation coming up and his mind was on that."

"When was the vacation?"

"He's still on it actually. Last week and this week." Mark shook his head. "Bad timing, too. If he'd been at work, he would've been able to fix that stupid computer glitch we had the other day..."

Mark said more, but Calvin missed it in the rush of excitement that was coursing through him. Could it be only a coincidence that this guy not only fit the profile but had a vacation the same week Emily vanished?

Well, he supposed it *could* be a coincidence. He had better gather more info.

"How exactly was he spacey?" Calvin asked.

Mark shrugged. "I dunno. Just kind of distracted. You know, like his mind was elsewhere. Sometimes I'd tell him something and it was like he wouldn't even hear me, like his mind was a million miles away."

"Huh."

"Come to think of it, he does frequent the park a lot."

"Really?"

"Yeah, he goes out to eat his lunch over there. Always struck me as kind of antisocial, actually." He grunted. "Still, I can't picture him going all crazy like that. He's always a very calm, collected guy."

"Could he be having problems in his personal life? Maybe he's got issues with his wife or kids or something?"

"Oh, Grey's not married. And he doesn't have any kids." Mark sounded almost envious.

Calvin was nearly exploding with excitement. Every single piece of data about Roger Grey matched Mr. May's profile.

"Well, maybe it wasn't him after all," Calvin said, trying to sound blasé. "The kid I was talking to might have been exaggerating anyway."

"Yeah…" Mark glanced at the TV, saw that the race was back on, and resumed watching it. After a few seconds, he glanced back at Calvin. "Let me know if you hear anything else about this. I'm curious."

"Okay, sure."

Calvin remained there watching the race with his dad a while longer, but he wasn't really seeing it. He was still buzzing with excitement. He wanted to call Mr. May right now and tell him the news. But no: The meeting was only about two hours away. Besides, if he waited till the meeting, he could reveal his big discovery in front of Cynthia. He smiled as he imagined how impressed she would be that he had come up with a suspect so quickly…

2

At that moment Cynthia was heading upstairs to Donovan's room to ask him if he knew who had been in the park on Thursday afternoon. She didn't expect he would, but she felt obliged to ask anyway, especially since she hadn't learned much from her parents.

She had been afraid to ask at first, worried that her mom and dad would find the question suspicious and demand to know why she was asking. But when she finally conquered her fears last night and asked her dad while he sat sipping a beer and watching an old *Remington Steele* re-run, she had received not suspicion or an interrogation but a tirade about how the goddamn police and FBI weren't telling him a goddamn thing about goddamn anything. So, no, he didn't know who was in the park that day. He seemed to regard the question as merely natural curiosity about her sister's disappearance. It was too late by then to ask anyone else, since her mom and Donovan had gone to bed early. Or rather, Mom had gone to bed and Donovan had claimed he was going to bed but was probably actually doing things he shouldn't have been.

It had taken Cynthia nearly all morning to find an opportunity to ask Mom. Ever since dawn Mom had been prepping the house for Aunt Wendy's arrival, a task of truly Herculean proportions. The guest bedroom, where Wendy would be staying, hadn't been cleaned in years, and the rest of the house was cluttered with painful evidence of the family's recent stupor: Chinese takeout boxes and empty beer bottles covered the coffee table; the kitchen sink was heaped high with food-crusted plates; the wastebaskets were overflowing with Kleenex; the floors were filthy with chunks of mud and bits of gravel from the passage of countless well-wishers and law enforcement officials. For hours Mom had been scrubbing, mopping, vacuuming. The washer and dryer had been rumbling almost constantly. The smells of dust and stale soy sauce had slowly been replaced by the lemon scent of furniture polish. The trash cans in the garage filled up one by one.

It was clear that this cleaning frenzy was a way for Mom to take her mind off the painful realities of the situation for a little while. Cynthia felt like a cad to remind her again.

She felt like even more of a cad when she discovered she needn't have bothered. Mom didn't know much more than Dad. The one and only piece of information she had to offer was that she had heard one of the local cops mention that some junior high school kids had been playing a baseball game at the west end of the park.

That left Donovan.

He was in his bedroom with the door closed. She rapped on the door hard enough to make sure he heard it over the drone of the vacuum coming from downstairs.

"Just a second!" Donovan called.

Fifteen seconds passed. Cynthia was raising her fist to knock again when the door opened, and Donovan looked out at her. Despite the open window and the sinus-clearing scent of the peppermint Binaca on his breath and the freshly lit stick of incense burning in its holder on the dresser, the odor of cigarette smoke was unmistakable. For that matter, the incense hadn't been burning long enough to account for the thick stratum of smoke that hung in the air behind him.

"Oh, it's you," he said, disappointed that his frantic effort to hide his guilt had been unnecessary.

"Can I come in?" she asked.

"Uh, sure."

He waved her inside, then shut the door behind her. She sat down on the edge of his bed. He pulled out his desk chair and sat down facing her.

Cynthia flapped a hand in front of her wrinkled nose. "God, it reeks of tobacco in here."

"Is it that strong?"

"Are televangelists lying crooks?"

"Crap."

"At least its just tobacco this time."

Donovan's eyes slid away from hers."Um, what's that supposed to mean?"

"Sometimes I can smell the weed from down the hall. I'm surprised Mom and Dad haven't busted you yet."

"Oh."

"You need to be more careful. For that matter, you shouldn't even be smoking that shit in the first place."

"Which shit?"

"Both shit! Neither one's healthy." When he opened his mouth to protest, she waved a placating hand. "Look, just forget it for now. I didn't come here to get on your case. I just need to ask you about something."

"What?"

"I'm trying to find out who was in the park on Thursday afternoon when Emily was there. I was wondering if you've heard anything about it from the cops. I asked Mom and Dad, but they hardly know anything."

"Oh, um, actually yeah. I mean, I don't know anything from the cops, but I know some of the folks who were in the park."

"You do?"

"Yeah. Violet was there. Violet O'Donohue? I don't know if you know her, but—"

"You mean your not-so-secret girlfriend? Yeah, of course I know who she is. I only see her sneaking across the porch roof to your room, like, every other night."

Donovan gaped at her. "What? That's, um, that's…"

"Don't worry. I won't tell Mom and Dad. But only if you tell me who she saw in the park. It's important."

"All right, all right. Violet said there were kids playing baseball and a couple of chicks with babies. None of them sound like they had anything to do with anything. But she said she also saw two other people. Men. Adult men. By themselves. One was a dude named Theodore Walsh. He's that big fat guy who runs the antique store on Horst Road."

Cynthia stiffened. The antique store was practically right across the street from the park. And though Walsh was older than Mr. May's profile demanded, it couldn't be by very much. "Oh, my God."

Donovan waved a hand dismissively. "If you're thinking it's him, it's not."

"How do you know?"

"Um…" Donovan frowned, looked down, scratched the back of his neck. "Well, you know, we, um, Violet and me, we sort of ruled him out." He nodded, smiling, as if to convey to her that this was a satisfactory answer and she needn't ask any more questions about it.

But she did. "What does that mean exactly?"

Donovan grimaced. "Well, um, we kinda checked out his house. You know, when he sorta wasn't there."

Cynthia stared at him, blinking, as the meaning of his words sank in and she realized they didn't admit of multiple interpretations. "You broke in?"

"That's kind of, you know, a harsh way to put it. We just sort of briefly invited ourselves in while he was out. Um…" He trailed off with a frown, realizing his euphemism didn't really improve things very much.

She closed her eyes and shook her head. "I don't believe this. Donovan, you could've gotten arrested! You could've wound up in jail."

"Maybe."

"Think what that would do to Mom and Dad! I mean, they're fucked up enough with Emily gone. What, you think it's gonna help if they get a call and find out you're in jail now, too?"

"Damn it, Cyn," he snapped. "I'm just trying to help Emily." He glared at her a moment, his brown eyes filling with tears. Then he lowered his head and sleeved his eyes clear.

Her shoulders slumped.

"Yeah, I know," she said gently. "I know, I know." She heaved a sigh. "And that's good. You just need to do it...better. Let me guess, the whole thing was Violet's idea, right?"

"Well..." He shrugged. "Kinda. Mostly. But it seemed solid."

"Donovan, she's not a good influence. I mean, admittedly, I don't know her all that well, but what I do know isn't good. She's got an IQ of, like, negative six or something. She's irresponsible. She's vulgar. I mean, isn't she the one who covered over the M in the May High School sign with the big pink cardboard G right before the Homecoming game?"

Donovan couldn't restrain a grin at the memory. Seeing his sister's scowl, he forced his smile down and opted not to tell her that he had been the one who supplied Violet with the cardboard.

"Look, just watch yourself," she told him. "She's bad news."

"Yeah, okay..."

She could see he was just telling her what she wanted to hear, but she decided to drop the matter. For now.

"You said there was someone else in the park," she said. "Another man besides Theodore Walsh. Who was it?"

"A guy named Roger Grey."

"Who's he?"

Donovan shrugged. "I don't really know. Violet says she knows him. He lives, like, practically right around the corner from her. She says he's an uptight, dweeby, sexually repressed loser type, which makes him a prime suspect."

"And you haven't, um, paid his house a visit?"

"No…" Donovan looked away with a sheepish expression. "Not yet. We were kind of thinking about it tonight."

"Well, don't." She jabbed a finger at him. "Just don't, okay? I'm serious."

"Yeah, but if it is him, the cops aren't doing shit, you know? They can't. They're, like, all wrapped up in laws and stuff and won't be able to do anything."

She rolled her eyes. "Look, I'm not gonna get into a debate with you about this. Just don't do anything. And keep Violet on a really short leash."

"Fine," he sighed. "I—" He frowned and eyed her closely. "Wait a minute. What's going on? You're up to something yourself, aren't you?"

A small, proud smile flickered on Cynthia's lips. In spite of Violet O'Donohue and gallons of booze and entire forests of weed and who knew what else, her brother could be pretty sharp sometimes.

"Yeah, we kind of are," she said.

"We?"

"Yeah. Do you know Calvin Beckerman from school?"

Donovan shook his head. "Never heard of him."

"He's in my grade. He's my lab partner in Chemistry."

Donovan smirked. "Is he, like, your boyfriend?"

"No!" Cynthia said emphatically. "It's just…look, if I tell you something, you have to promise not to tell anyone else. Not Mom and Dad. Not the cops. Not anybody."

"Well, yeah, okay." He shrugged. "I mean, you've got the whole breaking-and-entering thing hanging over my head, so what the fuck can I do, right?"

"Well, me and Calvin, we've been sort of working together with old Robert May next door—"

Donovan's jaw dropped. "Weird old Mr. May? He's, like, some kinda mental case or something, isn't he?"

"No! That's just stupid gossip. He's actually a pretty cool guy. And he has some investigative experience, so he's helping us out with a sort of private search for Emily."

Donovan clucked his tongue. "So you're, like, doing the same thing you're telling me not to do!"

"We're not breaking into people's houses!"

"Not yet."

"Look, I think we're actually making some headway. Just don't tell anyone, okay?"

"Okay, but…"

"But what?" Even as she asked it, she realized what was coming.

"I want in on this, too."

"Donovan—"

He raised his head defiantly. "She's my sister, too. I wanna help."

Cynthia hesitated. Though Donovan could sometimes be easily swayed (usually by bad influences like Violet O'Donohue), he could also be very stubborn and determined when he wanted to be. Now was clearly one of those times. She couldn't blame him.

"I'll have to take it up with the others," she said. "I mean, it's not just me who's involved, you know?"

"Uh-huh. Well, take it up with them, then, and make sure they say yes. Because I'm not just gonna sit around and wait for other people to do what needs to be done."

She nodded. "I'll do what I can."

Just then Mom's voice came shouting up the stairs.

"Aunt Wendy just pulled in!"

Chapter 18

Wendy Crow

1

When Cynthia saw Aunt Wendy walk in the front door, it was like she was seeing a whole new person. It wasn't because Wendy had physically changed. Wendy looked the same as she had when the family visited her during their summer vacation in New England: same steely gray hair; same thin, angular face; same quick, green eyes peering out from the shade of the same wide-brim black hat. What was different was that Cynthia now knew the details of Wendy's painful history, the details no one in the family ever talked about. She knew now why Wendy wore black. She knew now why Wendy wasn't married. She knew now why Wendy rarely visited her birthplace anymore. She knew now that the thin lines that seamed Wendy's forehead and bracketed her eyes and mouth were due as much to pain and tragedy as to advancing age. She saw Wendy's dark eyes briefly fix on a section of the hardwood floor in the front hall, and she felt her chest and throat tighten in sympathy and sorrow.

After an exchange of greetings and hugs, everyone headed into the living room and sat down.

"Has there been any news?" Wendy asked.

"No," Hannibal said. "Nothing."

She tutted and shook her head. "Do the police have

any suspects?"

"We don't know. They're not telling us much."

She grunted, then frowned slightly and rubbed her forehead.

"Everything okay?" Brenda asked. She sounded a little excited. Cynthia realized her mom was hoping Wendy was having a vision.

"Just a slight headache," Wendy said. "I don't fly well."

"Oh," Brenda said, trying to hide her disappointment. "Donovan, why don't you get your aunt some Tylenol and a glass of water."

"Oh, no," Wendy said. "There's no need to go to any trouble."

"It's no trouble at all." Brenda nodded at Donovan, who had started to get up but then froze uncertainly when Wendy objected. "Go on."

He hurried away.

"Is Krezchek still the chief of police?" Wendy asked.

"Yeah," Hannibal said.

She snorted.

"The FBI have taken a big role in the investigation, though," he told her.

"Thank goodness for that."

"Is Chief Krezchek, like, not cool or something?" Cynthia asked.

"He's an idiot," Wendy said.

"Now, now," Brenda said. "He's doing his best."

Cynthia couldn't help but wonder why Aunt Wendy disliked Chief Krezchek so much. Had he been in charge of the investigation into Eugene Scott's death? No, wait. That wouldn't make sense. He would have been in his early twenties at the time, the same age as Wendy and Eugene. Maybe he had been a rookie patrolman and did something stupid that compromised the investigation. Or maybe he and Wendy had known each other personally. Maybe they had even dated. *There* was a freaky thought.

Donovan returned with a glass of water and two Tylenol. Wendy gulped them down.

"Thank you," she said. She set down the glass, then heaved a deep breath and said, "All right. Show me Emily's room. Let's see if I can pick anything up."

"Are you sure?" Hannibal said. "I mean, this soon? You haven't even—"

"I'm sure. Bear in mind, I can't guarantee results, though. My talents aren't something I can turn on and off. The visions come when they come."

"We understand," Brenda said. But there was a brittle, hopeful gleam in her eyes that suggested she felt sure this grim situation would soon be resolved.

They trooped upstairs to Emily's room.

Cynthia hadn't visited Emily's room since the morning they had found her missing, and Cynthia's heart hurt to see her sister's untouched things: the black cat coverlet on the bed; the pajamas neatly folded on the seat of her small white rocking chair; the jump rope draped over the knob of the closet door; the paperback copy of *Harry Potter and the Chamber of Secrets* on her desk. The placement of her glow-in-the-dark jack-o'-lantern bookmark showed she had been nearly done with the book.

Cynthia wasn't the only one affected by the sight of Emily's room: Beside her her mom began to weep silently. Hannibal put an arm around Brenda's shoulders. She clutched him tight.

Everyone watched in tense, expectant silence as Wendy slowly made her way through the room, pausing here and there to touch or handle something.

"Normally my visions come to me out of the blue, independent of anything," Wendy said as she paused next to the closet. She grabbed one of the jump rope's orange plastic handles, held it a moment, let it go. "But occasionally I can pick up feelings and images from specific objects or locations. That's what's called psychometry. That's what I'm hoping to do here."

She headed over to the desk and studied the papers and pens and knickknacks that littered its surface. Her gaze settled on one of the papers, and she frowned. She picked it up. It was a drawing of a coyote howling at the moon with the words "Happy Birthday John" at the bottom. It had clearly been intended as a hand-made card for Emily's friend John Coyote, whose birthday was the same day as Emily's: Halloween, a week and a half away. Wendy studied the drawing intently, her frown deepening.

"Are you, um, getting something?" Brenda asked.

Wendy didn't respond for a moment. Then she shook her head slightly and set the paper back onto the desk.

"Just a feeling," she said. She shrugged her black shoulders. "I don't know. It's probably nothing."

She moved on to the rocking chair next to the bed and laid a hand on Emily's pajamas, which were dark purple and adorned with images of cartoon fairies with dragonfly-like wings.

Wendy grunted.

"What—" Brenda began.

"Quiet, please," Wendy said. She shut her eyes and held very still. Her breathing slowed. Ten seconds passed. Then fifteen. Twenty. Everyone glanced at each other, wondering if this was it.

Wendy opened her eyes.

"A yellow box," she said.

"What?" Brenda said.

"I saw a large yellow box of some kind. That's all. But I saw it very clearly. It felt important somehow."

"How large was it?" Cynthia asked.

"It's hard to say. Maybe about the size of a crate or a trunk. Except I think it was made of metal or plastic. Something shiny and artificial."

"And it was yellow?" Hannibal said.

Wendy nodded. "It doesn't mean anything to any of you?"

Everyone shook their heads.

Brenda heaved a shaky sigh. "Oh, well." Her voice wobbled with emotion.

"Don't despair," Wendy said. "We're not defeated yet. Just because I didn't pick up anything on the first go-round doesn't mean I won't pick up anything later. Besides, I still have to try the clearing. There's a much better chance of getting a result there. All things considered, the clearing's more likely to have retained an impression."

"An impression?" Cynthia said.

"Of emotional energy. Some people think that's how psychometry works, that people's psychical or emotional energy somehow imprints itself upon objects or places and lingers there for a long time afterward. Some people think that's what makes so-called sick houses feel that way: that there was a big imprint of negative emotional energy sometime in the past that tainted the whole place."

"Interesting." Cynthia wondered if the concept of psychic-emotional imprints could be somehow connected with what had been going on in and around the woods over the last two hundred years. Could Turner and Hamilton's vision of the dragon have been a lingering psychic imprint of the Mima's belief in Wakansa? Could a massive buildup of negative psychic energy be driving people to murder and suicide? If so, where did it come from? And why didn't it affect more people? And why did it affect the people it affected in such extreme and focused ways? No, there had to be something more at work. She should try to remember to bring this up with Mr. May. Then again, he had probably already considered it.

As they headed back downstairs, Wendy frowned and touched her forehead with the tips of her fingers.

"You okay?" Hannibal asked her.

She nodded. "My headache. It's a little worse."

"Do you want another Tylenol?" Brenda said. "We could—"

"No, no. I should probably give these more time to work." She went into the living room and grabbed her purse and her wide-brim hat. "Let's head out to the clearing."

"Now?" Hannibal said.

Wendy nodded and clapped her hat on her head. "Let's get this done."

2

Five minutes later Wendy, Hannibal, and Cynthia were tromping through the woods on their way to the clearing. Brenda and Donovan had opted not to go. Cynthia didn't blame them. She wasn't sure she wanted to be there if her aunt saw something. But she felt that she *needed* to be there. Not just to keep tabs on things for Mr. May, but for herself. And for Emily.

They crossed the river at the stepping stones, then headed north toward the clearing. They were halfway there when Wendy paused, frowning. She leaned against a tree trunk with one hand.

"Are you all right" Hannibal asked her.

"My headache…"

"Do you want to go back?"

She didn't answer. Instead she peered north, squinting like someone trying to see through a heavy rain.

"There's something there," she murmured.

"What?" Cynthia said. "What do you mean?"

Wendy continued squinting into the distance for a moment, then shook her head.

"I don't know," she said. Her voice was low, puzzled.

Cynthia and her dad exchanged a baffled glance behind Wendy's back.

"Are you sure you don't want to head back?" Hannibal asked Wendy. "We could—"

"No, no." Wendy pushed herself off the tree trunk and strode forward. "Let's go. Emily needs us."

They headed on. Less than a minute later Wendy paused again to lean against a tree. Her face was drawn and pale. She rubbed her temple with one hand as she stared north toward the clearing.

"What *is* that?" she muttered.

"Wendy," Hannibal said, "why don't we just stop? We can come back later."

"No. We need to do this. We need to do it for Emily. And I need to know what this is."

"Is it, like, a psychic thing?" Cynthia asked.

"Yes. At least I think so. It's not like anything I've ever encountered before. It's—it's like…" She shook her head. "I'm not even sure how to describe it. It's like…static. Or heat. It's like there's a huge furnace up ahead and I'm feeling its heat. I'm pretty sure it's what's giving me the headache, too. It's not jetlag. It's…" She tilted her chin toward the clearing. "That. Whatever it is. I need to know."

"And it's connected with Emily?" Hannibal asked.

Wendy opened her mouth, shut it, shook her head. "I don't know."

She walked on. Cynthia and Hannibal followed. They barely took their eyes off Wendy, partly out of concern, partly out of hope that she would suddenly fling up her hands and cry, "I can see it all," and announce where Emily was. But she didn't. Instead her steps grew unsteady and her breathing grew labored and irregular. By the time the first glimpse of the yellow police tape that ringed the clearing came into view up ahead, her face was the color of chalk and sheened with sweat.

She froze about thirty feet from the clearing, her eyes fixed straight ahead. Cynthia followed her gaze. Through the foliage she saw bits and pieces of the clearing—swaths of green grass, a few fallen red and yellow leaves, an edge of the burned circle.

"My God," Wendy whispered. "What is that?" Her purse slid from her shoulder and thumped to the dirt beside her. She didn't even notice.

Hannibal looked down at the purse, then at Wendy, then at Cynthia, then back at Wendy. He stooped and snatched up the purse.

"Wendy—" he began.

"A dome," Wendy said. "It's a dome."

"What?"

She lurched forward. Hannibal and Cynthia hurried after her. Wendy stumbled over tree roots and tore through brush, and all the while she never once took her eyes off the clearing up ahead.

When she reached the police tape, she kept walking,

seemingly unaware of the yellow ribbon pressing against her belly. The tape stretched farther and farther, and bit deeper and deeper into her stomach. The black letters that read "Crime Scene Do Not Cross" grew elongated and barely readable. Just when Cynthia felt sure the tape would snap, Wendy stopped.

Wendy looked up and down, then from side to side as if she were studying some vast object in the center of the clearing. Then her gaze dropped to the grass midway between her feet and the burned circle.

"I think it's underground, too," she said. Her voice was thick and slow as if she had been drugged. "It's…" She looked up and all around again. "A sphere." She frowned. "Or is it a hole?" She cocked her head. Her eyes narrowed. "I think it's both."

"Wendy," Hannibal said gently. He took her elbow. "Why don't you—"

She wrenched her arm away and stalked forward. The tape snapped. The two halves fluttered to the grass as she plodded into the center of the clearing. She stopped with her feet planted squarely on the burned circle.

"Oh, my God," she gasped. She raised her arms and let her head fall back as if she were basking in applause or sunshine. Her black hat fell off and landed upside-down on the grass. She let out a long, low, almost orgasmic moan that dissolved into a breathy laugh. "This is incredible. This is…this is…"

Her words were replaced by a thick gurgle from deep in her throat. At the same moment she began to shudder violently as if she had touched a live wire.

"Wendy!" Hannibal screamed.

She toppled backward onto the grass, crushing her hat beneath her. She writhed about, her arms and legs flailing, her gurgles growing louder and shriller. Her eyes had rolled up so far that only the vein-squiggled whites were visible.

"Do you have your phone?" Hannibal cried.

For one weird moment, Cynthia thought he was talking to Wendy. Then he seized Cynthia's arm and yelled, "Your phone! Do you have it?

She tore her eyes from her aunt's thrashing, gurgling form. "I—" She touched her pocket to make sure, and felt the bulge there. "Yeah."

"Call 911! She's having a seizure!"

"But…"

But she hasn't had one of those since she was a little girl, she wanted to say.

Instead she turned away and made the call. She had to stride a dozen paces out of the clearing to hear the dispatcher's voice over the horrible turkey-gobble noises Wendy was making. By the time the dispatcher assured her that help would arrive soon and Cynthia hung up, Wendy had fallen silent.

Cynthia returned to the clearing. Her dad was kneeling on the grass next to Wendy, who now lay on her side. She wasn't gurgling and thrashing anymore. She wasn't doing anything. For a moment Cynthia thought that that was a good thing, that the seizure had passed and Wendy was exhausted or unconscious but otherwise okay.

But then her dad threw his head back and let out a horrible wail. Tears spilled from his eyes. The cords in his neck stood out like cables. And that was when Cynthia noticed Wendy's eyes were still wide open and showing white, and Wendy's chest was still.

Cynthia felt her own eyes burn with tears. She was about to hurry over and join her dad on the grass when she became aware of a faint silvery light suffusing the clearing.

At first she thought the light was a byproduct of her tears—some kind of weird shimmery halo effect or something—but when she swiped the tears from her eyes, the light was still there. It was real. Or at least it *looked* real. Her dad was kneeling right in the middle of the light and he didn't seem to notice anything. But then, his eyes were shut, and his mind was on other things.

The light grew brighter and more defined, and Cynthia discerned that it didn't quite fill the whole clearing; it stopped about ten feet from the edge. And it was curved along the top...

A dome! That was how Aunt Wendy described what she had been seeing! Somehow Cynthia was seeing the same thing.

And then she wasn't. In the space of a heartbeat the light vanished. The clearing was normal once again.

Cynthia stood there, stunned and scared, while her father's anguished cries echoed through the woods.

Chapter 19

Black and White

1

Roger Grey stood at his living room picture window and looked out at the sunlit street. He didn't know what to do. Twenty-four hours had passed, and Emily Faux had not returned. Neither had the FBI. Which was good, of course. But Roger couldn't help fearing that the FBI *had* returned, just not openly, that Emily Faux's assistance yesterday hadn't helped as much as he had thought, and the FBI had pegged Roger as a prime suspect and set up surveillance on his house.

His eyes returned for the umpteenth time to the Stillson house across the street. Or rather the *ex*-Stillson house. The Stillsons had moved out three weeks ago. The house's windows were dark and empty, and a For Sale sign stood on the front lawn. That would be the most logical place for a surveillance team. He hadn't noticed any signs of activity there, but he wasn't sure if that meant anything one way or another.

Hell, he wasn't sure of anything at this point. He wasn't sure if he was still under suspicion; he wasn't sure if he should try to dump Emily's body; he wasn't sure if Emily Faux would ever return; he wasn't sure what she was or why she had helped him. His uncertainties immobilized him. He felt like a blind man in a room full of bear traps.

"I can help you solve your problems," Emily's voice said behind him.

Roger spun around. Emily Faux sat on the couch in the spot where Agent Rowan had sat yesterday afternoon.

"Where did you go?" Roger said, his voice surly. "You disappeared."

"I had things to do," she said. "Responsibilities. But I'm back now. To help you. Now please sit. We need to talk."

She gestured at his recliner with one small, slender hand. Her nylon jacket rustled with the movement. Her long glossy black hair swayed gently. He could see the life-line and loveline creasing her open palm. She seemed perfectly real in every way, yet he knew with absolute certainty that if he tried to grab her, his hands would close on empty air.

"What are you?" he said.

"Sit," she repeated.

He stared at her a moment. He wanted to refuse. He wanted to deny all of this. He wanted none of this to be happening. But it was.

Scowling, feeling resentful and manipulated, he sat.

"What are you?" he asked again. "You're not Emily. She's dead. She's in the basement with a hole in her."

One of her eyebrows rose slightly.

"How do you know I'm not a ghost?"

"I..." He had been about to say, "I don't believe in ghosts," but he foresaw the philosophical sinkhole that would lead to. He was already granting credibility to apparently clairvoyant intangible entities. That wasn't really very far from ghosts, was it?

"You're not her," he said. "You don't talk like her."

She nodded as though pleased. "No, I'm not her.

You're right."

"Then why do you look like her?"

"To show you what's possible. To show you what you can have again."

"I don't understand."

"I'm here to help you bring her back."

"What?"

"If you do what I tell you, you can bring her back. She can be alive again. Real. *Fleshy.*" Her lips spread in a slutty smile that made Roger's penis stir despite the weirdness of the situation.

"Fleshy..." he muttered, hypnotized by the train of thought that word and that smile had set in motion. Then he frowned, realizing she had set that train moving on purpose. "And how exactly do you propose to bring a corpse back to life?"

"Magic."

Roger barked out a laugh. "Riiiiight." He began flinging his hands about like a hammy magician poofing things into existence. "Presto-chango! Abraca-pocus! Watch me pull a rabbit out of my ass!"

She simply watched him with a small, patient smile. In the face of it, his excitable behavior made him feel foolish and juvenile.

"Magic is very real, Roger," she said.

"Bullshit," he snapped.

"I'm proof of it, aren't I? I'm here, I'm real, but only you can see me. I've told you things you couldn't have known on your own."

"Maybe." He folded his arms and glowered at the TV as if he were hoping this inane conversation would end soon so he could watch something. In the TV's blank gray screen he could see the hazy, distorted reflection of her body perched on the edge of the couch. Her face was only a pale featureless blur, but he knew she was watching him.

"The magical worldview is equally as valid as the scientific one," she said.

"Don't be ridiculous," Roger said, turning to glare at her. "They're opposites. They can't both be true."

"Black and white are opposites. They cannot coexist in the same space. If they try to, they become something else. And yet neither black nor white is wrong or false in any sense. They simply cannot coexist. Likewise, a mind can hold a scientific view of things, or a magical view of things. Never both. Alternatives exclude."

"That's nonsense. Science has proofs. Tests. Empirical evidence."

"And magic has its own proofs that are equally valid for those who view the world through its lens. Science says Emily is dead and gone forever, but magic proclaims otherwise. If you choose to, you can bring her back. To be yours to do with what you will."

Roger eyed her narrowly.

"Why would you even want to help me? What's your angle? And what the fuck *are* you, anyway? You never really answered that."

"There isn't a language in the world that has a word for what I am. You might say I am…an adjustor. A corrector of errors. I am here to make right what was wrong. Emily was not supposed to die. Not then. Not in that way. The error must be corrected. Reality must be reset."

"Reset? What does that mean? That doesn't sound like just reanimating a corpse."

"Time will be reset to the moment of the error, and events will be adjusted to ensure the error does not occur. Emily will no longer be dead. She will be alive. She will be yours. Your slave. Your plaything."

Roger sucked in a breath at the delicious thought of Emily chained and imprisoned in his basement. But then he gave Emily Faux a sidelong look. "Or maybe you're just saying that. Maybe *she's* supposed to kill *me*, or something. How do I know that's not what will happen if I help you to…to *reset* things, or whatever."

"You don't. For that matter, I don't either. I'm here only to correct the mistake. I'm only a functionary, if you will."

"Who do you work for?"

She shook her head. "Even I don't know that."

He grunted, then just sat there a moment, deep in thought. Emily watched him in silence, her face unreadable.

Finally he said, "If—*if*—I choose to go along with this magic nonsense, what exactly would that entail?"

"Magic requires balance," she said. "A life for a life. In this case, though, the magnitude of the proposed changes will require two lives."

"Whose lives?"

"Two similar and connected lives. You remember those two children you saw Emily with in the park?"

"The boy and the girl?"

"Yes. His name is John Coyote. Hers is Anna West. Both of them must die so that Emily may live again. They must die in the clearing, in the same spot you killed Emily so that their blood may replace hers." She smiled lewdly again. "You may, of course, do what you wish with the girl before you kill her."

Roger remembered his vivid dream of raping Emily in the clearing, and then imagined doing the same to Anna West. His cock stirred again.

He shut his eyes, shook his head.

"I'm not killing anyone!" he said. "You're trying to set me up or something, in revenge for killing Emily! This— this makes no sense! This resetting reality garbage is complete and utter bullshit! Stuff like that just doesn't happen!"

She smiled. "It happens more often than you might think. Besides, like I said, the magic will reset reality, and none of them will be dead any longer. Not John, not Anna, and not Emily."

"I have only *your* word for that."

"True. But you also have the fact of my existence as proof that there are other realities than the one you know. You have a choice to make, Roger. Take some time to think it through. But don't take too long. This must be done soon or it cannot be done at all. And by the rules of magic, only you can do it."

She vanished.

Roger slumped back in his chair and stared out the window. Ms. Souter from down the block passed by, walking her poodle. Her permed curly white hair matched the dog's fur. The ordinariness of the scene made him ask himself if he had really just been talking to a ghostly entity that wanted him to kill two children in order to reset reality.

But no. He knew better. It had been real, at least in some sense. The offer had been real.

The question was, what was he going to do about it?

Chapter 20

Reconnaissance

1

Calvin was breathing hard as he rang Mr. May's doorbell. He had run most of the way here, eager to share his discoveries with Mr. May and Cynthia.

But when Mr. May answered the door, Calvin's ebullient greeting died on his lips. He could tell from the grim look on the old man's face that something was very wrong.

"Ms. Crow will not be joining us," Mr. May said as he led Calvin to the parlor.

"What?" Calvin's voice was high with alarm. "Is she okay?"

"Her aunt died this afternoon."

"Oh." Calvin relaxed, relieved that Cynthia was okay, then felt a stab of guilt that he didn't feel more saddened about Wendy's death.

While Mr. May settled into his claw-and-ball chair, Calvin sat in the same spot on the couch where he had sat yesterday. He glanced at the empty cushion where Cynthia had sat. It wasn't going to be the same without her.

"What exactly happened?" Calvin asked.

"About an hour ago I was having a cup of tea when I heard a siren and a vehicle racing up my driveway. Wondering if I was about to be arrested for some obscure reason, I looked out and saw an ambulance screech to a halt at the end of the drive. Two paramedics leaped out and sprinted into the woods with a stretcher and various equipment. I went outside to find out what was happening. I could hear faint voices in the distance, in the direction of the clearing. I started to head that way, but I hadn't even made it halfway there when I nearly collided with the paramedics, who were heading back to the ambulance with Wendy's body on the stretcher. She was dead. Cynthia and her father were following along close behind them. I'm not sure Hannibal even noticed me—he looked pretty dazed—but Cynthia did. While we headed back to the ambulance, she told me what had happened. They had gone to the clearing to see if Wendy could psychically learn anything about Emily's disappearance. Wendy had already had a vision earlier, in Emily's room—an image of a large shiny yellow box, possibly made of metal or plastic. Does that mean anything to you?"

"No."

"Me either. Anyway, they went to the clearing, and before Wendy even got there she was acting strangely, staggering about and breathing irregularly. She claimed she sensed something up ahead in the clearing, something that was giving off psychic energy like heat from a furnace. When they got there she started babbling about a dome and a sphere and a hole."

"A dome!" Calvin exclaimed. "The underground chamber Turner May wrote about was a dome!"

Mr. May nodded. "True. But in this case I think it refers to something else, as you'll soon see. No sooner had Wendy said all this than she had a seizure, just like when she was a little girl. Only this time it killed her."

"Did she, like, swallow her tongue or something?"

Mr. May shook his head with a small laugh. "That only happens in movies. No, nobody seemed to know exactly why she died. Given her age, I wouldn't be surprised if it was a heart attack or a stroke. At any rate, right after she died, Cynthia briefly saw a faint dome or hemisphere of silvery light in the center of the clearing."

"Does that mean Cynthia's psychic, too?"

Mr. May hesitated. "I…I don't know. Her father didn't notice anything, but Cynthia said his eyes were shut at the time, so I guess there's no way to know for sure whether the light was a psychic manifestation visible only to sensitives or just a display of normal energy that would have been visible to anyone."

"What does it all mean? What do you think's going on?"

"If I had to hazard a guess, I would say that energy of some kind is manifesting in the clearing whenever…certain events occur there. I don't want to say 'deaths,' given that Emily's fate is unknown and I would prefer to remain optimistic. Let's just say 'traumatic events,' shall we? Though the light that Cynthia saw didn't appear to leave any physical traces in the clearing, it's hardly a stretch to posit a connection between that light and the peculiar burned circle found in the wake of Emily's abduction. But as intriguing—and worrying—as that is, it's something we must set aside for now."

"What? Why?"

"It's most likely a matter of the macro-level, of the larger patterns at work. As we discussed yesterday, our focus right now needs to be on the micro-level, on finding Emily. And on that score, Cynthia managed to tell me one other thing before she and her father headed away. She learned the names of some of the people in the park on Thursday. She learned them from her brother, of all people, who wishes to be included in our future plans."

"Hm," Calvin said with a small frown. He knew their goal was to find Emily, of course, but he couldn't help feeling a bit put out that he and Cynthia would no longer be the only ones working with Mr. May to solve the case. It had been a unique connection between them, setting them apart from everyone else.

Mr. May noticed Calvin's sudden glumness and raised an eyebrow. "Is there a problem with young Mr. Crow that I don't know about?"

"Oh, uh, I don't know. I don't really know him, but..." Calvin shrugged. "Well, I've heard he's kind of a stoner."

"Be that as it may, he has helped us immeasurably already. He provided a rundown of people who were in the park, including a couple of actual names. Based on what Cynthia told me, the only one that seems like a viable suspect at the moment is a man named Roger Grey."

Calvin shot bolt upright. "What? Roger Grey?"

Mr. May sat forward, eyes agleam with excitement. "This means something to you?"

Calvin told him about his talk with his father that morning. When Calvin related how he got his father to identify bank employees who fit the profile Mr. May had come up with, Mr. May laughed.

"Excellent," Mr. May said. "Very clever. Very well done."

Calvin swelled with delight.

After Calvin finished telling what he had learned, Mr. May nodded slowly as if the info confirmed what he had already suspected.

"You think it's him?" Calvin asked.

"I think he is by far the likeliest candidate. All lines of investigation are pointing his way. He matches the profile to a T. He was in the park at the right time. He no doubt saw Emily fairly often. He has been acting in a peculiar manner recently. He's on vacation but still chooses to hang around the park, a place he visits nearly every workday."

"Should we tell the police?"

"They're privy to most of the same information we are. I'm sure they already know about Mr. Grey."

"Then why don't they do anything?"

"I imagine they don't feel the evidence is strong enough. Which, from a legal standpoint, it isn't. It's wholly circumstantial."

"So what do we do?"

Mr. May said nothing for a moment. He just gazed off into space, thinking.

Then he smiled.

"We look for more evidence," he said. He cocked an eyebrow at Calvin. "Up for a little reconnaissance this evening?"

2

After dinner Calvin told his parents he was going for a walk, then strode briskly toward eastern May. He didn't have a lot of time. The sun had set about ten minutes ago, so there was only about twenty more minutes before dusk fell and it got too dark for him to do what he needed to do.

It took him about ten minutes to reach Grace Road where Roger Grey lived. The road was deserted except for a paunchy middle-aged male jogger puffing his way down the opposite side of the street. The jogger looked too busy trying not to collapse from exhaustion to pay much attention to Calvin. Good.

Calvin kept a close eye on the house numbers as he

walked along. When number 452—Grey's address—came into view, he got out his cell phone. He silenced it so it wouldn't ring while he was using it, then turned on the video recorder. He put the phone to his ear on the side facing Grey's house and started talking as if he were having a conversation with someone. He made sure to hold the phone so the camera lens was level with the house.

He didn't rely only on the camera, though; he took a good, long look at the house out of the corner of his eye as he strolled past. After all, if the video quality wound up sucking, he wanted to be able to give Mr. May a decent description of the property.

It was a simple one-storey white bungalow. The driveway was empty, but the garage door was closed, so the car might be parked inside. All of the house's windows were curtained tight. A light was on in one of the front rooms. Probably the living room. But the light didn't mean Grey was home, or even in town. He could be away on a trip, and the light on a timer.

The lawn was green and well-maintained. The high bushes separating Grey's house from the house on the south were nicely trimmed. The low white wooden fence separating it from the house on the north looked like it had been recently painted. There was nothing here that said "psycho" or "pervert." It was, in fact, the paragon of suburban normalcy. But outward appearances meant nothing.

Calvin's heart was hammering as he passed the house, and the phone slid a little in his sweaty grip. He feared that the front door would fly open and Grey would storm out, having somehow discerned what Calvin was up to. But the door stayed closed the whole time, and Calvin saw no signs of life from inside.

Despite his nervousness, Calvin did a good job maintaining his end of the fake conversation. He kept it simple by pretending to be doing most of the listening, interjecting only occasional brief comments like, "Uh-huh," and, "Yeah, that's what I thought, too," and, "So what did she say?" He made sure to move the phone about just enough to get a thorough view of the front of the house and both sides.

That left the back. After he had passed Grey's house, he pretended to end the conversation, saved the video footage, and then stuffed the phone into his pocket. He strode north to the end of the block, then east down Wilsey, then south down Elmwood, the street behind Grey's. He walked quickly since it was getting darker by the moment. Too much longer and there wouldn't be enough light to film anything.

Elmwood Road was slightly busier than Grace Road: An old lady was walking a poodle on the other side of the street, and two little blonde girls were doing cartwheels on the front lawn of a house near the far end of the block. TVs flickered in living room windows. A dog barked somewhere.

As Calvin headed down the block, he got out his phone again and repeated the video/fake conversation procedure. When he drew parallel to Grey's house, he looked between the houses until he found a spot where the back of Grey's house was visible.

There were no signs of life anywhere on Grey's property. The house's rear windows were curtained and unlit. Even the two small glass panels high up on Grey's back door were curtained. The backyard was as plain and well-maintained as the front. The patio was empty save for a single aluminum-frame lawn chair.

Calvin turned face-forward again with the phone to his

ear so that the camera was filming the back of Grey's house. Then he paused, frowning, and raised one of his shoes to look at its underside.

"Aw, man," he told his imaginary phone friend. "I think I just stepped in something." He examined his sole with a sour expression, occasionally turning slightly this way and that to make sure he filmed the entirety of the back of Grey's house. When he felt he had enough decent footage, he lowered his foot and started to walk on.

"Okay, bye," he said into the phone, then saved the footage and put the phone away.

He couldn't help taking one last glance back at Grey's house before it passed out of sight. When he saw it, his breath caught in his throat.

The window to the left of the back door was now lit up. Crap. It must have come on while he was filming.

As Calvin gawped at the lit window, a shadow passed across the curtain. Grey *was* home! Or at least *someone* was.

Calvin lowered his head and strode away as fast as he could.

3

Back home, he emailed the videos to Mr. May. (He was inordinately pleased that Mr. May had given him his email address. He felt as if he had been admitted into some exclusive club.) Then he called Mr. May.

"Mission accomplished," Calvin said.

"Yes, I see," Mr. May said. "I'm watching the videos right now. You did a good job."

"Thanks."

"Was there any evidence that Mr. Grey was at home? I

see the living room light was on, but—ah, there we go. I see the light came on in back, and someone's moving around inside."

"Oh, good. I wasn't sure if I caught any of that on film."

"That was why I wanted you to go during twilight, when it was still just bright enough to get some usable footage, but dark enough that he would have his lights on. Of course, I was secretly hoping we would have a stroke of incredibly good luck and catch him coming home from somewhere, and you would discover that he keeps a spare house key inside a fake rock out front, the way I do."

"So what now?"

"Now you get a good night's sleep and have a fine, educational day at school tomorrow. Meanwhile I will examine this footage and ponder what we know so far and try to come up with some ideas to, ah, gather more evidence."

"Does that mean, like, break in?"

"We can discuss that tomorrow. I'm officially calling a meeting for tomorrow afternoon—you and me and Cynthia and her brother. We can all sit down and discuss our next move. If all goes well, that move will take place tomorrow night. And if all goes *really* well, this whole situation will be resolved before tomorrow night is through."

Chapter 21

The Old Witch

1

Anna West pretended to watch Miss Dryer scrawl a math problem on the blackboard, but in truth her eyes were on John Coyote.

She was worried about him. Again. They had spent most of the weekend together, working on homework, commiserating, talking. And connecting. After a rough start, she had begun to get through to him. She had been easing his bitterness and hostility over Emily's disappearance. She was helping. She was healing.

But this morning all her good works began to unravel. When she tried to chat with him at his desk before school started, he barely seemed aware of her. He kept staring at Emily's empty seat, and he scowled any time someone laughed or roughhoused or displayed any other outward sign that they weren't thinking about their missing classmate. It pained and offended him to see life going on as usual. Anna didn't think he should have come back to school so soon. He wasn't ready.

But here he was anyway.

Miss Dryer turned from the blackboard and looked at the class. She was a tiny, withered old woman with horn-rimmed glasses and a face like Yoda's. Everyone hated her. She was prim and humorless and issued homework over holiday weekends. Emily once said that Miss Dryer was the sort of person who had probably acted like an old lady even when she was a little girl.

"Who can solve this problem?" Miss Dryer said. Her icy blue eyes scanned the room.

Anna glanced at John again—he was slouched in his seat, his chin in his palm, his eyes on his desktop, obviously not listening—and she suddenly felt sure that Miss Dryer was going to call on him.

She was right.

"John," Miss Dryer said. "Perhaps you can show us how to solve this problem."

John didn't budge. He didn't even raise his eyes from the desktop.

"I don't know," he said.

Miss Dryer peered at him over the top of her glasses. "Don't know? I spent the last ten minutes explaining it. How can you not know?"

He glanced at Emily's empty seat, then dropped his gaze back to the desktop.

"I don't care," he muttered.

Miss Dryer's eyes narrowed. She crossed the room and stood beside his desk.

"You *should* care," she said. "You should care very much. Without an education you will be an ignorant savage. Without understanding how the world works, you will be its victim. Is that what you want?"

"I don't know." His voice was barely audible.

Miss Dryer pursed her wrinkled lips. "I know you are troubled by the disappearance of your little friend. It is troubling for everyone. But that is no excuse to wallow in willful ignorance and defeatism. We must soldier on. Life must continue. Growth must continue. We can't stop the world for one person."

John's head shot up. His eyes were so dark and steely with hate that Miss Dryer drew back, one hand rising to her chest. Even Anna shrank back in her seat. She had never seen him look like that. Heck, she had never seen *anyone* look like that. She realized with a sick, sinking feeling that she had absolutely no idea what was going on in his mind. Maybe she never had.

John's upper lip drew back. "Go fuck yourself, you evil old witch."

A collective gasp rose up. Anna gaped in horror. He had said the F-word to a teacher! There was no telling what they would do to him for that. They might even expel him. What would he do then? What would *she* do?

For a moment Miss Dryer only stared at him, her face blank, as if his words deviated so far from the natural order of things she couldn't make sense of them. Then she seized his arm in one liver-spotted hand, yanked him from his seat, and hauled him toward the front of the room.

At the door she stopped and turned to the class.

"I will be gone for a short while," she said. "I expect no shenanigans in my absence."

She flung open the door and dragged John out into the hallway. The door banged shut.

Anna heaved a deep, shaky breath. She had to keep blinking quickly to keep the tears from her eyes.

It seemed like everything just kept going wronger and wronger.

2

John didn't say a word as Miss Dryer dragged him down the hall. He merely stared straight ahead, his face set and grim. He had said what he had to say. He had no regrets. Let the cards fall as they may.

Miss Dryer threw open the door to the main office, stormed past the startled secretary, then barged right into the principal's office without even knocking.

Principal Powell sat behind his big dark desk. He was a tubby, red-cheeked man with receding brown hair and a mustache. Miss Hubbard, the school's guidance counselor, stood next to his desk holding a pair of hand puppets. Miss Hubbard, John knew from experience, was big on puppets. She seemed to think that kids learned best when you spoke in a funny voice and demonstrated things with soft, fuzzy toys. She talked a lot about feelings and "we-ness." He had once heard Miss Dryer call Miss Hubbard a "ditzy little hippie girl" under her breath, though John wasn't entirely clear what that meant.

"What's the meaning of this?" Principal Powell cried as Miss Dryer marched John up to the big desk. "I'm in the middle of a meeting!"

"I want this child expelled," Miss Dryer declared. "Now."

"What's he done?" Miss Hubbard said.

"He said…" She glanced down at John with a small frown. "He told me to fornicate with myself, though he used much crasser language. I'm sure you can guess what."

Miss Hubbard nodded. "I'm sure I can."

Principal Powell fixed John with what was probably supposed to be a stern, level gaze. John thought it looked more constipated than anything.

"Is this true?" Principal Powell said.

"Yep," John said.

Principal Powell didn't seem to have been expecting such a simple, affirmative response. He sat back in his big leather chair, looking a little baffled, and said, "Ah."

There was a long silence.

"Well?" Miss Dryer said.

"I don't think we should be so hasty to expel him," Miss Hubbard said to Principal Powell. "I mean, Emily Crow was one of his best friends, and he's obviously having a tough time dealing with things. I'm surprised he's even in school. I'm sure he must be really scared and worried." She bent down until her face was level with John's and gave him a broad sympathetic smile with her eyebrows drawn high and her head tilted to one side. She reminded him of one of her puppets. "Isn't that right?"

John looked down at the floor. "Um, I guess."

Miss Hubbard turned back to the principal. "See? He's suffering enough as it is. He's hurt and confused, lashing out in fear at a world that's become threatening and hostile."

Miss Dryer cocked an eyebrow. "You describe him as if he were an animal, when he is in fact a human being capable of rational thought. He is able to logically weigh his actions and must be taught that foolish actions have certain consequences that cannot be avoided."

"*You* describe him as if he were Mr. Spock. He's a child. He's ten years old."

"And coddling him now will instill erroneous notions that will last a lifetime."

"These are unusual circumstances."

"His behavior was far beyond what should be tolerated

even in the worst of circumstances."

Miss Hubbard rolled her eyes and heaved an exasperated sigh.

Principal Powell stared off into space for a minute, his fingers absently drumming on his desktop.

The fingers froze in mid-drum. His eyes swiveled to John.

"Why did you say what you said?" he asked.

John's eyes narrowed. His jaw clenched. "She said it wasn't important, what happened to Emily. She said we should forget about her."

"I said no such thing," protested Miss Dryer to the inquiring glances of Principal Powell and Miss Hubbard. "I merely impressed upon him the fact that when tragedies happen, we must continue to soldier on as best we can."

"That's a lie!" John spat. "She's a witch! She's an evil old witch!"

"No," Miss Hubbard muttered, almost inaudibly, "but it certainly *rhymes* with 'witch.'"

"What was that?" Miss Dryer snapped.

"Oh, nothing," Miss Hubbard said with an innocent smile.

Miss Dryer flashed a frosty smile in return.

Principal Powell watched the two women closely. When it became clear they weren't going to attack each other or do anything else that might require his intervention, he cleared his throat and turned to John.

"Yes. Well. I think it is safe to say that Miss Dryer is neither evil nor a witch. And, um, that such language as you used is thoroughly inappropriate in an educational context, and indeed in most contexts one could reasonably imagine. Under normal circumstances such language would indeed be grounds for the consideration of expulsion.

However"—here Miss Dryer frowned—"given that this is an unusual and very stressful time for both students and faculty alike, and given moreover that you are obviously greatly anguished by recent events, I feel that a certain modicum of leniency is called for. But not complete leniency, of course." Here Miss Hubbard frowned. "Allowing this regrettable incident to pass without anything more than a token response from the administration would only incite further examples of such behavior and fail to instill the proper mind-set in its charges." He leaned back in his chair. "Therefore, my decision is that you will be suspended for the remainder of the week and placed in lunchtime detention for the two weeks after that. Also I am going to recommend to your aunt that you see a counselor to aid you in this unfortunate time. Do you understand?"

"Um, yeah, I guess." In truth, he didn't understand half of what the principal had said (which wasn't surprising; Principal Powell always talked like that when he was making announcements and big decisions). But John understood the gist of it: He was being punished because Miss Dryer had essentially said that a bunch of math problems were more important than Emily, and John had responded to this in the only appropriate manner.

What made everything worse was that Miss Dryer and Emily had always despised each other. Miss Dryer had openly scoffed at Emily's love of fairies. One time she had even made Emily cry. And now this horrible old creature was still here, still thriving, and Emily was gone. The only person he had ever felt a real connection to—the only person who had ever made him feel that everything was okay—was gone, and the bullies were winning again.

His hate was a black gem inside him.

Chapter 22

See Emily Play (III)

1

"Holy shit," Violet said, looking up at the May house. The late-afternoon sun had slipped far enough behind the trees that only the topmost tip of the tower was still lit. "This place looks like a haunted house or something."

"Yeah," Donovan said. He headed up the front steps to the porch, the boards creaking under his black leather boots. He glanced back at Violet. She had stopped on the front walkway that connected the steps to the driveway. The way she was leaning back to study the house's façade made her breasts strain roundly against her tight black tank top. The sight made Donovan briefly forget what they were here for.

He shook his head to clear it.

"Come on!" he said.

"I bet all those stories are totally true," Violet said, trotting up the steps to join him on the porch. "I bet there really are bodies in here and shit. Skeletons sealed in the walls. Bloodstains under the carpets. Satanic symbols carved into the basement floor."

Donovan had raised a finger to ring the doorbell, but now he paused and looked at her, frowning.

"What the fuck are you talking about?"

"I'm just sayin'."

"Yeah, well, be nice. He's helping us find Emily."

"Yeah." She shrugged. "Course, we woulda found her on our own eventually. They're just tryin' to hog our action."

"It's not about who gets the action. It's about finding her."

He rang the bell.

Almost immediately he heard footsteps striding quickly toward the door. Somehow he recognized them as his sister's.

Indeed, a moment later the door opened, and Cynthia looked out.

And then she scowled.

"What the hell is *she* doing here?" she cried. "She wasn't invited."

"She wants to help, too," Donovan said.

"Yeah," Violet said. "You guys oughta be glad I'm here! I got lots to offer!"

Cynthia snorted. "Like what? Beer farts and cleavage?"

"Hey, at least I've *got* cleavage, toothpick."

"Why, you little—"

"Violet was the one who told us who was in the park on Thursday," Donovan interjected. "She's helped us already."

"Yeah, by accident," Cynthia said. "She was probably only in the park to feed Alka-Seltzer to the pigeons or something."

Violet planted her fists on her hips. "I haven't done that in years!"

"What seems to be the problem?" It was Mr. May. He was peering at them from a doorway halfway down the corridor.

"We've got an uninvited guest," Cynthia said.

"So I see." Mr. May waved them forward. "Well, bring them in. Let's see what's what and who's who."

Cynthia led them into the parlor. Mr. May stood waiting for them just inside the doorway. A blond kid Donovan recognized from school sat nearby on a leather couch. No doubt this was the Calvin dude that Cynthia had mentioned.

The room's elegant furnishings made Donovan's jaw drop in surprise. This wasn't at all what he had been expecting to find in the supposedly loopy old hermit's house. He had envisioned stacks of yellowed newspapers and scrawny cats everywhere.

"Welcome," Mr. May said, extending a hand. "I am Robert May."

"Uh, yeah, hi." Donovan shook the old man's thin, wrinkled hand. The touch of the ancient, spotted skin creeped him out a bit, but he didn't let it show. "Thanks for, you know, letting us team up with you. And for helping look for Emily and everything."

"It's the least I can do. We're all in this together." He turned to Violet, who was prowling around the room examining various items as if estimating their value. Donovan hoped she hadn't palmed anything. "And who is this?"

"I'm Violet," Violet said. "Nice to meetcha."

"She's the one who was in Indian Hill Park on Thursday," Donovan said. He tilted his chin up bravely, ready to defend Violet and her involvement if need be. "She's in this, too."

"Yeah," said Cynthia. "She's also the one who talked you into breaking into an innocent man's house the other night."

"And what exactly is it we're planning to do tonight, huh?" Violet said. "From the sound of it, you don't have a shred of actual proof this is the guy."

"We have way more reason to suspect Roger Grey than you guys did with Theodore Walsh!"

"Now, now," Mr. May said. "Let's not squabble. Are we not all pursuing the same end? Let's pool our knowledge and resources and strive to resolve this situation as best we can."

Donovan was afraid Cynthia would continue to protest Violet's involvement. But though she rolled her eyes, she didn't say anything else. She just sat down on the couch next to Calvin and crossed her arms over her chest.

"Please sit," Mr. May told Donovan and Violet. He motioned at a loveseat. They sat. "I trust you two know Mr. Beckerman here?"

"Yeah, I've seen you in the lunchroom," Violet told Calvin. "You're always reading books." She said this a little sadly, as if reading books were an irredeemable character flaw.

"Hey," Donovan said, giving Calvin a nod. He wondered again if Calvin and Cynthia were going out. Cyn had denied it before, but he wasn't sure if he should believe her. She kept her private life very private, even with family. Donovan knew practically nothing about her lovelife, not even if she had one. In fact, for a while there last year he had been wondering if there was something going on between Cyn and her friend Jessica Asher, given how much they had been hanging out together. Not that there was anything wrong with that, of course. Actually, lesbians were kinda hot. Well, mostly; if it turned out Cynthia was one, that would just be weird.

"I know you two are new here," Mr. May said to Violet and Donovan. "So do you have any questions or concerns before we begin? Or would either of you like anything to eat or drink?"

"Um, I don't suppose you have any beer?" Donovan said.

"Sadly no. No alcoholic beverages whatsoever, I'm afraid."

"I have a question," Violet said.

"Yes?" Mr. May said.

She pointed at the floor. "Are there, like, really bodies buried in the basement? Cuz, you know, I've heard stories at school that there are."

Cynthia muttered something to herself and put her face in her palm.

Mr. May just smiled. "No. I have to put the bodies upstairs. The torture devices take up too much space in the basement."

Violet blinked at him with uncharacteristic surprise for a moment, then burst into laughter.

"You're pretty funny for an old dude."

"I'm so glad you approve."

Donovan watched Mr. May closely, sure that underneath his good humor the old guy must be pretty peeved at the comment. But instead Mr. May was regarding Violet with a small, almost wistful smile. Donovan wondered if she reminded him of someone he used to know. A guy his age must have met pretty much every type of person there is.

Mr. May sat down in an antique armchair and said, "Let's call this meeting to order,"

And then there was lots and lots of talk. Donovan tried to follow most of it, but the fact was, Mr. May and Calvin and Cynthia were the kind of people who liked piling up huge towers of information and hashing over facts and details, and Donovan always had trouble keeping up with stuff like that. His eyes started glazing over shortly after Mr. May said, "First of all, let's review what we know…" Within five minutes all he could think about was how badly he wanted a smoke. A quick glance around the room showed not a single ashtray in sight. The increasingly restless stirring beside him indicated that Violet was jonesing too.

Still, he caught the gist of the discussion: Roger Grey was the most likely suspect in Emily's disappearance. The plan was to find a way into his house to look around. There was a lot of debate about how to get into his house without his being aware of it. Violet's main contribution to the discussion—namely, why not just wear masks, bop Grey over the head, tie him up, and search the place?—was met with an awkward silence and then, to Donovan's surprise, a polite explanation from Mr. May as to why that wouldn't be a good idea (primarily because it was hard to bop someone over the head without potentially causing them serious injury). "We want to do this stealthily and without violence, if possible," Mr. May explained. To Donovan's further surprise, Violet didn't protest or snark at him, but accepted this explanation with a thoughtful nod.

"We mustn't forget that we are on the side of the angels," Mr. May added. "We mustn't cause any harm unless absolutely necessary. We're the good guys, after all. We don't do things like that."

Donovan frowned. Mr. May's comment, in combination with the whole rallying-of-the-forces thing that was going on, dislodged a memory in his spacey, nicotine-starved brain. A memory of Emily. Of the speeches she gave while mustering her troops during the Zoo Wars…

2

The Zoo Wars began two years ago when Donovan decided he was too old to still own over four dozen green plastic army men, and subsequently bequeathed them to Emily, then eight. She wound up employing the army men in an elaborate game she dubbed the Zoo Wars (even though it technically had nothing to do with zoos).

The Zoo Wars pitted the army men against Emily's menagerie of stuffed animals. The army men represented the evil Mr. Mudge (the five-star general) and his henchmen (the lesser ranks), who had kidnapped the animals from their idyllic jungle home and taken them to Mudge's sinister circus where they were starved and beaten and forced to perform dangerous stunts for the amusement of boorish spectators. But one day Otto the elephant, Emily's favorite stuffed animal, incited the animals to revolt. The animals escaped into the wild with Mudge and his henchmen in hot pursuit.

Over the course of several months Emily enacted numerous encounters between Mudge's men and the animals. She would spend hours at a time setting up and then playing through each battle, the furniture in her bedroom serving as an exotic geography—the chair a mountain, the edge of the bed a cliff, the wastebasket the lava-spitting caldera of a volcano.

Before each battle, Emily would pretend to be Mudge as he mustered his troops. Cackling and rubbing her hands together in stereotypical bad-guy fashion, she paced back and forth before the assembled army men and exhorted them to capture the wicked anarchistic animals in the name of revenge, orderliness, and mucho profits. She hatched plans of attack and barked orders to her silent green troops and instructed them to win by any and every means possible, no matter how cruel or underhanded.

Then she would take Otto's role. He, too, paced about and talked to his troops, but in a gentler, more humane fashion. He urged them to avoid cruelty, to play fair, and to refrain from taking life. "Unless they leave you no choice," Emily/Otto would add. "Then you can kill the crap out of 'em." Emily always ended Otto's speeches with the line, "Don't forget: We're the good guys, and the good guys always win in the end."

Indeed, the battles bore this out. No matter how outmatched the animals were, no matter how bleak things sometimes appeared, Otto and his crew wound up winning every time, and hordes of generic henchmen died in gruesome and painful ways, though Mudge always escaped death to return next time with a new batch of generic henchmen. In fact, the outcome was always so certain and invariable that Donovan wondered why Emily even bothered. Everything was predestined. Why act it out?

Emily eventually came to agree. After a few months she got bored with the Zoo Wars and ended them with an epic battle on a mysterious island "all the way at the farthest end of the Earth." The last of Mudge's generic henchmen died, a few animals perished bravely (usually while sacrificing themselves to save other animals), and at the very end Mudge's own greed proved his undoing when he refused to let go of the basket of the huge hot-air balloon that was carrying the animals away from the sinking island. "No!" he cried. "You will be mine! Mine!" Then he lost his grip, plummeted "a hundred thousand feet" to the island below, and was impaled on the needle-sharp peak of the mountain at the center of the island.

With no further use for the army men, Emily started sticking them in odd places for people to find. For the longest time they were popping up everywhere—inside shoes, on pillows, in the fruit bowl. The general/Mr. Mudge turned up inside the toilet tank. Emily denied all responsibility and faux-innocently speculated that ghosts or elves were doing it. Eventually she ran out of army men, and that was the end of it.

3

"Do you understand the plan?" Mr. May said.

Donovan looked around, blinking. Everyone was looking at him.

"Uh, what?" he said. He realized he had been so immersed in his recollections that he hadn't heard a word anyone had said in the last few minutes.

"Do you understand what we're going to do?" Mr. May said.

"Um..." Donovan winced. "Do you think maybe we could go over it one more time?"

Mr. May grimaced. Cynthia rolled her eyes. Beside him Violet muttered, "Dude, zone much?"

"All right," Mr. May said with a small sigh. "This is the plan..."

Chapter 23

An Incident on Grace Road

1

Roger sat in his recliner staring at a TV show about life on the ocean floor but not really watching it. He was mulling over the proposition Emily Faux had presented to him yesterday afternoon. She hadn't reappeared since then. Which was just as well, since Roger wasn't any closer to reaching a decision.

On the face of it, hitting some temporal reset button sounded like a fantastic idea. Emily would be alive again, and Roger would be off the FBI's radar. Even if magically resetting time meant letting the real Emily go and forsaking any chance to live out his fantasies, it would be preferable to the present situation. But murdering two more children on nothing more than the word of a phantom was a price he wasn't sure he was willing to pay. Though the phantom had helped him with the FBI and had proven its reality several times already, Roger couldn't shake his fear that the whole thing was a set-up, a trick to redden his hands even further before unleashing the authorities on him.

"They're coming," Emily's voice said.

Roger started, but only a little. He was getting used to this. He wasn't sure if that was a good thing or a bad thing.

He turned. Emily Faux sat on the couch again. He felt both relieved and distressed to see her.

"Who's coming?" Roger said.

"People who suspect you. You need to get ready."

"What? You mean the police? The FBI?"

"No, not the police. Though the police will be here soon, since you're going to call them."

"What?"

She smiled. "Just do what I tell you, and everything will be fine."

2

Cynthia, Donovan, Calvin, and Violet—the Grace Road Housebreaking Squad, as Cynthia couldn't help mentally dubbing the group—squatted in the line of thick bushes that separated Roger Grey's house from his neighbors' to the south. Calvin and Cynthia wore black ski masks, and everyone except Violet wore headsets linked to long-range walkie talkies that were clipped to their belts. The walkie talkies kept them in constant contact with each other and with Mr. May, who sat in the tower of his house halfway across town. Mr. May had supplied the walkie talkies and the headsets. He said he had used them on countless anomaly investigations in the past.

The quartet in the bushes looked out through the foliage at Roger Grey's house. Night had recently fallen, and Grey's curtained living room window was lit up. The rest of the house was dark.

Calvin glanced at the others and whispered, "Okay, we all know what to do?"

"Dude, we've only been over it, like, sixty gazillion times already," Violet said.

"All right, all right. Let's get started, then. Agent Four,

go." Violet was Agent Four. Calvin, Cynthia, and Donovan were Agents One, Two, and Three, respectively. Mr. May was Shepherd. Mr. May had insisted they use code names just in case anyone was listening in on their transmissions.

Violet wriggled out of the bushes and strode toward Grey's front steps. The others watched.

"She's gonna fuck this up," Cynthia said as Violet rang the doorbell. "I just know it. We should have given her a more specific plan."

"No, I told you," Donovan said. "This is perfect. Without a plan, she has nothing to fuck up."

Cynthia frowned. "I think that's one of those things that only *sounds* like it makes sense."

"No, I think he's right," Mr. May said, his voice coming in loud and clear over the headsets. "I haven't known Agent Four for long, but I get the distinct impression that if we had given her a specific plan, she wouldn't have followed it anyway. She's one of those people who works best extemporaneously."

"Extemper-*what?*" Donovan said.

Before anyone could reply, Grey's front door opened, revealing a thirtyish man with glasses and neatly combed light brown hair.

"We're going," Cynthia whispered to Donovan. "Remember: Keep us informed. Tell us what Grey's doing." She remembered who she was talking to, then added, "Not, like, everything, of course. Just whether he's inside or outside or whatever. You don't have to tell us if he picks his nose or something."

"Aw, but that might be funny," he said with a smile. But though his mouth was smiling, Cynthia could see the worry in his eyes. He was cracking jokes to hide how nervous he was.

"Just stick to the plan," she said.

"Right."

She and Calvin slipped out of the bushes and onto Grey's neighbors' lawn. The lights were on in a couple of rooms in the neighbors' house, but all the blinds were shut tight. Hunching low and sticking to the shadows at the edge of the bushes, they scurried toward the rear of the house.

3

"Can I help you?" Roger asked with a small frown. He recognized this girl. She lived nearby. Sometimes he heard her yelling things late at night. Once he had spotted her rummaging through Ms. Souter's trash can. Another time he had seen her sprinting down the middle of the street with an overweight cop in panting pursuit.

"We need to talk about your lawn," she said.

"What about my lawn?" He pretended he didn't hear the faint rustle from the bushes on the south side of the property.

"You need to do something about the crab fungus."

"The what?"

She rolled her eyes as if she thought he were being willfully obtuse.

"The crab fungus. It's already starting to spread to the neighbors' lawns. Everybody else is too chickenshit to talk to you about it (you know how these suburban dweebs can be), but I'm not. So here I am, and I'm talkin'."

"Crab fungus?"

"Yes. Crab fungus. You know."

She looked and sounded so convincing that he caught

himself wondering if she might not be telling the truth after all. But then he heard Emily Faux say, "She's just trying to lure you out of the house."

He glanced down. She stood next to him in the doorway.

"Play along," she said. "Just like I told you."

Indeed, just then the teenage girl said, "Come on, I'll show you." She made a "follow me" gesture, then turned and trotted down the steps. She didn't even glance back, as if she were sure he would follow.

He did.

4

Calvin was starting to wonder what was taking so long when Donovan's voice came over the headset: "Okay, he just followed her down the steps and onto the lawn."

"Perfect," Mr. May said. "Agents One and Two move in."

Calvin and Cynthia pushed through the bushes and hurried across Grey's backyard to the rear of the house. There they paused and looked around at the neighbors' houses to make sure they were unobserved. Several windows in the houses were lit and uncurtained, but no one was in sight. Thankfully Grey didn't have any outside lights on, and only faint light came from inside his house, which meant Calvin and Cynthia were mostly in shadow. Even if a neighbor looked out, he or she likely wouldn't be able to see the black-clad duo at all.

Calvin and Cynthia tried the windows. They were locked tight. The back door was, too.

"Everything's locked," Calvin said.

"Can you see in through the windows?" Mr. May said.

"Yeah, the curtain's parted a little in one of them," Cynthia said, peering in. "It's a kitchen. There's just…kitchen stuff. There's a single light on over the sink."

"Go ahead and use the glass cutter, then. But be quick."

Calvin took out the glass cutter and the putty Violet had given him. He stuck the putty onto the glass, then started to cut a circle around it, wincing at the occasional screech it made. Grey was too far away to hear it, but Calvin couldn't help fearing that someone else might be in the house. An accomplice or a girlfriend or something. If Calvin and the others got caught, they would be in huge trouble. Of course, the authorities might be willing to overlook a few well-meant illegalities if it turned out that Grey was indeed the man who had abducted Emily. But what if he wasn't? What if they were wrong?

When Calvin had voiced these concerns at the meeting earlier, Mr. May had dismissed them, saying, "I am all but certain Grey is the culprit. And if I'm wrong and if you get caught, I'll take care of things. Though I rarely travel far from home these days, I still have considerable sway in this community, plus enough funds to grease as many wheels and official orifices as necessary." At the time, in the cozy comfort of Mr. May's parlor, this reply had been enough to assuage Calvin's doubts. But now, as he watched his shaking, black-gloved hand swing the glass cutter around to complete the circle (more like a scalloped oval, really), all of his doubts and fears returned, and new ones surfaced. Maybe Mr. May could get them out of jail if they got caught, but what if they didn't survive long enough to get caught? What if Grey had a gun and shot them? It was legal for homeowners to shoot intruders, wasn't it?

He popped out the circle of glass, then reached in through the hole and unlatched the window.

"Okay, it's unlocked," he said.

"Go in," Mr. May said. "Hurry."

Calvin pushed up the window, then grabbed onto the ledge and boosted himself up and through. Inside, he paused a moment and looked around this strange kitchen, his heart pounding. He was officially a housebreaker, a criminal. But it was for a good cause, right?

He heard a grunt behind him, then turned and helped Cynthia climb inside.

"We're in," he whispered into the headset, his voice lower than ever. He was still afraid that someone other than Grey was in the house.

"Now go and unlock the back door," Mr. May said.

"What? Why?"

"Because if you have to flee quickly, it will be easier to flee out a door instead of having to climb through a window."

"Oh. Yeah. That's a good idea." He smiled. Mr. May's expert guidance made him feel a little calmer, a little less worried. He felt that they were in good hands.

"It sounds like you've done this sort of thing before," Cynthia said.

"No comment," Mr. May said.

The back door was in line with the archway that led to the living room. Peeking around the arch, Calvin had a clear view straight to the front entrance. The main door was open, though the storm door was closed. Through the storm door's screen he could see the top of the house across the street, a swath of autumn leaves on a tree illuminated by a nearby streetlight, the black sky. He faintly heard the strains of Violet's voice in the distance.

"Is Grey away from the front door, Agent Three?" Calvin asked.

"Oh, uh, yeah," Donovan said. "He's way over across the lawn with Vi—I mean, uh, Agent…Number Whatever."

"Okay."

Calvin leaned forward and unlocked the deadbolt on the back door. Then he drew back out of sight of the front door.

"Done," he said.

"Now search," Mr. May said. "Search quickly."

Cynthia began quietly opening cupboards and cabinets. It was her job to search the kitchen and the basement. The rest of the main floor was Calvin's. He peeked around the archway again and listened carefully. He heard Violet say something. Then he heard a lower, more masculine voice. Grey.

"Is Grey still in the same place, Agent Three?" Calvin said.

"Yep."

"All right."

Calvin entered the living room.

5

"I don't see anything," Roger said, examining the blades of grass Violet had plucked from the lawn and handed to him. She stood facing him with her arms folded. Emily Faux stood on the grass nearby, watching the scene with a blank expression.

"Probably cuz it's dark," Violet said. "Come over here under the light." She motioned for him to follow then started to head toward the cone of light streaming down from the streetlight that stood between Roger's house and that of his neighbors to the north.

"Why don't we just go inside?" he asked, jerking a thumb at his front door.

Violet turned and regarded him with a raised eyebrow. "Riiiight. Cuz I'm gonna enter some strange guy's house."

"I'm not a stranger. I'm a neighbor. I'm not gonna do anything."

"Well, even if you did, it wouldn't matter. I could take you down easy."

Roger snorted. "Oh, really?"

"Fuck, yeah! I know Krav Maga! Watch this!" She started flinging her arms and legs about in a manner that made her look more like she was directing airplanes than fending off attackers.

"That's not Krav Maga," Roger said. "That's a silly teenage girl showing off stuff she doesn't know anything about."

"Oh, like you'd know. Cuz bank nerds are so fuckin' knowledgeable about the martial arts."

"I know more than you," he said.

"Oh, yeah? Prove it!"

"How?"

Violet spread her arms and waved him forward. "Bring it on, bitch. Let's rumble."

6

Calvin started his search in the living room. The lights were on in here, so he left his flashlight in his pocket for now. He peered behind furniture, looked inside the cabinets of the entertainment center, and even flipped up the cushions on the couch. He found nothing of note.

Next he got out his flashlight and checked the front closet (coats, boots, gloves), the bathroom (towels, toilet paper, moldy grout), and a broom closet (a vacuum cleaner, dust rags, cleaning products). That left two closed doors at either end of a short hallway off the living room. One was probably Grey's bedroom. What was the other one? He imagined opening one of the doors to find Emily tied to a bed, or locked in a cage. He imagined rescuing her, saving the day…

But what if it was too late for that? What if she was already dead? What if he opened the door and discovered her dismembered corpse on a steel table? What if he found a room full of skulls and bones and masks made from human skin?

He paused before one of the doors, closed his eyes, and took a deep breath. It didn't slow down his racing heart one bit. Before he could chicken out, he twisted the knob and pushed open the door.

It was just a computer room, nothing more. A desk sat against the far wall. Atop it sat a computer (shut down), a printer, general clutter. There was a shelf above the desk full of computer manuals. On a small table sat a second computer, one side of its casing removed to expose its intricate innards. Next to it sat a small black leather case opened to reveal rows of specialized computer tools. The room had one closet, which contained two boxes full of flowery china wrapped in newspaper.

Calvin moved on to the last room. As he had suspected, it was the bedroom. There was a full-size bed, a dresser, a bedside table, a closet full of clothes, a small bookshelf full of books on math and economics.

And that was it. Calvin's shoulders sagged. His search had failed to turn up a single shred of evidence that would suggest Roger Grey was the man behind Emily's abduction.

Had they made a mistake, then? Was this the wrong guy? Had all of this been for nothing?

7

Cynthia eyed the two doors that faced each other across the corridor in the basement. It was eerily silent down here, and the air was cool and still. It was like a crypt. Or a morgue. She really, really didn't want to be here, but there was nowhere else left for her to look. She had given the kitchen a quick once-over, checked a small closet, and shone her flashlight through the glass panes of the door that led to the garage. It was only a one-car garage, and there wasn't room for much beyond the car, a mower, and assorted lawn care tools. Now here she was in the cool, silent basement with two closed doors.

Anything could be behind them. Anything at all.

A floorboard creaked directly above her, and she jumped, her heart slamming into her throat. Then she realized it was only Calvin prowling around upstairs. At least she hoped it was Calvin.

She drew in a long, slow breath, then let it out as quietly as possible, hoping no one could hear it over their headsets.

She tried the door on the left first. Muscles tense, ready for anything, she turned the metal knob, pushed the door open, and then shone her flashlight inside.

A washing machine. A dryer. A chipped, cracked sink.

She went in and gave the room a quick but thorough

search, checking every corner, looking behind the door, even peeking inside the washer and dryer. Nothing.

She crossed the corridor to the other door. Just one more room and she was done.

She laid a hand on the knob, then paused and stared at the door. For some reason, her heart was pounding harder than ever. She suddenly wanted to be done with this and far away from here.

But she couldn't be. Not yet.

After taking another long, silent breath, she closed her fingers around the knob and turned it.

8

"You must be joking," Roger said. "I'm not going to fight you."

"No joke, nerdcakes," Violet said. She waved him forward again. "It's time for you to put your money where your mouth is!"

Emily Faux glanced at the house, then looked at Roger.

"It's time," she said. "Go."

Roger spun around and strode straight toward the house.

9

"Shit, where's he going?" Donovan said. "He's—"

"What is it?" Mr. May said. "What's he doing?"

Donovan didn't reply for a second. He just stood there in the bushes, head cocked, listening. He could hear sirens in the distance. Lots of them. And they were getting louder by the moment.

"Oh, shit," he said. "I hear sirens. And Grey's heading back to the house."

"What?" Calvin said.

"Get out of there. Now."

<h1 style="text-align:center">10</h1>

Cynthia started to whirl around to flee the house, but then she stopped herself.

She couldn't go without checking the last room. Not if there was a chance Emily was in there.

Forcing her fears away, she threw open the door and stepped into the room. She started to raise her flashlight, then frowned. Fuck the flashlight. She didn't have time for that. She flicked on the overheard light.

There wasn't much to see. Shelves. An old, scarred wooden table. A few bits of miscellaneous junk.

And a yellow chest freezer, humming away quietly at the north end of the room.

Since the freezer was the only place in which to hide something (and why did the sight of the freezer trigger something, some faint fleeting memory? Had someone mentioned a chest freezer recently?), she headed toward it. She hadn't gone five paces when she heard the clatter of running footsteps directly above her. A moment later something big and heavy crashed to the floor hard enough to send dust sifting down from the rafters.

"Agent Two, get out of there!" Calvin yelled. "Abort!" His voice came to her both over her headset and down the stairwell in a weird stereophonic effect.

She looked at the freezer again. She could still quickly

check it. She—

"Let go of me!" Calvin cried.

"Damn it," she muttered, and raced upstairs.

11

Calvin had still been in Grey's bedroom when Donovan issued his warning. Galvanized by panic, Calvin sprinted straight for the back door. As he emerged from the hallway that connected the bedroom to the living room, he heard the storm door open. He didn't look around. He just ran harder, sure he could make it to the back door in time. Maybe then he could lure Grey out into the backyard and thus allow Cynthia the chance to slip out the front. Or something. His thoughts were a frightened, jumbled mess.

But Grey was faster than Calvin anticipated. Calvin had barely made it to the kitchen when Grey tackled him, and they crashed to the linoleum, the force of the impact making the burners on the stove rattle. Calvin's headset came off and tumbled away across the floor.

Just in case Cynthia hadn't figured out what was going on—and he wasn't sure she had; he didn't hear a peep from the basement—Calvin yelled at the headset: "Agent Two, get out of there! Abort!"

He fought and wriggled to break free, but Grey had him pinned to the floor.

"Let go of me!" Calvin cried.

Grey just grinned, his mouth a wall of teeth, his eyes gleaming ferally behind his glasses.

And then he yelped in surprise as Violet leaped on his back. She hooked her legs around his waist and wrapped an arm around his neck.

"You stupid fuck!" she said. "I'm gonna Krav Maga your nerd ass all the way to Nagasaki!"

Grey made a gagging sound as Violet tightened her grip on his neck. His face turned as red as a beet, but he remained squarely atop Calvin, holding him in place.

The sirens grew ear-splittingly loud, and tires squealed as a police car screeched to a halt outside. Beyond Grey's head, Calvin saw blue and red lights flashing on the living room ceiling.

Footsteps pounded up the basement stairs and across the kitchen floor.

"Let go of him!" Cynthia shouted. Calvin felt a surge of relief that she was okay.

She grabbed Grey's arm and tried to pull him off Calvin. Snarling, Grey yanked his arm from her grasp.

The storm door flew open. A figure stood silhouetted against the red and blue lights outside. The figure was crouched down a little and was aiming something at them that gleamed metallically in the strobing lights.

"Everybody freeze!" the figure bellowed.

From the dislodged headset, Calvin faintly heard Mr. May's voice say, "Oh, dear."

Chapter 24

Aftermath

1

Calvin, Cynthia, Donovan, and Violet sat in a line on one side of a long wooden table, an arrangement that made Calvin feel as if they were contestants on a game show. But instead of a gaudy set full of games and prizes, they were in a white-walled, gray-carpeted conference room in the police station, and instead of Pat Sajak or Wink Martindale, their "hosts" were Chief Krezchek and FBI Agents Rowan and Schmidt. The trio stood conferring in low inaudible voices beside the door, one of them occasionally casting a humorless glance at the seated quartet to make sure no one was violating the order to remain silent.

Violet violated it anyway. She leaned over to Donovan and whispered, "Don't worry, if they were gonna arrest us, they wouldn't have put us all together like this. They would've separated us and locked us up already. They're probably just gonna give us a big bad warning and let us go."

Cynthia, who sat on the other side of Donovan, leaned around him and said, "And how would you even know this, exactly? You're, like, fourteen."

"I got street smarts." She scowled. "Besides, I'll be fifteen in a month."

Chief Krezchek shushed them. He and the FBI agents

exchanged a few last murmurs, then sauntered over to the table. They didn't sit down. They just stood in a line on the opposite side of the table and regarded the teens with stern, humorless expressions.

"All right," Chief Krezchek said. "What the hell did you kids think you were doing?"

"We were looking for my sister!" Cynthia said. She was surprised at how righteous and unafraid her voice sounded. She certainly didn't *feel* unafraid. Her guts were twisting themselves up so much she was worried she might puke.

The three men glanced at each other.

"Do you have some particular reason why you were looking at Mr. Grey's house?" Agent Schmidt asked.

"He was at the park the day Emily met her abductor."

"So were a lot of people," Agent Rowan said.

"Yeah, but most of them don't fit the profile of the sort of person who would have abducted Emily," Calvin said. "What is it? White male in his thirties, introverted, lives alone—"

Agent Schmidt laughed. "So, what, you're a profiler now?" He shook his head. "Let me guess: You saw some documentaries about serial killers on TV or something, and now you think you know as much about the subject as we do."

Calvin's face flushed. He wanted to tell them that the profile had been created by Mr. May, a man thrice Schmidt's age, a man who had more investigatory experience than anyone in this room. But so far the cops seemed unaware of Mr. May's involvement in all of this, and Calvin wanted to keep it that way.

"Is his profile wrong?" Violet said, leaning back in her seat with her arms folded.

The three men looked at her. No one said anything.

She cocked an eyebrow. "Well?"

"Whether he's right or wrong, or what the profile is or is not, is not your concern," Agent Rowan said.

"The hell it's not!" Donovan cried. Everyone stared at him in surprise. Till now he hadn't said a word, or looked like he would say a word. He had just sat quietly and placidly with his head down. But now he glared at the men, his eyes gleaming with tears. "It's my damn sister that's missing."

The men looked at each other, and some tacit agreement seemed to pass between them. Their hard expressions softened, and they pulled out chairs and sat down across from the teens. Calvin got the impression they had decided to skip ahead in the program.

"Listen," Krezchek said, looking first at Donovan, then at the rest of them, "I know you want to tear up the planet in search of Emily. And I sympathize. I really do. I have to admit, I don't know what it's like to go through what you're going through. But these things have to be done a certain way. There are laws and rules and procedures that are there for a reason. And, no, we haven't found her yet. And despite everyone's best efforts, sometimes people don't get found. Or they don't get found alive. And that's awful and it's tragic, but that's just what happens sometimes. But don't think for a second that we're not trying. We're doing everything we can within the limits of the law."

Cynthia tensed up, expecting Violet to interject some snarky comment about the law's limits being the problem. But Violet said nothing. Cynthia glanced over and saw that Violet was sitting still and at attention, her face calm. Then Cynthia noticed that Violet was holding Donovan's hand under the table, and her attitude toward the girl softened. A little.

"I understand your wanting to get out there to help," Chief Krezchek went on, "and I certainly can't fault you for that. But breaking into people's houses, damaging property, scaring people, starting a regular little crimewave—and don't try to tell me it wasn't you guys who broke into Mr. Walsh's house, too—"

Calvin opened his mouth to protest that the Walsh break-in had been purely Donovan and Violet's doing, but then he shut it. He wasn't going to throw them to the lions. They all had to stick together. Besides, parsing out each individual portion of blame wasn't going to make much of a difference at this point anyway.

"Stuff like that just isn't productive," Krezchek said. "It complicates everything. I mean, how are we supposed to look for Emily when we're busy looking for masked burglars, too? To be blunt, all you've really done is make things worse."

The quartet hung their heads. The room was silent for a minute.

"Now, we're not gonna officially charge you," Krezchek said. "Your parents"—he nodded at Cynthia and Donovan—"they're going through enough as it is without you two winding up in juvie. And trust me, we've got more than enough on all of you guys to put you in orange jumpsuits for a very long time. But instead, you're going to apologize to Mr. Grey, and you're gonna pay to fix the damage to his window."

"What?" Cynthia's voice was shrill with outrage.

"Is there a problem?" Agent Rowan said.

She wanted to reply that, yeah, there was one hell of a problem: There was no chance in hell she was going to apologize to Roger Grey, and if she saw him on fire she'd hide the nearest fire extinguisher. But saying any of those things wouldn't be terribly productive.

"It's just, he's involved somehow," she said. "I know it."

"What makes you so sure?"

"Because everything points to him."

"Like what?"

"For one thing, he works at the bank, which is right near the park, and he spends some of his free time in the park, so he has to have seen Emily there. He was definitely in the park at the time she met her abductor. Plus he was on vacation last week and this week, which seems a little too perfectly coincidental, you know?"

"Is that all?" Agent Rowan said. He sounded somehow both amused and disappointed.

"My dad said he was acting funny right before his vacation," Calvin said.

Agent Rowan cocked an eyebrow. "Funny how?"

"Distracted. Spacey."

"That doesn't mean much," Agent Schmidt said.

"Well, I know for a fact it was him," Violet said.

"How?"

She shrugged. "Just by talking to him. I can tell these things."

"That's a lovely talent," Agent Rowan said dryly. "We should sign you up for the Bureau."

She snorted. "Forget it. I ain't workin' for the pig system."

Agent Schmidt looked at his partner with feigned amazement.

"Golly, I didn't realize I was part of the pig system."

"That must be why I like truffles so much," Agent Rowan said.

"Hey, make fun of me all you want," Violet said. "But I'm right about Grey. You'll see."

Agent Rowan's good humor faded, and he eyed Violet in silence for a moment. Then he swept his gaze over the whole group.

"Do any of you have any actual hard evidence to support your suspicions about Mr. Grey?" he asked.

No one spoke. Calvin and Cynthia glanced at each other, both of them realizing the same thing at the same time: They *didn't* have any solid proof. Even the circumstantial evidence, which had seemed so convincing when they set out from Mr. May's house, now felt weak in the face of cold law-enforcement logic. Was Grey innocent after all? And what about Mr. May? Was he really not the ace investigator he had led them to believe?

Then a thought struck Calvin.

"Did he call you guys?" he asked.

"Who?" Chief Krezchek said.

"Roger Grey. Did he call you?"

"Yeah. He called to report intruders in his house."

Cynthia stiffened, seeing where Calvin was going with this. "But we couldn't have been in his house at that point," she said. "He must have called you before we even approached the house! Because Violet went to the front door before any of the rest of us did anything, and he didn't make any phone calls after that."

"Well, he probably just saw you lurking about and, you know…" Agent Schmidt shrugged. He had sounded sure of what he was saying when he started to say it, but at the end the words trailed off uncertainly.

"He knew what we were going to do?" Calvin said.

Agent Rowan gave a derisive laugh. "When you see folks in black ski masks lurking in the bushes next to your house, it's not hard to divine their intent. Besides, I don't recall the precise phrasing of the phone call. He probably just said there were suspicious characters lurking about, or something like that. I think you're making too big a deal out of this."

"Did you search his house?" Cynthia asked.

"Why would we? He hasn't given us cause to. He's not the guilty party here, don't forget. You are."

"Besides," Agent Schmidt said, "didn't you guys already search it pretty thoroughly?"

"Not everything," Cynthia said. "We didn't really check his garage. And I didn't get a chance to finish looking through his basement." She wanted to mention her feeling that there was something important about the chest freezer she had seen, that it meant something. But she still wasn't sure what, so she held her tongue.

"And he might own property somewhere else, too," Donovan said. "I mean, he might have a cabin or—"

Chief Krezchek shook his head. "Just drop it, kids, okay? We're letting you go. Mr. Grey has been kind enough not to press charges—he understands how freaked out you all are about Emily going missing—but like I said, you'll still have to pay for his new window and give him your personal apologies. In fact, he's waiting in the lobby for those apologies right now."

"Oh, fuck you!" Violet said.

Chief Krezchek's cheeks went bright red. He scowled at Violet.

"Unless you want to spend the next week in the city jail," he said. "Do you?"

Violet regarded him with narrow eyes. It seemed like she was about to say yes, but then Donovan gave her hand a small squeeze under the table. She glanced at him, then rolled her eyes and looked away at a framed photo of the May police force from 1985.

"Fine," she said. "We can make with the kissy-face shit."

"Good." Krezchek settled back in his chair and hooked his thumbs into his belt. "I'd say we're about done here, then. We've notified your parents to come pick you up. They're waiting for you outside."

A collective groan rose up.

"Before you go," Agent Rowan said, "is there anything else any of you guys have to say? Any questions?"

Heads shook. Shoulders rose in preoccupied shrugs. Everyone was too busy fretting over their parents' impending outrage to think of much else.

But as the three men started to rise from their seats, Calvin remembered something.

"Yeah," he said. "I have a question, actually."

The men glanced at each other in surprise, then sat back down.

"What is it?" Chief Krezchek said.

"Did you ever figure out how the clearing got burned?"

The men glanced at each other again.

"We can't speak about the details of an ongoing investigation," Agent Schmidt said.

Calvin nodded. He didn't need them to speak. He could tell from their reaction the answer was no.

2

Five minutes later the four teens stood before Roger Grey, who was regarding them with a small, smug smile.

"I'm sorry," Calvin told him, hating the words, hating

the man.

Roger's smiled widened and he gave a crisp nod. He turned to Cynthia, the next in line, eyebrows raised expectantly. He was clearly enjoying their humiliation.

"I'm sorry," Cynthia said tersely, her narrow eyes fixed on Grey's in hopes of conveying the message: *I know you're behind this, and you won't get away with it.*

If he got the message, he didn't seem to care. He just nodded again like a king receiving tribute. He turned next to Donovan.

"I'm sorry," Donovan mumbled, the words barely audible.

Grey nodded again. He turned last to Violet.

Violet grinned at him, her teeth white and gleaming, her eyes glinting evilly.

"I am so, so sorry," she said. Despite the words, it didn't sound anything even remotely like an apology. Instead the message conveyed by her tone and expression was, "I am going to ass-rape you with a rusty chainsaw and cackle while you scream."

Grey's smile flickered. He glanced at Chief Krezchek as if about to protest this violation of protocol, but then apparently thought the better of it. He swept his eyes over the foursome.

"I accept your apologies," he said. "And I hope we have put any misunderstandings behind us."

"All right, then," Krezchek said. "Let's return you kids to your parents." He hustled them toward the door. He was clearly in a hurry to finish this up. In his view, the police had more important things to deal with.

3

"I don't believe this," Mark Beckerman said as he pulled out of the May Civic Administration Building's parking lot. "This is…" He shook his head and heaved an angry sigh, as if his outrage with his son were too great for words.

In the passenger seat Calvin's mom Mary Beckerman glanced at her husband, then turned and looked at Calvin, who sat meek and quiet in the back seat.

"You were just trying to help that little girl, right?" she asked.

Calvin nodded. "Yeah. She's my…my friend's sister. We were just—"

"You were breaking the law, is what you were doing!" Mark growled. His knuckles were white on the steering wheel. The back of his neck was bright pink. "You were humiliating me in front of the whole damn community. A community I have to deal with on a daily basis. But you didn't give a thought to that, did you?"

"Mark—" Mary began.

"Don't!" He swatted away the consoling hand she had stretched out toward him. "Just don't. There is nothing you can say that will make this acceptable." Calvin watched his father's head shake atop its thick pink neck.

The houses rolled by outside in silence. Most of the houses were dark. Calvin peered at the clock on the dashboard. It was nearly eleven p.m.

Calvin thought that the dressing down was pretty much done, but after they pulled into the driveway, his dad turned off the engine, then twisted around in his seat to look at Calvin, the imitation leather upholstery creaking loudly in the closed and freshly silenced car. Mark didn't look angry anymore. He didn't look anything. His face was blank, as if he had quashed any feelings he had for his son.

"You're grounded for the next month," he said.

"What? But—"

"Mark—" Mary began.

"No debate," Mark said. He opened the driver's side door. Cool night air spilled in, diluting the warm, tense atmosphere that had built up in the car during the drive home. He looked back at Calvin. "Now go to your room and don't come out till it's time for school tomorrow."

4

Calvin waited until his parents went to bed, then called Mr. May.

Mr. May answered midway through the first ring.

"Yes?" he said. "What happened? Is everyone all right?" His voice was tight with worry. Calvin wondered if this kind of excitement was healthy for a guy his age.

Calvin told him everything that had happened at Grey's and at the police station.

"I'm sorry," he said in conclusion.

"For what?" Mr. May sounded baffled.

"For...I mean, we kinda messed this up, didn't we?"

To Calvin's surprise, Mr. May laughed. "Hardly. You successfully searched most of his house and got away with having only to give an unfelt apology and pay for a window. Which all seems quite onerous, I'm sure, but trust me, it's much better than spending time in jail. I know. I've been there."

"You've been in jail?"

"In seven different countries, actually. When you're in-

265

vestigating things that lie beyond society's accepted bound-aries, you find that you have to cross some of those boundaries yourself from time to time."

"Wow." Calvin smiled, buoyed up by the sense of ac-ceptance and confirmation he was receiving from Mr. May. Calvin felt that he had done right and well and that every-thing was going to be okay. Which was exactly the opposite of what his dad had made him feel. Calvin found himself wishing that Mr. May had been his father instead of bland, button-down Mark Beckerman.

"Well, we still have recourses," Mr. May said.

"We do?"

"Certainly. I have a few more ideas about things we can do. But…"

"But what?"

"Will you and Cynthia be free to visit tomorrow after-noon? And I suppose we should consider her brother and his, um, interesting little friend to be part of the team at this point."

Calvin grinned at the idea of being part of a team. It was like something out of a comic book or a TV show, only for real. Then his grin faded as he remembered other, less pleasant aspects of reality.

"I dunno," he said. "I'm technically grounded. Cynthia probably is, too. I might be able to visit, though. After all, my dad was the one who grounded me, but he doesn't get home from work till close to six, and I think my mom'll cover for me. I'll probably be okay as long as I'm back be-fore my dad gets home from work."

"Good."

"What exactly would we do, though? Do you still think it's Roger Grey, or should we investigate someone else now?"

"I am more certain than ever that Roger Grey is the culprit. As you said, he seemed to know the four of you were there before you made your appearance."

"Well, it's possible he spotted us in the bushes or something..."

"But why play along with Violet then? And why go back into the house if he knew there were mysterious masked intruders inside? He didn't act as if he were worried about his safety. He didn't act as if he saw you as any kind of a threat at all. He acted as if he were trying to entrap you."

"Holy crap! That's exactly right." Calvin wished he had thought to frame the situation in those terms to Chief Krezchek and the FBI guys.

"So, no," Mr. May said. "We're not done with Roger Grey just yet..."

5

When Roger unlocked his front door and stepped into his house, his nose wrinkled. He could still smell strangers, unfamiliar bodies, the scent of leather cop belts. He hated it. It was a violation of his space, his selfhood.

He wasn't entirely surprised to see Emily Faux sitting in her usual spot on the couch.

"Now do you see?" she said. "Now do you believe me? If I had wanted to hurt you, I wouldn't have warned you about those children. I wouldn't have helped you at all. Yet I did. And my help was flawless. My advice was correct in every respect. Everything occurred exactly as I said it would."

"I guess," he muttered. Much as he hated to admit it,

she was right. All throughout the incident Roger had dreaded that something would go wrong, that Emily's advice and assurances would prove incorrect either by mistake or on purpose, that one of the kids would find the body or one of the cops would decide to search the house. But everything had gone perfectly. The chest freezer had not been opened. The cops hadn't even gone downstairs. They had been more interested in busting the kids than in looking around.

Roger's eyes narrowed. "Then again, maybe you're only helping me just long enough to reanimate Emily. Maybe you'll find a way to dispose of me once you're done with me. Maybe..."

He trailed off with a frown. He was talking about performing reality-altering magic as if it could be true. The trouble was, by this point he was more than half-convinced it *was* true.

"My word has been reliable so far," Emily Faux said. "You have no evidence to believe it will ever be otherwise. As I told you before, my task is only to correct an error. That's all. You're being needlessly paranoid." She smiled reassuringly. It looked like a real smile.

But then, she looked like the real Emily.

"Whatever you decide, you must do it soon," she told him. "Think hard. Think well. The next time you see me, you must give me your answer."

Roger opened his mouth to ask how long he had. But by then she had already vanished.

PART FOUR

The Other Side
of the Door

Chapter 25

See Emily Play (IV)

1

"No, I don't think I'll be able to meet up today," Cynthia told Calvin on the phone the next day. He had called her during his lunch period at school to see if she could make it to Mr. May's proposed meeting. She could hear the usual lunchroom din in the background. She was surprised to find herself missing school. She wondered how soon it would be before she and Donovan went back, before normal life resumed. If it ever did. "I'm kind of under house arrest for the foreseeable future."

"You can't get out at all?" He sounded heartbroken. She winced to hear it.

"I'd like to," she said. "But it's just not possible. My parents are watching Donovan and me like hawks. Besides…I don't know, maybe this situation *should* be left to the police."

"Are you serious?" His voice was high, almost outraged. "How can you say that after everything we've done, everything we've learned."

"I said *maybe*. I don't know."

"But she's your sister."

"No shit, jackass!"

"Sorry. I didn't mean…um…you know…"

"I know," she said in a soft, conciliatory tone. "It's just,

I want to do what's best for her, but I'm not quite sure what the best thing is anymore. After what happened last night, I can't help wondering if maybe the cops were right: Maybe we're just making things worse."

"Yeah, but don't forget: If Mr. May's right, then there's a lot more going on here than just a child abduction. There's a whole history. The cops aren't equipped to deal with that. Besides, at the moment they all seem to think Grey's an upstanding citizen who can do no wrong."

"I know, I know. I just—"

The school bell rang.

"I gotta go," Calvin said. "I guess…well, I guess I won't see you later, then." The heartbroken tone was back. God, he had no ability to hide it, did he?

She decided it would be best to end the conversation on a light, humorous note.

"As much as I might want to go," she said, "I don't think I'll be able to evade the guard dogs and the land mines my parents have set up around the house."

She was relieved to hear him laugh.

"All right," he said. "I'll talk to you later."

"Right. Bye."

After hanging up, she sat there on her bed a minute, lost in thought, then got up and headed for the door. She hadn't had a chance to talk with Donovan about the Roger Grey debacle last night. Maybe discussing it, and the hunt for Emily in general, might help her sort out her feelings.

She opened her door, stepped out onto the balcony, and then stopped, staring at Donovan's closed door across the way.

He was playing music, some death metal band she didn't recognize. Crap. He eschewed his headphones for his iPod dock only when he was in a really bad mood. Or when he had Violet in there and he was trying to hide the sound of her voice. It was too early in the day for Violet to be visiting (or to be conscious, for that matter), so he was probably only cranky or depressed. Either way, he wasn't going to be very talkative.

Her eyes slid to the door to the left of Donovan's. Emily's door. Taped to it was a sign with a skull and cross-bones and the words "Keep Out" in big red letters. Emily had made the sign herself.

Impelled by an urge she didn't understand, Cynthia circled the balcony to Emily's door and stood there gazing at the sign. She could feel the bass from Donovan's music thumping along the floorboards and up through her feet. She heard the TV chattering away in the living room downstairs. The cutlery drawer rattled open in the kitchen.

Cynthia grasped the doorknob, then looked at the sign again. Keep Out. She felt a twinge of guilt about going in. She had gone in there with everyone else when Aunt Wendy was here the other day, but that was different. That intrusion had had a point. Cynthia was here for no reason she could understand. It was pointless. Yet it was also somehow psychologically necessary. She didn't know why, though.

"Sorry," she muttered at the sign, then opened the door and stepped inside.

The music was louder in here. Donovan kept his iPod dock right up against the wall that separated his room from Emily's. That was one of the few causes of discord between Emily and Donovan. Cynthia couldn't begin to count the times she had heard Emily pounding on the wall with one fist and shouting, "Turn it down!"

Cynthia shut the door behind her, then stood in the middle of the room a moment, looking around at Emily's things. Her gaze finally settled on Emily's stuffed elephant, which lay on the floor next to the bed. Cynthia picked up the elephant and sat down on the edge of the bed with the elephant in her lap.

This had been one of Emily's favorite animals. She had named it Otto and given it a fanciful history, making it the leader of the animal army in that weird Zoo Wars game she was obsessed with a couple of years ago.

But Cynthia remembered it better from another context, one much more recent…

2

One day in mid-September Emily had come home from school in a rotten mood. For the rest of the afternoon she shut herself in her room, an odd thing for her to do on such a pleasant, sunny day. When she came down for dinner at six, she was quiet, almost surly, responding to questions with terse monosyllables, her eyes rarely rising from her plate. She claimed nothing was wrong and said she was fine. No one believed a word of it. After dinner she vanished back into her room.

Concerned, Mom asked Cynthia to check on her.

"Why me?" Cynthia asked.

"It might be something she doesn't want to discuss with, you know, parents. Besides, you're good at that kind of thing."

"What kind of thing?"

"Helping people feel better."

Cynthia was flabbergasted. "I am?"

"Oh, don't be silly. Just go on."

Cynthia went upstairs and knocked on Emily's door.

"What," Emily said, her voice small and muffled through the door.

"It's me. Can I come in?"

"Whatever."

Cynthia went in and shut the door behind her. Emily sat on her bed. She had lain one of her old Monster High dolls on the coverlet and was moving Otto the elephant back and forth over it, manipulating the elephant's gray legs in an imitation of walking. With each step Otto took, Emily blew a short, sharp raspberry: Pppp. Pppp.

Cynthia watched this in bafflement for a while. Otto went back. Otto went forth. Pppp. Pppp. Emily never once looked up at her sister.

"What are you doing?" Cynthia finally said.

"This is Miss Dryer," Emily said, nodding at the doll. "Miss Dryer is slowly being stomped to death by Otto the elephant. She is in horrible, horrible pain, but nobody cares, and nobody will help her, and they will just laugh and watch as she bleeds all over everything and gets turned into mashed potatoes."

Cynthia sat down on the bed next to Emily. Up close she could see that Emily's eyes were red and her cheeks were faintly shiny with tear tracks.

"Okay, what did Miss Dryer do?"

Otto stopped walking.

"I dunno…" Emily mumbled. She absently plucked at one of Otto's big floppy ears.

"Come on. You need to tell it to somebody; otherwise you're gonna end up going on a tri-state shooting spree or something. I can tell."

Emily let out a choked giggle. "It's nothing," she muttered. "It's just stupid stuff."

"Well, of course. If it has to do with Miss Dryer, it

must be stupid. I remember her. She was a dried-up old bag."

Emily's head shot up. Her eyes were bright with relief that she had found someone who understood.

"Yeah!" she exclaimed. Then her eyes narrowed into black slits. The points of her jaw bulged as she clenched her teeth. "She's a *cunt.*"

Cynthia was too shocked to respond. She had never seen Emily look so hateful. And she had never heard Emily use the C-word before. Cynthia fumbled about for something to say, but then she found she didn't have to: Emily's outburst had opened the gates, and the whole story came pouring out.

"Miss Dryer wanted us to write an essay about what we did this summer, right? So I started writing about our trip to New England, but it didn't turn out long enough. It had to be three pages, and all the stuff about the trip came out to only one and a half, so I had to think of something more. But I couldn't. I mean, I wanted to write about something cool, something worth reading, you know? What was I gonna do, write about going to the dentist? So I made up a story about going into Spirit Cave and finding a doorway in the back and going down underground and having adventures with fairies and trolls and visiting a city made of crystal and stuff like that. I mean, I know it didn't really happen, but it was better than writing about getting my teeth scraped. So I turned it in yesterday, and then today, when we were going to recess, Miss Dryer told me to stay behind. I didn't know what for, but then she pulled out my paper."

Emily dropped her voice to a peevish, geriatric rasp in uncanny imitation of Miss Dryer. "'What is this?' she said. And I told her, 'It's my paper.' And she was like, 'It's nonsense. It's garbage. This is not an acceptable paper. You did not do this over the summer.' And then…"

Emily paused to take a deep breath.

"Then she ripped it up right in my face, ripped it in half and threw it in the trash. And I started crying. I couldn't help it. But she didn't care. She just said, 'I want you to write it again, only this time I want you to write it without monsters and fairies and other infantile nonsense. I want a real paper, not this imaginary hogwash. Ten-year-old girls are old enough to know the difference between reality and fantasy.' So I said, 'I know the difference. I just wanted it to be fun and interesting.' And she said, 'I don't want it to be fun and interesting. I want it to be true.' So then I told her I really did see fairies in the woods once when I was little. I told you about that, right?"

"Yeah."

"Yeah, so I told her the story, but she just huffed like an angry cat and said, 'No. You did not see such things, because fairies do not exist. What you think you saw was only the product of a childish, undeveloped mind. Fairies do not exist. Trolls do not exist. Dragons do not exist. Therefore you did not see them. A girl your age should know better. I want a real paper about real things on my desk tomorrow morning.' And then she sent me out onto the playground."

Emily hugged Otto to her chest and mumbled, "Stupid old bitch. I hope she drops dead."

"I wouldn't take it too much to heart," Cynthia said. "Miss Dryer's been pulling this stuff for years. Everybody hates her guts. And when she dies a bitter, lonely old biddy, she'll have no one to blame but herself."

"Yeah…" Emily glanced at Cynthia, her lower lip pinched between her teeth, then said, "So, uh…do you believe it?"

"Do I believe what?"

"Fairies and stuff. Do you believe in them?"

Shit. How was she supposed to answer that?

Cynthia thought it over carefully, weighing every word, then said, "I don't know. Honestly, my gut instinct is to say no. But that's probably just because I've never seen one. I mean, I've never seen Antarctica or an electron either, but that doesn't mean they don't exist. So..." She shrugged. "I don't know."

Emily nodded. The answer seemed to satisfy her. Then her eyes narrowed again.

"Yeah," she said. "Even if they're not real, I don't care."

"What do you mean?"

"I mean, like, why are true things supposed to be so much better than not-true things? And how can you say something's not true if it *feels* true, you know? If it makes a person feel something, then it must be true somehow, right? A feeling's a true thing, isn't it? So how can something that isn't true produce a thing that is?"

"Um..."

"And besides, if something's really cool, who cares if it's true or not? Just because something's true doesn't mean it's any good." Emily frowned. "Of course, I still have to write my stupid paper anyway."

Emily looked more annoyed than depressed now. It was definitely a step in the right direction. Telling her story to a friendly ear had had a cathartic effect. Cynthia remained with her a while longer to help her take a few more steps out of Miss Dryer's drab shadow and to help her with her paper by showing her how to artfully pad out the tale of their New England trip to a full three pages...

3

Cynthia held up Otto in one had. He was threadbare and stained, one glossy black eye was coming loose, and his trunk was limp and floppy where some of the stuffing had fallen out through a gap in the stitching.

"I'm sorry," she said.

She was sorry because she had lied. Deep down, she hadn't really believed in fairies. Like Miss Dryer, she had regarded Emily's claimed sighting of them to be nothing more than childish wishful thinking. Now she knew that she had been wrong. She knew that there were more things in heaven and earth than she had ever thought possible. She knew that Emily could very well have seen fairies. Especially in *these* woods. Hell, Cynthia herself had seen that weird silvery light in the clearing the other day, though of course the light was only the merest glimmer of whatever Aunt Wendy had seen...

Cynthia shot to her feet with a gasp. Otto tumbled to the floor, forgotten.

Aunt Wendy. The visions.

Cynthia remembered Aunt Wendy standing right there in the middle of the room and having her seemingly meaningless vision of a yellow box. A big, shiny yellow box, maybe made of metal or plastic.

Just like the chest freezer in Roger Grey's basement.

That was the connection her mind had been trying to make ever since she saw the freezer last night.

Then the full implications of this connection hit her. Her breath caught in her chest. Her eyes filled with tears.

If Wendy's vision was true and meaningful, it meant

that Emily was probably dead. You don't put a live body in a freezer.

But maybe there was another explanation. Maybe Grey was keeping Emily somewhere else, and the freezer contained something else of importance, like...like...

She couldn't think of anything.

A teardrop slid down her cheek and dripped off her chin.

"God damn it," she said in a husky voice. She suddenly didn't want to believe in Wendy's visions. Maybe everyone was wrong about them.

Maybe. But she had to do what she had to do.

After knuckling her tears from her eyes and snuffling back the snot that was threatening to drip from her nose, she got out her phone and dialed the number for the police station. A woman with a high, chirpy voice answered. It wasn't Anna West's mom.

"May Police," the woman said. "How can I help you?"

"I need to talk to somebody involved in the Emily Crow case. I'm Cynthia Crow, her sister. I need somebody who's, like, in charge or something. Chief Krezchek or—"

"Special Agent Rowan of the FBI is right here. Would he—"

"That's fine."

"Hold, please."

There was a hollow clunk as the phone was handed off. The woman said a few words in a voice too low for Cynthia to make out.

Then Agent Rowan's calm, even voice said, "Hello, Ms. Crow. How can I help you?"

"Um, hi. I just remembered something. Or, well, I made a connection about something."

"Yes?"

"When I was in, um, Mr. Grey's basement"—she grimaced at calling him "Mr. Grey"; it afforded him a measure of respect she felt sure he didn't deserve—"I saw a chest freezer in one room. A big yellow one. It was the only thing down there I didn't get a chance to check out."

"Uh-huh."

"And, um…look, I don't know if you believe in psychics, but my aunt Wendy, who died just a couple of days ago"—crap, did mentioning her aunt's death make it sound like she was fishing for sympathy or something? Oh, well; there wasn't anything she could do about it now except forge ahead—"she had a vision in Emily's bedroom. She said she saw a big yellow box that seemed to be made out of either plastic or metal. She didn't know what it meant. Nobody did. But just now it dawned on me that it sounds exactly like that chest freezer."

There was silence on the other end of the line. It went on so long she started to wonder if he had hung up or the call had been lost.

But then he said, "I see. Well, thank you for letting us know, Ms. Crow."

She could tell from his tone that he didn't believe it. Oh, he believed that Aunt Wendy had said she saw a yellow box, but he didn't believe in the validity of psychic powers.

"She's had lots of visions before," Cynthia blurted out. "And they always turned out true."

"I understand," he said. "Thanks again. We appreciate it."

He hung up.

"Son of a bitch," she said. He hadn't believed her. He wasn't going to check out the chest freezer. "Son of a bitch!"

Her gaze fell on Otto the elephant, who stared up at

her from the floor with one beady black eye. She remembered Emily spitting out, "She's a *cunt.*" Her lips curled into a grim and bitter smile.

"Those authority figures always let you down, don't they?" Cynthia said to Otto and, through him, to Emily.

She sat back down on the bed and called Mr. May.

The phone rang and rang. Five times. Eight. Ten. Didn't he have voice mail?

She was about to hang up when he answered.

"Yes?" He sounded winded and a little testy.

"Um, Mr. May? It's me, Cynthia Crow."

"Oh! Is everything all right?" His testiness was gone, though he still sounded out of breath. "I wasn't expecting to hear from you right now."

"Um, actually, I…" She heard a man's voice in the background. She couldn't identify any words, but the deep, hearty tone was clearly that of Stephen Krezchek, the police chief's son and the town's most prominent lawyer.

Mr. May put a hand over the mouthpiece and said something to Krezchek. All Cynthia caught was "won't be too long."

Cynthia frowned. "You're not busy, are you? I don't want to interrupt anything."

"Is it important?" he asked.

"Maybe. I think so."

"Then it's worth the interruption. What is it?"

She told him about the chest freezer and its possible connection with Wendy's vision. She also told him about her call to Agent Rowan, and the FBI agent's tepid response. When she was done, he was as silent as Agent Rowan had been, but when he finally spoke, his response was very different.

"Good Lord," he muttered.

"I wish I'd gone ahead and opened that freezer," Cynthia said. Then she thought about it and added, "No, wait. Maybe I don't."

"Yes. The implications are rather...distressing, aren't they?" He heaved a shaky sigh. He sounded as affected by this as she was.

She forced herself to ask the question she didn't want to ask: "Wendy's visions—are you sure they were always accurate?"

"I would love to say she was often wrong. But I can't recall her ever having had a vision that proved untrue. That said, I do remember a few that were somewhat misleading, suggesting one thing when the truth proved more complex. That, I suppose, could give us hope." He didn't sound terribly hopeful, though.

Stephen Krezchek spoke up again. He sounded closer and louder now, and this time Cynthia caught the words "more appointments this afternoon."

"Yes, yes." Mr. May called out to him. Then, to Cynthia, he said, "I'm sorry, but I have to go. I have...business to take care of. Can you come by later?"

"I don't think so. Donovan and I are grounded until we're, like, twenty-four. Calvin said he'd probably be able to stop by your place after school, though."

"Well, perhaps when Calvin gets here I can call you, and you can participate via telephone. Maybe your brother, too."

"That would be awesome."

"Till then, take care."

"Yeah. You too."

She hung up. She thought she was going to return to her room, but instead she only sat there staring down at the stuffed elephant on the floor with a blank, dead expression.

Then out of the blue her face crumpled up, and she burst into tears. She wrapped her arms around her chest and laid her forehead on her knees and cried till her eyes and throat were raw and the knees of her jeans were damp. She let it all out, every last drop of anguish, grateful that Donovan's music was there to hide the sound of her sobs.

Chapter 26

End of the Line

1

Calvin sprinted through the woods toward Mr. May's house, trees and bushes blurring by, his sneaker soles pounding on the dirt, his backpack with its load of books and notebooks jouncing on his back. He had hurried straight here the moment school let out. He knew he had only a limited amount of time before he had to hurry home and pretend he had been in his bedroom all afternoon, and he meant to spend as much of that time at Mr. May's house as he could.

He wished he could have ditched school altogether and spent the whole day at Mr. May's. As it was, he barely heard a word any of his teachers or classmates had said. He had been too busy mulling over every aspect of the Emily situation, everything from Firebird's suicide to the incident at Roger Grey's last night. He had even spent most of seventh period study hall compiling a list of everyone who was known to have seen a vision in or near the woods, and then looking for any commonalities among them.

What did he need school for anyway? He knew now what he wanted to do with his life. He wanted to be an anomaly investigator like Mr. May.

He could see it all so clearly: Mr. May would be his mentor, his intellectual and spiritual father, instructing him in the ways of the anomaly hunter. And Cynthia would be there too, his fellow anomaly-hunter-in-training, at least until they were ready to strike out on their own and trot the globe together in search of mysteries and weirdness.

Calvin couldn't help grinning at the thought. He finally felt as if his existence had a purpose, a direction. He could see his future stretching out ahead of him, straight and true...

When he bounded out of the woods and onto the wide, rolling lawn of the May estate, his steps slowed to a walk and his grin faltered. The front door was ajar. He could see a dark swath of the house's interior through the crack.

Calvin looked all around as he crossed the lawn, but saw no one anywhere. His gaze returned to the open door. He was close enough now to make out the rectangular shape of one of the dorky bucolic paintings on the hallway wall. He kept expecting the door to swing wide and Mr. May to hobble out with his cane, but the sliver of hallway remained dark and silent and still.

He ascended the front steps, then paused on the porch, listening. He heard the woods stirring softly in the breeze. He heard birds chirping. He heard the in-and-out of his own breath, which was deep and ragged from his run. He heard nothing from inside the house.

"Mr. May?" he called. He was pleased at how strong and sure his voice was. He didn't sound worried at all.

There was no answer.

He began to fear that someone had broken in. Maybe Roger Grey. Maybe Grey had somehow figured out that Mr. May had been the organizer of last night's home invasion, and come here for revenge.

Then again, the door didn't look like it had been forced. The lock was undamaged. Maybe Mr. May simply hadn't shut it firmly enough.

Maybe.

Calvin crossed the porch, his steps resounding hollowly on the wooden boards. As he neared the open door, he smelled the usual odors of Mr. May's house—furniture polish, old leather—but he also caught a whiff of a sharp, unpleasant scent. Urine.

"Mr. May," he called again. And this time his voice was high and scared.

His heart was pounding as he pushed on the door. It opened six inches and then stopped, blocked by something inside. But it had opened far enough to reveal the silver handle of Mr. May's cane on the burgundy carpet, and next to it, one wrinkled and immobile hand.

"Mr. May!" This time his call was met by a barely audible moan from behind the door.

Calvin pushed against the door hard enough to overcome the resistance of whatever was blocking it. There was a heavy, complex rustle from inside, and the hand began to slide across the carpet, a sight that made Calvin wince. As soon as the door was wide enough for him to pass through, he stopped pushing then wriggled inside.

Mr. May lay on the floor, the top half of his cane beside him, its end splintered. The bottom half must be underneath him. His face was pale and waxy. His eyes rolled behind half-shut lids. His mouth hung open and a line of drool connected his lower lip to the carpet. The crotch of his trousers and the carpet beneath it were dark and wet. The stench of urine was overpowering. It didn't look like he had been attacked. There were no visible injuries, no blood, no signs of a struggle. This looked more like a heart attack, or something of that sort.

Calvin knelt beside Mr. May and gently shook his

shoulder.

"Mr. May! Can you hear me?"

The eyelids fluttered. Another, fainter moan rose up.

Calvin sprang to his feet, got out his phone—nearly dropping it twice in his panic—and called 911. After calmly listening to Calvin's frantic outpouring and asking a few questions, the dispatcher told him an ambulance would be there shortly and advised him not to try to move Mr. May.

While he had been talking to the dispatcher, Calvin had turned away from Mr. May out of the probably silly notion that Mr. May wouldn't want to overhear himself being talked about. Now Calvin heard Mr. May's weak, rasping voice behind him: "Emlee…"

Calvin looked back. Mr. May's eyes had opened fully and were fixed on him. His jaw opened and closed in short jerks as if he couldn't remember how to use it properly.

Calvin stuffed his phone back into his pocket and knelt down next to Mr. May again.

"The ambulance is on its way," Calvin said. He was trying to make his voice sound upbeat and reassuring, but it came out quavering and half-hysterical. "They didn't say exactly how long it would be, but—"

"Emlee…"

"What? Emily?"

"Vile…" Mr. May said.

"Vile? What's vile?"

Mr. May's tongue swabbed at his lips then sank back into his mouth.

"Pain…" he said.

"You're in pain?"

Mr. May grunted. He almost sounded angry.

"Paining," he said.

Calvin frowned, and was about to tell him he didn't

understand. But then he did understand.

"Painting? Is that what you're saying?"

Mr. May nodded. "Paining..." His eyes closed and his head lolled to one side as if he no longer had the strength to hold it upright. "Emlee..."

Calvin shook his head. "What about Emily?"

Mr. May didn't move, except for the faint rise and fall of his chest. Too faint, Calvin thought. Calvin didn't think Mr. May would say anything else for now, but then the thin lips twitched, drew back, painstakingly shaped words.

"Vile..." he said.

Back to that again. And it still made no sense.

"I don't know what you're trying to say," Calvin said.

"Vile...paining...binded..."

"What?"

"Safe. All...safe..."

"Mr. May, I—"

Through what must have been a supreme effort of will, Mr. May opened his eyes and lifted his head a couple of inches off the floor. He fixed his eyes on Calvin's.

"Bromst...her..." he said through teeth that were gritted against the pain this effort was costing him. "Took... care..." The effort was too much; the head dropped back to the carpet. He kept his eyes locked on Calvin's, though. "Took...care..."

Calvin shook his head, the motion dislodging one of the tears that had built up in his eyes. It shot down his cheek and dripped onto the carpet. He wanted to ask who the "her" was and what "bromst" meant, but he was afraid to speak lest he miss anything else Mr. May said.

The old man smiled.

"Yours...now..." The words were barely audible. "For...Emlee..."

Calvin shook his head again. "Mine? What's mine?"

Mr. May's eyes drifted slightly to the right of Calvin's face. At first Calvin thought that Mr. May was looking at something over his shoulder, but then he realized that the mouth and lips had stopped moving, and the slow, silent rise and fall of Mr. May's chest had ceased.

"Mr. May! Mr. May!" Calvin gave the old man's bony shoulder a shake. Mr. May's body moved in a horribly reactive way. The head wobbled like a ragdoll's. The unfocused eyes swung back and forth across the ceiling.

Calvin moved his hands to the center of Mr. May's chest, ready to perform CPR as he had seen done a thousand times on TV. But his hands froze atop the rumpled suit jacket. He didn't know exactly where to place them. He had horrible images of his pumping hands shattering the old man's fragile ribcage and driving splintered bit of ribs into the heart and lungs.

Calvin shot to his feet, his hands raised uselessly before him. He looked up and down the hallway as if he might find something there that would give him instructions.

"I don't know what to do!" he wailed, hating the whiny sound of his voice but unable to modulate it. "I don't know what to do!"

He heard sirens coming down Oaks Road. The sound calmed him a little. He looked down at Mr. May's body. The old man hadn't moved or changed one bit, but perhaps the paramedics could change that. It wasn't too late. He had heard of people being resuscitated many long minutes after the heart had stopped.

Tires squealed as the ambulance veered off Oaks Road and onto Mr. May's long driveway. The roar of the engine echoed up the corridor of trees.

Calvin wiped the tears off his face and peeked out the

doorway just in time to see the ambulance shoot from the woods and screech to a halt at the end of the driveway, leaving black tire marks on the concrete. Two paramedics leaped out and raced up to the house.

"Who needs help?" asked one of the paramedics.

"In here." Calvin showed them.

The next several minutes were a blur of activity as the paramedics tried to get Mr. May breathing again and bombarded Calvin with questions about what had happened and about Mr. May's medical history, virtually none of which Calvin could answer. Nothing the paramedics did produced the slightest response in the body on the floor.

A May cop arrived. It wasn't a cop Calvin had ever seen before. The cop asked Calvin a lot of questions, then took down his phone number and told him he could go. The paramedics had already left in the ambulance.

As Calvin trudged toward the driveway, he heard Cynthia's voice call out, "Calvin!"

He looked up and saw her hurrying toward him across the lawn, her red hair flying.

"What happened?" she asked when she reached him. "I heard the ambulance. I tried to get away as soon as I could, but—" Her words stopped dead when she looked over his shoulder and saw the sheet-shrouded form through the open doorway. "Oh, God."

"He died," Calvin said with a sob. "Right in front of me. I couldn't do anything. I just...just watched him. He just...he was..." He couldn't talk anymore. He hung his head. There were still bits of leaves caught in his shoelaces from his eager run through the woods earlier.

Cynthia put her arms around him and held him close. A moment later his own arms rose up and returned the embrace. They held each other in silence for a while. At the end of the driveway the cop watched them as he radioed for the coroner.

"What're we gonna do now?" Calvin said. He drew away from her and looked her in the face. "What's gonna happen? With Emily. With the Collection. With everything."

She shook her head.

"I don't know," she said. "I just don't know."

Chapter 27

The Golden Key

1

Calvin was horrified to see himself in the bathroom mirror as he brushed his teeth the next morning. His face was pale and puffy, and there were purple bags under his bloodshot eyes. Which wasn't surprising, considering he had barely slept a wink all night. He had lain there for hours in the silent darkness, replaying Mr. May's death over and over and wondering if there were something more he could have done. When sleep came, it was brief and fitful and full of nightmares about slack, dead faces gaping at him from shadowy corners, about imminent disasters he was helpless to stop, about wandering lost through dark empty rooms the size of warehouses.

He didn't know how he was going to make it through eight interminable hours of school. The only thing he had to look forward to was talking with Cynthia. Before they parted late yesterday afternoon he had promised to call her after school today so they could discuss their next move. Or whether they should even bother with a next move. Calvin wasn't sure anymore.

His dad's "Bad to the Bone" ringtone jangled in the kitchen. Calvin paused to listen, the toothbrush jutting from his mouth, a froth of blue-white foam on his lips. He heard the clunk of a coffee mug being set on the table, then the creak of a chair. Then his dad said, "Hello?" A pause. "Hey, Steve. What's up?"

Calvin rolled his eyes and resumed brushing his teeth. It was only dad's buddy and golf partner, Steve Krezchek, the stupid lawyer and son of the stupid police chief.

"What the hell are you talking about?" his dad said in a high, surprised voice.

Calvin stopped brushing again and leaned toward the half-closed bathroom door, listening.

"But...but..." It seemed that Mark Beckerman was actually at a loss for words. Calvin almost smiled. He wished he could hear what Krezchek was saying.

"Yes, I understand that," Mark said. "But why Calvin? It makes no sense."

Calvin stiffened and stared wide-eyed at his reflection. A blob of toothpaste foam slid down his lower lip and dangled off the bottom edge on a rope of bluish saliva, ready to drop onto his shirt. He saw it, watched the rope slowly elongate, but made no move to stop it. If he moved, made noise, he might miss what his dad said next. His suddenly felt as nervous and rubbery-stomached as he had before the break-in at Roger Grey's the other night.

Wait, was that what this was about? Was Grey suing them or something? The cops had told Calvin and the others that Grey wasn't going to press charges, but that didn't preclude a lawsuit, did it? Oh, God, that had to be it! Calvin could think of no other reason a lawyer would call to talk about him.

"It's insane!" Mark said. "It's...well, yeah. Of course. But it's still just...crazy."

The rope snapped. The toothpaste plopped onto his shirt.

After a long pause Mark said, "Yeah. We'll be there.

See you soon."

He hung up. Calvin quickly finished brushing his teeth, wiped the toothpaste off his shirt, and left the bathroom. His father was sitting in the living room, waiting for him.

"Calvin, come here," Mark said. He was trying to sound strong and fatherly, but his eyes were full of confusion. "We need to talk."

"But I have to get ready for school."

Mark shook his head. "Forget about school. I'll call them later, tell them you won't be in."

Calvin's heart was pumping madly now. Forget about school? He had never heard his dad say something like that before. This *was* serious.

"Sit down," Mark said, motioning at the sofa. Calvin sat. Mark opened his mouth to speak, shut it, frowned. He couldn't seem to figure out what to say.

"Who was that on the phone?" Calvin asked. He knew who it had been, of course, but he figured this would give his dad a place to start.

"Oh. That was Steve. Steve Krezchek. He—he had some important news." Mark grimaced and ran a palm over his blond crew cut. If Calvin hadn't been so full of anxiety, he would have enjoyed the sight of his father acting so uncharacteristically rattled. "Well, you know that Steve's an attorney, and, um…" Mark gave Calvin a sidelong look. "Did you know Robert May?"

"Uh, yeah."

"Did you know him very well?"

"I don't know. Sort of. I just met him a few days ago." Calvin shrugged. "Why? What's going on?"

"Well, he, um, apparently he passed away yesterday. It looks like he had a stroke."

"Oh. A stroke…" So that was what it had been.

"It turns out, um, he left some things to you. In his will. Well, actually it's a trust. He was one of Steve's clients."

"He left me something?" He wondered if it included anything from the Collection. His dreads and sorrows were washed away in a flood of excitement. Then he felt a stab of guilt for feeling excited about profiting from Mr. May's death. Great. Yet another twist of the emotional corkscrew. He noticed that his father had fallen silent and was looking confused again.

"What things?" Calvin asked.

Mark opened his mouth to reply, then looked at his watch. He stood up.

"Come on," he said. "We're supposed to meet Steve in ten minutes. He'll tell us all the details."

2

Ten minutes later Calvin and Mark sat in big leather chairs facing a well-polished, conspicuously uncluttered cherry-wood desk behind which, in an even bigger leather chair, sat Stephen Krezchek. He was a slim fortyish man with a long nose, a jutting chin, and a head of brown hair that was starting to turn the same shade of gray as his father's.

"As I told Mark," Krezchek said, "Mr. May named you as one of the beneficiaries in his trust. In fact, he just called me out to his house yesterday afternoon to amend the trust. I can't help but wonder if he somehow knew what was going to happen."

Calvin couldn't wait any longer. "What about the Collection?" he blurted out.

Krezchek pursed his lips and flipped through the pages

of a binder that lay open on the desktop before him. "I don't recall anything about a collection..."

Calvin was stunned. If Mr. May hadn't left the Collection to anyone, what would become of it? Would it be thrown out? Calvin pictured a swarm of burly, uncaring workmen hurling seven-headed rattlesnakes and coffins and giant footprint castings into a huge industrial dumpster on the May house lawn. But, no. That couldn't be right. Mr. May would have known better than to leave his life's work unaccounted for in the trust. He must have called it something else.

"No," Krezchek said, settling back in his chair. "No collection is mentioned. But whatever it is you're referring to is no doubt included in one of the properties."

"Properties? What do you mean?"

"Heh. Well, I'll spare you the legalese and just give it to you straight." He cleared his throat, glanced at Mark, and said, "You are named as the recipient of the property—the house and land—on Oaks Road, including, with a few exceptions, the contents of the house, as well as the sum of one million dollars."

There was a long silence that was finally broken when Calvin said, "What?" Krezchek chuckled. Mark shifted in his seat, a nervous smile stretched across his face.

"I should tell you up front," Krezchek said, "there are certain stipulations—"

"He left me everything?" Calvin said.

Krezchek laughed. "Oh, no! No no no. Mr. May possessed quite an impressive list of property and investments. The man knew how to make his money work for him, I'll say that much. I cannot, of course, give you any specifics, but what you're receiving is maybe only half of the full fortune."

"Hold on," Mark said. "You said earlier that he'd receive the contents of the house 'with a few exceptions.' What are these exceptions?"

"Oh, nothing substantial. Mostly single items earmarked for various individuals. Old friends, I guess. Let's see..." He flipped through the binder again. "An antique chest, a pair of cufflinks, an old May-Crow Brewing Company sign. Things like that."

"But no Collection, or, like, a batch of items or anything like that?" Calvin asked.

Krezchek shook his head. "No..." He frowned then peered at a page in the binder. "Well, there's a complete set of Dickens going to a lady in England. Is that what you mean?"

"No. It's...no. Nothing like that. It's okay."

Krezchek settled back in his chair again, eyes on Calvin. "Of course, there remain various formalities to go through. And as I was about to say earlier, the trust stipulates that you complete college before receiving the full inheritance. You do plan on continuing your education, right?"

"Uh...yeah."

"Couldn't this be contested?" Mark asked.

Krezchek shook his head. "As far as I know, there are no surviving relatives. And I'm sure Mr. May's friends will have no cause for complaint."

"Even so, if he was ill when he made the changes..."

"What do you mean?"

"I mean, when he added Calvin yesterday. If he had a stroke right afterward, couldn't people claim that, um..." He trailed off, noticing that Krezchek suddenly seemed reluctant to look him in the eye. Mark frowned. "Isn't that when he left all this to Calvin? You said he made some changes."

Krezchek flashed something halfway between a smile and a wince. "That, uh, that wasn't exactly what he changed. Calvin has been named as a beneficiary for several years now."

Mark looked at Calvin. "I thought you said you just met him a few days ago."

"I did!" Calvin said.

Nobody spoke for a moment.

"I…I don't understand," Calvin said.

Krezchek spread his hands apologetically. "I can't help you. He never explained it to me."

Mark glared at him. "But you knew about it all this time! I thought we were friends. I thought—"

"Damn in, Mark! It's confidential information. You know that."

Mark opened his mouth to deliver some no-doubt profane retort. Then he glanced at Calvin and muttered, "We'll talk about this later."

"Fine," Krezchek said.

Calvin barely paid attention to the rest of the meeting. His father and Krezchek babbled at great length about property appraisals and homeowner's insurance and value-oriented funds and a million other things, but he barely heard a word of it. He just sat there in a daze while conflicting emotions tore at his mind.

On the one hand, he felt as if he had just won the lottery. The house, the woods, the money, the Collection—it was a dream come true.

But the price he had paid to get it was too high. How could he be happy about any of this when it meant Mr. May was dead and gone? Calvin felt as if he had finally found his real father only to have him cruelly snatched away before they could really get to know each other.

And he had so many questions. Surely Mr. May had a lifetime of acquaintances, many of them older and with decades of experience dealing with anomalies. So why leave the Collection to a teenage boy? And maybe not even that: If Mr. May had added him to the trust several years ago, Calvin might not have even been a teenager yet. And how could Mr. May have known him at all back then? Had they met at some point when Calvin was too young to remember?

If Calvin was going to have a future as an anomaly investigator, this would have to be one of the anomalies he investigated. It was almost as if Mr. May had lain it in his path as a challenge.

It would be a few hours before Calvin learned that he wasn't the only one faced with such a challenge.

Chapter 28

Closed Doors

1

Anna's heart was racing as she dialed John's number. They had barely spoken since the Miss Dryer incident on Monday, but it wasn't for lack of trying on Anna's part. She had called him after school that day, but he was glum and unresponsive and told her he didn't feel like talking. Nothing she said would change his mind. She tried again after school yesterday, with the same disheartening results.

She felt sure that things would be different today. She felt sure that he would want to meet up once he learned the big news she had to tell him.

His phone rang once, twice, three times.

"Yeah?" John said. His voice was terse, remote, just like yesterday and the day before.

"Hey, John," she said, making her voice as bright and chipper as she could.

"Hey."

"Guess what?" she said.

"What?"

"You'll never believe it."

"What?"

"Old Mr. May, that guy next door to Emily? He just died the other day, and it turns out he left me a hundred thousand dollars in his will! Can you believe it?"

John was silent for a moment. Then he grunted.

"You too, huh?" he said.

"What, he left you money too?"

"Yeah. A hundred thousand, just like you. But I have to go to college and stuff before I can get most of it."

"Yeah, same here." She was smiling. This was the most John had said to her since Monday morning. She felt more certain than ever that he would want to get together. "That's so weird. Why do you think he did it?"

"I don't know."

"I mean, I don't think I ever even spoke to him. I only ever saw him a few times when I was out with Emily in the woods."

"Yeah. Me too."

"My dad said that maybe he did it because he felt bad about what happened to Emily and he wanted to do something for the people who cared about her."

"Yeah, maybe. I guess that makes sense."

"So have you thought about what you want to do with your money? When you get it, I mean?"

"Not really."

"I was thinking about using some of mine to set up some kind of fund for missing kids like Emily. I mean, even if it turns out she's okay, it's still a good thing to do. Don't you think?"

"Uh-huh."

"So, um, I was wondering, would you like to get together and talk and stuff? It sounds like we have a lot we could talk about."

He was silent for a few seconds. Then he said, "I'm not really in the mood."

"But, John—"

"Look, not right now, okay? I'll talk to you…later."

She opened her mouth to tell him that avoiding things wasn't going to help. But then she shut it. She knew it wouldn't make a difference.

"Okay," she said, struggling to keep her voice level. "Take care. Bye."

2

Anna's tears had stopped by the time her mom poked her head into Anna's bedroom. Karen West was wearing the khaki pants and white polo shirt that constituted her dispatcher's uniform.

"I'm off to work, honey," she said. Then she peered more closely at Anna's face. "Is everything okay?"

"Mom, what do you do if someone you care about is hurting really bad, but they're not talking about it and they're not letting anybody help?"

Karen walked over and squatted down next to where Anna sat on the bed.

"Is this about John?"

Anna merely nodded. She wasn't sure she trusted herself to speak. She might start crying again.

"Some people just react to things differently," Karen said. "They handle bad things differently. Some folks are more social about it, and others need to deal with things more privately."

"But what if they can't deal with it by themselves? What happens then?"

"Then I guess it would be time for someone else to help."

"How do you know when that time is?"

Karen glanced at the clock on Anna's wall.

"I hate to say it, but I really need to go to work. I'm off tomorrow, though. Why don't we talk about this then? Remind me, okay?"

"Okay."

"Don't worry." She smiled and placed one hand atop Anna's head. "We'll sort this out. You wait and see."

Anna smiled back. Inside, though, she couldn't shake the horrible feeling that she had already lost both of her best friends.

Chapter 29

House of Secrets

1

After dinner Calvin told his parents he was going to take a walk because he wanted some time alone to think about everything that had happened. Calvin's dad was cool with Calvin going out. Calvin's being grounded was ancient history now, his trespasses forgiven and forgotten. Mark Beckerman was even acting unwontedly chummy with his son, all bluster and bear hugs and manly advice. Calvin told himself he should be pleased with his father's about-face, but instead it only depressed him. His dad was acting like this only because Calvin was now richer than he was. If it hadn't been for that, Calvin would still be consigned to his room every night. He found himself wishing more than ever that Mr. May were still alive.

Technically he *did* take a walk, but instead of aimlessly roving about as he had implied to his parents, he headed straight to Mr. May's house. Or rather, *Calvin's* house. Or, well, not really that either. Stephen Krezchek had explained that it would be quite a while before Calvin could officially take possession of it.

Officially, perhaps. But unofficially, Calvin had other ideas.

When he reached the house, he tried the front door. As expected, someone—probably the cop from yesterday—

had locked it.

Calvin descended the porch and scanned the ground on either side of the front steps, hoping Mr. May hadn't been kidding when he mentioned keeping a spare key inside a fake rock.

In no time, Calvin found a rock that looked real but was actually made of plastic. When he picked it up he heard something small and hard shift inside it. A few seconds of fiddling with the pseudo-rock revealed that the top half popped up and swung open like the lid of a box. Inside was a house key.

Calvin felt a chill. When Mr. May had made the comment about the key, Calvin had thought it an odd and graceless thing to say, either a bad case of too much information, or too far to go for a lame joke. Now he couldn't help wondering if Mr. May had made the comment solely to tell Calvin there was a key available if he needed it. He remembered Steve Krezchek wondering aloud if Mr. May had known he was going to die, and he felt that chill again.

After confirming that the key did indeed unlock the front door, he got out his phone and called Cynthia. He hadn't had a chance to call her earlier, and he was eager to tell her about the inheritance.

He was shocked when she said she had already heard about it.

"How?" he asked.

"Stephen Krezchek met with my parents earlier. You're not the only one to get something from Mr. May. He left everybody in my family a hundred thousand dollars each. Even Emily."

"Holy crap."

"I know. Trouble is, none of us kids are allowed to touch anything more than the interest until we graduate from college."

"Yeah, I got stuck with a similar stipulation. So, um, are you free right now? I'm at the house right now. If you can get away, I was thinking we could explore the place and then maybe discuss our next move."

"Yeah, I think so. It'll take me a little time to get away, though."

"See you then."

He hung up, then went inside. He felt strange and criminal entering the house alone, but also excited. And guilty for feeling excited. The emotional corkscrew kept twisting.

The dark stain on the hallway carpet was still there, and the stench of urine was still strong. Mr. May's broken cane still lay there, too. It didn't look like anyone had done anything except remove Mr. May's body and then lock the door.

Calvin snatched up the two halves of the cane and set them on the coffee table in the parlor. Then he went in search of something to clean up the stain. He wasn't sure he should—though Mr. May's cause of death had already been labeled a stroke, there was still a chance there might be some kind of an investigation—but he couldn't leave the stain and the stench in the hallway like that. It was sickening. And it was insulting to Mr. May's memory.

He doubted there would be any cleaning products in the room across the hall from the parlor, but he figured he should check anyway. The room turned out to be a library. Every wall was lined with shelves, and every shelf was packed solid with books. Most of them were hardbacks, and few of them looked like they were less than fifty years old. Calvin wished he could linger and browse, but he needed to clean up that stain.

He moved on. There was a bathroom at the end of the hallway, right before the center circle, but a search of it turned up no cleaning products suitable for carpets. He went out and stood in the circle and looked down the west, north, and east wings in turn, wondering which of them to search first.

North, he decided.

Halfway down the north wing he came to two doors that faced each other across the hallway. The one on the right led to a large, ornate dining room dominated by a long mahogany table. A dozen matching high-backed chairs surrounded the table, and a crystal chandelier hung above it. Spaced around the walls were paintings, vases on pedestals, cabinets with leaded glass doors, and a mahogany sideboard that looked like it would give the guys on *Antiques Roadshow* week-long orgasms.

Calvin felt a little queasy at the thought that all of this was now his. His to take care of. His to insure and protect and clean (and how the hell were you supposed to clean a crystal chandelier anyway?). Part of him balked at the responsibility. It meant he had to grow up fast. It meant he could no longer maintain his safe adolescent sense of separation from the "real" world.

He decided he didn't want to think about it anymore, so he resumed his search.

Opposite the dining room was a kitchen four times the size of his mom and dad's. There was a squat black iron stove that looked at least as old as the house. Next to it sat a modern electric stove. There were shelves full of more herbs and spices than Calvin knew existed. Pots and pans hung from hooks. Cabinets and drawers lined the walls and the spaces beneath the counters. Various appliances had been installed wherever there was room.

A quick check of the shelves and cabinets revealed plates and cookware and cutlery and nonperishable food. No cleaning products.

Calvin moved on. Farther down the hallway was another pair of doors. The one on the left led to a pantry, most of whose shelves were bare and dusty, which wasn't surprising given that Mr. May had been the house's sole occupant for most of the last half-century.

Across the hall was the laundry room he and Cynthia had peeped into when they suspected Mr. May of Emily's disappearance and were looking for clues. Calvin smiled a little at the memory. It was hard to believe how much had changed in only five days.

There was a cabinet in the wall between the washing machine and a stainless steel sink, and when Calvin opened it he discovered a plethora of cleaning supplies. Bleach. Detergents. Sponges. Rags. Towels. Buckets. Brushes. Gloves.

And Formula 409 Carpet Cleaning Solution. Bingo.

He got out a bucket and filled it a third of the way with warm soapy water, then tossed a soft-bristled brush into the water. After putting on a pair of rubber gloves, he carried the bucket, the Formula 409, and a couple of towels back to the stain beside the front door. He sprayed the carpet with the carpet cleaner until it was saturated, then drew the brush from the bucket and scrubbed at the stain for a few minutes. When he was done, he laid the towels over the wet area and pressed them against the carpet to soak up the moisture.

Footsteps thumped on the porch stairs. Calvin looked up just in time to see a figure appear on the other side of the front door, a figure made ghostly and hazy through the thin white curtain that covered the window in the door's upper half. Despite the figure's ghostliness, he immediately recognized the slender physique. And the curtain couldn't fully block out the fiery color of the figure's hair.

Ugh. He had hoped to be able to clean up a little before she got here, to wash the stink of labor and Formula 409 off him. Oh, well. Maybe she would appreciate his manly sweat, or at least his dutifulness.

Cynthia knocked.

"Hold on," Calvin called out.

He moved the bucket out of the path of the door, then tugged off the gloves and tossed them into the bucket. After wiping his sweaty palms on his jeans, he opened the door.

His heart swelled at the sight of her. She was lit up by the light spilling out from the hallway, and her red hair and green eyes and smooth, pale skin stood out starkly against the dark wall of trees behind her and the darkening twilight sky above. He thought she had never looked half as beautiful as she did at that moment. He had never wanted to kiss her so badly. The feelings were intensified somehow by their new circumstances: This was his house now, and her visiting him, standing there on his threshold, held all kinds of subtle significances.

"Hey," he said. He stepped aside and waved her in. As she entered, she took in the bucket and the damp towels with a small, approving nod. He felt pleased.

"So how are you?" she said as he shut the door.

"I don't know. Overwhelmed, I guess."

She nodded. "I can relate."

He motioned at the parlor door. "Do you want to sit down or—"

"Actually, I was thinking you could show me around your new digs while we talk." She shook her head. "It's weird to think you're my neighbor now."

"I'm not, really. Not yet. Technically the house isn't mine yet. Or, well, it is, but it isn't."

"Is that one of the things that's conditional on your completing college?"

"Yeah. I'm not entirely clear on all the details, but I think it's like, the house is gonna be held for me by some kind of legal entity. But I'm still technically the owner, and I'm responsible for its day-to-day upkeep."

"Maybe so no one else would handle the Collection."

"Probably. In any case, it'll be a long time before I can actually move in here."

"Still." She looked down the hallway toward the center circle. "Have you gotten a chance to look around yet?"

He nodded at the bucket. "Only while I was looking for that stuff. There's a big, fancy dining room and a huge kitchen back there."

"Well, let's check the place out. We can talk about things as we go, maybe discuss our next move."

First he showed her the rooms he had already seen. The library proved a huge disappointment to Calvin. Instead of the obscure tomes on magic and anomalous phenomena he had been expecting, the selection consisted of the usual classics of literature and various nonfiction subjects. Then Calvin remembered that Mr. May had mentioned a library upstairs where he kept Turner May's journal. That must be where all the cool stuff was, the stuff Mr. May didn't want the casual visitor to see.

After Calvin showed Cynthia the kitchen and the dining room (she whistled in awe at both of them), they headed down the west wing. On the north side was a music room with periwinkle-colored wallpaper, a grand piano and a harp draped in white cloths, lots of plush chairs and couches, and a fireplace that looked big enough to fit a car inside. Across the hall was a game room that was decorated in dark reds and greens and contained a pool table, a large round table ringed with eight high-backed chairs, two smaller chess tables, and another huge fireplace.

As they headed for the east wing, Calvin said, "Did Stephen Krezchek say how long you guys have been named in Mr. May's will?"

"No, why?"

"Apparently I was added to it several years ago."

"But how? You only just met Mr. May last week!"

"Don't ask me. But he must have known me *somehow*. He wouldn't leave his life's work to a total stranger."

"Do you think maybe, um..." Cynthia gave him a hesitant look. "I mean, I don't want to cast aspersions or anything, but could Mr. May have been, you know, related to you? I don't know a lot about your family, but maybe he got all cozy with your grandma when they were young, and, you know..."

"I thought of that, too. And I guess it's theoretically possible. But honestly, I just don't see it. I look too much like my parents, and my parents look too much like *their* parents. Seriously, if you saw pictures of everyone, you'd know exactly what I mean."

"Maybe your great-grandma, then. Mr. May was old enough."

"I guess. But that still doesn't explain why he left stuff to you guys."

"Yeah, but with my family it makes more sense because we were neighbors, and our families had a tangled history together. But you—you're sort of..." She shrugged. "No offense, but you're kind of the odd man out here."

"Yeah. Story of my life."

They took only a quick look at the room on the north side of the east wing since they had already seen it through the window five days ago. The room across the hall was done in rich browns and tans and contained leather-upholstered chairs, Tiffany lamps, paintings of hunting scenes, another huge fireplace, and lots of dust.

"I don't even know what the hell some of these rooms *are,*" Calvin said. "I mean, what do you call this? A smoking room? A study?"

"It doesn't matter. It's yours now, so it can be whatever you want it to be. You can make it a study, or a meditation room, or you can tear it up and convert it into a bowling alley."

"A bowling alley?"

"Just an example. The point is, it's up to you. The possibilities are endless."

They left the whatever-it-was room and headed to the spiral staircase.

"Basement first?" Calvin asked.

"Sure."

They went down and found themselves in a small, square, concrete-floored room with a door in each wall. One door led to a wine cellar filled with cobweb-shrouded wine racks, all empty. A faint stink of vinegar lingered in the room. The next door led to a room that contained the furnace, the water heater, and a small stack of firewood.

Calvin grunted. "I don't think there's much down here."

The last two rooms proved him wrong. Both of them were crammed with a bewildering variety of items, apparently things that Mr. May hadn't known what to do with but wasn't comfortable getting rid of. There were stacks of yellowed tax forms dating back to the 1960s, bags full of books, boxes of china, old furniture, antique metal contraptions that neither Calvin nor Cynthia could identify, and various oddities, such as a stuffed and mounted crocodile and a barrel full of salt.

"You're gonna have a hell of a time sorting through all this stuff," Cynthia said.

"You could help."

"Oh, no. This is all yours. Your silver lining, your cloud."

As they explored the maze of items, Calvin noticed a box of small glass vials with black plastic screw tops.

"Vials!" he said. He grabbed the box and rummaged through it. His excitement died when he discovered that all the vials were empty, and there was nothing else in the box except a receipt from the North Coast Medical Supply Company dated 1974.

"Crap," he said.

"What are you looking for?" Cynthia asked.

"Remember the stuff I told you Mr. May was saying right before he died—'Emily' and 'painting' and 'vile' and all that? What if he wasn't saying 'vile' as in 'reprehensible'? What if he meant 'vial,' like one of these?"

"Calvin, are you sure you're not reading too much into all that? I mean, he might have just been delirious."

"Maybe. But remember, one of the last things he said to me was 'yours now.' I didn't know what that meant then. It sounded like more gibberish. But now it's obvious what he was trying to tell me. Which makes me wonder about everything else he said."

"Even so, if it was something important why didn't he tell you before?"

"Maybe it was something he just found out about. Or, I don't know, maybe he simply didn't want to tell me for some reason. I get the impression he played a lot of things really close to the vest, that he knew a lot more about stuff than he let on. In fact I keep wondering if he knew he was going to die."

"What do you mean?"

He told her about the odd comment that had enabled Calvin to find the key to the front door, and about Krezchek's revelation that Mr. May had made an amendment to his trust only a couple of hours before his death.

"That's right!" Cynthia said. "Krezchek was over here when I talked to Mr. May on the phone yesterday. I forgot about that." She shrugged. "But it might not mean anything. Maybe he *did* know he was about to die. Sometimes people can just tell. Physically."

"I suppose."

"What, you think it was more than that? You think he was, like, psychic or something?"

"It's a possibility. I mean, it seems like nearly everybody who lives around here winds up having visions of some kind sooner or later. Maybe he foresaw his own death or something."

She wrinkled her nose. "God, I hope not. That would be really disturbing."

They returned to the stairs and headed up to the second floor. They had already seen the two Collection rooms in the north wing and the one Collection room in the east wing. But there were two more rooms in the east wing that May hadn't shown them. One of these was another bathroom. The other was a darkroom that didn't look like it had been used in years.

They moved on to the south wing. Once again, two doors faced each other across the corridor. The one on the right led to the library that Calvin had been hoping to find.

It was larger than the one on the first floor and nearly half the books were devoted to magic, demonology, parapsychology, cryptozoology, UFOs, and other anomalous phenomena. There were also sections on nearly every other subject under the sun.

"Some of these are really old," Cynthia said. She pulled a book from the shelf. It was sealed in an acid-free plastic bag, which was the only thing keeping the book in the shape of a book. The tome's spine had crumbled into fragments, the pages were loose, and swaths of the leather binding were flaking off. The gilt lettering on the front cover was almost completely worn away, forcing Cynthia to tilt the cover to the light to read the impressions of the letters.

"*Aenigma Mundi,*" she read.

Calvin glanced up from the first edition copy of Charles Fort's *Book of the Damned* he was flipping through. "Never heard of it," he said.

He set the book back on the shelf and looked around the room. "You know, Turner May's journal is in here somewhere, too."

"But where?"

"I don't know. Is there a local history section?"

His gaze settled on an oil painting on the wall nearby. He had been so awed by the books that he hadn't really paid much attention to anything else in the room. But at the sight of the painting he forgot all about the books. He strode over to it.

The painting's photorealistic style told him even before he saw the signature that it was another Randolph Crow painting. It showed a beautiful young woman with long chestnut hair and green eyes sitting on the ground between the gnarled roots of a tree, her back against the thick dark trunk. She wore a filmy white toga that exposed one shoulder and breast. In the grass around her bare feet danced a group of fairies, each about five inches tall, with willowy limbs, long hair, and shimmering butterfly-like wings. The woman was smiling up at and extending one hand toward another fairy that was hovering over her head. All of the fairies were naked and female (presumably; they had smooth hairless skin where their genitals should be, and only the smallest of breasts), and each one's hair was a different color: black, red, blonde, white, brown, and various shades in between.

"Hey," he said. "Here's another painting by your, um…what was he again? Your great-uncle or something?"

"I think so, yeah." She headed over and joined him in front of the painting.

"This must be one of the two paintings of Anna May that Mr. May mentioned."

"It's well done," she said with a crisp nod. "He was very talented."

"Yeah. And Anna May was…" He was about to say "smokin' hot" but he doubted a comment like that would go over well with Cynthia. "She was beautiful."

"Uh-huh," she said.

He glanced at her out of the corner of his eye. She seemed uncomfortable, antsy. Her eyes wouldn't settle on one spot of the painting for long, and she kept shifting her weight from one foot to the other. It was as if she didn't want to have to look at the painting anymore but was afraid it would look strange or rude to turn away from it too quickly.

Calvin wondered what was wrong. Was she embarrassed by Anna May's bare breast? It didn't seem likely; Cynthia didn't strike him as the prudish sort. What, then?

Then a thought struck him. Maybe it was the fairies. Maybe they reminded her of Emily. That had to be it.

"Come on," he said. "We'd better hurry up and finish the tour so we can work out our next move."

She looked relieved and a little surprised.

"Yeah, that's—that sounds good. Let's go."

Across the hall was the master bedroom. It contained a wooden four-poster bed, a rocking chair, a dresser, an old wooden trunk shut with a padlock, a glass-doored cabinet full of books and sundry knickknacks, and another of the house's omnipresent fireplaces.

The second Anna May painting hung on the wall directly opposite the door. In this one she lay on her side on a grassy riverbank with one bare foot dangling in the water. Her face was turned to the viewer, but her eyes had a distant, unfocused look as if she saw only some pleasant inner dream. She wore a diaphanous white gown and apparently nothing else; her nipples, dark and round, were visible through the fabric, though her artfully arranged legs hid her genitals. Behind her, huge dark trees loomed like a sinister fairy-tale forest.

Calvin wished he could spend a while examining the painting, but he didn't want to linger here long. Not only did he want to finish up the tour of the house for Cynthia's (and Emily's) sake, but he felt uncomfortable being in Mr. May's bedroom. Though the old man was dead, Calvin couldn't help feeling that they were violating his privacy.

He took a quick look around and was about to head out the door when Cynthia said, "I wonder who this is."

"Huh?" He turned. She was examining a framed photograph on Mr. May's bedside table.

He went over for a better look. It was a black-and-white portrait of a pretty young woman with soft, full lips, wire-rimmed spectacles, and dark hair pulled back in a bun. Judging by the woman's appearance and the quality of the photo itself, Calvin guessed the picture dated from the 1930s.

"The love of his life, maybe?" Calvin said. He couldn't help glancing at Cynthia as he said it, wondering if she would catch any deeper, personal meaning in his words.

She didn't respond at all. She just hunched down to look at the photo more closely.

"It's so old," she said. "I mean, why is the picture so old? Why does he have only this one ancient picture of whoever it was? I wonder if something happened to her."

"I don't know," Calvin said. He stared at the photo and imagined Mr. May gazing at it sadly before climbing into bed alone every night. Maybe he even talked to it. To her. Calvin suddenly wanted to be in here less than ever. "Let's check out the west wing. That's all that's left at this point."

There were two rooms in the west wing. One was a spare bedroom that obviously hadn't been used in ages. Every surface was thick with dust.

The other room, however, was one of the most-used rooms in the house.

It was an office. A black walnut desk faced the door. Atop it a computer sat amid a jumble of papers, pens, folders, and sundry office supplies. A satellite map of the block of land that contained the woods and the May and Crow houses was tacked to a large bulletin board on the wall behind the desk. A black push-pin marked the clearing where Emily had been abducted. Along the other walls were half a dozen metal file cabinets, bookshelves laden with bulky reference books, a fax machine, and a framed poster for a 50s movie called *The Terrible Dr. Eris.* The poster showed a huge, shadowy grinning face and a giant pair of hands, their fingers hooked into claws, looming in the darkness above a square-jawed man and a busty blonde.

"Huh," Cynthia said, stepping forward to examine the computer. "I never really had Mr. May pegged as the computer-age sort. I kind of pictured him tapping away on an antique typewriter or something."

"I never had him pegged as a big movie lover, either." Calvin said. He peered at the credits at the bottom of the poster, wondering if Mr. May had been involved in its production in some way. But Calvin didn't see a single name he recognized. Not even any of the actors. Was the movie simply a favorite of Mr. May's, then? Calvin realized he would probably never know. The idea depressed him.

He joined Cynthia beside the desk and scanned the clutter atop it: a coffee ring–stained printout about Easter Island, a bent paperclip, a scratchpad covered with sloppily scribbled numbers, a spray of pencil shavings in front of the electric pencil sharpener. These tiny reminders of a life now gone only depressed him even more. He imagined Mr. May sitting here in the dead of night, the old man's face bathed in the glow of the computer monitor as he pursued the latest anomaly.

This was it, Calvin realized. The final form of Mr. May's time upon the Earth. It had stopped forever in this messy and unfinished state. Had Mr. May hoped for one last, old-age meeting with the girl in the photo in his bedroom? Had he wanted to see *The Terrible Dr. Eris* one more time? Were there anomaly files half-finished amid the heaps of papers on the desk? Well, now they would never be finished, at least as far as Mr. May was concerned. All undone things would stay undone forever, all unanswered questions would remain unanswered, all loose threads would dangle eternally.

His thoughts were too much for him. His chest tightened. Tears filled his eyes. A choked sob escaped his throat.

Cynthia, who had been inspecting a pewter kangaroo paperweight, looked up at him in surprise.

"Calvin, what's wrong?"

Embarrassed, he turned away from her and tried to wipe his tears away with the heels of his palms. She came around beside him and laid a consoling hand on his back.

"What is it?" she said.

"I don't know. It's just...all his stuff..." He shrugged. He must sound like such an idiot, blubbering away over a bunch of paperclips and coffee stains.

"It's okay," she said gently. "I understand." Her hand began to stroke his back.

He nodded. But he suddenly found himself unable to focus on anything except that hand moving slowly up and down his back. Only the thin fabric of his shirt separated his skin from hers. Her face was barely six inches away, close enough to reveal a faint spray of freckles on the bridge of her nose that he had never noticed before. Close enough that he could see his own reflection in her eyes. Close enough to kiss.

His thoughts whirled in confusion. Was this a bad time to make a move? He wasn't sure. Tragedy often brought people together, didn't it? It happened in the movies, at least. Besides, would she have gotten this close to him if she didn't at least feel comfortable around him? Would she spend all this time alone with him?

He thought again of the forever-unfinished state of Mr. May's life. Of that mysterious girl on his bedside table—a lost love, a never-begun love, whatever. Of loose ends and desires unfulfilled.

He had to try.

Cynthia seemed to sense some subtle shift in his body or his emotions. Her hand stopped stroking, and she gave a small, puzzled frown, the smooth skin between her eyebrows buckling into a trio of folds. God, she looked so cute when she frowned like that.

He looked from her eyes to her lips to her eyes again. Her frowned deepened, then smoothed out as her expression went blank.

His heart hammering, he drew in a breath and leaned forward, propelling his lips toward hers.

Her eyes went wide. She jerked backward and thrust her hands up, palms out.

"Calvin, don't."

"What? But…"

"Just…don't. Please."

"I…" His face burned. "I'm sorry. I—I just…" He shook his head. "I'm stupid, I know. This isn't the right time, what with your sister and everything…"

Her shoulders slumped. She looked at him with a mix of pity and…was that guilt?

"It's not that," she said. Then after a pause she added, "Or it's not *just* that." She opened her mouth to go on, but nothing came out. She shut it.

"What, then?" he said.

She continued staring at him a moment longer, then looked away at the file cabinets. She shoved her hands into the back pockets of her jeans, then pulled them out a moment later and folded her arms across her chest. She swallowed. The click from her throat was audible in the otherwise silent room.

She was scared of something, he realized with surprise. But what?

Calvin remembered her odd reaction to the painting of Anna May in the toga. Did Cynthia have some kind of problem with sex, or men? Had she been raped or something?

She shut her eyes, heaved a shaky breath as if preparing herself to do something she didn't want to do, then looked at him again.

"If I tell you something, you have to promise not to tell anyone. And I mean *anyone*. Okay?"

"Um, yeah. I promise." He felt nearly certain she was about to confess to having been sexually abused.

For a moment she only continued staring at him in silence with large, frightened eyes. Then she took another deep breath and blurted out, "I'm a lesbian. I like girls." She closed her eyes and shook her head. "That's redundant, isn't it? God, I sound like a fucking idiot."

Calvin didn't say anything. He couldn't think of anything to say. He just stared at her, his mouth slack, while in his mind all the beautiful romantic fantasies he had constructed over the last couple of months came crashing down in awful, lonely silence. It felt as if a giant fist were slowly squeezing his chest.

He sat down on the edge of the desk, his eyes on the floor. He sensed Cynthia looking at him. He turned his head away from her. He felt small and embarrassed and resentful. He knew he shouldn't feel that way, but he did. He couldn't help it.

"I'm sorry," she said. "I know I should've told you before. I mean, I could kind of tell that, y'know, that you liked me. But I just…I didn't know how to tell you. I've never told this to anyone before. I—I don't know how to do this."

A quaver in her voice made him look up at her. Her

eyes were glimmering with tears. Seeing her distress, all his bad feelings vanished in a rush of empathy.

"You don't need to apologize," he said softly. "It's okay. I understand. This must be… difficult for you."

She gave him a small, sad smile. "It's difficult for both of us, I guess."

"Yeah," he said, giving her a small, sad smile right back. He felt proud that he was handling this in such a calm and mature manner. Still, he knew that he would probably cry himself to sleep tonight.

He turned to gaze at the movie poster again. She sat down on the edge of the desk an arm's length away and likewise gazed at the poster. Neither of them spoke for a while.

She broke the silence first. "So, um…are we…" She cleared her throat. "Are we still friends?" Her voice was small and nervous.

He looked at her, surprised.

"Of course," he said. "You'll always be my friend. That'll never change."

She started to say something, but her emotions welled up and choked off her words, so she only nodded.

There was another, longer silence.

Then she looked at him with a smile. "Don't worry. A guy like you should have no trouble finding tons of eligible and interested women. I'm sure someday real soon you'll bag some supercool, smokin'-hot girl who's a million times more awesome than me."

"Yeah," he said. But he thought: *Not possible.*

A gust of wind rattled the windowpane behind the desk, making Calvin glance over his shoulder at the window. As he started to look away, his gaze fell on the map of the woods and the black pin Mr. May had inserted into the clearing.

"All right," he said with a sigh, then pushed himself off the desk. "Let's get back to finding Emily."

Chapter 30

Red on Yellow

1

"This is a wild goose chase, you know," Officer Ronald Carter said as he and Officer Bob Thompson pulled out of the May Civic Administration Building's parking lot in Patrol Car Five. Carter flipped down the sun visor above the passenger seat and examined himself in the mirror on its back. He turned his head left and right, trying to see his thin face from every angle. "This psychic stuff's a bunch of crap."

"I dunno," Thompson said. "I've heard stories about Wendy Crow."

Carter snorted. "Yeah, they're *stories*. That's the point."

Thompson shook his head, then watched as Carter licked the tips of his forefinger and middle finger and used them to swipe back a lock of his blond hair.

"What're you preening for anyway?" Thompson asked. "It's not like you're going on a date. We're just going to check out the freezer Cynthia Crow called about."

"It's not *preening*. It's about public relations. It's about the fact that we as officers of the law are the law's public face. We need to look our best."

"Dude, you think about this shit way too much."

"Well, at least someone's thinking."

"Fuck you." He glanced at Carter, who was examining

a tiny reddish spot on his chin. "You look beautiful. Mr. Grey is gonna be so impressed, he's gonna wanna give you a big wet kiss."

"Fuck you right back." Scowling, Carter flipped up the sun visor and settled back in his seat. He watched the suburban homes on Potts Road slide past. A few of them had their drapes open, and happy families could be seen basking in the glow of TV sets as they digested their dinners. "It's kind of late to be doing this, isn't it? I mean, it's already after seven."

Thompson shrugged. "I dunno. I guess Krezchek felt too much time had passed already. Besides, I think he really has a lot of faith in Wendy's abilities.

"So what are these amazing stories about Wendy Crow, anyway?"

"I dunno. Just…stuff. She just saw some stuff, and it all came true."

"'Some stuff'? You don't even know?"

"Not specifically, no. It's just…look, you didn't grow up here. Everybody knows about Wendy."

"Yeah, well, I'll believe it when I see it. I mean, what, she says, 'a yellow freezer' and this is supposed to be evidence?"

"It's not evidence necessarily. It's something we need to check out. And it wasn't 'a yellow freezer'; it was 'a yellow box.' I think."

"That's only more vague. It just proves my point. Psychics spew out a bunch of shit and then everybody acts all gosh-wow surprised when a few things amid all the spew turn out to kinda-sorta resemble something in reality. It's a lot of bunk."

"Yeah, well, Krezchek doesn't think so."

"But Agent Rowan does." Carter chuckled. "Man, you

could smell the love between them."

"Yeah." Thompson shook his head. "I thought Krez-chek was gonna have a stroke when he found out Cynthia Crow called yesterday and Rowan didn't even mention it till now. And, hell, I can't blame the Chief. A lead's a lead. We need to follow it up."

Carter rolled his eyes. "It's not a real lead. It's not based on anything solid. Rowan didn't want to waste re-sources—us, that is—on some pseudoscientific nonsense when we could be out there looking for Emily."

"We are."

Carter flung up his hands and gasped in exasperation. "I mean in a useful, realistic way."

Thompson smiled. He enjoyed riling up Carter. It was almost too easy, though.

"Here we are," he said, pulling into the driveway of a small white house and parking behind a gray Ford Focus. "452 Grace Road."

"Let's hurry this up so we can get back to some real work," Carter groused.

2

Roger was rinsing off his dinner dishes when he heard Emily say, "They're coming."

He spun around, splashing water all over the counter. Emily Faux stood in the middle of the kitchen, her eyes fixed on him.

He sucked in a sharp breath. She had said that when he saw her again he would have to give her his decision. But he still wasn't sure what to do.

"Is—is this it?" he said. "Is it time?"

"There's no time to talk. Two policemen are on their way here. If you want to make it through this okay, you must do exactly as I tell you."

Roger shut off the water and toweled his hands dry. Part of him resented the influence she had over him, and was appalled at how ready he was to jump through whatever hoops she told him to. But she had helped him time and time again, hadn't she? She had earned his trust.

But if that were true, why did he balk at killing the two kids?

He shook his head. This wasn't the time for questions or analysis. He had more urgent matters to deal with.

"What do I do?" he said.

"Get a knife. A big one. A sharp one."

He opened the cutlery drawer and pulled out a carving knife. It was the longest, sharpest knife he had.

"Is this good?" he asked.

"It's fine."

The doorbell rang.

Roger looked in the direction of the front door, then back at Emily. He felt that he should be nervous, but he wasn't. Not with Her here.

"Hide the knife," she told him. "Tuck it under the back of your shirt. Then let them in."

Roger lifted the back of his shirt and slid the blade down the back of his pants, flinching a little at the metal's cold touch. He headed to the door. Thanks to the knife, he had to walk stiff and upright lest the blade bite into his skin. The knife's handle was a hard column against his spine.

The doorbell rang again just as Roger reached the door. He opened it to find two cops on the front steps—a skinny one with blond hair and a plump one with brown hair and a mustache.

"Be pleasant," Emily said beside him, unseen and unheard by the cops. For the thousandth time Roger found himself wondering what she, or it, really was. "Do what they ask. Give them no cause for suspicion."

"Can I help you?" Roger asked with the sort of concerned smile he figured a normal citizen would adopt in a situation like this.

"I'm Officer Thompson," said the plump one. "This is Officer Carter. How are you this evening?"

"Um, pretty good. Is this about the other night, when those kids broke in?"

"Not exactly, sir." Officer Thompson nodded at the living room behind Roger. "May we come in?"

"Sure," Roger said. He opened the door and led them into the living room. "Would you like to sit down, or—"

"Actually, we don't plan to be here long. We were just hoping to take a quick look at something, and then we'll be on our way, if that's okay with you."

"Sure. What is it you need to see?" Roger felt sure he already knew the answer.

"We understand you have a yellow freezer in your basement," Officer Thompson said. "Mind if we take a look inside?"

Roger glanced at Emily. She nodded.

Roger's heart began to pound. What was she doing? Was she planning to betray him to the cops after all? But no: If she meant to do that, why would she have warned him? Why would she have told him to grab a knife?

"No problem," Roger said, somehow managing to keep his fears and doubts from his face and voice. "Follow me."

He led the cops to the basement stairs. He made sure to walk upright and with a slight bow to his back so the contours of the knife handle wouldn't be visible under his shirt.

Halfway down the stairs, Roger realized that Emily wasn't with them. Where had she gone? Had she abandoned him? His heart pounded harder than ever. He felt sweat collecting along the top of the knife handle and trickling down the length of the blade.

When Roger entered the workroom and saw Emily waiting for them next to the chest freezer, he breathed a silent sigh of relief.

"Tell them to take a look inside the freezer," she told Roger. "And stay behind them when they do."

"Well, there it is," Roger said, stopping about six feet from the freezer and waving a hand at it. He hoped neither of the cops noticed how sweaty his palm was. "Take a look if you want, but there's nothing in there except some frozen meat."

The two cops stepped up to the freezer, Thompson on the left, Carter on the right.

"Get out the knife," Emily said.

As Thompson lifted the lid of the freezer, Roger reached back and slid the knife from his waistband.

The cops looked into the freezer.

"Holy shit!" Carter began. "That's—that's—"

"Stab him here," Emily said, pointing at a spot on the back of Thompson's shirt. Right about where the heart was.

Not allowing himself time to think or hesitate, Roger did exactly as she said. He drove the knife in as hard as he could. It sank in so deep the edge of the handle thumped against the cop's back.

Thompson stiffened for a moment, then began to shudder as if he were being electrocuted. The freezer's lid dropped from his hand and banged shut. Carter whirled around, his hand zipping toward his gun.

"Push him into the other one," Emily ordered.

Holding the knife in place with one hand, Roger seized the back of Thompson's shirt with the other and heaved the cop's still-shuddering body toward his partner. Thompson's body drove Carter against the freezer hard enough to make it rock backward against the wall. Pinned between the body and the freezer, Carter tried to elbow the body away, but Roger kept pushing it forward. After one final violent spasm, Thompson went limp, his upper body slumping over his partner's as if trying to give him a hug. Carter grunted and strained against the dead weight.

"Pull out the knife," Emily said.

Roger did. Blood gouted out after it, splashing Roger's pants and shoes and the concrete floor.

"Let go of the body."

Roger did. With a roar, Carter shoved his partner's corpse off him. Thompson's body crashed to the floor, the skull striking the concrete with a noise like a bat hitting a homerun. Carter's hand fumbled for his gun.

"Go for his throat," Emily commanded.

At the same moment that Carter tore his pistol from his holster Roger swept the carving knife across the cop's throat.

A lipless mouth parted in the middle of Carter's throat, and blood geysered out in quick, rhythmic pulses.

Blinking at Roger, Carter started to raise the gun. The muzzle rose one inch, two. Roger leaped back, fearing for one horrible moment that Carter would manage to shoot him after all.

But then Carter's arm went limp and the gun slid from his slack fingers and clattered to the floor. Carter's eyes rolled up, showing white. His body sank and turned at the same time, spraying the whole basement with blood—the walls, the shelves, Roger, the freezer. Carter collapsed in a heap atop Thompson's legs.

Roger gaped at the carnage before him. He had killed two men in ten seconds.

"There's...there's blood on the ceiling," he muttered. Then his face turned the color of cottage cheese, and a hot frothy ball of vomit rose up his throat. He tried to swallow it back but couldn't. He barely had time to lean over before it came gushing out his mouth. The sounds of his retches and of the vomit splashing into the puddle of blood on the floor were loud in the otherwise silent basement. The tan puke and the red blood mingled together in sickening swirls.

When there was nothing left to puke, and when his throat stopped trying to puke anyway, he wiped the specks of vomit from his lips with the cuff of his sleeve, then straightened up and looked around for Emily. He avoided looking at the two messy corpses beside the freezer. He realized his hands wouldn't stop shaking.

Emily sat on the old wooden table, her legs folded Indian-style. She flashed him a perky smile.

"It's time to make the magic happen," she said. "We'd better hurry, though. There's a lot we need to do." She motioned at the dead cops. "First of all, get their guns..."

Chapter 31

Convergence

1

"So what's our next move, then?" Cynthia said. She pushed herself off the desk and joined Calvin in the center of the office.

"We need to get back into Roger Grey's house and check out that chest freezer," he said. "That should be priority number one."

She nodded. "Yeah. Especially if the cops aren't gonna bother."

"We should probably call your brother and Violet and see if they want to join in."

She groaned. "I don't know…"

"They helped last time. He's your brother, after all."

"It's not him I have a problem with. It's Violet."

Calvin shrugged. "I thought she was very helpful."

"Yeah, well, you don't know her like I do."

"You don't really know her that well either."

"I know enough." She sighed. "Of course, I also know that if we include Donovan we're gonna *have* to include Violet. If we try not to, she'll tag along anyway."

"Well, do you want to make it just the two of us, then?"

She opened her mouth, shut it, sighed again. "No, you're right. We should call them over. This involves them, too."

She got out her phone and dialed Donovan's number.

2

With Officer Thompson's cop hat perched atop his head, Roger pulled Patrol Car Five onto May Road.

"Anna West's house is on the west side of the library," said Emily Faux, who sat in the cop car's passenger seat. "Only a line of bushes separates the two."

"Right."

He pulled into the library's parking lot. The building was ablaze with light, and a dozen cars sat in the lot. Thankfully the corner of the lot nearest the West home was far from the building and shielded from the nearby street lamps by trees and bushes.

Roger parked facing the bushes and cut the engine. Through the foliage he could make out a pair of lit windows in the West house. He opened the car door and got out. The movement made the stink of blood rise up from the splotches on his pants and shoes. He hadn't bothered to change. He had wanted to, but Emily had impressed upon him the need for urgency. The hour was late, and the time for niceties was gone.

"Just follow my instructions and everything will turn out fine," Emily told him. She stood beside him on the pavement now. She hadn't actually gotten out of the car. She had merely vanished from the passenger seat and appeared next to him like a ghost in a movie. "Remember: Once the deed has been done, you'll have nothing more to worry about. Everything will have been reset. But until then, you must maintain as low a profile as possible."

He nodded, then took a look around. A few figures moved about inside the library. No one else was in sight.

He checked the cops' belts, which he had stripped of everything except the guns and the handcuffs and one of the flashlights and now wore across his waist like a gunslinger's gun belts. After ensuring that everything was good to go, he ducked into the bushes.

3

Anna threw down her pencil and sat back with a frustrated sigh, her white desk chair creaking. How could she concentrate on her spelling homework with Emily gone, with John slipping away, with a hundred thousand dollars burning a hole in her mind? Everything was changing too much, too fast. She felt lost.

She looked up at the photo of her and Emily and John that was thumb-tacked to the bulletin board above her desk. It had been taken by Anna's mom during the ice cream social last spring, and it showed the three of them holding up their cups of ice cream and grinning at the camera. Anna had vanilla, John had chocolate, and Emily of course had mint chocolate chip. It was practically the only flavor of ice cream she would eat. She was weird that way.

Anna's eyes misted up at the sight of the photo. She suddenly didn't want to be alone anymore, so she got up and headed out of her bedroom and into the living room where her dad was watching the History Channel. Her heart sank to see that he was asleep in his easy chair, his head slumped to one side. Faint snores rose up in time with his slow, rhythmic breathing.

She sat down on the couch anyway. Even asleep, Dad

was better company than nobody. But then she saw that the show that was currently airing was about famous missing people. Amelia Earhart. Judge Crater. Jimmy Hoffa. Not what she needed to see right now.

She thought about calling someone, but who? The person she most wanted to talk to was John, but she didn't want to have to face the likely scenario that he wouldn't want to talk to her. Maybe Katie? Katie would probably be working on the spelling problems right now, too. They could chat about that. Yeah, Katie would be good.

She headed back to her bedroom for her phone. It sat on her desk, next to her homework. As she reached out for it she felt cool air moving across her face and heard the whoosh of a car outside, far louder than it should have been. Looking up, she saw her curtain moving gently in the breeze. Why was the window open?

She heard a faint creak behind her, the creak the closet door always made, even when you were trying really hard to be quiet.

She sucked in a breath of too-fresh, too-cool air to scream, but then a big sweaty hand closed over her mouth and another big hand waved a gun in her face and a voice hissed in her ear, "If you make a sound, I'll shoot you, and then I'll shoot your daddy, too."

4

Donovan sat on his bed staring down at the fringed beaded Native American medicine bag he had bought Emily for her birthday next week. He remembered how excited she had been when she saw it in the display window of the Whole Shebang gift shop downtown back in August. Even the fifty-dollar price tag hadn't dissuaded her from leaving finger- and nose-prints all over the glass while she raved on and on about all the cool stuff she would keep in it. Donovan had practically had to drag her away so they could meet Dad for lunch at Subway. He had returned to the Whole Shebang the next day and spent his entire doob fund on the pouch. He hadn't been able to afford any weed for nearly a month after that, but when he imagined her expression when she unwrapped it, he knew it was worth every penny.

He wondered what he would do with it if she never came home. Would he hold onto it? Probably. How could he get rid of it? He imagined himself as a little old man with the bag still tucked away in a drawer or on a closet shelf. It would become some weird and depressing family heirloom.

He felt tears threatening to form, so he thrust the medicine bag back into the Whole Shebang's plastic "Thank You Come Again" bag and shoved it back under the bed.

Shit, he needed a smoke. A regular one, this time. He got out his Marlboros and his lighter, then headed over to open the window.

He had just flipped the latches when his phone rang. It was Cynthia.

"What's up?" he asked, looking in the direction of her bedroom even though he couldn't see it through his closed door. "Why are you calling me? Why don't you just come over and—" He frowned. "Wait. You're not in the house, are you?"

"I'm with Calvin at the May house," she said. "We're thinking about resuming the investigation, if only to check something in Grey's house. Do you and Violet want in?"

"Hell, yeah."

"Well, do you think you can wrangle her up? I don't have her number."

"Um, actually, she'll probably be here in about ten, fifteen minutes. We were gonna, you know, hang out."

"Again? If Mom and Dad catch the two of you smoking and drinking and—and stuff..."

"They haven't yet."

"Well, look, if you think you guys can slip out without anyone knowing, then come on over here. Hopefully this won't take too long."

"I should be able to get out okay. Last time I looked, Mom was zonked out in front of the TV, and Dad was on beer number three."

"Great."

"I know."

She sighed. "One way or another, we need to end this soon."

"I hear you. Violet and me'll be over there as soon as we can."

5

Roger Grey pulled up at the curb outside John Coyote's house. He looked up and down the street. Picture windows shone in the darkness. Occasionally a shadowy form passed across a drape or curtain. The street itself was empty. Nothing moved under the cones of light cast by the streetlamps.

There was a faint scuff and thump as something moved inside the trunk.

"This one will be trickier," Emily Faux said from the passenger seat. "You'll have to deal with his aunt, too.

They're in the living room watching television. You can threaten them with the gun, but don't use it. Not yet."

Roger nodded. "Right."

He got out of the police car and softly shut the door. He paused beside the car, listening. He heard no more sounds from the trunk. Good. She must have been shifting position rather than trying to escape or attract attention. His slow and detailed descriptions of exactly what he would do to her mommy and daddy if she didn't do as he said must have done the trick.

He strode up the driveway and headed down the walkway past the picture window. The drapes were closed and too thick to allow him any glimpse of what was going on inside.

Emily was waiting for him at the top of the front steps.

"Remember what I told you," she said. "No gun, if you can help it."

"Yeah, yeah."

After one last look up and down the block to make sure none of the neighbors had decided that now would be a peachy time to take Snoogums for a walk, Roger rang the doorbell.

A few seconds later the inside door opened. A middle-aged woman smiled out through the screen in the upper half of the outside door. She was short and frumpy, with graying brown hair and a pair of small round glasses. Her eyes widened when she saw the policeman's cap on Roger's head.

"Can I help you?" she said.

"Yes, ma'am," Roger said. "We've got important information we need to share with you. Mind if I come in?"

"Of course."

She pushed open the door. He moved around it to step

inside. She started to edge out of his way, then froze, finally registering the civilian clothes he was wearing. And the bloodstains on his pants and shoes. And the gun in his hand.

"Oh," she said in a tiny voice. Her eyes, now huge and alarmed, rose to meet his.

Roger smiled and thrust the barrel of the gun in her face.

"Don't make a sound."

6

"It'll probably be at least fifteen minutes," Cynthia told Calvin as she put her phone back into her pocket. "Probably more like half an hour, given that it's Violet we're waiting on."

"Well, that'll give us some time to think stuff through," Calvin said.

"What stuff?"

"The big picture. The whole history of the woods and all the weird shit that's happened in and around them. If Roger Grey is part of it, then how does he fit in? How does it all tie together?"

"Do we really need to answer that right now? Shouldn't our main concern be figuring out how we're going to get into Grey's house and check out the chest freezer? I thought we were going to focus on the micro-level for now."

"I don't think we have that luxury anymore. I think it's all too tied up together to parse out like that. Remember how Grey seemed to know we were there before there was any way he could have seen or heard us? If that's what happened last time, it'll probably happen again. Which means we need to take it into account and figure out how he knew. And I bet it ties in somehow with all the macro-level stuff, all the dreams and visions and weirdness in the woods."

"What, are you thinking he's psychic or something?"

"Maybe. Or he's having, I don't know, outside help or something."

"Outside help?" She cocked an eyebrow. "Like what? The fairies are telling him stuff?"

"I don't know. But I think there's definitely something unusual going on. And if there is, it's something we need to know about if we want to try to get into his house again."

"But how do we know what it is? How do we even begin to figure it out?"

"I don't know." He thought for a moment, then circled around the desk and studied the satellite map up close. Cynthia joined him.

"Let's go over what we know," he said.

"Okay," Cynthia said. She gestured at the dark, blotchy green that covered most of the map. "First of all, it has something to do with the woods. Or something *in* the woods.

"Or under the woods. Let's just say something in this vicinity. Not necessarily the woods themselves."

"And it's connected with people seeing things that aren't there, or at least things that other people don't see."

"Right. So what causes people to see things other people don't see?"

"Lots of things. Insanity. Psychedelic drugs. Dreams. Brainwashing. Psychic powers…" She frowned. "What if all the people who saw weird things were psychically sensitive?"

"That would be an awful lot of psychics."

"Maybe a large proportion of the population *is* psychic. Maybe their psychic abilities are so minor they don't even realize they're psychic. At least not under normal circumstances."

"But if they're exposed to whatever is in the woods…"

"Right. Maybe whatever's in the woods is some kind of weird psychic energy source that's so powerful it affects people whose psychic abilities wouldn't normally be noticeable."

"But didn't Mr. May say he had some psychics come out here, and they didn't really detect anything?"

"Oh. That's right. I forgot. Crap. So what else causes some people to see things that others don't? Imagination? Optical illusions?"

Calvin didn't say anything for a moment. He just studied the map in silence. Then suddenly he stiffened.

"What about the obvious?" he said. "What about something that doesn't *want* other people to see it?"

"Like what? A ghost?"

"The Indians had lots of stories about shapeshifters. Things that could turn into whatever person or animal they chose. Maybe that's what this is. Maybe it all connects back up with the Mima."

"What, Wakansa was real, and it was a shapeshifter?"

"Why not? Maybe Turner and Hamilton were wrong. Maybe the dragon they saw didn't appear and disappear out of nowhere; maybe it turned from something tiny, like a spider, into a huge dragon, and then back into a spider."

Cynthia eyed the map, deep in thought.

"It's an interesting idea," she said finally. "And it would explain some things pretty well. But don't forget: A lot of people saw and heard things even when other people were present. Olive Crow heard music when no one else did. Luther Jones had conversations with people no one else could see or hear. And then there was the light my aunt and I saw. I didn't see it at first, and my dad didn't see it at all. All of which means we're talking about something primarily psychic or psychological."

"Oh, yeah. Shit." He looked at the map again and sighed. "Back to the drawing board..."

7

"Get moving," Roger growled. He gave John a hard shove between his shoulder blades. John stumbled forward and nearly fell. He couldn't steady himself very well because his hands were cuffed behind his back with Officer Carter's handcuffs.

John glared over his shoulder at Roger and said something that the silver rectangle of duct tape over his mouth reduced to "Mmmm *mmm.*"

The cold, hateful look in the boy's eyes conveyed his meaning well enough. Roger leaned down till his face was level with John's then pointed the gun at John's aunt, who lay on her stomach on the couch, her arms and legs bound with electrical cords torn off the room's lamps. Her cheeks were red and wet with tears, and a rill of snot glistened on the duct tape covering her mouth. Her fluttery skirt had gotten hiked up, revealing her pale, cellulite-dimpled thighs.

When she saw Roger point the gun at her, she emitted a shrill squeal. She sounded like a piglet.

"Remember," Roger told John: "If you don't do what I tell you, I'll shoot the old bitch. And then I'll go out and shoot your little friend Anna. And then"—he swung the gun around so that John was looking down the black tunnel of its muzzle—"I'll shoot you. Won't that suck?"

John's eyes shifted from Roger to his aunt, then back to Roger. The icy hatred in them never wavered, but nevertheless he turned and strode toward the front door exactly as Roger had demanded. Roger followed him out, one hand on the boy's shoulder. On the couch behind them John's aunt whimpered.

Outside, not a soul was in sight except a kid on a bike whizzing through the intersection at the end of the block. Traffic hummed on Potts Road two blocks east. Roger guided John to the trunk of the car, then kept the gun trained on the boy with one hand while he unlocked the trunk with the other.

He raised the trunk lid, revealing Anna West curled up on the carpet inside, her hands likewise cuffed, her mouth likewise taped, her tear-filled eyes white and gleaming in the shadows. John stiffened at the sight of her, then fixed that hateful look on Roger again.

"Get inside," Roger ordered. When John merely continued glaring at him, Roger shoved him against the back of the car hard enough to make the car rock on its springs, then waved the gun at the trunk. "In."

John glanced at Anna again. Her eyes were huge and scared and pleading. She emitted a small muffled sob.

John climbed inside. Roger slammed the trunk shut.

Roger sat down behind the wheel. Emily was waiting for him in the passenger seat. As he inserted the key into the ignition, the radio crackled and a woman's voice said, "Car Five, what is your status?"

Roger frowned, then craned his head out the window and looked at the 5 on the side of the door.

"Car Five, please report," the dispatcher said.

Roger looked at Emily.

"Ignore it," she said. She nodded at the steering wheel. "Just hurry. Things are starting to happen now."

8

Colleen listened to the police car start up and pull out of the driveway. Then she sucked in a deep breath through her nostrils and heaved herself off the couch. She crashed to the floor hard enough to make the picture window rattle. A spike of pain shot through her hip. She ignored it and rolled across the carpet to her purse, which sat next to her rocking chair.

When she reached the purse, she turned her back to it, then wriggled about until her cuffed hands came into contact with its imitation leather surface. She unzipped the main compartment and thrust her hands inside. A pencil tip jabbed her finger. She winced, but kept groping about until she found her phone.

She pulled it out of the purse, then felt about on its surface in search of the button to turn it on…

9

As the police car accelerated down May Road, John planted his feet against the side of the trunk and slid his cuffed hands down the back of his legs until they were even with his heels. He stepped one foot backward over the handcuff chain, then the other. Now his hands were in front of him., exactly the way a stage magician had done it on a TV special John saw last month. Who said watching TV was bad for you?

He raised his hands to his face and pulled off the duct tape. Then he scooted close to Anna and whispered in her ear, "I'm gonna take the tape off your mouth, okay?"

The interior of the trunk was too dark for him to see her nod, but he sensed the movement and heard a tiny, muffled, "Mm-hmm."

With much more care than he had used when removing his own tape, he peeled the duct tape off her mouth. While he did so, he faintly heard Roger talking. John couldn't catch any words, but the rhythms of Roger's speech and the way he kept pausing briefly made it sound like he was having a conversation with someone. But John didn't hear a second voice.

"What are we going to do?" Anna whispered as soon as her mouth was uncovered. Her voice was wavering and husky. She was close to panic.

"Do you have a bobby pin or anything?"

For a moment she was silent, no doubt baffled by the seeming non-sequitur.

"What?" she said.

"A bobby pin. Something I can pick the handcuff locks with."

"Oh, um…no."

The car jounced over a pothole. The force of the impact flung them up and down hard. Anna's head thumped against the floor.

"Ow!" she yelped.

"Quiet," John whispered. "We don't want him to know we're free. Or, well, kinda free."

"Sorry."

The car turned a corner, sending John sliding into the wall and Anna sliding into John. As the car came out of the turn and accelerated, they wriggled apart.

"What are we going to do?" Anna asked again.

"The next time he opens the trunk, I'll attack him. You jump out and start running."

"But he has a gun. He might kill us."

"Yeah, well, what do you think he's gonna do anyway?"

To that, Anna had nothing to say.

10

Special Agents Max Rowan and Russell Schmidt were on their way to a meeting with some of their fellow agents in the police station's conference room when Chief Krezchek intercepted them in the main hallway. Krezchek's aged face looked more lined and careworn than usual.

"Have either of you seen or heard anything from Officers Carter or Thompson?" he asked.

"No, why?" Agent Rowan said.

"They're not responding to calls."

"Where were they last?"

"I, uh..." Krezchek grimaced, then tilted his chin up resolutely. "I sent them to check out the Crow girl's tip about the chest freezer at Roger Grey's house. Their last call-in was about twenty-five minutes ago, when they reached the house. Since then, nothing."

Agent Rowan grunted. "We'd better—"

A wail rose up from somewhere in the station. All activity in the busy hallway ceased. Everyone looked around, stiff and wide-eyed. A moment later the dispatch room's door flew open and Karen West ran out.

"No!" she cried. "No no no!"

"Karen, what is it?" Chief Krezchek said.

"Anna!" she shrieked, clutching at his shirt. "She's been abducted. Right from her bedroom."

"What? What happened?"

In one swift, barely coherent outpouring, she explained that she had just gotten a call from her panicked husband Herbert, who had been at home alone with Anna. He had been in the living room watching TV. Anna had been in her room doing homework. When he got up to check on her, she was gone and her window was open. A man's footprints were in the flower bed outside.

"Oh, God," she moaned. "We have to find her be-fore—before—" She began to sob.

"Damn it," Krezchek muttered. He looked around. The hallway was packed now. Most of the people in the station had come running to find out what all the shrieking was about.

"Has anyone seen Carter and Thompson?" Krezchek called.

"Aren't they in Car Five?" asked Officer Murphy.

"Yeah."

Murphy jerked a thumb over his shoulder at the main entrance. "As I was coming in just a minute ago, I saw Car Five drive past. It was heading south down Potts."

"South?"

Alison Creech, another of the dispatchers, poked her head out of the dispatch room.

"Chief," she said, "someone just dialed 911 from the home owned by Colleen Brandt. That's—"

"That's John Coyote!" Karen cried. "He and Anna and Emily Crow are all best friends!"

"Any info with the call?" Agent Rowan asked.

Alison shook her head. "No one said a word. There were just some muffled scuffs and groans."

"Send two men there and two men to the West house," Agent Rowan said. "Send another two to Grey's house. Everyone else on the streets. Eyes out for Anna West, John Coyote, Roger Grey, Carter and Thompson, and Car Five."

As the crowd dispersed around them, Agent Schmidt asked, "So where do *we* go?"

Agent Rowan stared off into space, thinking hard. Then he stiffened and snapped his fingers. "South down Potts! The woods!" He raced toward the door. Agent Schmidt hurried after him. "He's going back to the scene of the crime! He's going back to where all this started!"

11

"Okay," Calvin said. "Maybe we should try a different tack. Let's get back to the basics here. Let's trace this back to square one."

"Square one?" Cynthia said.

"Everything begins somewhere, right? What's the first thing we know happened for sure?"

"Firebird. His vision quest." She frowned. "No, wait. The underground chamber." She jabbed her finger at the spot on the map where Spirit Cave was located. "If we believe what Turner May wrote, then it sounds like someone carved that chamber and put those bones there a long time before Firebird was even born."

"There's also the Stone Pillar," Calvin said, tapping the spot where the pillar was. "Everyone assumes it was a piece of stone left by the glacier or a marker for some old Indian trail, but what if whoever carved the chamber also put the pillar there? I mean, the pillar's on a straight east-west line with Spirit Cave, so it could be, uh…"

He had been about to suggest that the pillar was a marker pointing the way to the cave, but as he stared at his and Cynthia's fingers on the map and the black pin Mr. May had inserted into the clearing, he realized there was more to it than that. A lot more.

His eyes roved over the map as he recalled everything Mr. May had told them about the history of the area.

"Oh my God," he muttered.

"What?" Cynthia said. "What is it?"

He fumbled through the desk's drawers until he found a pencil and a ruler. Then he laid the ruler against the map and began to connect everything up. From the May house, where Turner May's family burned to death and Anna May succumbed to influenza, he drew a line northeast to Spirit Cave, where Hamilton Crow found his daughter's sodden corpse and Turner and Hamilton descended into the underworld; from the cave he drew a line west to the Stone Pillar, the mysterious obelisk of uncertain origin where Randolph Crow blew his brains out; from there, a line southeast to the Crow house, where Turner May performed strange rituals and Randolph Crow painted *Door* and Eugene Scott fell to his death; then a line from the Crow house north-northwest to Indian Hill, the holy site of the Mima, where Firebird led the ceremony that culminated in his suicide; and finally a line from Indian Hill south-southwest to the May house, where he had started.

The lines formed a perfect pentagram.

And right in the center of the pentagram was the black pin, the clearing.

Calvin and Cynthia looked at each other, their eyes big with amazement.

"What does that mean?" Cynthia asked.

"I don't know," Calvin said. "But there's no way that's

an accident."

The rumble of an engine grew audible. A car was coming up the driveway. They hustled over to the south-facing window and peeked out the blinds.

Headlights shone down the long tunnel of trees. The lights grew brighter and brighter, and then a police car rolled into view. It passed out of sight behind the house's south wing. A moment later the engine cut off.

"The police!" Cynthia said. "I wonder what's going on."

"Let's go find out."

Chapter 32

Full Circle

1

"That stupid old fuck," Violet said as she hopped off the last of the stepping stones and joined Donovan on the Kanseeka's west bank. They headed up the bank and through the woods toward the May house. "How come he only left me ten thousand bucks? How come everyone else got a hundred thousand, and that dweeb Calvin got a million plus a giant fucking house? I helped out just as much as anyone else. More, even. If that doddering old fuck wasn't already dead, I'd kick his wrinkled little ass."

"I think you're being too hard on him," Donovan said. "I'm sure the dude had his reasons."

"Yeah, the reason was, he was a dick."

"Violet, maybe you should...uh..."

He fell silent. Up ahead in the distance white light shone through the trees. He and Violet stopped walking and listened. They could faintly hear the rumble of an engine.

"Does Calvin own a car?" Violet asked.

"I don't think so. And I know Cyn doesn't."

The lights went out. The engine stopped. A few seconds later a car door slammed.

"Come on," Violet whispered. She motioned for him to follow, then slunk forward. "Keep in stealth mode till we know what's what."

"I got a bad feeling about this," Donovan muttered. Then he followed her into the darkness.

2

When the car stopped and the engine shut off, John whispered to Anna, "Okay, you know what to do."

Anna scooted against the driver's side wall. John positioned himself on his back under the center of the lid, then drew his legs up until his knees were against his chest. The plan was that when Roger opened the trunk, John would kick at Roger as hard as he could. While Roger was distracted, Anna would scramble out of the trunk and run. It wasn't the greatest plan in the world, but it was better than nothing. Maybe John could kick the gun out of Roger's hand. Maybe Anna would get away. Or maybe not. But they had to try.

They waited. Nothing happened for several long moments. Wherever they were, it was deathly quiet. John didn't even hear any traffic. That wasn't good. It meant there were few, if any, people around, which would make finding help more difficult.

Then Roger said, "Okay," as if someone had just told him something. The driver's side door opened and shut. A moment later keys jingled right outside the trunk. A key thunked into the trunk lock. The lock clacked, and the lid popped up slightly.

A second passed. Then two. Then three.

Then the lid flew up. John started to kick, but then saw that no one was there. There was only an expanse of stars, distant trees. His legs dropped back to the trunk floor. Beside him he heard Anna let out a despairing moan.

Roger stepped into view from around the side of the trunk. He had backed a couple of paces away from the trunk, out of John and Anna's reach. He trained Officer Thompson's gun on John.

"Do you think I'm a fucking idiot?" he asked.

"Yes," John said.

Roger's eyes narrowed. "Get the hell out of there."

3

Calvin and Cynthia drew back the curtain in the smoking room window and looked outside. A police car sat front-first against the garage door, its trunk wide open. Roger Grey was leading two handcuffed children north toward the woods. He held a flashlight in one hand and a gun in the other.

"Those're Emily's friends," Cynthia said.

"I'll call the cops." Calvin got out his phone and dialed 911.

"They might not get here in time," Cynthia said, hurrying toward the door. "We'd better do something ourselves."

"Agreed." Calvin hustled after her, the phone pressed to his ear.

4

"Fucking cops," Violet grumbled. She and Donovan were peering out the woods at the police car in the May driveway. "What the fuck are *they* doing here?"

"That's not cops, Violet," Donovan said. He pointed at the north end of the lawn, where Roger Grey and two kids were just disappearing into the woods.

"That's Roger Grey," Violet said. "That scumfuck! Let's get him!"

Violet raced north through the woods. Donovan followed.

"Um, shouldn't we, like, call the cops or something?" he said.

"Don't think that'll be necessary." Violet raised one index finger into the air. At first Donovan had no idea what she was talking about, but then he heard the sound of sirens in the distance.

5

Rather than bother with a car, Agents Rowan and Schmidt ran to the woods, bargaining that since it was only a couple of blocks, they could get there faster on foot. Indeed, by the time they heard the first sirens whine to life in the Civic Administration Building's parking lot, they were already sprinting across Indian Hill Park, their black shoes smashing flowers, their trench coats flapping behind them like drab flags.

"We try the clearing first?" Schmidt asked.

"He liked it once."

"What if he's not there?"

"We'll worry about that only if we have to worry about it."

They disappeared into the woods in a flurry of foliage.

6

"The dispatcher said the cops are on their way," Calvin told Cynthia as he put his phone back into his pocket. They were running across the rear lawn toward the spot where Roger Grey and the two kids had disappeared into the trees twenty seconds earlier.

"Good," Cynthia said.

"She said we should just stay out of the way and let the cops handle everything."

"Uh-huh."

She didn't slow down. Neither did he.

They plunged into the woods.

7

Violet stopped in her tracks and flung out an arm across Donovan's chest, stopping him too.

"What—" he began.

"Sh," she said. "Someone's coming."

Donovan listened and heard the thump of feet and the puff of breaths swiftly approaching behind them.

"Oh, shit," he whispered. "Is that Grey? Did we pass him by?"

Violet motioned for him to get behind a tree. They hunkered down and waited.

The footsteps and heavy breathing grew louder, closer. Then a bush rustled violently on the other side of the tree, and there was the sound of branches snapping.

"Ow," said a familiar male voice. It was Calvin. "I can't see shit. We should've brought flashlights."

"Too late now," said a female voice. Cynthia.

Donovan and Violet stood up and stepped around the tree.

"Hey, guys," Donovan said.

Cynthia and Calvin yelped and scrambled backward, then stopped when they realized who it was.

"Jesus, you scared the fucking shit out of us," Cynthia said. "What are you guys doing here?"

"We saw Grey," Violet said. "We're gonna kick his ass."

"Well, come on, then," Calvin said, hurrying off in the direction Grey had been going. "There's no time to waste."

8

When Roger pushed John and Anna through the last tangle of bushes and into the clearing, he was relieved to find Emily waiting for him there, her white sneakers stationed squarely on the circle of burned grass. He had been starting to worry; he hadn't seen her since he left the car. Yet for all his relief, he couldn't help feeling a sense of disorientation, as well. It was jarring to see the girl he had murdered looking healthy and alive in the very spot he had stabbed her.

Of course, this wasn't the real Emily. But soon enough, if everything went as planned, the real one would be alive again, and all of this would be over.

But he had to act fast. The sirens were louder now. They seemed to be everywhere. They were Dopplering down Potts and Indianview. They were massing on Oaks. He didn't have much time.

Emily knew this, too.

"Quickly," she said. "Kill them. Right here in the center of the clearing. You have to act fast."

She vanished. Roger stiffened. Why had she disappeared like that? He might need her help.

But no. He knew what to do. It was simple.

He tossed the flashlight aside. He didn't need it now. Not with the starlight illuminating the clearing. He holstered the gun, and before the kids could glance back and see their chance to run, he grabbed each one by an arm and pulled them into the center of the clearing. The kids understood what was about to happen. Anna screamed for help and pleaded with Roger to stop. John writhed and twisted, trying to tear free of Roger's grip. None of it did any good.

Roger flung the two kids face down onto the burned circle, the very spot where their friend had died five nights earlier. Then he drew both cops' guns and aimed one at each kid's head.

He heard a rustle in the bushes on the south side of the clearing. He started to look back over his shoulder, but the moment he took his eyes off John and Anna, John planted his chest and hands against the burned grass and kicked up and back with both feet. One foot slammed into Roger's left thigh. The other smashed into his balls.

Roger doubled over with a hoarse cry. He reflexively squeezed one of the guns' triggers and sent a bullet into the dirt half a foot from Anna's face.

He snarled at John. "You son of a—"

And then Calvin and Violet tackled him. The trio toppled onto the two kids. Anna screamed.

Calvin and Violet each seized one of Roger's arms and pinned it to the grass. Roger growled and tried to buck the duo off him. Then he saw that Donovan and Cynthia were pulling John and Anna out from under his legs.

"Don't!" Roger cried. He kicked at John Coyote's head,

hoping to crush the little fuck's skull. After all, Emily didn't specify *how* the kids had to die. But Roger's aim was off and his shoe only thumped against the small of John's back. As Donovan pulled him to his feet, John cast a hateful scowl at Roger.

Roger struggled harder. Calvin and Violet redoubled their efforts to hold him down.

"You're fucked, fucker!" Violet shouted into his face.

Roger headbutted her, his forehead smacking into her right eye socket with a sound like a pair of coconuts knocking together. Violet slumped sideways, groaning. Her grip on his arm slackened enough for him to wrench it free. She groggily grabbed for the gun he held in that hand, but she was too slow, too disoriented, and her hands closed on empty air.

Since Violet was currently too dazed to be a threat, Roger pointed the gun at Calvin's face. Calvin jerked his head to the side just as Roger pulled the trigger. There was a bang that made Roger's ears hurt, and Calvin tumbled away across the grass, screaming and trailing droplets of blood.

Roger sprang to his feet and looked around just in time to see Donovan, Cynthia, and the two kids disappearing into the brush at the east edge of the clearing.

"No!" Roger bellowed. He started to raise the guns, but then out of the corner of his eye he caught a blur of movement in the woods at the north edge of the clearing. He spun around and raised his guns at the exact moment Agent Schmidt burst from the foliage, his own pistol raised.

Both men fired simultaneously. Schmidt's shot traced a thin red line across Roger's left cheek then vanished into a tree trunk on the south side of the clearing. One of Roger's two shots likewise wound up in a tree, but the other one left a neat round hole in the center of Schmidt's forehead and a much larger hole in the back of his head. Gore splattered the bushes behind him, as well as the face of Agent Rowan, who had emerged from the woods a second after Schmidt. Rowan staggered backward, trying to wipe his partner's brains from his eyes, while Schmidt's corpse toppled forward onto the grass.

With a feral grin, Roger started to take aim at Agent Rowan, eager to finish off the FBI geek so he could turn his attention to recapturing the kids. But then he froze.

Silvery-white light was filling the air around him. Before Roger's amazed gaze, it grew brighter and brighter, reducing the rest of the world to a pallid phantom.

9

Calvin felt himself screaming, but all he could hear was a muffled ringing. Every atom in his head seemed to be vibrating from the gunshot. His left temple throbbed with pain. It felt as if someone had clobbered him with a sledgehammer. He touched a hand to his temple, and his palm came away streaked with blood.

When he saw the silvery light growing brighter around him, his first thought was that there was something wrong with his vision. Which didn't really surprise him, given that he believed Grey's bullet was lodged deep in his brain.

But then he saw Grey himself standing a few feet away and looking around with his mouth agape, his pistols hanging forgotten at his sides. Grey saw the light too.

So did Violet, who sat on the grass nearby, likewise gaping. She saw Calvin looking at her and said something.

He couldn't hear anything except that incessant ringing, but he could clearly lip-read the words, "What the fuck?"

10

When Agent Max Rowan cleared his partner's blood and brains from his eyes, he was stunned to see a silver-white light filling most of the clearing.

Max looked up, thinking it might be a searchlight from a helicopter.

But no. The light wasn't a beam. It wasn't streaming down from above. It was a discrete dome that stopped a few feet short of the clearing's edge. It engulfed Agent Schmidt's corpse all the way down to the calves. Max himself was just outside it.

Max trained his gun on Roger. Weird light or not, he had a job to do and a partner to avenge.

"Drop—" He meant to say "drop your weapons" but that was when he noticed hazy shapes in the light.

11

"This is it," Cynthia said. She and Donovan had barely gotten John and Anna to the edge of the clearing when the gunfire erupted behind them. They had all dove into the bushes, then peered out through the foliage. Cynthia had half expected to see Calvin and Violet dead and Grey charging after them. Instead she saw a familiar silver-white radiance. "This is the light."

"The what?" Donovan said.

"The light I saw when Aunt Wendy died. This is the

same thing. Only stronger. Brighter."

She glanced at Grey, who stood gawping at the light, then at Violet and Calvin, both of whom sat on the grass, likewise gawping. Calvin's head was bleeding, but only a little; it looked like Grey's bullet had only grazed him, thank God. Still, he might have a concussion. And Grey might regain his wits at any moment.

She was about to order Donovan to lead the kids away while she dashed back into the clearing to help get Calvin and Violet to safety, but then she noticed the shapes in the light.

As she watched in fear and wonder, the light brightened and the shapes grew clearer.

12

Anna averted her eyes from the light. She didn't want to see it. It was wrong. She didn't know how she knew it was wrong, but she did, and it was.

"John…" She laid a hand on his arm. "Come on. We should get to where it's safe."

He didn't move. He didn't speak. He didn't even seem to hear her. He just kept staring at the light and its increasingly clear contents as if he suspected they were something important, something he needed to see.

13

Roger turned in a circle. The light had stopped growing brighter, and the shapes within it were clearer now. Clear enough to see. Mostly. They overlapped and interpenetrated, occupying the same space like double exposures. Except they weren't double or triple or quadruple. They were infinite. They were everything.

Roger was standing in a graveyard and on a mountain-top and in a factory and at the bottom of the ocean and in a thousand other places all at the same time. A neon-green spider as big as a softball scuttled through Roger's left foot as if it were Roger who was the immaterial thing. A young woman ran past with a baby clutched to her chest. A team of bearded dwarves tended a blazing furnace, their faces grim and intent in the red glow. A pair of velociraptors mated in a fernbrake. A boxy silver robot whizzed over-head. A two-headed dog-like creature with dark gray fur and glowing red eyes tore at the carcass of a large animal, its twin muzzles dripping blood. A cavalry charged past, banners fluttering, dust billowing up from the horses' hooves. It was like a million movies all playing on the same screen at the same time. Roger could even hear some of the sounds these things made, though the sounds were faint and muffled and barely audible over the ringing in his ears.

14

Max watched the weird flickering images for a few seconds, then shook his head. Whatever this was, it wasn't why he was here.

He took a step forward, which brought him to the very edge of the shimmering, image-laden light. For all his de-termination and sense of duty, some primitive part of him balked at entering that light.

In his initial amazement at the spectacle, Max had low-ered his gun. Now he raised it at Roger again, who was barely visible at the heart of the bizarre display.

"Drop your weapons!" Max shouted. "Now!"

15

Roger didn't move. Roger barely even heard him. The FBI agent was merely one more detail in the endless flux.

Roger flinched as a gigantic jellyfish swam through him.

"This isn't real," he said through gritted teeth. He looked around. Where were those damn kids? He still had to kill the kids. He couldn't see them amid all the dolls and obelisks and sandstorms.

For that matter where was Emily? He hadn't seen her since she vanished. Had she abandoned him? Had she—

The images began to fade. The creatures and places and things grew fainter and hazier and blended back into the light, which likewise began to ebb. But while everything else faded, one thing grew crisper and clearer: Special Agent Max Rowan standing a few paces away and pointing a gun at Roger.

"No!" Roger cried. He started to duck down and raise his own guns at Max, but he was too slow. He saw the muzzle-flash of Max's gun, heard the bang, felt a brief pressure at the center of his forehead as if someone had tapped him with their fingertip, and then—

16

And then he was in a mill of some kind, a structure so vast its walls and ceiling were lost in distant shadow. A complex network of enormous wooden shafts and cogwheels filled most of the space overhead. The machinery's intricate, creaking movements drove a pair of millstones in the center of the floor. The stones were as big around as houses, and as the runner stone rotated slowly and inexorably atop the bedstone, it produced a low, deep rumble that Roger felt in the very marrow of his bones.

Emily stood between him and the millstones.

"There you are!" Roger cried, relieved. He had been afraid she had abandoned him. "What do we do now? What, uh…"

He frowned, trying to recall what had to be done. How had he gotten here exactly? He couldn't quite remember. But there were definitely things that needed to be done. There always were.

Emily didn't respond. She just stared at him, her face blank.

Her blankness made Roger stiffen, suddenly afraid. He sensed the presence of someone off to his right. He turned and saw a Native American man leaning against a pillar with his arms folded across his chest. The man wore a black suit and tie, and had hair as long and black as Emily's. He was regarding Roger with a small, sly smile.

Then Roger glimpsed another figure in his peripheral vision. He turned to the right again, which left him facing away from Emily, and saw a strange figure on a walkway a dozen feet above the floor. The figure wore a hooded pale-yellow cloak that completely shrouded its body. Beneath the hood, the entity wore a pallid mask made of a hard, smooth substance that for some reason Roger felt sure was bone. The mask was blank and featureless, with no holes or designs of any kind. The entity was so still that Roger thought for a second it might be a dummy or scarecrow.

But no: It was alive. He could feel it.

And then he caught a flash of movement out of the corner of his eye. Turning once more, he spied a figure barely visible in the shadows—a tall, burly man with a beard and what appeared to be a fur vest like a barbarian would wear.

And Roger sensed other entities watching unseen from the murky depths of the mill. What the hell was going on?

He turned to the right one last time, which brought him full circle back to Emily and the rumbling millstones.

Except Emily wasn't there anymore. In her place was a small, willowy female entity, about four-and-a-half feet tall, with long pointed ears, jet-black eyes, a pair of fleshy antennae sprouting from her forehead, and multicolored butterfly wings on her back. She was naked, and her pale skin glowed with a moony light.

"What's happening?" Roger said. "I don't understand."

"It isn't meant for you to understand," the entity told him in a voice that buzzed and warped in a manner Roger found almost physically nauseating. "It isn't *possible* for you to understand. Not with your pathetically limited human perceptions."

"What? But—"

"You were just one tiny cog in a vast and ancient machine. And now we're done with you." She smiled. It wasn't a friendly smile. It was the smile of something cold and inhuman. "Goodbye."

17

Roger's corpse collapsed to the grass, blood trailing from the small, neat hole in his forehead.

Max lowered his gun and looked around. "Is every-one—"

And then the light, which had nearly faded completely, flared back to life with redoubled intensity. It grew so bright that everyone present had to squint, and it ballooned well beyond its original limits until it extended a dozen feet into the woods, engulfing Max and Cynthia and Donovan and John and Anna. The thousand million images in the light took on a life and clarity they hadn't had before. But just when it appeared that these images would become real and solidify into one intermingled mass, the light and the images vanished with a bang of imploding air, revealing a small flock of birds in the air above the burned circle of grass. The birds fluttered about the clearing in a panic for a few seconds, long enough for everyone present to identify them as some kind of pigeon, and then they flew up through the hole in the trees overhead and disappeared into the night.

"Okay, I give up," Violet said. "What the *fuck* just happened?"

No one answered.

Donovan crawled out of the bushes to join her in the clearing, but when he planted one hand on the grass to push himself to his feet, something small and hard and angular dug into his palm.

"Ow," he said, yanking his hand back. He looked down. There in the grass was a green plastic army man. A radio operator with a handset held to his face and his mouth open as if he were in mid-report.

Donovan picked up the army man and stared at it. It looked like one of the army men he had given to Emily. Maybe it was. Emily had stuck them in all kinds of weird places. Why not here, too? It could have been sitting here for years. After all, who would notice a green army man amid the green grass?

Unless it had gotten here some other way. Unless...

He suddenly remembered Emily saying, *We're the good guys, and the good guys always win in the end.*

Donovan looked around at the FBI dude checking Calvin's head wound, at Cynthia and John and Anna emerging from the bushes, at Violet strolling toward him, at the bodies of Grey and the other FBI dude (he didn't allow his gaze to linger on them for long), at the cops and FBI agents streaming into the clearing from every direction—and then he looked up. Up where the birds had flown. Up at the sky. Up at the stars.

Violet came up beside him.

"You okay?" she asked.

"Yeah," he muttered. His fingers closed around the army man and he slid it into the pocket of his coat. "Yeah, I'm fine."

And all the while he kept staring at the stars.

Epilogue:

Two Endings
and Three Beginnings

1

Calvin was surprised at the size of the turnout for Mr. May's funeral. He wasn't the only one, either: When he entered the McLaughlin Funeral Parlor, the first thing he saw was Mr. McLaughlin and his assistant lugging armfuls of wooden folding chairs through the wide-open double doors that led to the viewing room, from which a loud and steady drone of voices emanated.

When Calvin himself stepped through those double doors and joined the crowd inside, the drone diminished, and he felt countless eyes upon him. No big surprise there, given the line of stitches bristling from the shaved pink patch on the side of his head, which made him feel at one moment like the poster boy for the Make-A-Wish Foundation and at the next like a rugged, battle-scarred man of action. Thankfully Roger Grey's bullet had only glanced off his skull, but even that had left Calvin concussed and in need of eight stitches.

Many of the funeral's attendees were residents of May, come to bid farewell to the last member of the town's eponymous family. But a substantial number of mourners were out-of-towners, strangers, presumably friends and associates of Mr. May's.

And an odd and diverse lot they were, too. A tall, animated Arab wearing a tailor-made suit with gold cufflinks conversed with a statuesque middle-aged blonde who had an eye-patch over her left eye and splotches of scar tissue on her left cheek and forehead. An obese bald man with skin as white as a cue-ball wept silently beside the open casket, his broad back blocking the contents of the casket from Calvin's view. A tiny old woman, who Calvin thought must be the oldest person he had ever seen, sat in the front row, her back erect and her hands folded in her lap like a conscientious child at an Easter Sunday church service.

As Calvin navigated the crowd in search of Cynthia, who had said she would be here with the rest of her family, he noticed some of these out-of-towners watching him out of the corners of their eyes, and this time he was sure their scrutiny had nothing to do with his stitches. He guessed they knew that Mr. May had left him the house and the Collection. No doubt they were wondering why. He hoped they didn't ask him to explain; he didn't understand it either.

Cynthia sidled out of the crowd to greet him. For a moment Calvin was struck dumb at the sight of her. She wore a long black dress that, while tasteful, showed off the lines of her body in a way her usual T-shirts and blue jeans never did. Seeing her like this made his heart ache as it never had before. He had hoped he had laid to rest his unrequited—and unrequitable—feelings for her, but he understood now that things like that don't just roll over and die because you want them to.

"There you are," she said. She gave him a quick hug, making sure only their arms and shoulders touched, which he was both grateful for and annoyed at. "How's the, um..." She waved a finger at his stitches. "The war wound?"

"It's okay. But how are *you*? How's your family holding up?"

She shrugged, her eyes misting and her chin dimpling. Calvin felt bad for even asking.

"We're dealing with it," she said. "As much as it can be dealt with, at least." She cocked her head. "You're coming to the funeral, right?"

"Of course."

"In fact, come on." She stepped back and waved him forward. "Sit with us."

"Oh, I don't want to intrude."

"No, it's cool. After all, you helped to try to find her and everything. Besides, you're our neighbor now. I think my folks are keen to get to know you. And think of it this way: It's like the May and Crow families are finally together again."

"Huh?" Calvin frowned in puzzlement and glanced at the casket across the room. The obese man had left, but a fresh clutch of mourners hid the body from sight.

"I mean, you're, like, the scion of the May family now, right?"

"Oh. I never really thought of it like that, but yeah. You're right." He glanced at the casket again. "Tell you what, I should, uh, go pay my respects first, you know? Then I'll join you guys."

She nodded, then turned and slipped back into the crowd.

Calvin's heart pounded as he made his way through the press of bodies toward the casket. He didn't want to do this. He was afraid of what Mr. May would look like. The only funeral he had ever been to was his Grandma Ellie's, and that had been a closed casket affair thanks to the condition of the body. She had been practically carbonized in a housefire.

By the time he reached the front of the room, the mourners had dispersed and he was alone with Mr. May. He took a deep breath and looked inside the casket.

Calvin had heard about how mortuary science had advanced to the point where dead folks looked like they were only sleeping. But seeing Mr. May's body, Calvin disagreed. Mr. May looked completely unnatural. His cheeks were obviously rouged, the shape of his face wasn't quite right, and his posture—lying there with his head propped up and his arms bent at an odd angle so that his hands could be folded on his waist—looked stiff and artificial. But the unnaturalness made it easier for Calvin to deal with the experience; it made it clear this wasn't Mr. May. This was a shell, a thing.

Calvin stood there a while trying to remember all of the things he wanted to tell Mr. May: that he was grateful for the inheritance even though he didn't understand the whys and wherefores of it; that he would treat the house and the Collection well; that he would continue investigating anomalies; that he would do his best to solve the mystery of the woods; that despite their brief time together Mr. May had made a profound and lasting impression on him.

But as he thought these things, Calvin realized they were ultimately for himself, not for Mr. May. Either Mr. May didn't know anything anymore, in which case there was no point in saying anything, or he already knew what was in Calvin's mind and heart, and again, their utterance was pointless. Calvin realized there was really only one thing left to say.

"Goodbye," he mumbled.

Blinking away his tears, he turned and headed back the way he had come to look for Cynthia and her family.

2

Emily's funeral was held two days later. It was a small, private affair. No press. No curiosity seekers. No uninvited guests.

Anna tried hard to maintain a brave face throughout the memorial service at the funeral home, but it was tough. The worst part was the eulogy given by Emily's dad. It wasn't the eulogy itself that affected her; it was when Hannibal Crow, whom Anna had always known as a calm, rational man, broke down into helpless, wracking sobs at the end. Anna wept quietly, not even trying to wipe away her tears, just letting them drip like rain into her lap, while Mr. McLaughlin ushered Emily's dad back to his seat.

John, who sat a few seats down from Anna, remained silent throughout the memorial service. He stared straight ahead the whole time, his eyes dark, his face stony. He maintained the same grim silence at the graveside service in the cemetery.

Anna hadn't had a chance to talk to him since that horrible night in the clearing. Neither of them had been in school since then. There had been too much to do—doctors to see, police to talk to, parents to reassure.

She finally got a chance to talk to him in the cemetery parking lot after the funeral. While Anna's parents stopped to chat with John's aunt and a few other people, Anna stole over to John and said, "How are you?"

"Okay," he muttered, not looking at her. He was looking at the grave they had just left: the steep-sided hole in which the casket lay out of sight; the trampled grass around it; the wreaths that marked the spot where the headstone would stand once it was done being carved; the mound of dirt draped with a grass-colored tarp. Some distance away a groundskeeper smoked a cigarette under the eaves of a small wooden shed. A dirt-caked shovel stood propped against the wall beside him.

"Um, do you want to get together later?" Anna asked. "Or maybe over the weekend?"

John kept staring at the grave in silence for a moment. Then his eyes narrowed a little, and he turned and looked at her.

"Do you believe in life after death?" he said.

"Um, yeah. I mean, not ghosts. But, like, I think Emily's with God now. And she's happy." She tried to smile to show him the happiness she thought Emily must be feeling, but it came out warped and wrong. Though she believed Emily was happy, she didn't feel such happiness herself. She still had to live here in this world, where Emily was gone, where men like Roger Grey lurked and preyed.

John looked up at the sky. A few dull gray clouds were scudding overhead on the chilly autumn wind. His eyes dropped back to the grave.

"Don't you?" Anna asked, troubled by his silence.

Before he could answer—if he was going to answer at all—Anna's parents disengaged from their chat with the other adults. Anna's mom took her hand and began to guide her toward the car.

Anna looked back over her shoulder at John. "I'll call you, okay?"

John said nothing. She wasn't sure he had even heard her. His eyes never wavered from the open grave.

3

That night John dreamed he stood atop a tall, round, crenellated tower built of snow-white stones. The cloudless blue sky stretched overhead, as vast and deep as the sea, and the sun blazed directly above him, reducing his shadow to a black oval beneath his feet. In the sunlight the tower's white stones seemed to glow with milky luminescence.

John peered over the battlements and gasped. The tower stood in the center of a lush, green forest that extended on and on in every direction, nearly mirroring the vastness of the sky. And though the tower itself was not as tall as the tallest trees in the forest, it rose far above their crowns for it had been built upon a high, grassy hill.

The view was incredible. He could see the curve of the earth in some places. (And yet he also realized that this was impossible: To see as far as he did would require his being many thousands of feet above the world. The fact that he saw what he saw from a tower that, even with the height of the hill taken into account, could not be more than a couple hundred feet tall, made him realize this had to be a dream.)

A tan stripe ran along the horizon in the direction John was facing. The edge of a desert, probably. To his right, a line of hulking gray mountains extended along the horizon, their snowy peaks bright in the sunshine. To his left, the forest ended countless leagues away in a green plain threaded with blue rivers. At a spot where several blue threads met was an irregular shape colored gray and black and brown and white. It was, he realized, a sprawling city, the towers and pinnacles of which, though surely enormous, were at this distance as thin and faint as the hairs on a spider's leg. And in the final direction, opposite the desert, a silver-blue glimmer along the horizon betokened the presence of an ocean.

"Do you like it?" said a voice behind him. A girl's voice. Emily's voice.

John whirled. Emily stood in the center of the roof, smiling at him.

John's eyes filled with tears, and a big, joyful grin split his face. He took an eager step toward her, then froze, his emotions suddenly plummeting.

"This is just a dream, isn't it?" he said.

She started to shake her head, but then stopped and shrugged.

"Well, yeah, kind of. But it's not a normal dream. It's a special dream."

"Oh." He pondered this, then gestured at the fantastic landscape around them. "Where are we exactly?"

She looked out at the scenery with a small, pleased smile. "Somewhere later. It's not a real place yet." She fixed her dark eyes on John again. "But you can help me make it real. We can replace the evil, broken world with one that's better."

John regarded her in silence a moment, then turned to look out at the breathtaking dreamscape again. A smile slowly spread across his face.

"Tell me how."

4

"God, my life has been nothing but funerals lately," Cynthia said. She and Calvin were strolling through one of the

Collection rooms on the third floor of Calvin's house. It was the first time they had had a chance to meet up since Emily was buried four days ago. "My parents even took us to Officer Thompson and Carter's funerals. Which was only proper. They died trying to find her. I think we even would have gone to that FBI agent's funeral. Agent Schmidt. But he was buried where he grew up. Somewhere in Utah."

"Did they ever determine what your aunt died of?" Calvin said.

"Oh. Yeah. Well, actually no. Not really. They officially chalked it up to something called SUDEP, which stands for 'sudden unexplained death in epilepsy.' It's basically just a clinical way of saying they have no idea what happened."

"Sort of like how they had no idea what caused her seizures in the first place."

"Exactly. Except *we* know that whatever happened to her probably had something to do with whatever is going on here in the woods. But that's the million dollar question, isn't it? What exactly *is* going on in the woods?"

Calvin shook his head. "I don't know. I just keep thinking about that pentagram on the map. If your aunt was right about how emotional energy can be imprinted on a place, then I wonder what happens when it gets imprinted in a specific way, when a few centuries'-worth of intense emotions gets concentrated in certain key spots."

"It might even be more than a couple of centuries if those skeletons Turner May wrote about are any indication."

"Yeah, and that's another thing: In Turner's account we had two skeletons in a dome-shaped room somewhere under the woods. Then in the present day we had Roger Grey, who couldn't have known anything about any of that, getting ready to kill two kids in a round clearing, where a dome of light appears every time someone gets killed there."

"And then there's the stuff we saw inside the light. I don't know about you, but I saw..." She gave a self-conscious laugh. "Well, I saw a lot of things, but one of them sure as hell looked like a walking tree with a face on it, like one of those Ents from *The Lord of the Rings*."

"I didn't see that. I did, however, see what appeared to be a Viking ship. And a flying Asian guy. And some giant penguins."

"Giant penguins?"

"What, is that weirder than an Ent?"

She opened her mouth to respond, then shut it again and shrugged. "No, I guess not."

"The question is, what were we seeing? Alternate realities? Hallucinations? Dreams? Disembodied ideas?"

Cynthia suddenly stopped walking and frowned. "A hole..."

Calvin stopped beside her. "What?"

"Aunt Wendy. That was one of the ways she described what she was seeing. Which was probably the same thing *we* were seeing. She said it was a hole."

"A hole in what?"

She shrugged. "Reality? I don't know."

Calvin pondered this, then sighed. "There are too many questions and not enough answers. I guess this is gonna have to be one of the things I look into as an anomaly investigator."

She cocked an eyebrow. "Alone?"

He looked at her, surprised. "Um, I don't know. I mean, I wasn't sure if you were still interested now that Emily's, you know, not missing anymore."

"She might not be missing anymore, and Roger Grey might be dead, and all the micro-level stuff might be sorted out, but we still don't understand the macro-level. The big picture. If there's a consciousness or some kind of purpose behind all this, then I damn well want to know what it is. But even if there isn't, even if it turns out that all of it—the tragedies, the patterns—if it was all just a bunch of random accidents—even then, I still want to investigate anomalies. I mean, all the stuff I saw I can't unsee. My world is different now. *I'm* different now. I can't go back to the way things were. So, yeah, I'm definitely on board with this. I'm ready to investigate all the damn anomalies the world has to offer."

"Awesome."

He grinned. She grinned.

Then they looked around at the rows of crowded shelves stretching away in every direction, and their grins faded.

"So…" Cynthia said. "Where do we start?"

5

From the *Kingwood Morning Star,* Sunday, November 10, page B3:

PIGEON SIGHTING SPARKS EXCITEMENT, CONTROVERSY

PHOENIX TOWNSHIP—The bird-watching community is all atwitter after a birder observed a small flock of what appeared to be passenger pigeons, a species long believed extinct.

Fred Birney, 60, a resident of Deermont, was bird-watching Friday in a heavily wooded area in southern Phoenix Township, one mile west of Route 7 and two miles north of the township line, when he spotted a flock of about a dozen birds perched in the upper branches of an oak tree.

"At first I thought they were mourning doves," Birney said. "But when I checked my field guide I realized they couldn't be. They were too big and a little too colorful, and they didn't have the black mark on the throat that mourning doves have."

He got out his camera to photograph the birds, but before he could do so, they flew away southward.

Since his field guide provided no clues to the birds' identity, he hurried home to consult his other bird books. In an antique bird guide published in the 1920s, he finally found what appeared to be a perfect match: the passenger pigeon.

"I was amazed," Birney said. "That was the last thing I was expecting."

Once the most common bird in North America, passenger pigeons were hunted to extinction during the nineteenth century. The last known wild passenger pigeon was killed in Pike County, Ohio, in 1900. The last captive specimen died in the Cincinnati Zoological Gardens in 1914. Birders, however, remained on the lookout for the birds for years, hoping against hope that a colony still remained somewhere and that the birds would one day make a comeback.

Sure that these hopes had finally become reality, Birney reported his sighting to fellow members of the Kingwood Audubon Club. From there, word quickly spread to birding groups across the country. Plans are already underway for a series of outings in Phoenix Township to search for the birds.

Despite the fanfare, many bird experts, such as Scott Brandenberg, an ornithologist affiliated with the Kingwood Zoo, believe that the whole business is much ado about nothing.

"They were almost certainly mourning doves," Brandenberg said. "There have been countless sightings of supposed passenger pigeons over the years, and they've always turned out to be mourning doves. The mistake a lot of amateurs make is forgetting that what you see in a bird book is not always what you see in the field. Minor variations in size or color sometimes occur, and minor variations are all that's needed for mourning doves to look like passenger pigeons.

"Of course I'd be lying if I didn't admit that part of me hopes he's right," he added, a little wistfully. "It would be like a dream come true."